W. A. Salisbury

Portugal and its People

A history

W. A. Salisbury

Portugal and its People
A history

ISBN/EAN: 9783337287498

Printed in Europe, USA, Canada, Australia, Japan

Cover: Foto ©Andreas Hilbeck / pixelio.de

More available books at **www.hansebooks.com**

PORTUGAL AND ITS PEOPLE

A HISTORY

BY

W. A. SALISBURY

T. NELSON AND SONS

London, Edinburgh, and New York

1893

PREFACE.

THE author of this volume believes that the history of Portugal and its people is not second in interest to the annals of any people past or present. In attempting to traverse a field so great, it was necessary to omit many details of consequence; but he has done what he could within brief limits.

The splendid story of the Arabian conquest and domination of the Peninsula, for instance, belonging to Portugal as well as to Spain, it was only possible to tell in the most meagre fashion, in order to preserve some degree of proportion in the whole chronicle. The author ventures to hold, let it be said by the way, that the redoubtable leader of the first Saracen invasion was not of African but of Arabian descent.

In the following account the idea has been adhered to, that the successful campaigning of Alfonso Henriquez against the Mussulmans was responsible for the foundation of the Portuguese kingdom, and hardly his conflict with the Castilian power, in which he was as signally disappointed as he had been fortunate in his engagements with the infidel. Some have been anxious of late to belittle the battle of Ourique, supposing that it can have been little more than a skirmish, since the defeated could gather head again in the course of a few months. But when one remembers the teeming and warlike population of the Mohammedan recruiting ground, one need not be surprised that even after a Christian victory on a large scale another horde of the enemy should be seen so soon in the field.

The *Cortes* at Lamego in 1143 has been, perhaps, too hastily relegated by certain writers to the domain of fiction. It seems to have as much evidence in its favour as the jousting at Valdevez, which they insist was the romantic means adopted for determining the claim of Alfonso Henriquez to independent sway.

The device of separating the sketch of Portuguese enterprise in other lands will be found convenient; and the appended chronological and genealogical tables will be useful as aids to the memory.

CONTENTS.

PORTUGAL AND THE PORTUGUESE.

◆◆

CHAPTER I.

THE HOME OF THE PORTUGUESE.

ON a map of the Peninsula Portugal looks like a Spanish province ; it is so small, and lies in such close contact all along its northern and eastern boundaries with the adjacent kingdom.   It reminds one, by its size and vicinity to Spain, of a child tucked under a nurse's arm.

The intimate and exclusive connection of Spain and Portugal as to their frontier would seem to afford a reason why these countries ought to be a political unit.   Moreover, not to speak about the radical identity in race and language of the two nations, nature has here imposed no great barriers to union, as she has done in the case of Italy and Germany.   No gigantic mountain chain frowns upon the intercourse of Spaniards and Portuguese.   No vast river draws a clear line between them. It is the study of its history which can alone show sufficient cause for the independence of Portugal.

Before beginning, however, the interesting story of the Portuguese people, let us take a glance at the physical aspect of their land.

The country is an oblong. Its length may be compared with that of England from London to Berwick—about three hundred and sixty miles. Its breadth, pretty uniformly maintained, is something like the distance between the mouths of the Humber and Mersey estuaries—say one hundred and forty miles. It contains, according to the latest computation, an area of thirty-four thousand square miles—less than one-fifth the superficial extent of Spain.

The whole line of the Portuguese coast on the west and south is washed by the Atlantic, the fury of whose attack upon this exposed portion of the Peninsula, when it blows hard from the west, can be easily imagined. Almost every haven of Portugal, too, has the disadvantage of a bar; and in stormy weather the dreadful surf, which thunders on the shore, renders navigation excessively perilous. Approaching from the ocean this most westerly kingdom of the European continent, it presents a sea-board indented with few bays, and these, with two exceptions, unimportant. The prevailing features of the coast are low hills of sand and flat wet ground, like those extensive and swampy heaths of Brittany which the French term *landes.* Here and there a bold cliff relieves the monotony of the level shore-line; but, as a rule, the mountains terminate some fifty miles inland, leaving a surface more gently undulating to the verge of the ocean. A great belt of pine woods, stretching north and south, shuts out the inland from the sea-board region.

The interior scenery of Portugal closely resembles that of Spain. Portuguese mountain ranges are the seaward spurs of Spanish chains. The great rivers of Portugal have their fountains on the other side of the frontier, giving her only their spacious lower reaches, which are brief compared with the entire length of the flow, since the trend of the land is towards the west. Indebted thus for its principal ridges and streams to the other country, the landscape must inevitably partake of the general Spanish character. Rugged elevations like those of Spain, though the altitude in the western kingdom is for the most part not so great, are seen also in Portugal. The picturesque Spanish valleys repeat themselves on the Portuguese side. The soil of Portugal, if lighter, is not essentially different from that of Spain. The same vegetation, therefore, which clothes the vales and the more sheltered mountain slopes in Portugal is to be found also across the border.

The climate of the little kingdom of Portugal is undoubtedly fine. It is, of course, affected and diversified by various causes —the elevation of particular districts, their proximity to the ocean or to lowland dead water and marsh. But speaking generally, there is no quarter of the Continent to which this country must give place as a healthful abode for man. The mean annual temperature of Lisbon is 60°, while that of England is 49·5°, and even at Ventnor only reaches 51·5°. In Tras os Montes and other lofty regions of the north, winter brings a "nipping and an eager air," snowfalls in those parts being frequent and heavy, particularly during the month of January, the coldest of the year in Portugal. But in the flat country of Beira and Estremadura snow is a rarity. And as for the more southern districts, it is said the natives once hurried panic-stricken to the churches when, in an exceptionally severe season, a snow-storm occurred.

The heat from the latter half of June to the middle of September is great, and would be more trying still were it not for the grateful humidity of the ocean breeze, which, sweeping, for instance, up the Tagus defile, is felt like a benediction. These winds atone in a manner for the almost total absence of rain during that period. They make even Algarve, the southernmost province, more tolerable in midsummer than Alemtejo, from whose interior the mountain chain by which it is traversed shuts out the cool breath of the Atlantic. When in autumn, however, the wind blows from the east, the vegetation is scorched and life becomes somewhat of a burden. The Portuguese are accustomed to say, "A Spanish wind and a Spanish match are two bad things." The only result of the Atlantic winds to be deprecated is the fog-banks which they often drive before them, obscuring the coast-line and putting vessels in peril.

When one thinks of Switzerland, or even of its own neighbour Spain, the scenery of Portugal cannot be said to be on a grand scale. But what is lost there in magnitude is gained in compass and variety. Climbing its jagged mountain walls, one can gather up more in the clear Portuguese air with a single sweep of the landscape than is possible where nature expresses herself in a greater manner. And although its salt-marshes and sandy plains are sufficiently dismal, there is much in Portugal to satisfy the most fastidious lover of the picturesque. Her sentinel peaks of granite, sheer and naked, her wooded chalk bluffs, her deep rich dales, through which flow silver streams, now hasting and brawling, now slowly wandering, the prospects from her heights of the long blue ocean line, afford pictures fit to touch with romance the dullest imagination. Nor can the gorgeous colouring of the country, the *nuances* of its verdure and the tints of its flowers, be surpassed anywhere in Europe. The travelled native of Portugal is not ashamed still to sing the praises of his fatherland. And for the development of its stirring history no theatre could have been more worthy than the home of the Portuguese.

CHAPTER II.

HISTORICAL INTRODUCTION.

WHEN the Romans had reduced their own peninsula they found themselves in unpleasant proximity to another power, as yet greater than they—Carthage, the then mistress of the seas. The Carthaginians having established themselves in Sicily, seemed on the eve of annexing the whole island, and thus, only a few miles from the toe of Italy, would have barred the progress and threatened the stability of Rome. A contest for supremacy was inevitable, and ere long hostilities broke out. The series of campaigns called the first Punic War ended disastrously for the African city, the loss of Sicily being one of its results. Carthage was much in need of a rich granary like Sicily, and for the sake of its future, required to be strengthened somehow and somewhere across the Mediterranean. Therefore a great Carthaginian general, Hamilcar, whose soubriquet was Barca (lightning), perhaps from the rapidity of his military movements, a statesman as well as a soldier, conceived the idea of turning Spain to the advantage of his city. Carthage had long been engaged in barter with the natives of that country, and had placed several marts upon the coast. In this respect the Carthaginians were only following the footsteps of their mother-country Phœnicia. They had also worked various mines in the Iberian Peninsula, as probably the Phœnicians had done before them ; and besides settling their factories, they had subjugated a certain portion of western

Spain.   But the aspiration of Hamilcar was not only to see the
ships of Carthage carrying away minerals and food stuffs.   His
ambition flew even higher than extensive conquest.   He wished
to unify the wild tribes and train them to ordered, national
life—to found a state there, subservient to the African metropolis, whose inhabitants should fight for her, and lay their
resources as they increased at her feet.   So in 238 or 236 B.C.,
Hamilcar crossed over into Spain by Gibraltar and addressed
himself to his difficult task.   Thus was the first deliberate effort
made to bring the rude people of south-western Europe into
abiding contact with civilization.

The tribes whom Hamilcar was bent upon educating were of
the Celtiberian race, a mixture of Iberians (from Africa, in all
likelihood) and Celtic immigrants who had come through the
passes of the Pyrenees and intermarried with the earlier inhabitants.   In some parts of the Peninsula the two elements,
Celtic and Iberian, had remained more distinct; but generally
the blend was thorough.   They were a rude, fierce people, no
doubt, resembling the "kerns and gallowglasses" of Celtic
Scotland long ago, separated into numerous clans by rivers or
mountain ridges, mutually jealous and revengeful.

The success of Hamilcar was signal.   He identified himself
with the people by marrying into a powerful clan, and by living
the rough life of the natives.   Yet he was careful to inspire
them with a desire to rise out of their mere animal existence.
He set them to develop such industries, mining and other, as
were possible to them, drilled them into soldiers, and endeavoured to reduce the friction among rival septs.   With the
forces he had disciplined, he marched victoriously over the
Peninsula, and what is especially important for us to remember,
his influence spread as far west as that part of Hispania which
we now name Portugal.

Barca's work was continued after his death by worthy successors, his son-in-law Hasdrubal, and his son, the famous

Hannibal, who managed so to maintain the policy of their relative that by-and-by, with the exception of the northern highlands and some Greek colonies on the coast, the entire country was in vassalage to Carthage, or on terms of friendship with her.

The exploits of the Barcine family, as it was called, were not unnoticed by the Romans, who naturally disliked the idea of their rival Carthage furnishing herself in Spain with an abundant supply of grain, a vast treasury of mineral wealth, and a practically exhaustless recruiting ground. The audacious attack of Hannibal upon Saguntum (Murviedro, in Valencia), a Greek emporium under the protection of Rome, supplied a pretext for a new war between the two great powers. The issue of this second struggle, not so protracted by a few years as the former, was much more decisively in favour of Rome. In Hispania, Carthage had her prestige put down for ever; and though she afterwards nerved herself for a final attempt to resist her formidable foe, it was but for self-preservation. She was too discouraged to indulge such dreams as that which filled the soul of Hamilcar.

The practical Romans immediately began to reap in the western peninsula all the fruits of Carthaginian sowing which were within their reach. Where the Carthaginians had sunk mines, the Romans wrought them further; where roads had been made, the Romans extended them. They improved every position their swords had won by erecting forts and throwing small garrisons into them. Towns grew up under their hands—imitation Romes, with temples, forums, baths, and every possible memorial of the metropolis. Thither flocked loyal families, some of them from far, to show the example of industrious, civic life, to strengthen the Roman dominion, and secure its permanence.

But it was only in the south where the progress of Rome was so smooth. The flight of its eagles was checked by the untamed tribes of the north and west, whose connection with Carthage had been of a looser kind. The legionaries had to contend through many years of petty but bloody warfare with those quasi-independent septs, who preferred death to a foreign yoke thus roughly thrust upon them.   For though Scipio Africanus, the illustrious Roman leader, inaugurated in Spain measures of conciliation, his countrymen were loath to continue a policy which they considered derogatory to their dignity.   In general they tried to be just with respect to subject races where justice was not inimical to the interests of the republic, but were mercilessly severe in smothering the desire for freedom throughout the provinces of their dominion.   So the Spanish tribes were ready to contrast unfavourably the new *régime* with the kindlier Carthaginian government.   And those of upper and western Spain, which, having been in friendly alliance with rather than in subjection to Carthage, had not felt the weight of her imposts, determined to bar the advance of the invader.   It was therefore only in 179 B.C., eighty-seven years after the Carthaginian forces were banished from Spanish soil, that Rome effected anything like a pacification of northern Spain.   And had it not been for the willingness to reason and the moderate dealing of Tiberius Gracchus, the representative of the republic, an honest and sagacious man, it is hard to say how long the struggle might have been protracted.

Difficult as it was to crush rebellion (as the Romans thought it) in the north, the men of the west, the ancestors of the Portuguese, were yet more intractable and prejudiced against the Roman influence.   For well-nigh one hundred and fifty years those stubborn tribes resisted the greatest power in the world.   As general succeeded general in command of the invading legions, fresh expeditions were undertaken against the western tribesmen ; but one commander after another had to confess himself baffled by the hardihood and even more by the cunning of the clans fighting for their rude altars and hearths. The tactics of these savage warriors must have resembled those of their descendants the *guerillas.*   We can imagine how

Roman vedettes were surrounded by superior forces of the enemy, who seemed to have risen out of the ground, so suddenly did they spring from their ambuscades; how stones were flung by hundreds of unseen hands and with terrific effect from the tops of defiles as the troops were marching through, unconscious of danger; how the very camps of the Romans were plundered under cover of night and the soldiers slain in sleep. A disciplined host, trained for the pitched field, might well be confounded by such a mode of warfare.

At length the unscrupulous Roman prætor, Sergius Galba, by fair speeches induced the clans to come out of their fastnesses and meet him in three divisions at different open spaces, where he proposed to fix boundaries and assign sites for towns, and otherwise satisfy their requirements. But, as he had secretly intended, he successively attacked in force and butchered each of the three Celtiberian detachments, which were totally unprepared for such an onslaught. Thus the tribes of the west were treacherously terrorized for the time into a cessation of hostilities. Only a few escaped. One of those, however, who found safety in flight from the swords of Galba's soldiery, lived to be the head of a wider insurrection in western Hispania. This man, one who had, as Wordsworth says, "lived unknown a shepherd's life," the "redoubted Viriatus," possessed all the qualities which mark men out as leaders—bravery, patience, considerateness, and generalship. The Roman annalists themselves admit his capacity and moral excellence. The pastoral calling was not in his case so opposed to the military as we might imagine; for in rude days and disturbed districts the shepherd is especially a man of war, ready to defend his charge against robbers, whether in the shape of wild beasts or of men. And no doubt the thousands who followed Viriatus were accustomed to the use of weapons from their youth, as indeed every man in a primitive state of society requires more or less to be.

Viriatus had devoted himself to the idea of avenging the day of Galba's treachery, and sweeping the aliens from his native land. With extraordinary enthusiasm he roused his fellow-countrymen to combine in taking up arms against Rome ; and being placed in command of the patriot troops, he carried on the war in the face of tremendous odds with undaunted spirit and consummate skill, until at length he fell under the dagger of an assassin bribed by the Romans for the purpose of despatching thus a noble enemy whom they could not defeat. Opposition to Rome in the west of the Peninsula, after the murder of the gallant Viriatus, virtually collapsed, at least south of the Tagus, the theatre, more especially, of that hero's contendings. The region between the Tagus and the Douro did not as a whole submit till Julius Cæsar effected its reduction in the year 60 B.C. Then western Hispania owned the sway of the republic without dispute. There was no new Viriatus to be the head and heart of a rebellion.

The Roman name for that division of their Spanish province which lay nearest to the Atlantic sea-board was Lusitania. But Camoens and Byron are not strictly accurate in making Lusian synonymous with Portuguese. For while ancient Lusitania excluded Minho and Tras os Montes, it comprehended portions of Leon and Spanish Estremadura. It is very doubtful, therefore, whether the Portuguese are justified in assigning Viriatus, as they are fain to do, a niche in their national temple of fame, because the Lusitanian shepherd may in truth have belonged to the other side of the frontier. But the facts remain that Portugal from the Douro to the southern Atlantic represents by far the greater part of ancient Lusitania, and that those stubborn hordes who kept the army of the republic so long at bay were the forefathers of the people who inhabit the centre and south of that kingdom.*

* Most modern peoples are hybrid, the Portuguese not less than their neighbours. But there is no reason to doubt that after all the infusion of Roman, Gothic, even Saracen and Jewish blood, the original Celtiberian element has remained the largest.

Only once during the republic, after Julius Cæsar's work in the provinces, was there an organized Lusitanian rebellion, and that outbreak was directed by the Roman general Sertorius, who, taking advantage of civil dissensions in the capital, and having, for his own purposes, made many friends among the native chieftains, planned an armed endeavour to repudiate vassalage to Rome. The Lusitanians crowded to his standard; but after a brief period of success, the Romans employed against him their frequent instrument, the assassin, and at one blow slew the ringleader and crushed the mutiny for which he had been responsible. Half a century later all Spain was subdued.

Under the empire, at least for its first hundred years, the hold which Rome had obtained in these, as in other parts of her world-wide domain, became firmer still. The emperors were able to impress their personality everywhere, and fully to carry out their schemes, uncontrolled by public opinion or the voice of a senate. Thus the realms of the Cæsars might be either an immense stage for the exhibition of consummate energy and sagacity or the plaything of a fool. History has recorded the good and the evil which accrued to the provinces from the imperial rule. This, at all events, is very evident, that the enlarged imperial notion of sovereignty, which consisted in thoroughly Romanizing the dominion, was fraught with great and far-reaching benefit to the peoples on whom the policy operated. In Hispania we see as well as anywhere else the action of these measures of statecraft. Road-making was carried on with the greatest assiduity, until the country may be said to have been fairly opened up for the passage of armies, and its peace thus, to a certain extent, guaranteed.

The immigration of Romans was encouraged to the utmost, and by these new settlers many towns and cities were founded, which exist under changed or sometimes only slightly disguised names at this day. The introduction of Roman customs curbed the rude manners of the Peninsula. The very dress of the

Romans became fashionable, and the Celtiberians learned to like being known as *togati.* The blood of these Roman immigrants was by-and-by mingled with that of the Celtiberian stock, and in this surest way a spirit of loyalty to Rome took root in the province. The language of Rome, too, supplanted in time the former barbaric speech of the inhabitants. And whatever value the tongues of the regions once subject to the Italian city may have in determining the depth of the impression she made upon them, it is undeniable that the Peninsula is the most Latin of all these former possessions of Rome. And it is particularly worthy of notice that Portugal, which so long provoked the Romans by its refusal to accept their government, and its readiness to revolt, has retained even more of the old Roman speech than Spain.

Traces of the Carthaginians are almost nowhere to be found in the Peninsula. Only one or two place-names speak with any certainty of the influence they exercised there.* And even these words may be previously-imported Phœnician expressions.

But relics of Rome are everywhere visible. Besides its towns and highways, antiquaries find abundant evidences of its occupation in the shape of ruined forts, walls, temples, aqueducts, and the like. It is even suggested that the primitive style of farming which is practised in some parts of Portugal, and the very songs of the Minhote peasantry, date from the old Roman time.†

The story of the empire's decline and fall is well known, and need not be dwelt on here. From its immense wealth sprang all imaginary luxury and vice; and the Sybarites, who represented the simple and public-spirited men of the republic, were unable to cope with the task of governing such a great dominion. The armies of Rome were by-and-by no longer completely sub-

* Tejo (Tagus), from *dagi,* fishy; Lusitania, from *luz,* almonds, *ana,* ewe (in Guadiana), etc. See M'Murdo's "History of Portugal from Portuguese Sources."
† "Travels in Portugal." By John Latouche.

ROMAN TEMPLE AT EVORA.

servient to its will, and, divided against itself, its decay became notorious. Nor did the formal sanction of Christianity by the state in the beginning of the fourth century preserve the realms of the Cæsars. Through the breaches in their defences poured barbaric myrmidons of various name. They spread panic and desolation everywhere, and had the audacity to thunder at the very gates of the imperial city.

The Iberian peninsula, too, was overrun by ferocious hordes from the east, till the emperor, despairing of his ability to expel them, was fain to ally himself with one of these predatory peoples, and to use it against the others. He summoned therefore the Visigoths, whose home was on the shores of the Danube, to drive out the invaders. The Visigothic leader succeeded in this enterprise, and with surprising honesty handed over to the Romans the province which he had cleared of their enemies. Since, however, they had become acquainted with a country where they had fought so hard for others, the Visigoths longed to possess it for themselves, and entered a second time to stay. They were indeed vanquished by the brave Emperor Majorianus; but no sooner was that last capable wearer of the purple removed, than the Visigoths, in defiance of Rome, erected in Spain a sovereignty of their own, destined to be maintained for three hundred years. So once more the Peninsula changed hands, after having been in the power of Rome for more than six centuries.

The Visigothic monarchs were Christian after a fashion, like those whom they had displaced. But the conduct of Christian Romans did not, on the whole, reveal any marked superiority to that of their heathen fathers. Nor were the principles of the gospel very vividly illustrated by the manners and morals of the Visigoths. There were honourable, wise, and courageous men among them, as among the Roman prætors and governors. Yet the record of many in the list of Gothic rulers is stained with crimes as great as any with which the Peninsular officials of heathen Rome could be indicted.   There was the church now in Spain, to be sure, according to the Roman model; but one finds its priests little apt to manifest the "sweet reasonableness of Christianity."   They are seen seeking their own in the council chamber, and sometimes with armed hand in the field; developing also that spirit of persecution which in after times used for its fell purpose the elaborate machinery of the Inquisition.   Nevertheless there were other and better elements than rapacity and bloodshed in the church, even as it was then and there.   Learning was being prosecuted with such light as had been given, and the leaven of gracious precepts and gentle lives led here and there was no doubt doing its work.

There are two or three outstanding names among the Visigothic kings.   There is Euric, the second Spanish sovereign, who was filled with an earnest desire to see his realm law-abiding.   He himself framed a set of enactments, giving proof of an acute and enlightened mind; and although the religious intolerance which he many times displayed was a patent blot upon his character, it must be admitted that he distinguished his reign by the persistent efforts he made to secure for his people the advantages of civilization.   Another notable man who later occupied the throne was Theudis.   In his time— the earlier part of the sixth century—that combination of Teutonic tribes which called itself the Frankish nation had been making extensive conquests, and now crossed the Pyrenees with the intention of annexing Spain.   But Theudis covered himself with glory by the generalship and heroism he displayed in stopping their progress and holding the field till they were compelled to retire behind their mountain wall, whither he indeed followed them and seized a rich district of their territory.   Wamba, too, a Visigothic Andrea Doria, revealed even as a veteran a martial spirit and a fertility of resource which might have put many a younger man to shame.   He caused a navy to be constructed for the defence of his coasts, and his sea-fights against depredators from northern Africa won him perhaps more renown than his engagements on land.

The last king of the Visigoths was Rodrigo (Sir Walter Scott's Don Roderick), whose career was one of the most shameless immorality. It was Rodrigo's profligacy, according to tradition, which not only wrought his own ruin, but put an end to the Visigothic sway. We are told—though historians have thrown some doubt upon the matter—that the king in his wanton insolence grossly insulted Florinda, the daughter of Count Julian, an influential noble of his own race. The enraged father, who, as an experienced soldier, was defending in his monarch's interest the African fortress of Ceuta, determined upon the direst retaliation for the outrage. For this purpose he did not hesitate to play the traitor, and called upon the enemies of his country to aid him in wreaking his revenge.

Those allies of Julian were the Moslem Arabs, sometimes more vaguely called Saracens (Orientals), who, carrying out their programme of conquest in the prophet's name, had thrown themselves into north Africa, and occupied Barbary.*

The Visigothic commandant, it is said, filled with reckless fury, betrayed his charge of the coast castle to the Moslems, and guided their forces by Gibraltar to Spain. This was Hamilcar's old route, and the natural one. Whatever truth there may be in the story of Julian, it is certain that the Arabs would welcome any opportunity which offered for opening with advantage a campaign in the Peninsula. Their own chronicles tell how the news of its delicious climate, its clear

---

* These people are often styled Moors, but that is a misnomer. The Moors were a heterogeneous folk, composed of Libyan, Phœnician, Roman, and other elements, with a strain of heathen Arab blood, dating from a long-past immigration. It is a mistake to speak of the Mussulman invasion of Spain in Rodrigo's time as Moorish. For though the Arabs held the land of the Moors, as the Romans held the Peninsula, set out thence for Spain, and no doubt recruited their ranks from among the able-bodied Moors, the expedition was directed, officered, and chiefly manned by Arabs. It is true that the Moors, converted then to Mohammedanism, flew to the aid of their Arab co-religionists in Spain three hundred years later, and thereafter founded a kingdom in Granada, of which the Alhambra is a splendid memorial. But they never had a footing in the western or Portuguese portion of the Peninsula.

and serene skies, its inexhaustible riches, the fine qualities of its fruits, its numerous towns, and so forth, had made them hungry for possession.*

So Musa, Emir of Africa under the caliph at Damascus, despatched Taric, his best general, in 711 A.D., to subjugate the goodly land across the sea. The army of Rodrigo, much superior in numbers, the Arabs say, to the Mohammedans, encountered the invaders at Xeres de la Frontera, in the valley of the Guadalquivir. For two days the bloody conflict raged, but on the third the Christian host was totally routed. Rodrigo was slain, and his head sent to the emir. The Arabs pursued their victory, and bore down all opposition. The power of the Visigoths was broken to pieces. But among the northern mountains many fugitives found a home from which their descendants should one day emerge and recover the lost land.

The rule which thus came to a disastrous end was on the whole better than that of Rome, although it was of unquestionable benefit that the Visigoths should have been preceded by a people who had ineradicably impressed the minds of their subjects with the idea of order, and had left behind them so many monuments of civilization, and particularly a language which was the key to much and various knowledge. The Visigoths, however, bringing with them some Roman notions, and learning many more in the Peninsula, improved upon the Roman notion of government by acknowledging certain popular rights which their predecessors' absolutism never dreamed of conceding except to the favoured *municipiæ* and *coloniæ*. The landlordism established under the Visigoths tended to the serious prosecution of the farming industry; and in the development of trade they were aided by numbers of that wonderful race, the Jews, who have been mixed up with European politics for so many centuries.

Peaceful, unarmed invaders, these "tribes of the wandering

* See Condé's "Dominion of the Arabs in Spain."

foot" stole into the Peninsula in considerable numbers during the Visigothic period, and their unassuming influence then and afterwards was incalculable. There, as elsewhere, with incredible patience and assiduity, they kept the wheels of commerce moving, and made themselves useful in manifold ways. Occasional outbursts of persecution they had to endure even from their earliest settlement in Spain. But they bore the cruelty of man as no other people could, and still lived on in this as in all their adopted lands, asking no lordship, only to be let alone that they might worship the God of Abraham, and quietly husband their gains.

The Arabs quickly overran the best and most cultivated parts of Spain, Lusitania also being impotent to dispute the passage of the Moslem troops; and had not the forces of the intrepid *Maire du Palais*, Charles Martel, constructed a rampart more insurmountable than the Pyrenees, the human tide would have covered the fair fields of Gaul. Crowned with success, they began to administer the affairs of the country in the spirit of absolute sovereignty. Like the Romans, they did not admit that their subjects had any rights of their own, or even held their lives by any other tenure than the pleasure of the caliph. But the natural kindliness of the conquerors, it must in justice be said, ameliorated greatly the condition of the conquered. The inhabitants of the Peninsula, perforce accepting the situation, obtained many immunities *ex gratia*, and were treated by their masters in the main with courtesy and honour. Unscrupulous medieval chroniclers have done their best to vilify the "Moors;" but it may be questioned, considering the oppression with which Israelitish sojourners were visited, and the intolerance displayed to the heretical Arians, whether any so-called Christian monarchy of that age would have ruled an alien race with a tithe of the forbearance shown by the Arabs in Spain to its subjugated people.

For about fifty years after the Mohammedan invasion, the

Peninsula was held under the Eastern caliphs, but at the end of that period their control was repudiated, and an independent government founded in the person of Abderrahman I., first of the Spanish caliphs. The cause of this disruption of the Moslem dominion was the sanguinary dispute in the East about the succession to the caliphate between the rival families of the Ommiades and the Abbasides, terminating in the defeat of the former and the almost complete extermination of the Ommiade family. Abderrahman, one of the fugitive Ommiades, coming to Spain, was acknowledged as their monarch by his co-religionists there who were faithful to the old dynasty. The line of the Spanish Ommiades, which continued for three hundred years, was a brilliant one. Abderrahman I., a great warrior, who immortalized himself by defeating Charlemagne at Roncesvalles, was not less distinguished by his sagacious and amiable rule. Most of his successors were remarkable for courage, wisdom, and humanity towards their subjects; and the prosperity of the country, during the continuance of this famous house, was as remarkable as could possibly be imagined under the yoke of foreigners whose Book forbade the granting, to any except Mohammedans, of those liberties which alone enable a people to develop its idiosyncrasies, and rise to the height of its powers.

But all this time the Christian remnant in the north was gathering strength. It could not be dislodged from its mountains. On the contrary, by perpetual raids it began to spread panic among the Moslems. The Arabs had considered those mountaineers barbarians, and, not dreaming that a nation was in process of construction up in the heights of Asturias, persisted in making light of the Christian incursions; while they cherished the impossible project of adding Gaul to their peninsular domain, and busied themselves with futile endeavours to make the whole of north Africa subservient to them. So they paid the penalty of lightly esteeming the banished Goths.

There were, however, other forces at work to vex and weaken the Mohammedan power. Scandinavian kinsfolk of the Goths came in their war-galleys to pillage the western coast; and the walis, or Arab governors of provinces, quarrelled violently among themselves, frequently taking the field against each other. These attacks of pagan Goths from the sea, and more especially of Christian Goths from the hills, shook the Mussulman despotism. So, blinded by its own schemes of conquest, its realm distracted by internecine commotions, the splendid dynasty of the Beni Omeyas was gradually undermined, and fell with a crash in 1031. There was thenceforth no such strong and central Mohammedan authority.

A number of walis assumed therefore sovereign functions, and turned their provinces into sultanates, each one pursuing the policy which he deemed most suitable.

From the downfall of the Ommiades the complete humiliation of the Moslems in the Peninsula was only a question of time. Their kingdoms could now be separately attacked, and by setting the Mohammedan rulers at variance, war could be declared against one without fear of seeing him defended by his neighbour. But it was above all the audacious and determined valour of the Christian leaders, without which their diplomacy would have availed nothing, which brought, amid many repulses, the hope of expelling the aliens every year closer. And, notwithstanding that swarm after swarm of Mohammedans arrived in the Peninsula from Africa, either to help their co-religionists or to push them aside and fight on their own account—at all events to reinforce the Mohammedan power, and dash the expectations of the Christians—the vigour of the native party was generally sufficient to repel the advance of the Crescent by the wiles of the guerilla, if not in battle array.

As Islam in Spain degenerated, a Christian people pent up in the highlands was being educated to occupy its room. While the Mussulman was looking in other directions, a process of consolidation was taking place among the men of the north. Their sudden swoops upon their foes were not the instinctive rushes of barbarians, but part of a resolute plan to rid the land of the swarthy usurper. They had the feeling that the future was theirs. Therefore the discouragement of temporary disaster never deepened into despair, but with admirable elasticity of spirit they returned again and again to the contest. This northern nation was one in race, language, religion, and deadly antagonism to the devotees of the prophet; and if it had remained one politically, complete triumph over the common enemy might have been easier and nearer. But, unfortunately, instead of one, four, and eventually five, independent Christian states were formed in the Peninsula. Of these states, consisting partly of peninsular districts which the Mohammedans had not touched, and partly of tracts recovered from them as their sway declined, four—Leon, Navarre, Castile, and Aragon—are now provinces of Spain; the fifth is the kingdom of Portugal.

The circumstances in which the Portuguese state arose will be described in another chapter. Meanwhile let us sum up in a few words the characteristics of the Moslems in the Peninsula.

The horrors of their incursion have been painted by the older writers in very glaring colours. And it is not to be expected that a power so foreign and, for various reasons, hateful should have been allowed to march through a country populated by a courageous race, and overturn a throne established for three centuries, without making good its way by sword and fire. But nothing is more certain than this, that the Arab in Spain has been grossly misrepresented. So soon as he assumed the reins of government he acted upon the principles of humanity. He did not offer the alternative of Islam or death, for his heart was better than his Koran. He scrupulously avoided interfering with the Christian religion, and generally refrained from damaging Christian edifices. The inhabitants were not oppressively taxed; their persons and property were protected.* Far from being a truculent ruffian, as the monkish caricatures of him which have been handed down to us insist, he was promise-keeping, more than just, and distinguished by a high-bred courtesy, which, stiffened into a form, has been preserved in the elaborate etiquette of the Peninsula. It would be difficult, however, to bring a Spaniard or a Portuguese to see that his ceremonious politeness is a burlesque memorial of the old Arab suavity.

Nor were the Arabs an uncultured people. They were fond of mathematics, and studied with avidity astronomy (after a superstitious manner, to be sure). They were industrious and graphic chroniclers. They produced much poetry of a luscious, dreamy sort. Their architectural work, with its elaborate though rather fantastical ornamentation, points to a patiently cultivated love of the beautiful. And it may be questioned whether there was any people of their day so advanced in chemistry and the healing art. The Jews during the Ommiade supremacy, it may be said by the way, multiplied greatly ; and the Mussulmans were sagacious enough to observe their talents, and encourage them to employ themselves, not only as merchants, but in the capacity of mathematicians, physicians, and in other learned professions. The Mohammedans made their mark upon the language of the Peninsula. There are about two hundred Arabic words in Portuguese, chiefly relating to the use of herbs, medical science, chemical processes, and various arts, the vocabulary affording valuable information regarding the kind of debt under which its rulers laid the country.†

In art and science the Arabs had much to teach, and in morals particularly their schooling was precious. But, like the Romans, they could not inculcate political progress, because they themselves did not understand it. Genial as was their rule, at any rate in its best days, it was too paternal to be perpetual. The wonder is that it lived so long.

* See Condé.   † See Latouche.

CHAPTER III.

THE height of Gaya, at the mouth of the Douro, on its southern side, opposite Oporto, was once crowned with a castle named Cale, and the little harbour which the fortress guarded was known as Portus Cale (the port of Cale). By-and-by the name of the haven was applied to the surrounding district. And when, in the eleventh century, a new state came into existence in the west of the Peninsula, distinct from the other Christian kingdoms, it was looked upon as an extension of the Porto Cale region, and so styled. Nor, though bit by bit it grew till it reached the ocean on the south, did it ever lose the medieval designation, which is found only slightly modified in the word Portugal.

The boundaries of Portugal as it is are very different from those of Portugal eight hundred years ago. At that time we find Alfonso VI. of Leon and Castile holding as a dependency the western portion of the Peninsula as far south as the Tagus, the territory from the left bank of the river to the southern coast of Algarve being still in the hands of the Moslems. The upper division of this Castilian domain was called Galicia; the lower, from the Douro to the Tagus, Portucale or Portugal. To the aid of Alfonso in his wars against the Mohammedans there had come a number of knights from Burgundy, and upon one of these, Count Henry of Besançon of the French royal house,* the king had conferred, in token of his gratitude and confidence, the governorship of Portugal and the hand of his illegitimate daughter Theresia. (Another Burgundian noble, Count Raymond, appointed Governor of Galicia, wedded Urraca, Alfonso's younger and legitimate child.) The governorship, as held by Count Henry, began to resemble more and more the state of a sovereign. As commander-in-chief of the forces within his province and supreme judge, and especially as the son-in-law of the Castilian monarch, he came to be regarded as an authority little inferior to the person from whom he derived his power, and the Portuguese got to speak of him in legal documents and elsewhere as reigning count, or sometimes even *prince*. Henry's connection with the royal family, his honourable character, and the comparative poverty and insignificance of the region which he ruled, hindered any feeling of political jealousy from taking possession of Alfonso. And, indeed, it cannot be denied that the Count of Portugal, so long as his father-in-law lived, administered his office as a vassal of the Castilian king.

But from the death of Alfonso VI., in 1109, the relationship of Portugal to the crown of Castile was changed. In that very year Henry styled himself "by God's grace, Count and Lord of all Portugal." So 1109 may be considered the date at which Portugal became independent. Two things led Henry to formally separate his dominion from the Spanish power. In the first place, a deadly quarrel in Castile about the succession to the throne constrained him to take up a position where he could as a free ally embrace the cause of either party, as it should suit the interests of Portugal. And secondly, as the Saracens, emboldened by the removal of the valiant Alfonso, the champion of Spanish Christendom, and by the consequent strife in the realm of the deceased monarch, began to force

* Grandson of Robert I., Duke of Nether Burgundy, and great-grandson of King Robert of France.

their way northwards, and to take town after town belonging to the Christians—Lisbon, Cintra, Santarem—Henry, thrown upon his own resources for the defence of his frontiers, seemed to himself to have gained, after unaided and on the whole successful resistance of the invaders, as good a right to sovereignty as any potentate in the Peninsula.

The complication in Castile arose from the assumption of lordship over that kingdom by Alfonso of Aragon in right of his wife Urraca, daughter of Alfonso VI., with whom he had been united after the death of her first husband, Count Raymond. Urraca, who was at odds with her husband Alfonso, resented his interference, and desired to rule Castile in her own name, and to conserve the sovereignty for her child Alfonso, the son of Raymond. Count Henry of Portugal at first decided for the Aragonese king, but afterwards furthered the claim of Urraca. This change of sides was extremely diplomatic, for having made his weight felt as an opponent, Henry was in a position to sell his friendship at a good price. What he wanted was an extension of territory, and it is certain that there was an arrangement in his favour between him and Urraca regarding the land north of the Douro. Some places in Galicia were even granted to the Portuguese count—or rather, having taken them, he was permitted to remain in possession. Yet with all this increase of influence, although he himself no doubt thought the Portuguese power by this time independent, the Castilian throne had not given up the idea of its suzerainty over the western province.

What would have been the result to Portugal if a great soldier like Alfonso of Aragon had been left with a free-hand to prosecute his claims upon Castile, it is hard to say. But the Mussulmans were stirring in the Peninsula, and Castile and Aragon were forced to patch up their differences for the sake of defending themselves against the unbelievers. The only real gainer from this unseemly bickering between a husband and wife was Count Henry, who obtained for the part he took in it an enlargement of his borders, and while the eyes of his neighbours were fastened upon the Castilian-Aragonese difficulty, was able to secure his seat in Portugal and prepare the nation for formally shaking off allegiance to any superior.

Henry died in 1112, and was succeeded by his widow Theresia, as regent of Portugal and guardian of her son Alfonso Henriquez, a child of tender years. Theresia drew out an ambitious programme for herself. She was bold enough to assume the title of queen, and proclaimed her intention to hold those towns and castles north of the Minho which had become Portuguese, in pursuance of a bargain with her late husband. But her sister Urraca was not disposed to make much of a promise given to Count Henry during her trouble in Castile, and suspected that Theresia desired to be mistress of Galicia. Therefore the Castilian regent refused point blank to comply with her sister's wishes, and war immediately broke out between the two powers. It was an unequal struggle. Theresia, notwithstanding her determination and capacity, could make no headway against the forces of Castile. She damaged her cause, too, by imprisoning the Archbishop of Braga, who had shown himself unfriendly to her plans. The Pope, Calixtus II., had to threaten her and her adherents with the ban, and her realm with the interdict, before she would set the archbishop free. But even though she thus capitulated, her reputation suffered severely from her audacity in seizing the person of an ecclesiastical dignitary. Yet she clung to her purpose, and, after the death of Urraca, continued the contest with her nephew, the young King of Castile, Alfonso Raymondez. The Castilian monarch resolved to strike a decisive blow, and summoning all his vassals to the field, marched to Portugal and wasted the country for six weeks. The enemy were in such overwhelming force that Theresia was glad to conclude a peace, whose exact terms, however, are not preserved. What we do know is that whatever penalty the king may have exacted, the question of Portuguese independence was left in the kind of undetermined state in which it had been for years. Still, with all her efforts, Theresia had not advanced her interests in the slightest—had only spent blood and treasure, and brought down the foe upon the fields of Portugal.

Theresia ought to have learned discretion after her prolonged and disastrous campaigning, but wilful and oblivious of danger as ever, she proceeded to destroy any respect which her own people might still entertain for her by uniting herself (if indeed there was a legal union, for that is doubtful) with a Galician count, Ferdinand of Trastamara. This arrogant and dissolute man was elevated to the highest place in the state next to the regent herself, and the more she showered honours upon him, the more did the people detest him. The nobles were of the opinion that the sooner the unworthy favourite should be crushed the better, and consulted about measures for curbing his unscrupulous ambition.

They had an instrument at hand. Alfonso Henriquez, the son of Theresia, was growing up to manhood. He was a youth of great promise. His appearance and manners were captivating; and the early unfolding of his intellectual powers gave the Portuguese notables confidence in the future of their country, should he be spared to succeed his father. Already, in his fourteenth year, Alfonso Henriquez had dedicated himself to the profession of arms, kneeling in panoply of steel before the altar; and during the fifty-seven years of sovereignty to which he was destined, he may be said to have almost never laid down his weapons, so constantly surrounded with danger was his growing realm.

He was just eighteen years of age when he received an invitation from some of the most important of the nobility to enforce his rights as hereditary Governor of Portugal. He acceded to the request, and appeared at the head of an army for the purpose of compelling his mother to surrender the regency, which she had in a great measure delegated to the foreigner, Ferdinand of Trastamara. Theresia's forces encountered those of her son at Guimaraens, about forty miles north-east of Oporto, and after a sanguinary fight the regent was defeated, Ferdinand escaping to Galicia. Theresia herself was taken prisoner, and though treated with consideration by the conqueror, was never afterwards allowed to interfere in public affairs. Thenceforward Alfonso Henriquez took the reins of government into his own hands as Infant of Portugal.

Of course many of those who assisted Alfonso at this crisis made him pay dearly for their aid, particularly the Archbishop of Braga, Theresia's old enemy, who extracted from the victorious Infant large immunities for his see, the granting of which set up an unfortunate precedent and caused endless trouble between church and state. But Alfonso was young and inexperienced, and in the happiness of his first triumph was naturally inclined to be indiscreetly generous.

His cousin, Alfonso Raymondez of Castile, had so increased in power that almost all the other Spanish kingdoms were more or less in subjection to his throne, and had, in the cathedral of Leon, been formally acknowledged as Emperor of Spain. Thereupon the Portuguese Infant determined to show that he for one would not do homage to the new empire, and revived the old claims of Count Henry to those Galician towns said to have been ceded to Portugal by Urraca. Alfonso of Castile, however, in the brand-new pomp of the imperial purple, was not at all inclined to concede any demand whose justice was in the least doubtful, and opposed the Infant with all his might. The cousins took the field against each other, and notwithstanding the heroism and strategy of Henriquez, he would certainly have been severely beaten, as he was greatly outnumbered, had not a fresh attack upon Christian territory by the Moslems, whose incursions often stopped the mutual slaughter of the Christians, necessitated a truce between the opposing leaders. The Portuguese agreed to evacuate Galicia, and the Castilian gave up the towns he had taken in Portugal. The subject of Portuguese independence does not appear to have been discussed, but it seemed written in the book of Providence that Portugal was not to press farther north than the Minho.

Alfonso Henriquez now began his campaigning against the unbelievers, by which he gained for himself one of the most eminent places in the roll of honour. Small though his army was, each man imagined himself to be doing the work of Heaven in resisting the followers of the false prophet; and Alfonso was a host in himself, brave to rashness, and yet uniting the courage of the lion with the wisdom of the serpent. Always foremost in the fight, his genius and presence of mind was able to take advantage of every opportunity for baffling and outwitting the foe.

If the Portuguese power might not extend itself northwards to the sea, it might expel the Mohammedans from the land south of the Tagus, and plant itself there, where the Castilian had no claim. So, impelled by land-hunger, and panting for laurels, Alfonso Henriquez and his forces cut their way with the sword through the Mohammedan population south of the Tagus, and found themselves on the frontiers of Algarve. There, in the plain of Ourique, the great battle was fought which decided the fate of Portugal. All the available Saracen strength confronted the Portuguese. The Mussulmans, say the patriotic chronicles of Portugal, were to the soldiery of Alfonso as at least twenty to one. But setting aside such exaggerations, it is clear that the numbers of the Mohammedans must have been vastly superior to those of their antagonists. It seemed as if the Portuguese were about to be swallowed up. But the desperate valour of the Christian knights, animated by their matchless leader, filled their enemies with terror. The

Saracen host was utterly discomfited and put to ignominious flight. The day of the battle of Ourique, July 25th, 1129, was the birthday of the kingdom of Portugal, for from that date Alfonso assumed the royal title.*

But in order to perpetuate the kingship, Alfonso sought better guarantees than the acclamations of his troops. So, without fully accomplishing the large design he entertained against the Mohammedans, he hastened northwards and called a meeting of the notables and representatives of the nation at Lamego, some forty miles to the east of Oporto. Before this parliament, or Cortes, he laid a number of statutes for the administration of national affairs, and of justice between man and man. Regarding the nobility also, a code was submitted which bound them to the royal house, and made provision for the punishment of individuals who, through treachery or other unworthy conduct, should bring dishonour on their order. Many useful regulations were approved by the assembly, and questions of great importance to the king were settled as to the authority of and succession to the throne of Portugal. Concerning the succession, sons of the sovereign were to succeed, and failing them, daughters. But a daughter's husband should not succeed until a male child had been born of the marriage. And if a daughter were wedded to a foreigner, she deprived herself and her posterity of any right to the crown. The Cortes impressively closed by the king and all the members standing up, and, with drawn swords uplifted, vowing to maintain the freedom of Portugal, and to inflict the penalty of death upon any who should be the means of subjecting their land to foreign control.

Alfonso breathed more freely after the Cortes of Lamego, for

* The Saracens who were thus defeated were the Almoravides, or servants of God, a fanatical people of Africa, whose capital was Morocco. They had entered the Peninsula ostensibly, and at first no doubt really, to stand by the Ommiades in defence of the Crescent, but afterwards drove that dynasty from power, and now represented in south-western Europe the Mohammedan cause.

now he knew that a united people was willing to support him in the exercise of his prerogative, and in the work upon which he had set his heart. Yet, still further to take hostages of fortune, he appealed to the Pope for his benediction. For he dreaded lest the emperor's opposition should smother the infant kingdom in its cradle, and ardently desired that the Papal power should stand between it and the strength of Castile. After a time the king's wishes were granted from Rome. The new monarchy was acknowledged by the highest authority in Christendom, and in return Alfonso engaged to contribute a sum of money for the support of the Pontifical chair.

Now the Portuguese king was prepared and fain to resume hostilities against the Saracens. It may be remembered that on the decease of Alfonso VI. of Castile the Mohammedans took several towns on and about the Tagus. Of these, Santarem, Cintra, Lisbon, and more besides, remained in possession of the unbelievers. These places Alfonso Henriquez was bent upon restoring to Portugal. His first attempt was made at Santarem, which by a determined night-attack he took and garrisoned, so that he might have a strong place to fall back on in case of need. Then he addressed himself to the more difficult task of laying siege to Lisbon. This town was one of the strongest bulwarks of the Saracens in the Peninsula. Protected on the north and south by steep heights, and on the east by the Tagus, it had been strongly fortified on the western side, where access was easiest. It would have been well-nigh impossible for the Portuguese to have taken it alone; but it so happened that just at that time a fleet, transporting crusaders— English, Lorrainers, Flemings, and a great number of German pilgrims—took shelter at Oporto from stress of weather. This multitude was bound for the Holy Sepulchre, under vows of hostility to the unbelievers. They were entreated to delay their voyage until they had rendered assistance at the siege of Lisbon. They were glad to take part anywhere against the foes of their faith, and sailed for the Tagus without delay. Thus it came about that Alfonso was provided with large reinforcements in carrying out what was, if we except Ourique, the most important military performance of his life. The siege nevertheless was long, and attended with great loss of life and terrible privations. The garrison defended themselves with stubbornness, often repulsing the besiegers; but after five months the Christians, on October 25th, 1147, forced an entrance and made themselves masters of the town. The Mussulman population of this and other captured places were generally treated well, at all events after the fury of the successful besiegers was spent. They were allowed to remain in certain quarters of the towns, and not compelled to change their religion.

Lisbon, in this way recovered, was afterwards to become something far greater as a centre of political and commercial life than at that time could have been conceived; but even as it was, an astute mind like Alfonso's, considering its splendid situation on the Tagus and its excellent harbour facing the western ocean, must have seen in it a factor of incalculable moment for the furtherance of his far-reaching plans. He was careful, therefore, to foster the shipping trade of the place, and to do everything else in his power for its material advancement, while its erection into an episcopal see gave it ecclesiastical visibility.

The taking of Lisbon paved the way for other conquests. One of the prizes which fell into his hands was Evora, the principal town of Alemtejo. It surrendered to a certain Rinaldo, named the Fearless, a famous freebooter, who sought to rehabilitate himself by doing some signal service to the king. In the most daring manner he and his band climbed the walls one dark night, slew the sentinels, and in an incredibly short time had the place at their mercy. Rinaldo obtained from the king, delighted with his brilliant success, pardon for his former crimes and the governorship of the town which he had so adroitly captured.

Alfonso was a Knight Templar, and therefore bound to do lifelong battle with the unbelievers; but apart from the vows of his order, he deemed it imperative for the future security of his kingdom to suppress the Saracens on every hand. So we find him by-and-by engaged in besieging the Mohammedan town of Badajos. But that place was in vassalage to Ferdinand of Leon, one of the heirs of Alfonso VII. of Castile (the emperor), whose realm after his death was divided among his sons. Ferdinand, then hearing of the siege, hastened to relieve it, and, although son-in-law to the King of Portugal, did not hesitate to measure swords with him. It was an unfortunate encounter for Alfonso. His horse fell in the fight, with the result that the king shattered his thigh and lay helpless on the ground. His followers seemed to lose heart when they saw their leader fall, and soon the day was Ferdinand's. The Leonese sovereign was, however, too generous to press his advantage far. He only required that the Portuguese forces should retire from Badajos, and that Alfonso should finally renounce what had been so long a bone of contention between Portugal and Leon—the Portuguese project, namely, of obtaining a foothold in Galicia. The King of Portugal agreed to these conditions, and was carried homewards. But the great Portuguese hero was, in consequence of his injury on the battle-field, a cripple for life, and was never able to mount a horse after the fight at Badajos. He had for the most part to let others carry out the warlike designs which he framed. Nevertheless, when campaigns were protracted, and when strong places would not yield to his besieging troops, he caused himself again and again to be borne in a chariot to the scene of action, and his appearance hardly ever failed to turn the tide of victory in his favour. Taking part thus in battle against the Almohades, another fierce Mohammedan tribe who had by this time displaced the Almoravides, his fiery spirit impelled him to leap from his carriage and engage personally in the fray till he saw the enemy take to flight. And just the year before his death the venerable king hurried to succour his son Sancho, who was shut up in Santarem by the Saracens, and in a wretched case. No sooner, however, did the besieged garrison see Alfonso approaching than they sallied out and threw themselves upon their foes with such fury that the unbelievers were utterly routed.

In 1185, at Coimbra, Alfonso I. of Portugal, perhaps the most heroic figure in the story of his country, departed this life. He was, in a sense, the creator of Portugal, and it was the greatest possible blessing to the land that a man so resolute and enlightened should have been spared so long. To his successors he served as a pattern of all that is manly and kingly; and it may be said, without fear of contradiction, that none who ever wore its crown did more than he for the state whose foundation he laid so well as to defy all efforts to overthrow it.

Sancho, the son and immediate successor of Alfonso, although gifted with his father's indomitable courage, had a somewhat different part to play. The land stood greatly in need of rest after so much carnage and devastation. Alfonso had, no doubt, in the brief intervals between his campaigns, employed himself in settling and civilizing the realm. His pious zeal was displayed in the founding and endowing of numerous churches and religious houses, such as Alcobaça and Coimbra; but what was done in time of truce was often undone when the fighting recommenced. Now, however, Portugal from the Minho to the Tagus was won and strongly garrisoned for the Portuguese, and Sancho's *rôle* was mostly that of a cultivator and builder, with his weapon, however, lying handy to resist invasion, and an open eye for any advantage which could be secured without much risk of bloodshed.* He was an ap-

---

* The south was still the Saracen Gharb, and was not considered Portuguese any more than Mexico is looked upon as part of the United States.

proved soldier, but with admirable self-control he curbed the passion for adventure, and preferred the ploughshare to the sword. The feet of invading and defending armies had trampled down many times, in Alfonso's day, the fruit of patient labour. The cavalry who had often spread panic in the Paynim ranks were many of them yeomen withdrawn from their farms. The infantry who had withstood so well the shock of the Paynim charge were the hinds and vinedressers whose absence left the fields of Portugal languishing. The homes of the people had been everywhere razed by ruthless hands. The people's wealth had been devoured by the insatiate spirit of war. It was time for the slaughter-house to be transformed into an abode of peace and plenty.

The crusading spirit, roused once more by the fall of Jerusalem in 1187, sent many knights to Palestine, and a fleet of crusaders appearing in the Tagus, Sancho bethought him of the aid his father had received from these foes of the Saracen in the, taking of Lisbon. So he prevailed upon the knightly voyagers to help him in clearing Algarve of the infidels who held the province. They were successful, with the help of Portuguese auxiliaries, in invading Algarve and storming Silves, its chief town. His use of the pilgrim soldiers in the, to them, congenial work of pushing back the Mohammedan power, was a wise measure on the part of King Sancho. His stake on the enterprise was small, and the gain should be his country's.

But Providence willed that he should make little or nothing of the crusaders' campaign. The destructive forces of nature manifested themselves, after his allies' withdrawal, in an unprecedented manner. A prolonged rainfall spoiled the grain as well as the fruit of the vine and olive trees. This wet weather was succeeded by an extraordinary drought, effectually preventing vegetable growth. A plague of worms ensued which consumed what the rain and the drought had left. And to crown all these misfortunes, a deadly epidemic appeared among the people, making numberless victims whom hunger and thirst had spared. The Mussulmans were not slow to turn the misery of the Portuguese to their own advantage. Silves was recaptured by the Mohammedan Governor of Cordova; and Sancho, in view of the unfortunate state of his land, was compelled to conclude a five years' truce with the enemy.

It was in these woful circumstances that the king fairly earned for himself the title "father of his country." The finer qualities of his nature were conspicuous at a time when many men would have given way to despair. His wonderful activity and sympathy in the mitigation of distress are worthy of the highest praise. He travelled from district to district, personally inspecting the condition of his farmers and peasantry. He visited many towns, and made such arrangements as were necessary for their welfare. He put premiums upon industry, specially encouraging, by the promise of privileges, the reclamation of wastes, and the restoration of towns and villages which had been destroyed in the vicissitudes of warfare. He gave freedom to many serfs, and showed such compassion for the poor in the ceaseless efforts he made to better their state, that he lived in their hearts as a Portuguese king of the commons.

For the defence of the land he relied much on the various societies of knights which had been established in Portugal, some of them in his father's time. These orders, such as the Templars, the Knights of St. John, of St. Michael, and of Avis (a member of which last body was by-and-by to sit on the Portuguese throne), Sancho warmly supported by pecuniary allowances, and by the granting of rights over certain towns and districts. He did not forget, however, to stipulate in these settlements for the subordination of the orders to the plans and wishes of the throne.

One thing vexed the king exceedingly, and troubled the last years of his reign—the growing arrogance, and assumption of almost supreme power within their dioceses, of certain ecclesiastical magnates; their disposition to interfere, moreover, in matters of state. Unfortunately Alfonso I. had, in his earlier days, surrendered more to the church than was safe for the realm and the crown. Some of its prerogatives, indeed, dated from the time of the regent Theresia. So the privileges of the church were old already in Sancho's reign. But the bishops' exercise of their feudal rights was not always tempered with the policy and kindliness which so endeared the king to his subjects. It happened, therefore, that the citizens of Oporto, feudatories of the bishop, deeming themselves oppressed, wished to be released from a rule so much stricter than the king's. But Sancho, unwilling to encourage resistance to the church, exhorted the people to submission. Yet the proud prelate was not satisfied with the king, who he thought might have more thoroughly put down the spirit of revolt, and showed on a future occasion how much he resented Sancho's half-hearted advocacy of the episcopal claims.

The occasion was the marriage of the Infant Alfonso in 1208 with a distant relative, daughter of Alfonso VIII. of Castile. The Bishop of Oporto refused to attend the wedding, and declared it illegal, as it was, according to him, within the prohibited degrees. This conduct was so much more than the king could endure, that he cast the bishop into a dungeon, and only after some months' incarceration did the prisoner manage to make his escape by night. The Pope, when he came to hear of Sancho's proceedings, demanded satisfaction for the dishonour done to the church. But Sancho had made up his mind to stand firm, and would not apologize. On the contrary, he invited the further hostility of the clergy by wedding his daughter to her cousin Alfonso IX. of Leon. Pope Innocent, therefore, ordered the dissolution of the marriage, and as no heed was paid to his command, laid the interdict upon both kingdoms. The suspension of religious exercises which this sentence involved was felt by the people to be a great deprivation ; so, as the murmurs of Leonese and Portuguese alike became loud, the union, attended by such disagreeable consequences to two nations, was broken in five years. But such tardy submission, and to the clamour of the people rather than to ecclesiastical authority, was not very gratifying to the representatives of the church.

However indiscreet Sancho may have been as to the latter, at least, of the two royal marriages, and perhaps in other instances, there is no doubt he was doing a useful work for the state in suppressing the high-handedness of the prelates. His behaviour is detailed, of course from the clerical point of view, in a letter from the Bishop of Coimbra to the Pope, wherein the king is said to be guilty of summoning clergy before secular judges, meddling with diocesan and other church estates, entertaining persons who were under the ban, and so on. The Pope describes Sancho's letter of self-defence to him as full of immodesty and presumption. But the king had, on the whole, his people, the knightly orders, and even some of the bishops with him in his efforts to set bounds to the ambition of haughty churchmen. The candid and enlightened believed that in insisting on his sovereignty in the secular sphere, Sancho was not animated by selfish motives.

Although he did not often, after his accession, appear like his father at the head of an army, Sancho I. had, we see, sufficient warfare of another kind. Yet at his death-bed stood the ministers of that church whose encroachments he had so stoutly resisted, and his legacies to religious establishments showed that he was weary of logomachy, and desired, in prospect of the other world, to say that he died in the Catholic faith. The Pope sent him in 1211, the year of the king's death, a letter of reconciliation and benediction, but whether it reached him before he departed cannot be ascertained.

His son, Alfonso II., signalized his assumption of the government by bitter contention with his sisters, whose rights to the possession of certain towns and lands, bequeathed them by his father, he declined to homologate until they had first done homage to him as overlord. Perhaps mistaking his meaning, and imagining that Alfonso would not permit them to hold their legacies on any terms, they appealed for aid to the Pope, who had confirmed their father's will, and to the King of Leon, the husband (though now judicially separated from her) of Theresia, one of Alfonso's sisters. The Portuguese monarch, irritated at this call for help from abroad, sought a meeting with his sisters, and explained that he only desired to secure his royal supremacy; offered to garrison the towns in question, and to allow the royal ladies the privilege of raising their annual dues. But they would not listen to him. So he resolved to let matters take their course. The Infant of Leon entered Portugal with troops, and began to lay waste the country; while Alfonso also proceeded to take, by force of arms, the places belonging to his sisters. An unwillingness was manifested on the part of the Portuguese nobles to take the field with their king in this cause. He was not personally such a favourite as his father had been, and compassion for females who seemed to be treated with harshness cooled their loyalty. Yet, notwithstanding the opposition and the degree of unpopularity with which he was met, and in spite of the Papal ban which, in addition, was hurled at his head, Alfonso persisted in seizing the towns, and not till he had them in his hands did he announce that he was prepared to treat. The Pope, as umpire, appointed him a fine so large that he could not possibly pay it. He refused to plunge into debt, and the ban was again let loose. After troublesome negotiations, the towns were, with the king's consent, given in charge to the Knights Templars, the royal superiority to be acknowledged, and the incomes paid to the sisters. So the unnatural strife, which occupied more than a third of Alfonso's reign, was outwardly healed, but the relations of the king to the other members of his family had been too much strained ever to become cordial.

He was relieved of the ban, but only for a short time. Disputes with the clergy, such as had engaged so much of his father's attention, were in like manner the lot of Alfonso. He commanded the bishops to contribute their share of the national imposts, and when they declined boldly possessed himself of their goods. Even the primate, the Archbishop of Braga, he dealt with in this masterful style. The new Pope, Honorius, could not choose but ban the king. But the anathema does not seem to have been much of a burden to him, for he carried it to his grave.

Alfonso II. gave proof of his physical courage in a number of minor engagements with the Saracens, at one of which he was drawn out beneath a heap of Mohammedan slain. But a remarkable obesity with which he was afflicted, and which brought him to his end, rendered him incapable latterly of much bodily fatigue. So, although a brilliant victory was achieved in his reign at a place in the Saracen south named Alcazar do Sol, where fourteen thousand of the enemy are said to have been killed, and an exceedingly strong castle was taken, the king himself was not present at the fighting. Those who won that great day were Portuguese, led (strange to say) by Martin, Bishop of Lisbon, and crusaders who had run into Lisbon on their way to Palestine. The capture of Alcazar do Sol was of great moment to the Portuguese, since from thence frequent raids had been made for years upon their fields and villages to their no small fear and loss.

What, however, we are sure the king had to do with was a code of laws which received the approval of the Cortes at Coimbra in 1211. The special note of this code was the respect it paid to the notion of individual liberty. Although it was much too early to expect the abolition of serfdom, yet the power of the feudal superior was defined, to the great

advantage of the vassal. The king also renounced the right
to the third part of all food-stuffs sold in the market, and the
higher nobility possessing such a right were in like manner by
the code of Coimbra deprived of it. One is pleased, too, to
observe in these laws a section forbidding the taking aught
without the owners' consent from shipwrecked vessels or persons, whether Portuguese or foreigners; "for it seems wrong
that the unfortunate should suffer further injury from men."
A portion of this admirable code was transcribed two centuries
later into the statute-book of Portugal, with the remark that
the laws of Alfonso II. were "full of wisdom and humanity."

Alfonso II. died in 1223, and his son Sancho II. ascended
the throne. The new sovereign lost no time in putting an end
to the dispute between the crown and the clergy, so persistently
carried on by his father; and finally settled, besides, that question of his aunts' holdings, which had caused such a fierce conflagration in the kingdom. Thus he was at liberty to give his
undivided attention to the business of making war upon the
Saracens in Alemtejo and Algarve. The Pope assisted him
greatly by issuing a bull promising forgiveness of sins to all
who should take part in the enterprise, just as if they had gone
to recover the Holy Sepulchre. Nearly the whole of Sancho's
reign was occupied with these endeavours to expel the unbelievers from the south, and much progress was made with
the work.

But to counterbalance his success in the field, from the third
year after his coronation a storm was brewing in the church
which eventually made shipwreck of his fortunes. As the
royal treasury required to be frequently replenished in order
to furnish the sinews of war, Sancho made requisitions on
clerical funds for the purpose. The consequence was a com-
plaint to the Pope against the sovereign on the part of the
Bishop of Oporto, the Archbishop of Braga, and others. The
king tried to settle the matter as best he could, but after all

his efforts found it next to impossible to meet the wishes of the clergy. Altercations were continually arising between royal and ecclesiastical officials regarding the collection of taxes. The king's servants insisted upon the payment of state dues, and the church as vehemently protested against what she called insolent demands. Things came to such a pass that the prelate, to teach the throne a lesson which should not be forgotten, concocted a subtle plot to pluck the crown from Sancho's head.

There was a certain amount of discontent in the country with the conduct of the king, of which churchmen readily availed themselves. A noble Biscayan lady, Dona Mecia de Haro, had gained considerable influence with Sancho. Some said she was actually married to him—and undoubtedly she more than once in documents subscribed herself queen; but there is no record of a legal union. At all events, Dona Mecia was thought to hold the sovereign in leading strings; and those members of the royal family who—Sancho being childless— had an eye to the succession, were easily infected by the bishops with jealousy of her and persuaded to join in the conspiracy.

A terrible indictment was drawn up against the unfortunate Sancho for presentation to the Pope. The king, it declared, was being led astray by a wicked woman. He was neglecting public affairs; keeping at a distance those relatives who were able and willing to assist him with advice and otherwise; and, above all, was bent upon robbing the church. The Bishop of Oporto also insinuated in a letter of his own to the Pontiff that the king was too much of a monk, and destitute of that martial spirit which was necessary for a monarch who was expected to lead his army in person. This allegation was without doubt a libel, because Sancho, though brought up under the care of monks, and wearing in his boyhood the Augustinian cowl, was, like his predecessors, a soldier who had borne the brunt of many an engagement.

These charges were, however, held to be proved, and Pope Innocent IV., in 1245, issued from Lyons, where he was sitting in general council, a bull dethroning the sovereign and appointing his successor. There were three persons who hoped for the throne—Alfonso, the elder of the king's brothers, Count of Boulogne in right of his wife; a younger brother Ferdinand; and the Infant Pedro, uncle of the king, a headlong, fiery knight, whose romantic escapades would fill a volume. But Alfonso had hitherto shown himself an obedient son of the church, and was, in view of the crown, ready to promise her everything, and, besides, stood next in right of succession. So there was no good reason for passing him by in favour of candidates like the Infants Pedro and Ferdinand. As for Pedro, his reckless bravery was the theme of many a tale, but no one could trust him in a responsible position; while Ferdinand had more than once laid violent hands on ecclesiastical property. There was really only one possible candidate; but churchmen had, for the purpose of spreading the agitation against Sancho, encouraged in all three the dream of succession. The Count of Boulogne, then, received from the Pope, who had no business to grant it, the right of stepping into a throne which was not yet vacant.

The count proceeded with a considerable following to possess himself of the power, which might have cost him no little trouble and bloodshed. But to the regret of Sancho's adherents, and to the very agreeable surprise of the count, the king lost heart on hearing of the doings at Lyons, and left the country for Castile. So Count Alfonso found the way to the throne comparatively clear. He charmed the people by his affability, and the Sancho party organized no resistance, but reconciled themselves to the situation. The runaway monarch obtained an asylum in Castile; but no more, for the Papal bull paralyzed the arms of every secular power which might have interfered in his behalf. So Alfonso was speedily master of Portugal.

A few fortresses, however, held out for Sancho till the king's death, which occurred in 1248 or 1249. The defence of some of these places reveals a loyalty and heroism on the part of their commandants well worthy of record.

The stronghold of Celorico, on the Mondego, for instance, seemed impregnable, so Alfonso sat down before it with the view of starving the garrison. In a short time the want within the walls grew oppressive; still the stout-hearted governor would not open his gates. One day a heron flew over the castle from the river with a freshly-caught trout in its mouth, which it happened to drop inside the battlements. The commandant, who was gifted with a ready wit, had the fish dressed, and sent it with some fine bread as a present to Alfonso. The count, believing his antagonists had some secret means of communication with the surrounding neighbourhood, despaired of capturing the place, and, raising the siege, departed.

Coimbra also repelled his repeated attempts to storm it, and on no account would the warden surrender, although his men were threatening mutiny on account of his stubborn resistance when their provisions had gone down to the lowest ebb. Coimbra was still besieged when the news came from Toledo of Sancho's death. Alfonso informed the commandant of Coimbra, but he refused to credit the report till he should have gone and convinced himself of its truth. Alfonso gave him safe conduct to Toledo, and there the devoted soldier caused the grave of his late master to be opened. He addressed the corpse, formally giving up his charge, and placed the keys of Coimbra in the dead hand; then taking them again, he travelled back to Coimbra, and acknowledged the Count of Boulogne as rightful sovereign of Portugal.

The count, as soon as the decease of Sancho became an established fact, called the estates of the realm together at Lisbon, and caused solemn homage to be done him as Alfonso III., for hitherto he had considered himself merely the guardian of the kingdom.

In the first year of his reign he resumed hostilities against the Mohammedans of the south; and attacking them on land, he was careful also to cut off their supplies from the sea by watching the coast with a Portuguese fleet. He was so fortunate in these operations that the apprehension of Alfonso the Wise of Castile, who disliked to see the Portuguese state crossing the Guadiana and approaching his western limit, was greatly excited. The Castilians had been in the habit of looking at Portugal as a comparatively insignificant country; but now that it was so rapidly extending, it bade fair to rival its eastern neighbour. So the Castilian king declared against his namesake a war which lasted a whole twelvemonth. In the treaty with which the war concluded, the King of Portugal, holding to the lordship of the territory he had won, gave up to his opponent the income of the province for his lifetime; and in a second clause of the compact promised to wed Beatrice, the illegitimate daughter of Alfonso of Castile. The cool audacity of such a promise will be seen in the fact that the queen of Alfonso III., Matilda of Boulogne, still lived. But the Portuguese monarch wished a male heir, and Matilda had borne him only one child, a girl. This desire, together with the idea that the new marriage would avert the jealousy of Castile, seemed to him sufficient justification for bigamy. The union took place; but the cause of the forsaken Matilda was espoused by the Pope, who put Alfonso III. under the ban. On the death of Matilda, however, the prelates of Portugal procured the removal of the Papal sentence and the legitimization of the marriage, with that of all Beatrice's children.

After the successful pleading of the bishops, the boundaries of southern Portugal were fixed with reference to Castile; and from this example we see how the formation of the country as a whole proceeded. The expansion of the bordering kingdoms westward was stayed by a massive wall of Mussulman defence, and they were compelled to accept that wall as their frontier. Then Portugal, the new state, began, as the Mohammedans weakened, to sweep them out of its area. It was let alone so long as there was a space between it and the eastern states; but whenever it had cleared the intervening room and threatened to collide with them, the territory had to be adjusted by treaty, Portugal claiming as much to the east as it dared, its neighbours pressing it back as far as they could.

Alfonso III. is to be considered first king of the Portugal which we see in the maps of the present day, for the result of his warring and treating was the final delimitation of the country. He became in reality sovereign of Algarve as well as of the land between the Minho and the Tagus. But while admitting his own contribution to this triumph, which was considerable, we must not forget that he was largely reaping what others had sown. Even the dethroned Sancho II., the memory of whose services was well-nigh buried in the ruins of his fall, had pushed the work vigorously forward. In fact, every crowned member of the Henriquez family had done something which made for the ultimate conquest of all Portugal.

But now that the Portuguese could congratulate themselves on uncontested possession of the land which so many hands had laboured to win, there remained the difficult task to which Sancho I. had been so well inclined, but because of the "Moors" had not had peace to make way with—the task of setting the land in order, of building and planting, of peopling empty spaces. There was great need, also, for making this business hopeful by framing a set of laws, on a more extensive scale than those of Lamego or Coimbra, for the secure and peaceable existence of a growing community. To necessities of this sort Alfonso III. was very much alive. His reign is distinguished by the well-framed arrangements which the Cortes sanctioned for the safety of persons and property, and by measures, which, though deficient in political economy, were full of good-will, for regulating prices of food-stuffs, and of exports and imports, raw and manufactured. These canons closely followed the measures of Alfonso the Wise of Castile, a man whose reputed " wisdom " was indeed like our English James's, rather erudition than intellectual power, but who must be allowed the merit of paying earnest attention to the internal condition of his kingdom. Provided with such statutes, the people fell in the more cheerfully with the designs of Alfonso III.; and authorities speak favourably both of him as an intelligent and considerate law-giver, and of the contemporary Portuguese as a generation which saw and diligently improved its opportunities.

Strife between church and state becomes somewhat tiresomely frequent in the story of the Burgundian house. But one might expect to miss it in the chapter which is occupied with the reign of Alfonso III. For at the time of his assignation to the succession he was full of submission to the Romish power. Yet as a king he greatly disappointed those who looked for a policy more favourable to ecclesiastical interests than his predecessors had followed. He did not object to mount the throne with the church's help, but he had no intention of occupying it for the church's behoof. So to their sorrow and displeasure the prelates saw the man of their choice walking in the footprints of his humiliated brother. Alfonso made requisitions upon them no less boldly than Sancho had done. But Alfonso sat too firmly in his seat to be dislodged. His people were united in their praises of the steps their king had taken for the national weal. His advantage in having a subjugated south to operate upon was great, and he had known how to make the best use of his means. As the bishops, in these circumstances, found it impossible to shake his popularity, seven of them travelled to Rome and accused him there. The Pope, Gregory X., issued at their request a bull of admonition, and Alfonso, whose moral character was certainly not very high, made vague promises of amendment. But for the fulfilment of these engagements Pope and prelates waited for three years in vain.

Then the death of Gregory in 1275, and the rapid succession, within the following year, of three Popes (the last of these being John XXI., of Lisbon, the only Portuguese who ever wore the tiara), enabled Alfonso to delay obedience by raising subtle points in writing and in audiences, till his own fatal illness in 1279. Then, as at the beginning of his career, he expressed himself ready to comply with all the demands of the church, and was released of the ban with which his countryman, John XXI., had loaded him.

Alfonso's *régime* was characterized by consummate sagacity. He does not seem to have shown much heart or scrupulousness, but as a politician he was generally shrewd and far-seeing. Only once does one find him making a great mistake in public affairs, when, to relieve the embarrassment of his treasury, he debased the coinage. But it was not long before he saw his error, and retrieved it in the best available way. And this exception only proves the rule in the case of Alfonso. He was a man of the world who knew what he was about, and his *savoir faire* redounded to the profit of his land.

His son Dennis, who followed Alfonso III., was, as the future monarch, trained with the greatest care from his childhood. Alfonso, judicious and calculating in this matter as in everything else, selected as governor of his son Lorenzo Magro, an extremely prudent and scholarly man, who devoted his whole heart to his pupil's education. For this preceptor of his youth Dennis cherished through life the greatest affection. But, besides Magro, the Infant had instructors in special subjects, chosen from France, a country where culture was much more advanced than in the Peninsula. Dennis was a hopeful subject. From his childhood he disclosed a striking aptitude for learning; and when Alfonso died, the prince, then a young man of about seventeen, had so profited by his education as to raise little doubt of his being able to wield the sceptre with credit. Men thought they complimented Dennis when

they professed to see in him a reproduction of his grandfather,
Alfonso the Wise; but the mental qualities of the Portuguese
Infant were of a much higher kind than those which distin-
guished the scholar of Castile.

Dennis was the first heir to the Portuguese throne who had
as Infant an establishment of his own. Alfonso reared for his
son a palace in Lisbon, the king's favourite residence, the town,
too, where Dennis was born and brought up. From his sixteenth year the prince lived in that house, having a special income and retinue. In this arrangement Alfonso had a twofold
purpose. In the first place, he wished to accustom his heir to
the business of the nation, and, secondly, to accustom his people
to the idea of Dennis as their prospective sovereign; for the
horizon of the prince royal was a little clouded by the existence of a younger brother, Alfonso, born after the decease of
Matilda of Boulogne, who, it might be surmised, would be disposed to regard Dennis as illegitimate.

For a short time after his coronation in 1279, the successor
of Alfonso III. shared the government with his mother. In
less than twelve months, however, Dennis took the reins into
his own hand. Alfonso the Wise was dissatisfied with this
proceeding of the young king, and requested a conference at
Badajos. Dennis rather unwillingly travelled thither as far as
Elvas. Then, pausing, he determined to assert his independence, and made the best of his way homewards. The venerable Alfonso had to give his precocious grandson up.

The Castilian Queen Beatrice, mother of Dennis, withdrew to
her own land, and the youthful monarch of Portugal immediately began to give evidence of a genius for government, completely justifying the hopes which had been built upon him.
The kingly office was in his case no sinecure. His frequent
progresses through the country to see with his own eyes the
civil and agricultural life of the people, his assiduous efforts to
stimulate their diligence in every branch of industry, revealed

the patriotic prince, whose chief concern and happiness lay in the prosperity of his subjects. He nursed the farming interest so carefully as to get the name of the "husbandman," * and mining operations had his lifelong attention.

But it was the shipping trade which, with prophetic instinct of Portugal's future, he was above all things eager to promote. The long stretch of the Portuguese ocean strand betokened that the nation was to be, if anything, a maritime power. And probably his birth and upbringing in Lisbon would lead the king to ponder the problems of seafaring. At all events, he thoroughly realized the importance of that occupation, and, by building harbours and granting privileges to shippers and mariners, provided for its maintenance and development. To this end also he strove to populate the coast with a hardy class acquainted with the deep, who should man the vessels of Portugal. For the defence of the merchant marine the fleet was better organized, if indeed the name of fleet borne by the few small vessels which beforetime carried the royal commission were aught else than a courtesy title; and the armament was officered by experienced Genoese, which nationality produced at that time the best sailors afloat.

The Portuguese rhyme—

> " El rei Dom Diniz
> Fez tudo o que quiz "

(King Dennis can do as he pleases), however applicable to the uninterrupted success of his plans for the well-being of the industrial population, does not hold good in respect of all his affairs. He had the usual quarrel with the church, which cannot be said to present in his reign any unique features. Only, one is struck with the self-control and the lucidity of his communications to the clerical authorities. There were serious

---

* He planted, for instance, to protect the fields from sand-storms driven eastwards, that line of pines, now a vast forest, running parallel with the shore, on which the fury of the blast is spent.

dissensions, too, between him and the grandees, who were loath to give up the notion of ruling as petty sovereigns within their domains, and it required all his mingled firmness and suavity to bring about a *modus vivendi.* Nor could he avoid being involved in the agitation which prevailed throughout Europe in his day against the various knightly orders, and particularly against the Templars.

Those orders had done great military service in the states where they had been established. It is impossible to overestimate the value of the work they had done in the Peninsula— for example, in putting down the Saracens, and so giving the people peace and room to grow. But the lands and privileges which they had acquired as rewards for their deeds of valour had made them, their accusers said, intolerably overbearing, and there were besides grave charges against them of immorality. The king investigated these accusations, so far as they concerned the Portuguese societies, and declared that he found them for the most part trumped up and inspired by the jealousy of the great landlords, seigniors and churchmen, whose greedy eyes had fastened on the heritages of the knights.

The fact is, Dennis would fain have protected the orders, since they curbed the rapacity of others, and might furnish him with a loyal contingent in case of a struggle with the nobility. But the hostile movement, whose headquarters were in France, and had the Pope for its patron, was too strong for the king to resist or ignore with safety. So he made the best possible terms for the societies. The Templars, as the most powerful order in Christendom, had to bear the brunt of the attack. Elsewhere they were treated with the greatest harshness, many of them being tortured and executed. But from Portugal they were quietly suffered to escape for the time. Then in 1319 Dennis, with consent of the Pope, founded the new Order of Christ, to which the Knights Templars, reappearing in the country, in large numbers attached themselves. Thus the king succeeded in virtually reviving Templarism under another name, stultifying its enemies, and behaving with admirable tact through the whole *imbroglio.*

But these were not the worst troubles of King Dennis. Discord in the royal family itself was the most bitter ingredient in his cup. The fears of Alfonso III. concerning his younger son were only too prescient. Prince Alfonso would not submit to the succession of his brother, because Dennis was born while his father's first wife was yet alive; this notwithstanding the acknowledgment of all children of Alfonso III. by Beatrice which accompanied the Papal sanction of the second marriage. The prince retired in dudgeon to his castle of Portalegre, on the frontier of Castile. There he was joined, as civil war was then raging in the neighbouring kingdom, by numbers of disaffected Castilians. The King of Castile objected to the proximity of such a force, and Dennis was compelled to besiege Portalegre before the rebellious Alfonso could be brought to his senses.

Much more painful and prolonged, however, was the king's differences with his own son, also an Alfonso, who by-and-by followed the mutinous example of his uncle, kept on plotting, and on more than one occasion actually took the field against his father. Unfortunately, Alfonso's unfilial courses cannot be explained without discovering a blot on the conduct of Dennis. The Infant's discontent was aroused by an illegitimate son of the king, Alfonso Sanches, to whom his father showed the warmest affection. Mischief-makers whispered that Dennis had secretly applied to the Pope for a bull of legitimization in favour of Alfonso Sanches, so as to name him for the crown, to the ruin of the Infant's hopes and right. The conjecture was false, but the prince royal gave ear to it, and his anger knew no bounds. He ingratiated himself with some of the nobles, and raised a force by means of which he entered into a distressing and sanguinary conflict with the king. Repeatedly an arrangement was sought to be made on the part of Dennis; but as he was unwilling to banish Alfonso Sanches, an essential matter with the rebel prince, hostilities were as frequently resumed, and it was but a short time before his death that the king consented to the demand of Alfonso, and accordingly put an end to the unnatural strife.

One who did much to accomplish the reconciliation of father and son was the queen, the beautiful Isabel of Aragon, a lady celebrated for the purity, the gentleness, and the unselfishness of her character; one of those ministering angels, those loving and gracious wives and mothers, whose lives, though medieval story takes too little account of them, brighten here and there its pages, made so gloomy with the details of men's greed and cruelty. Queen Isabel's is a delightful record. She had "a tear for pity, and a hand open as day for melting charity." A constant friend of the sick and poor, she visited them in their own homes, distributed much alms, and performed the duties of a nurse with sweet patience and humility. Her efforts were unremitting to heal the horrid rupture between her husband and her son, and hers was the peaceful victory when both laid down their arms. Her remarkable piety was of course marked by the austerities of the Romish idea, and she appears to have closed her life as a strict religieuse.

Dennis retired from the distressing contest with Alfonso only to learn to die. He had profited by the rough lesson the war had taught him. As the time of his departure approached he was much occupied with spiritual exercises, and frequently referred with the deepest regret to the sin from which he had reaped such a harvest of suffering. His queen waited upon him with the most tender solicitude, and his dying farewell to her and the repentant Alfonso who stood at his bedside was extremely moving and affectionate.

The *quondam* rebel was at once crowned as Alfonso IV. in 1325. The suspicious temper he had shown as expectant monarch manifested itself afresh after his accession. He decreed the exile of Alfonso Sanches, who, according to agreement with his father, resided in Portugal. In vain did his brother protest his loyalty. His declarations were discredited. Alfonso Sanches therefore raised an armed force for the support of his declinature to withdraw from Portugal. The royal troops sent to expel him were worsted; and Queen Isabel, hearing how matters stood, interfered at this juncture, and procured a treaty by which Alfonso Sanches retained his right of residence and property in the country.

As Castile had befriended his brother's cause, Alfonso IV. deemed it wise to put himself on a good footing with that country. The King of Castile seemed to reciprocate the desire, and soon two royal marriages were arranged to seal the friendship of the sovereigns. Alfonso XI. of Castile wedded the daughter of Alfonso IV.; and Pedro, Infant of Portugal, took to wife Blanca, daughter of the Infant Pedro of Castile. These unions were unhappy, which is not surprising since they were simply political transactions. Alfonso XI. dishonoured and grieved his queen by giving his heart to a certain Leonora de Guzman; and the Portuguese Infant, tired of a wife who was always sick, obtained, with consent of the Cortes, a separation from her, and was thereupon betrothed to Constance, daughter of the Duke of Villena. Mutual recriminations followed the behaviour of Alfonso XI. and of the Infant. Physical force succeeded polemics. The soldiery of Castile and of Portugal were called upon to shed each other's blood because their princes had married without love. The Pope, then, and the King of Aragon successfully negotiated a treaty which provided that the Castilian king should dismiss Leonora, and that the Portuguese prince royal should be allowed to wed Constance. Blanca retired to a convent.

The treaty also contained an article concluding an alliance between Castile and Portugal against the Saracens. The expediency of such an alliance was erelong demonstrated. In the course of the next year, 1340, the King of Morocco roused the suspicions of the Castilians by the extraordinary military preparations he was reported to be making. The small Castilian armada was ordered to be on the alert, and soon a powerful Moorish fleet was seen beyond a doubt making for Spain. The admiral of Castile exceeded his commission and gave battle in the most foolhardy manner. The result was the almost total destruction of his vessels. The war was begun, and this stupid move on the part of Castile laid bare the Strait of Gibraltar for the transport to the Peninsula of sixty thousand Africans. The foe was in the land, and Alfonso of Portugal was loudly summoned. When he arrived with his Portuguese and joined the King of Castile, he found the Moors beside the little river Salado, before the neighbouring town of Tarifa, the most southerly point of Spain, opposite Gibraltar. An Aragonese force occupied a height at some distance, prepared to support the two Alfonsos.

Anticipating a siege of Tarifa, the garrison had been strengthened by Alfonso XI. The King of Granada had by this time joined the African Mussulmans, and their united strength is said to have reached the amount of four hundred and sixty thousand men, while the allied Christian army numbered less than sixty thousand.* Nevertheless, after a hard day's fighting, in which the beleaguered garrison took part by a sally, the Mohammedan forces were thoroughly beaten with tremendous slaughter, and left behind them on their precipitate flight a camp full of splendid booty. The King of Portugal declined to share the spoil, and only consented upon urgent solicitation to bear home with him as souvenirs of the day a few small articles of value and one or two distinguished Saracen prisoners. He contented himself with his laurels, and with the consciousness that Mohammedan attempts on the

* These figures, out of old records, are to be taken *cum grano*.

independence of the Christian kingdoms had received at the battle of Salado the *coup de grace*.

Alfonso of Castile, out of gratitude for the military aid of Portugal, broke, on his return from the field, with Leonora de Guzman, and reinstated conjugal peace at his court. So the joy of Alfonso IV. was full; but only for a time. A dark fate hung over his house. As he himself had been estranged from his father, even so was his own son to turn against him. In the suite of the Infanta Constance was a certain Dona Ignez de Castro, a lady whose beauty and grace captivated the inflammable Pedro. The king becoming aware of his son's passion, conceived a great dislike to Ignez. Alfonso's distrustful spirit, which has been noted more than once, dreaded the influence exercised by some members of the Castro family, who for the sake of Ignez had been made welcome at court and were now fast friends of the Infant. The root of the mischief, the king thought, was Ignez. The Infanta was not blind to her husband's affection for her maid-of-honour, and although her union with the Infant was very much like his former one with Blanca, a marriage of convenience, felt, notwithstanding, greatly wronged by her treatment at Pedro's hands. Of a reticent disposition, she was consumed by a grief which she concealed, and died within five years of her wedding day. It is impossible to gauge the actual guilt of the Infant, but it is certain that Ignez was the principal object of his love, and the permanence of his affection demonstrated how deeply her image was graven on his heart.

After the death of Constance, Pedro was privately married to Ignez, but, though his father suspected as much, persistently denied the fact, because he knew that the king would never look with satisfaction on such a union. This equivocal position in which he permitted himself to leave his wife cost her her life and him all the pleasure of his own. Alfonso's courtiers busily fanned the king's hatred of the Castro influence, and of

Ignez as its source. They suggested putting her out of existence, and Alfonso was weak enough to acquiesce in a foul conspiracy for this purpose, to be carried out at some time when it should be known that Pedro was absent from her. Accordingly one day the king, attended by the ringleaders in the plot, went, the Infant being out of the way, to the religious house at Coimbra where the victim was residing. The unhappy Ignez at once guessed their fell design, and with her arms clasped round two of her children knelt at Alfonso's feet weeping and suing for mercy. Alfonso was overcome, and quitted the place. But his companions were not to be balked in this way. So they hastened after him, plied him with the old arguments, and prophesied all manner of danger to the realm unless the Castros' power were destroyed; and at last they wrung from the lips of the sovereign a permission to do their will. Ignez was slain.

The wrath of Pedro, when he returned and looked upon the bleeding corpse of his beloved, was ungovernable. He gathered an armed force and broke into Tras os Montes and Minho, plundering and killing with blind fury wherever he went. His career, however, was checked at Oporto, which refused him admittance ; and the Archbishop of Braga, seizing the moment of his discomfiture, persuaded the prince to bury his enmity and go to court again. But that enmity was buried alive, to be exhumed in full vigour at some convenient season. Nor could the father get over the murder of Ignez de Castro any better than the son. He realized

> " The deep damnation of her taking off,"

and is said never to have had a happy hour after that fatal day. He died in 1357, two years after the unfortunate being who, at his word, was hurled into eternity.

Alfonso IV. has been handed down to posterity as a thankless son, an unjust brother, and a cruel father, and certainly in all these relations he was worthy of blame. But if it be any palliation of his sins, one may remember his ingrained spirit of distrust from which the most patent of them sprang—a spirit too easily played upon by the crafty for their own ends. It is in evidence that his government was good. The quick recovery which the people made from two terrible visitations—an earthquake at Lisbon in 1344, and the black death, which ravaged Portugal like the rest of Europe in his day—proved his capacity for administration and his interest in the common weal. His bravery and unselfishness need no better illustration than the field of Salado. Nevertheless, however justly much of his career as a sovereign demands our respect, the man can win from us no warmer feeling.

When King Pedro came to the throne he was not long in showing that he had neither forgotten nor forgiven those assassins who had robbed him of his beloved Ignez. As they had settled in Castile, he did not rest till he had constrained its sovereign to extradite them. To accomplish this purpose Pedro bargained that his children should marry into the Castilian royal house, not considering, by the way, that thus he was repeating the very thing which had spoiled his own life. Whenever the murderers arrived in Portugal he "supped full of horrors" in executing his revenge. He had the hearts of the conspirators torn out of their breasts, and their still quivering bodies burned in his presence. One only of these objects of his hate escaped him by fleeing in a beggar's disguise, being warned of the fate intended for him; and Pedro by-and-by did not regret that in this particular instance he was foiled, for satisfactory evidence was laid before him of the man's complete innocence.

But the king had still something to do for the sake of Ignez de Castro. He swore publicly on the Gospels that he had been married to her seven years before, and two witnesses took oath that they had been present at the ceremony. Then proceeding with a great retinue to Coimbra, the place of her interment, her remains were brought forth from the crypt, decked in the insignia of royalty, and placed on a throne. Whereupon all the grandees who were present did obeisance to the corpse as Queen of Portugal. Then the body was laid in a rich coffin, borne by nobles to a splendid mausoleum at Alcobaça, and deposited there, no more to be disturbed. Thus Pedro in the strangest way did honour to one, the memory of whose love and suffering seems to have haunted him night and day.

It is almost certain indeed that the king's mind had become unhinged by the loss of Ignez, and especially by the cruel manner of it. For a full narrative of his eccentricities we have not space, but here are one or two instances which show what manner of man he was. He used to carry a whip in his girdle in order to personally castigate evil-doers. And this instrument of correction he was wont to apply without respect of persons. Having occasion to be in Oporto, he learned that the morals of the bishop were not what they ought to have been, and resolved to take him under discipline. So he sent a messenger commanding the ecclesiastic's presence at the royal castle. Highly flattered, the bishop obeyed the order, whereupon the king, getting him alone, reprimanded him for the wicked example he was setting, and chastised him besides within an inch of his life.

Another time it was reported to him in the town of Santarem that a certain priest had taken the life of a citizen; and coming across a herculean stone mason in the street, the king asked the man whether he knew that priest by sight. "Quite well," was the reply. "Then," said Pedro, "I bid you kill him." It was done, and the murderer arrested. At the trial the king appeared and presided. He inquired casually what had been done to the murdered priest for the similar crime which *he* had committed, and was informed that the ecclesiastical tribunal had sentenced him to be forbidden the performance of clerical duty for all time coming. "In that case," said the king, "I sentence the prisoner to be hereafter prohibited from hewing stones;" and ordering the mason to be discharged, he took care to provide him with a comfortable income. Because of such dealings as are noted in anecdotes of this kind men called him *O Justiceiro*, "the Justiciary;" but the ferocious style in which he gave effect to his views earned for him the name *O Cru*, "the Severe."

He appears to have been liable to paroxysms, not only of rage, but also of riotous hilarity. He kept a number of trumpeters, and would suddenly summon them before him and order them to blow together with all their might. The deafening clamour seemed to fill him with ecstasy. On occasion he would call for his trumpeters and for torch-bearers in the middle of the night, and make them march through the streets, he dancing and leaping, while the fanfaronade of the instruments roused the slumbering city, till he was perfectly exhausted. Then he retired to rest. Pedro presents a curious psychological problem. May not his outbursts of riotous mirth have been desperate efforts to dismiss the demon of melancholy?

Yet if we were to label Pedro "a maniac," we should undoubtedly libel him. He reigned only ten years, but when the grave closed over him people said, "We have not had in Portugal ten such good years." To be candid, we cannot endorse this unqualified encomium; but it must be conceded that with all his caprices and alternate fits of savagery and buffoonery, he could see the needs of his kingdom, and take steps to supply them as well as the wisest man in Portugal. He did not oppress the poor. He pressed impartial laws upon the Cortes, and dispensed them without fear. He kept the peace with his neighbours. Even when the internal commotions in Castile might have tempted him to interfere, he adroitly maintained his neutrality; and when the rejected Castilian king would have involved him in the strife, coming himself to Portugal for the purpose of personally enforcing his plea, Pedro promptly conveyed him back to his own border. So, as the land flourished under his rule, the people laughed at his unkingly pranks; and as he never hurt the law-abiding, they were ready to excuse his ruthless measures with the criminal.

When Ferdinand, son of Pedro and Queen Constance, began to reign in 1367, everything promised well. He himself was a young man of considerable personal attractions. He was esteemed the handsomest man of his time, and had a bearing most graceful and kingly. For feats of strength and agility he had few equals. He was noted for generosity. His manner to his inferiors was affable, and won him golden opinions from the commons. He had understanding, too, for state business, and a power of quickly unfolding feasible plans. The growth of the nation and its commercial prosperity had filled the royal treasury; and Portugal had, in 1367, no quarrel in hand with other nations. Never had a king a smoother path before him than Ferdinand. Yet there was hardly anything he touched, during his sixteen years' reign, which he did not mar. He flung away many advantages to which he had fallen heir. He greatly reduced the wealth accumulated by his ancestors for the necessities of the crown, entangled the country in foreign war, and generally mismanaged affairs at home. The reason of his failure was his instability of character. He laid out schemes, and left them; gave orders one day, and countermanded them the next; made promises, and lightly broke them. He ignored recent treaties of alliance, and bound himself without scruple, when he pleased, to the enemies of his former friends. He took no trouble to investigate the gravest matters. So his projects often miscarried, being founded on imperfect knowledge.

There was still trouble in Castile when Ferdinand assumed the sovereignty, and less prudent in this matter than his father, who was often thought crazy, he unhesitatingly took a side in the controversy. Pedro of Castile had no male heirs, and the Count of Trastamara, his illegitimate brother, the claimant of the succession, was in arms against the king, in order to immediately oust him, as the majority of the Castilians were thoroughly tired of their monarch's cruelty. The count, indeed, already called himself Henry II. of Castile. Ferdinand, with unnecessary celerity, acknowledged the claimant as a sovereign neighbour, and entered into a treaty of friendship with him. But no sooner did fortune seem to smile on Pedro in the course of the contest than the King of Portugal repudiated his alliance with Henry. By-and-by, however, the tide turned in favour of Henry, who secured himself upon the throne after slaying his antagonist with his own hand. It occurred now to Ferdinand that he himself had a right to the Castilian crown through his grandmother, Beatrix of Castile. That right he resolved to prosecute, and for this purpose signed a bond of alliance with the King of Aragon, and also with the Mohammedan King of Granada. Both of these princes were pleased to have a reasonable excuse for invading Castile with some prospect of success. The King of Portugal made his cause unpopular in his own land by harbouring a number of Castilian nobles, partisans of the late king, making them rich presents and treating them with more distinguished honour than the Portuguese aristocracy. As for the people of Castile, they could not entertain with satisfaction the idea of a Portuguese ascending their throne. However, the struggle began. Ferdinand led an army into Galicia. The King of Aragon was prepared to make a diversion in the east, and the King of Granada had already marched into the south of Castile. Indeed, Henry was surrounded by foes, and even while advancing to meet Ferdinand, was recalled to join battle with the Mohammedans, who had promptly taken from him an important town. What did Ferdinand do in this most favourable juncture but change his mind about the whole affair and make a treaty with Henry, and that without troubling himself to consult his allies! They, too, were in consequence forced to conclude a peace with Castile. The King of Aragon, however, retained in revenge a large sum of money that Ferdinand had deposited with him, for defraying the expense of the war to the Aragonese treasury, which was rather low.

The king had lost his character in this escapade, and so much of his money that he bethought him of that device which had been tried before in Portugal when times were bad. He issued gold and silver coins of comparatively little value, and gave them by statute an artificial worth. The result was, as might be expected, not encouraging, and more extraordinary measures had to follow. The value of all money was depreciated, and as prices did not fall, they were fixed at an absurdly low level, and selling made compulsory. The people were greatly incensed. All this had come of a war for which they did not care a straw; which, nevertheless, since he had commenced, Ferdinand might have carried on to a point where he could have been able to demand compensation for relinquishing his claim. The fickleness of the king was unpardonable. Alas, future events should amply corroborate the popular verdict.

Before his treaty with Castile, Ferdinand had been betrothed to an Aragonese princess. Now he stood in the same relation to the Castilian Infanta. Within five months the wedding was to take place. But the charms of Dona Leonora Telles, who was visiting his court, caused him to determine upon breaking off the Castilian marriage and taking her to wife. Leonora was married to an influential vassal of his own. This notwithstanding, Ferdinand worked his will. He procured a dissolution of her union, and the King of Castile's consent to give up his daughter. The Portuguese of all classes were shocked at the king's behaviour; and one day in Lisbon, the usual royal residence, and already in a measure the capital, three thousand armed citizens, led by a valiant tailor, appeared at· the palace and demanded that Ferdinand should refrain from marrying Leonora, whose husband, in terror of his life, had fled to Castile. The king consented to their request, and promised to make a satisfactory public statement on the morrow. That very night he escaped to Santarem with his intended, leaving directions for the apprehension and punishment of the ringleaders in the uprising. In a few days Ferdinand and Leonora were actually united at a convent in Minho. Everybody murmured when the fact was made known, but nobody ventured to express his mind publicly except Dom Diniz, the son of Ignez de Castro, whom the king would have stabbed on the spot had he not been forcibly withheld. The new queen was a clever woman, and understood, by flattery and gifts, by affability and assumed sympathy, how to win a strong party to her side.

In 1371 Ferdinand had given up his claim to Castile and made friends with King Henry of that country. Within twelve months the Portuguese harlequin was in alliance with John, Duke of Lancaster, son of our Edward III., who in right of his wife, the eldest daughter of the late Pedro of Castile, called himself " King of Castile," and proposed to make good his pretensions by invasion. The contract was made in secret, for Ferdinand knew that it would be disapproved by the Portuguese. In pursuance of this understanding with the duke, Ferdinand caused the disaffected Castilians who had taken up their abode in Portugal to make a hostile demonstration in Galicia, and gave orders for the capture of some Castilian vessels. The King of Castile, thoroughly enraged by his neighbour's faithlessness, declared war. His fleet appeared in the Tagus, broke through the Portuguese war-galleys, took and plundered Lisbon, and thereafter set it on fire. The best part of the city was destroyed. On land the success of the

Castilians was as complete; and as the promised help from England was not forthcoming, the Portuguese king was forced to capitulate. He bound himself to aid Henry of Castile against the English duke. Ferdinand endeavoured to engage the assistance of Castile against the King of Aragon, from whom he wished to recover his money, but in vain. The friendship of Aragon was just then required by Castile. So the King of Portugal treated with France for a combined attack upon Aragonese territory. While negotiations of this kind were going on, however, a dreadful tragedy at his own court absorbed all his attention.

His half-brother, Dom John, younger son of Ignez de Castro, had married the sister of the queen, Dona Maria Telles, a virtuous lady, whom the queen, nevertheless, or on that account, detested with all her heart, especially as she had been foremost in attempting to dissuade Leonora from wedding the king. The queen, with almost incredible wickedness, insinuated to Dom John suspicions of her sister's fidelity, and fabricated reasons for her belief. The miserable husband listened at first with surprise and then unhappily with confidence, till in a passion of jealousy he rode away to Coimbra. He arrived as the morning dawned, and flying to Maria's chamber, for she had not yet arisen, despatched her with his dagger. The murderer learned ere long that his wife, like his mother, had fallen a victim to malevolence, and so, tossed between remorse and fear that the avengers were on his track, he rushed hither and thither until at length in Castile he found rest for his wearied head, but none anywhere for his blood-stained soul.

This nefarious piece of work does not appear to have troubled much the seared conscience of the queen, notwithstanding all the excitement which it caused in Portugal, and although she was well aware that every one saw the sin lying at her door. On the contrary, her successful plotting against her sister was only the preface to the exhibition of her treacherous and mischief-making spirit in the political sphere. Ferdinand had a daughter, Beatrix, now eight years old. This child he looked upon as simply the tool of his policy—or political whims, for he had no policy. Accordingly he had betrothed her to the infant son and heir of the new King of Castile. But the ink was hardly dry upon the bond when Ferdinand sent to Castile a declaration of war. Leonora was responsible for the caprice. One of the disaffected Castilians secretly harboured in Portugal, but supposed to be banished thence under treaty to that effect with Castile, a man named Andeiro, had been sent by the queen to England to make fresh arrangements for an invasion of Castile in combination with Portugal, and had just stolen back with an engagement of this kind in his pocket. Thereupon the King of Portugal, with his customary bad faith, in spite of his profession of friendship so lately made, threw down the gauntlet once more. John I. of Castile was not a man to be trifled with, and promptly took up the challenge. His fleet met the Portuguese war-galleys, which were poorly manned, many field labourers having been pressed into the service. The Castilians were victorious, taking captive twenty Portuguese galleys, all their crews, and the admiral of Portugal.

Then appeared before Lisbon, a day too late, the promised English vessels, and landed three thousand men, at their head the Earl of Cambridge.* To the son of this nobleman Ferdinand therefore betrothed the Infanta Beatrix, and bound himself to provide pay and horses for the English troops. The soldiers who came to fight the Castilians made themselves exceedingly disagreeable in Portugal. They acted towards the natives as if these had been the foes against whom they were to act. Plundering continually, and slaying if any ventured to resist them, they roused in the people a deadly hatred, which found vent in frequent assassinations of the English.

* Edmund of Langley, afterwards Duke of York.

The queen shared with the foreign mercenaries the bitter animosity of the Portuguese. It was she to whose intrigues Portugal owed the plague of the English. That was notorious. Nor was she anxious to deny what seemed to her a triumph of diplomacy. But there was something else besides her management or mismanagement of public affairs which moved the wrath of those who were cognizant of it. They who had access to court gossip were talking of her friendship for Andeiro, for whom she had procured the Lordship of Ourem—a friendship too intimate to be innocent. The two had been closely watched, and many were convinced of her guilt. Yet none dared remonstrate with her. At length a noble named Azevedo ventured to call her attention to the scandal, of which the king seemed perfectly oblivious. The result of Azevedo's candour was the issue of a warrant for his incarceration on a false charge of treasonable dealing with Castile. That warrant contained another name—the name of one whom Leonora had cause to fear more than any man in the kingdom—one who knew Azevedo well, and would be likely to inquire into the reason of his apprehension.

This person so obnoxious to the queen was Dom John, an illegitimate son of the late king, appointed in his childhood to the Grand Mastership of the knightly Order of Avis; a man of great intelligence and firmness of character, and of influence daily growing in the court and with the people. He it was whom Providence had destined to step into the throne when Ferdinand should vacate it, and to inaugurate a magnificent epoch of the national history. His wonderful future was veiled from the queen and from himself also; but Leonora dreaded his ambition and his popularity. She knew, too, that though the Grand Master could hold his tongue and bide his time, he saw through her, and would compass her downfall if he could. So she, no doubt in concert with Andeiro, included Dom John in the accusation against Azevedo, and had both flung into a dungeon. An order for the execution of the prisoners quickly followed the apprehension. But the governor of Evora, where they were confined, was too prudent to execute such an important personage as the Grand Master off-hand, and betook himself to the king for confirmation of the mandate. Ferdinand was apparently astonished, for—so he said at least, and perhaps with truth—he was ignorant of the whole affair. The queen, to whom her husband appealed for information, seemed equally amazed, and now that the game was up, pleaded for the prisoners' release with tears in her eyes. They were set free. The king's brother returned to court and acted as if nothing had happened, receiving with thanks Leonora's congratulations on his acquittal. But Andeiro trembled as he saw the Grand Master looking at him and playing with his dagger.

After this interlude, which disturbed for a little time the progress of the war scheme, Ferdinand plunged once more into the business with great ostensible zeal. He gathered his army, appointed the various officers, and arranged with the English for the conduct of the campaign. The Castilians also lay in camp, prepared for fighting. Need it surprise any one that in the midst of all this bustle Ferdinand despatched a messenger by night to treat for peace with the King of Castile? At any rate, that was actually the case. And he was successful. King John agreed with the King of Portugal to restore the captured Portuguese fleet—ships, crews, and admiral—and to accept the Portuguese Infanta as a bride for his son. It was announced to the English that they should be shipped home in Castilian vessels. They were highly displeased, but there was no help for it ; and as they departed from Lisbon the people knelt on the quay and thanked God that they had been delivered from their friends.

Her engagement to the Castilian Infant was not the last of the much-betrothed Beatrix. Before the marriage could be consummated the Queen of Castile died, and the fertile mind of Ferdinand conceived another plan for his daughter. Why should she not become at once Queen of Castile by marrying the father instead of the son? The proposal was made, and John fell in with it. He stipulated, however, that Beatrix should on her father's death be nominal queen, the King of Castile to have the right of calling himself King of Portugal, and that their son or daughter should be actual sovereign. The wedding this time really took place in Badajos with great pomp, and as quickly as possible, lest King Ferdinand might again resile from his bargain. But indeed the King of Portugal was rapidly approaching the end of his career. That very year (1383) he sickened, and speedily succumbed to his malady. To prepare for himself a peaceful journey to the other world, he had himself clothed in the dress of a Franciscan; but after taking the sacrament his conscience awoke, and he said to his attendants, weeping bitterly the while, "I shall have a bad account to lay before God." In this miserable state of mind he passed away.

So ended the legitimate line of that famous Burgundian house under whose auspices Portugal had advanced from next to nothing to a position of national solidity and respectability which promised yet greater things. Ferdinand's predecessors had been, if not admirable in all respects, at least men whose character had a certain largeness and force which command our regard. They were frequently in peril, physical or political, yet they did not flinch. But their last representative was the shame of his line, for his shiftiness was the despair of his advisers and the foreigner's scorn. The few useful enactments which in his day were added to the statute-book were irrevocably approved by the estates while he was in the mood, or simply extorted from his fear. His heart spoke well on his death-bed, and unless compassion overcame candour, no one could help homologating the sentence.

CHAPTER IV.

HOUSE OF AVIS.

1385-1495.

JOHN of Castile had the settled purpose of annexing the kingdom of Portugal so soon as Ferdinand should pay the debt to nature. But there were three obstacles which remained even now that Ferdinand was out of the way. The first was John de Castro, brother of the late king, who, although a fugitive criminal, was not positively excluded from the succession. He had lived in Castile ever since the murder of his wife. Him, therefore, John could easily lay hands on. This he did, and put him in prison. So one hindrance was removed. Another difficulty was the treaty with Ferdinand, which provided that the King and Queen of Castile should be only nominal monarchs of Portugal. It was their child who should succeed, and till that child reached the age of fourteen years, Leonora was to be regent. These terms he meant to ignore, for he scorned the shadow of sovereignty. Forgetting altogether the third obstacle, which, indeed, made the treaty mere waste paper, that clause in the laws of Lamego, still valid, enacting that a Portuguese princess marrying a foreigner deprived herself of the right to succeed, John therefore pressed the widowed queen to have him and Beatrix proclaimed King and Queen of Portugal, quietly intending such proclamation as a prelude to his appropriation of substantial power.

Leonora complied with the request of her son-in-law, but whenever the announcement was made an uproar ensued.

"Have our forefathers," said the indignant people, "wrested Portugal from the Moors at the cost of so much blood that we should hand it over to the Castilians?"

The commons of Portugal felt themselves to be like sheep without a shepherd. The son of Ignez de Castro had been long out of their sight. His hands, besides, were stained with the blood of his innocent wife. They detested the regent and the King of Castile. To Queen Beatrix they would have had little objection, but her husband they could not accept. Their eyes turned to the Grand Master as the outstanding personage whose hands were strong enough to take the helm of affairs. Few nobles were prepared as yet to yield him such a post, but among these few some of the best. The people, however, idolized him. The Grand Master was not a man who "wore his heart upon his sleeve," and one knows not what he was thinking. Yet, no doubt, he was watching the course of events. Whether ambition moved him more or patriotism, who can tell? But if he were ambitious, his ambition was capable of the most heroic sacrifices; and he cannot be found guilty of abusing the power with which he was at any time intrusted. He was the greatest figure on the page of Portuguese history since the days of Alfonso Henriquez—the one man capable, so far as we know, not only of setting right the disjointed time, but, like the great Burgundian king, of inaugurating a new and hopeful political departure. The *vox populi* calling Dom John to undertake the government—a voice which by-and-by became so loud as to drown the fearful or jealous dissent of the nobles—was but the echo of a providential summons.

The late king's obsequies, held, according to the usual practice, a month after his death, brought together in Lisbon an immense multitude from all parts. Much discussion took place there and then about the situation and future of the country. The Grand Master and his friends held by themselves a serious consultation. One thing they were convinced was necessary as a preliminary to further public good—the removal of the queen's mischievous favourite Andeiro. A sentence of death was passed upon the Count of Ourem by this informal tribunal. But how should it be executed? "I shall find a way," said Dom John. The Grand Master's name had been mentioned by the populace too frequently and unreservedly to have escaped the quick ears of the queen. She had thought it best therefore to issue an order despatching him to guard the frontiers of Castile without delay; and, in pursuance of his project against Andeiro, he sent a message to Leonora, begging for an audience on the next day for more explicit directions before taking up his military duties. She could not deny him. Knowing then that the Count of Ourem would be present at the audience, he proceeded to the palace with an armed retinue. Leaving his followers in the ante-chamber, he entered the queen's presence, where he found Andeiro, as he had expected, and talked over his business. But on leaving he said to Andeiro, "I should like to say something to you," and led him to the ante-chamber. There unsheathing his weapon, the Grand Master plunged it into the wretched man, who fell mortally wounded. Some of Dom John's party rushed forward with drawn swords to strike the odious courtier, but their leader bade them refrain, lest they should turn an execution into a butchery. So perished a creature of exceptional wickedness, who had brought disgrace on the royal family, by whose means the Grand Master had been condemned to the block, who was believed to be plotting the destruction of all the patriotic leaders, and was known to be in treacherous fellowship with Castile. Still "the deed was foully done." Though the situation was difficult and the times were bloody, we cannot help seeing the shadow of Andeiro's murder thrown across the picture of the Grand Master.

The exasperation of the queen was extreme, but Dom John's popularity rendered her impotent to take vengeance upon him. The people were jubilant. The report of the tragedy had

somehow, at first, got turned upside down, and it was Andeiro
who was said to have slain their hero. They came, therefore,
in thousands to the palace, shouting for the murderer, that they
might tear him in pieces ; but when they learned the truth
they broke out in yells of triumph. Yet the mob would not
disperse. They were stirred up to such a pitch of furious
resentment against all Spaniards that they rushed away together to find some object upon which their patriotic fury might
spend itself. They made their way to the cathedral. The
Bishop of Lisbon, a Castilian by birth, and a learned and upright man, had retreated to the tower for safety on hearing
the tumult. A number of ruffians ascended to his place of
hiding, and threw him down upon the street, along which the
lifeless body of the venerable ecclesiastic was dragged by a
rope outside the town, and left there to be gnawed by dogs.
After this sacrifice to their furious temper the multitude were
contented for the time to separate. But the spirit of violence
spread beyond Lisbon, and many acts of violence were perpetrated in other quarters. It was only the presence of the
Grand Master which could avail to restrain the populace. The
authority of the regent was nowhere. Her person would not
have been secure but for Dom John. He was from the hour
of Andeiro's assassination the uncrowned King of Portugal.
The inhabitants of Lisbon greeted him with cheers whenever he
rode out. "Why did you not kill the traitress too ?" they cried.
" Rule over us yourself ! What do you wish us to do ?"

The queen felt so uncomfortable in Lisbon that she retired
to Alemquer, a strong place of hers some miles northwards.
This step was perhaps necessary, but it gave the friends of
Dom John an opportunity to move more freely. The regent
had deserted her charge, although, as every one knew, it was
very unwillingly. Nevertheless there seemed now occasion to
supply her place, and a great popular assembly was held in
Lisbon for the purpose (December 1383). The conclusion was

foregone. Whom could they choose but the Grand Master? Some nobles who were present demurred; but a sturdy cooper of Lisbon coming to the front asked them what their objections were, and whether any other were fit to defend them from the Spaniards. "I have only my neck to venture," said he. "Let him who will not accept the Grand Master take care of his own." Stormy applause followed this speech, and the dissentients were compelled to surrender. Dom John was appointed Defender of Portugal, and clothed with little less than royal authority. He had refused once and again to let his friends nominate him for such a position, though he could not disguise from himself or them that the state was without a head and must procure one. He had said that the power of Castile was great and his means were small; and that, if the commons were with him, he was conscious of many nobles hanging back from him. He was once on the point of embarking for England, lest, seeing the pressing need, he should be tempted to engage the nation, not united, in an unequal contest with the Spanish might. But after the assembly at Lisbon he threw his scruples to the wind, and accepted the honours and perils of office in a public address characterized at once by modesty and resolution.

A Castilian invasion was indeed imminent. The nation had declined to suffer the proclamation of the Spaniard's sovereignty, and they knew that he would not be easily baffled, but would proceed to thrust it upon them at the sword's point. Leonora had written her son-in-law to make haste to defend his right. That was not known to the people, but they were aware that preparations for resistance were urgently necessary. The Grand Master therefore chose his officers of state, and the excellence of his choice in every instance showed his powers of accurately appreciating men. He himself should remain in Lisbon to await the enemy there, and to the command of the forces which were to operate in the country he elected one who was a host in himself, Nuno Alvares Pereira, a young but already experienced and distinguished soldier, and a man whose rare virtues were as conspicuous as his generalship. Dom John also bethought him of sending an ambassador to England inviting co-operation. His representative returned with a large sum of money and the promise of an English contingent. The money was very welcome, for that was the Grand Master's weak point. After all he could borrow he was still in financial straits; but this and every other trial his cheerful and self-reliant spirit overbore.

Meantime the Castilians were, as the Portuguese expected, advancing. But as King John did not think his whole available strength was required for crushing what he imagined to be a faction, he sent only a small army into Portugal. To these troops Nuno Pereira gave more than sufficient occupation. His encounters with the Castilians were exceedingly fortunate, though his force was even less than the enemy's; and each success of the Portuguese brought over waverers to the side of the Grand Master. Another Castilian detachment, which ventured to sit down before Lisbon, was ignominiously driven thence by the garrison.

But now the King of Castile had found out that he had underestimated his task, and at the head of a well-armed host, including many grandees of Spain, marched to the siege of Lisbon. The regent met him at Santarem, whither she had now gone, and joined his army. To encourage King John she renounced the regency, and thus left him free to fight for actual and immediate possession of the supreme power in Portugal. Leonora and her son-in-law were hand and glove. But their amity did not endure. With that lust of power which had all along characterized her, she sought to exercise the very authority she had surrendered. The king firmly resisted her, and her revengeful heart immediately set about concocting a conspiracy against him. It was discovered; and King John, determining she should make no more trouble for him thenceforward, immured her in a convent. Thus she vanished from the scene where she had been so long a power for evil. It is to be hoped that in her solitude she addressed herself to the duty of repentance, for if her husband's was a blotted record, her own was more hideous still.

In Lisbon they had made every possible preparation for a protracted siege. A great store of provisions had to be gathered, as many had taken refuge in the city from the surrounding district. The defences had to be strengthened in several places. War galleys and vessels had to be made ready for sea. In these dispositions every one took part, priests as well as laymen ; and even priests anticipated using carnal weapons in defence of the town. The Archbishop of Braga, who was within the walls, went about in harness, over which was thrown his episcopal dress, exhorting the clergy to prepare, like him, for fighting. If any one objected that he was a priest, the bishop replied, "So am I, and an archbishop into the bargain." There was no lack of cheerfulness and hope among the thousands in Lisbon. The walls were strong, provisions were plentiful, and more were expected by a Portuguese fleet from Oporto, to meet which, and convoy it to the capital, the Lisbon ships ran out as soon as they were ready. An English fleet, transporting the promised contingent, was coming also to their aid. And above all, they had in the Defender a man on whose watchfulness and courage they could implicitly rely.

John and his Castilians came and pitched their camp on both sides of the river for the simultaneous siege of Lisbon and of Almada, just across the Tagus. About the same time the fleet of Castile sailed into the harbour of Lisbon. Thus the city and the town opposite were completely encompassed ; yet the king designed no storm, but trusted that hunger would soon reduce the places. So he sat still. After two months Almada gave out. Water failed first. They drank the stored-up rainwater, which had become exceedingly bad. Thereafter their only available supply was from the Tagus, and that could only be obtained in small quantities by men fastened with ropes slipping down in the darkness. But the bucketfuls which were thus conveyed tantalized rather than satisfied ; and those men were often caught, and paid with their lives the penalty of their temerity. The Defender sent a messenger, who swam across the Tagus, to ask how they did, and bade them open their gates, as he could give them no help. They did so on honourable terms, and the king was at liberty to give his undivided attention to Lisbon. There also they were beginning to feel the pinch of want. Water of a kind they had, but the stock of eatables was alarmingly small ; yet they knew that Lisbon was the key of the situation, and that if the siege were raised, Almada could be recovered and all Portugal preserved for an independent people. Therefore they looked down on the white town of the Castilian tents, hoping against hope, and no one breathed the word " surrender."

At last the Portuguese fleet, laden with provisions from Oporto, accompanied by the Lisbon vessels of war, approached the estuary of the Tagus. The Castilians, having intelligence of its coming, dropped down the river to stop it before it entered the firth. The two fleets met, and a most determined fight ensued, which resulted in the loss of three Portuguese galleys and a number of lives, including that of the brave and skilful Portuguese admiral, who was struck in the face by an arrow as he raised his visor for a moment to take breath. But the ships of Portugal, with the exception of the three which fell into the hands of the Castilians, broke through the enemy's line, and were moored in triumph at the quay of Lisbon. By-and-by, however, this new supply was nearly exhausted, for there were many mouths in the city ; and King John, guessing the distress of the Defender, tried to negotiate with him for a capitulation. His conditions, however, would have sacrificed the independence of Portugal, and they were decisively rejected, although all expectancy of further help, unless the English made their appearance, was gone. Negotiation having failed, the king tried a less honourable means of gaining access to the town; and having established communications with an officer of the garrison, to whom was committed the watching of a certain gate, he bribed the weak man to admit his troops by night. But the danger was exposed before its accomplishment, and the Defender's merciful conduct in dealing with the traitor, and all who were concerned in his perfidy, redounds to his credit. Dom John simply put their arms in their hands and had them thrust out of the gate, bidding them, if they wished to serve the Castilians, go where they could do so without disgrace. Thus, whether treating or plotting, the king's attempts equally miscarried.

By this time they were dying of hunger in the city. Bread could not be bought for money. The people were eating roots and olive husks. Still the spirit of defiance showed no signs of breaking; and whenever the bells signalled that the enemy seemed about to attack, the gaunt, famine-stricken garrison grasped their weapons and tottered to the ramparts. But the Portuguese had an irresistible ally in the Castilian camp. A dreadful plague laid hold of the king's troops, and spread so rapidly that the army was in a short time decimated. The Spanish nobles, and even the queen herself, who was in camp with her husband, were not spared. Long did the stubborn king resist this ruthless enemy. At last he confessed himself beaten, and gave orders for striking the tents, after a five months' siege, in October 1384. His homeward march resembled a funeral procession, so many were the coffins carried with the army to Spain. "O Lisbon," said the King of Castile, when he was taking a last look at its walls, "I shall yet live to see the ploughshare making furrows over thee!" A rash prophecy, but it was his only consolation as he led the remnant of his splendid host back to Spain.

The joy in Lisbon over the retreat of the Castilians was, says a chronicler, "like that of those who should return from death to life." The citizens had bought their freedom at a great price. They made history; they were the heroes of a chapter in the national annals about which the Portuguese to the latest generation could think with pride and thankfulness. Above all, it was the Defender himself who had been the soul of their resistance. His example of fearlessness and ceaseless activity had banished despair from their breasts and made tolerable the pangs of hunger. Their enthusiasm for him knew no bounds. What reward was too great for the saviour of Portugal? His defence of Lisbon had cleared his path to the throne.

Discovering and punishing a conspiracy against his life, instigated by the King of Castile, who saw that Dom John rather than Lisbon was the bulwark of Portugal, and after his futile siege conceived that coward's scheme of conquest, the Defender proceeded to Coimbra, where a meeting of the Cortes was appointed to be held. As he approached the town a great procession came forth to do him honour, and he was conducted first to the cathedral, where a *Te Deum* was sung, thereafter to the royal palace. At the Cortes it was found that all towns not under the power of Castile had empowered their delegates to choose "Dom John, Master of the knightly Order of Avis, to be lord and king of the realm." It was resolved accordingly, and a deputation waited on the Defender at the palace to lay before him the conclusion of the Cortes. He thanked them heartily, but refused the honour, on account both of the bar sinister upon his arms and of his knightly vow. When his answer was conveyed to the assembly it produced universal consternation. Without the sceptre he could not command abiding fealty from the vassals, and the kingdom which he alone seemed able to maintain in its entirety would certainly be ruined. They offered him their lives, their property for his official needs, and pledged themselves to procure a Papal Bull for the cancelling of his vows. Such pleading and promises he could not withstand. He was conscious of his own calling and of the nation's necessities, and accepted the dignity pressed upon him by a trustful and grateful people.

In April 1385 he was proclaimed King of Portugal amid unspeakable rejoicing, and immediately appointed the high officers of state, naming the faithful Nuno Pereira constable and mayor of the palace. The adjourned Cortes reassembled, and arranged a series of requests, to which they wished the king's assent. They stipulated especially that the sovereign should not declare war without the consent of the estates. He subscribed the articles, except one, which would have prevented him from marrying without their approbation of his choice. That, he said, was a personal matter, and he would only agree to inform them of his intention in that regard. Lisbon also presented a petition that it should be the recognized capital of the kingdom. This he granted, as it was already the most important town, and had deserved so well in the late war.

The Cortes having accepted the king's large concessions with his reservations of private rights, there remained for the estates and their newly-elected monarch the duty of vigorously prosecuting the work which had been only well begun by the obstinate defence of Lisbon. Many vassals in Minho, Estremadura, and elsewhere still held for Castile, and it was necessary to thoroughly purge the land of the Spanish influence. The constable, with an army, small but fresh and confident, conducted a fortunate campaign in Minho, and had succeeded in putting its principal fastnesses into the power of King John of Portugal, when the Castilian armada once more appeared before Lisbon. As these ships could only be intended to act in conjunction with a land force coming from Spain, the Portuguese collected their fighting strength to oppose the invasion. So the frontiers were carefully watched. The precautions were justified, for two Castilian forces had been ordered to enter

Portugal. One, the smaller, appeared in the direction of Ciudad Rodrigo, and was vanquished by the Portuguese. The other, a large army, was seen soon afterwards marching by Badajos upon Lisbon.

Whether the troops of Portugal could withstand such a host in the open field was a fair question for prudent soldiers. Various were the voices in the camp of King John. Some suggested a Fabian policy till the arrival of the English auxiliaries. But the stout Nuno Pereira held that the Castilians must not be allowed to draw near the capital and subject the inhabitants to another siege, wherein, without the king, and their garrison withdrawn to the field, they must inevitably yield or perish like dogs from sheer hunger. "The might of Castile is great, but God's is greater," said this Christian warrior, "and our cause is just." At last the constable, unable to endure any longer the hesitancy of the war-council, dashed off, without asking leave, with his battalion to intercept the Castilians. Some were indignant, and insisted on his recall; but King John smiled, and gave orders to follow his trusty Pereira. Overtaking the constable, the whole army of Portugal met the enemy in tremendous force at Aljubarotta, a village in Portuguese Estremadura. The Spanish king was with his soldiers, but in such poor health that he had to be borne thus far on a litter. Arrived in sight of the Portuguese, however, he mounted a mule with assistance, and made ready to take part in the fight.

It was another crisis in the history of Portugal, whose troops were here greatly outnumbered. But their king told them that a hundred Portuguese spears were worth a thousand Castilian—a piece of patriotic flattery, the exaggeration of which those who heard it were tempted to lessen by their prowess. Encouraged also by the benediction of Pope Urban, which he had sent the Portuguese, they overlooked the odds against them. Even the two pieces of ordnance, the first ever used in the Peninsula, with which the Castilians were provided, did not turn them by a hair's-breadth from their purpose of flinging themselves upon the foes of their country's liberty. The Spaniards, too, were resolute, trusting in their superior numbers, and in the blessing of Clement, the rival claimant of the tiara. The fight was short (half-an-hour is said to have decided it), but very determined and bloody.

The Portuguese leaders were foremost in the conflict. King John himself leaped from his charger, and armed with a battle-axe performed miracles of bravery. Nuno Pereira flew over the field like an angel of destruction. The standard of Castile was taken, and their cry, "Castile and St. Jago," was drowned by victorious shouts of "Portugal and St. George." The King of Castile was lifted on a swift horse, and in a half-fainting condition conveyed from peril which he should never have courted. What remained of his host saved itself by flight, and left an enormous booty for the conquerors in gold and silver, weapons and horses. The royal invader and his grandees had richly provided themselves with all manner of necessaries and comforts for that long sojourn in Portugal they were so vain as to expect. The decisive victory of Aljubarotta, gained on the 14th of August 1385, was improved by a seizure of those places in Portugal, such as the strong town of Santarem, which persisted up to that date in rejecting their lawful sovereign, and by an invasion of Castile, wherein Nuno Pereira took Badajos, and in various encounters with the foe added lustre to his renown.

With this work the Portuguese were still occupied when John of Gaunt, Duke of Lancaster, and an English army landed at Coruña. A treaty of mutual support was speedily entered into between the great English noble and the King of Portugal; and the king, some six months later, took to wife Philippa, the duke's daughter, for confirmation of the bond.*

---

* In order to this marriage King John had been released by the Pope from his vow of celibacy, taken as a knight of Avis.

Lancaster's attempt to lay hold of the Castilian crown, in right of his wife, Pedro of Castile's daughter, was little better than a *fiasco.* The pest which so frequently attacked medieval camps, through the absence of sanitary regulations, laid many of the English low, and crippled the duke's operations; and affairs in his own land urgently demanded his presence there. He was glad, therefore, to beat an honourable retreat, having made peace with his antagonist on the basis of a marriage between the Infant of Castile (afterwards Henry III.) and his daughter Katherine.

. Hostilities were nevertheless continued against Castile by Portugal, intermitted by truces, for a quarter of a century, at the end of which period both nations, becoming impressed with the folly of maintaining so long a warfare wherein, as it happened, neither party gained much, were equally anxious to sheathe their swords. In accordance with this feeling, a lasting settlement of the differences between the two countries was arrived at in 1411.

Meanwhile three sons of King John by Philippa—Edward, Pedro, and Henry—had grown to young manhood, and thirsted for military adventure. The "piping time of peace" following the cessation of the struggle with Castile, offering only the mock warfare of the tournament, was too tame for their fiery spirits. So they resolved to ply their father with arguments in favour of a new campaign. The coast of Africa opposite southern Portugal was considered a portion of Algarve. "The two Algarves" was a phrase to which Portuguese and Mohammedans had been long habituated. It seemed then to the princes, and to many in Portugal, that the conquest of the Mussulman Gharb beyond the sea was but the natural termination of that enterprise against the power of the Crescent which their fathers had carried on with such zeal and success. Prince Henry, however, had aspirations for his native land which his brothers were hardly fitted to comprehend. He was a thinker and a scholar who had few equals among the contemporary Portuguese. Especially had his interest in geographical knowledge stirred his imagination, and led him to sketch a career for Portugal which should lift it far above the position it had hitherto held as a European power. The country was hemmed in by the sea on two sides, and on the other two by Spain; and yet it evidently required more territory, that it might hold its own among neighbouring states. There was no room for its expansion in the Peninsula unless it seized Granada, the last stronghold of Mohammedanism in south-western Europe. But the annexation of that kingdom would inevitably lead to another war with Castile, which looked upon Granada as its legitimate spoil. How then should Portugal lengthen its cords? Africa, Henry thought, solved the problem. There should undoubtedly be found one knew not how much land teeming with various vegetation and mineral wealth—land unoccupied or populated by unbelievers, whom to dispossess and trample under foot would be a religious privilege and responsibility. The subjugation of the Gharb was in Prince Henry's eyes only the initial step towards the making of greater Portugal. Therefore, while sharing the enthusiasm of his brothers for feats of arms, his own deeper views rendered him all the more willing to bring the matter of an African expedition under his father's notice, and press for the royal assent.

The first object which the princes had set before themselves was the taking of Ceuta, that strongly fortified town near Gibraltar, once held by the Visigoths, and recovered by the Mohammedans in the time of Don Roderick. Ceuta was reckoned the most beautiful and populous town in the Moorish land. It was distinguished for its fine public buildings and private residences, and had a very pleasant and fruitful neighbourhood. The town carried on a lively trade with Alexandria, Spain, France, and Italy, and indeed was, by reason of its situation, an excellent emporium for Africa and Europe. It held out, therefore, the promise of rich reward to its captors. There were two reasons which particularly recommended an attempt upon it to the Portuguese. In the first place, an excessive toll was levied from their ships, as from those of all foreign nations, by Ceuta on their passing through the strait; and secondly, there was a possibility of reinforcements crossing thence into Granada for the support of the Mohammedans there. That was, of course, rather the affair of Castile than of Portugal. But the strengthening of Moslemism in the Peninsula would be dangerous for Portugal too.

King John was persuaded, by the representations made to him, that the adventure was worthy and called for, and that the King of Castile would not oppose it, since he would see in its success his own advantage in respect of Granada. The King of Portugal only doubted his ability to permanently hold the place. But on referring the whole matter to his queen, to whom he always paid that respect which her noble character and sound judgment deserved, she encouraged the project, bidding the king trust the Providence who should favour his enterprise to furnish him with means to retain his prize, and expressed, with the current fanaticism, her joy to think of her sons going forth "to wash away their sins in the blood of unbelievers."

While the armament for the siege of Ceuta was being prepared, Queen Philippa died (1423). Deep was the sorrow of her family and of the Portuguese nation, for she had been greatly beloved. An Englishwoman of distinguished birth, she was one of whom any people might be proud. Her dutiful, devout, and benevolent life had given a decided tone to the society of her adopted country. She was renowned for her attention to her children's mental and moral education, and to the duties of her household. She drew around her a circle of pure-minded women, so that her court was known as a school of virtue. Her opinion was much valued on account of her candour and discretion, and it has been carefully noted by ancient authorities that "she spoke little." The occasion of her death was a prevailing plague, to which many in Lisbon and its neighbourhood had succumbed. His sons endeavoured to induce the king to remove himself from the peril of being infected by the fatal disease with which the queen had been seized; but in vain. "She has been a faithful companion to me in life," said he, "and I will not leave her on her deathbed." Among her last words were an earnest exhortation to her eldest son to rule the realm in righteousness when he should be called to succeed his father.

After the days of mourning for the lamented Philippa were ended, the fleet (the largest armada which had ever set sail in the name of Portugal), commanded by the king in person, weighed anchor, and a favourable wind soon brought it within sight of Ceuta. The inhabitants were not only in great alarm at the spectacle of so many ships of war approaching them, they were also thoroughly surprised, for the contemplated expedition had been kept a profound secret. The plan had been drawn up on the report of some Portuguese officers, who had, without exciting suspicion, minutely examined the fortifications of Ceuta in the course of a voyage upon a bogus mission to Sicily from the King of Portugal; and the armada was got ready for the pretended purpose of attacking the Count of Holland—a stratagem which that sovereign connived at, in the interests of Christian Europe, knowing well the real destination of the fleet. The inhabitants of Ceuta were therefore astounded when they saw the Portuguese ships bearing down upon them; but they were shrewd enough to take in the situation, and hastily summoning some thousands of warlike Numidians to strengthen the garrison, shut their gates. A violent storm, however, compelled the Portuguese, just when they were within reach of the town, to steer for safety in the direction of home. Yet the apparently hostile elements were in reality friendly;

for the Ceutans, reassured by the supposed departure of the
enemy, dismissed their auxiliaries ; and the fleet, favoured by
a sudden change in the weather, once more hove in sight, and
ere long cast anchor within convenient distance of the shore,
before the Numidians could be recalled.   A landing was
quickly effected, one of the first to leap on *terra firma* being
Prince Henry.   The garrison sallied out, and a terrific hand-to-
hand encounter followed.   The Portuguese were victorious,
and entering the town, prepared to storm the citadel.   But as
they were about to attempt.an assault, they found that the
governor and the remnant of the garrison, together with a
multitude of women and children, had escaped by another gate
whenever the defeat of the defenders outside the walls became
evident.   Ceuta thus fell into the hands of the Portuguese
(August 21, 1415), and was never recovered by the Moslems,
notwithstanding all their strenuous efforts to dispossess the
invaders.

It was a great triumph to King John, who was such an
uncompromising foe of the Mohammedans that he would not
accept the loan of a single spearman from the King of Granada
during his contest with Castile.   But his hostility to the unbe-
liever did not constitute the sole element in his joy over the
taking of Ceuta.   He entertained, though he did not express
them with the unguarded enthusiasm of youth, some of those
hopes as to the expansion of Portugal which animated his son
Henry, and bore in after-days such abundant fruit.   "This is only
the beginning of conquest," said the king when he had mastered
Ceuta.   Prince Henry not only reciprocated the sentiment, but
deemed it advisable to pursue the victory at once.   So he prevailed upon his father to fit out several expeditions of African
discovery, each of which encouraged to new effort, until there
was created in the Portuguese nation a spirit of maritime adventure which became its predominant characteristic.   A con-
secutive account of these enterprises will be found on another

page, but it may be noted here that, under the auspices of Henry, Portuguese ships rounded the African cape Bogador, and made their way to the Guinea coast, discovered Porto Santo, Madeira, and the Azores. Such results are trivial compared with those which have been achieved in modern days; yet they seemed very wonderful in the time of Henry, and for his promotion of this kind of work the prince was justly distinguished by the name of the "Navigator."

On 14th August 1433, the anniversary of Aljubarotta, King John died, after a reign of nearly half a century. Seized with his fatal illness in the country, he requested to be conveyed to Lisbon, that he might breathe his last in a place for so many reasons dear to him. He was buried in the chapel of the Monastery of Batalha, the most magnificent building in Portugal, which he had reared in memory of the glorious victory over Castile.

He left a state on good terms with its neighbours. There were commercial and extradition treaties with Castile, and with England the Portuguese had the most friendly relations. The home policy of the king was favourable to the commons, and notwithstanding the enormous expenditure attending his expeditions of war and discovery, which made great inroads on the wealth of the kingdom, the title "of good memory" by which the people distinguished him shows that he never lost his early popularity. He managed to allay that inveterate controversy between church and state which had been the plague of many Portuguese sovereigns, by getting the assent of the ecclesiastical authorities to a definition of their territorial and judicial limits. And it is interesting to note that, according to a statute of King John, time ceased to be reckoned from the era of Cæsar. Thenceforward, after the example of Aragon and Castile, the year of Christ's birth was invariably used.

Two years before his master, Nuno Pereira, constable of

Portugal, was carried to his grave. He had supported King John with the arm of a hero and the heart of a warm and constant friend. It does not seem that the king could have won and kept his position without the constable. And so disinterested was Pereira that he was glad to forego the rewards of his valour that others who less deserved them might be satisfied. He was a man of few words, but every one "like a well-aimed arrow." In the field fearless, he was blameless in his home, and at all times and places a devout Christian. He might have sat for the portrait of Chaucer's "very perfect gentle knight." Nine years before his death he gave away all his property and retired from the world to a hermitage simple as his own soul. Little did he dream that his posterity should wear the crown of Portugal. But so it happened. His daughter Beatrice wedded a natural son of the king, the Count of Barcellos and first Duke of Braganza, and was thus the ancestress of the present reigning family.

The reign of Edward, eldest of John's sons, was a very brief one, only five years long, and full of misfortune. Like his four excellent brothers (for besides those who shared with him the honours of Ceuta, two others were now grown to manhood), he had been well trained by his mother. The depth of his religious convictions, impressed upon him by the precept and example of Philippa, was revealed by the whole tenor of his life. His statements and promises were so reliable that "the word of the king" was a current synonym for truth. In public he was mild and unaffected, and his private life was entirely admirable. He dressed simply, and restricted to the utmost the expenses of his household. His inclination to learning had been sedulously cultivated, and in his orations, wherein he displayed an extraordinary fluency, which obtained for him the *sobriquet* of "the Eloquent," he was able to draw upon a large fund of literary wealth. He was among the earliest of royal authors, his chief work being "The Faithful Adviser" (*Leal*

Conselheiro), a book full of earnest exhortation to good living, and only seldom expressing medieval prejudice and superstition. His proficiency in manly sports was remarkable ; his valour was well proved at Ceuta. But all that has just been said of him might be repeated regarding the other princes, except that none of them showed that talent for public speaking for which he was so famous. They were indeed a noble band of brothers, in whom Philippa might as reasonably exult as did Cornelia in the Gracchi. Henry, to be sure, must be singled out as possessing those characteristics which have been summed up in the word genius. He was the original thinker ; he was the master spirit without whose counsel none of them ventured to carry out a project. Still all were exceptional in talents, accomplishments, and moral worth ; and though history is said to repeat itself, it would be hard to find in the records of royal houses a parallel to the case of these five good and gifted brothers.

Edward, on account of the late king's increasing infirmities, had, for a year or two before his father's death, to perform various royal duties, and so was somewhat exercised in his office ere he was called upon to undertake the administration in his own name. But, his experience in state matters, his goodwill and capacity notwithstanding, the nation was not the better of the new king. His reign was too short to effect much, and from the very beginning of it he was launched into a sea of troubles. The pest ravaged the country at brief intervals during the whole of his kingship, and there was a year of grievous famine. The royal exchequer, too, had very little left in it after the enormous drafts necessary to defray the expenses of the African war and the expeditions of discovery.

But what afflicted the king most of all was the luckless issue of an attempt to take Tangier. The Infant Ferdinand, who, as he was only fourteen years of age at the time of the expedition to Ceuta, had been excluded from a share in the work, was dying to reap the honours of war. He consulted Henry, and that prince encouraged him in his idea, which was thereupon laid before the king. Edward was rather averse to the proposal, considering the state of the royal finances, and the impossibility therefore of equipping an army large enough to attack Tangier and resist efforts to raise the siege. But Henry pointed out the immense advantage of the place to Portugal, for the purpose of fully commanding the strait, and expressed his willingness to execute the task of reducing it even with a few. So the king, yielding to his importunity, managed to obtain from the Cortes a sum of money, and fitted out a small fleet supposed to carry fourteen thousand men. The Princes Henry and Ferdinand sailed for Ceuta, and there numbering the troops, found their strength less by some thousands than they were aware of ; but they resolved to push on and run all risks.

When they pitched their camp near Tangier, the governor of the town (the same who had been governor of Ceuta at the time of its capture by the Portuguese) drew them from their good position by opening the gates, but shut them again when the enemy was under the walls. While the besieging army waited there, a swarm of Mohammedans coming to the relief of Tangier attacked them in rear. The Portuguese, nevertheless, keeping their antagonists at bay, attempted a storm ; but the ladders were of insufficient length to reach the top of the ramparts. It was hard work to resist the Moslem reinforcements and carry on the siege at the same time. Yet this was done. The ladders were lengthened, and a tower of wood constructed, when a Mohammedan prisoner brought to the princes reported that a host led by the Kings of Fez and Morocco was on its way to the scene of action. The information was true, for ere long the fresh Mohammedan army appeared, an overwhelming force which precluded all thought of continuing the investment of Tangier. The Portuguese withdrew to their camp, which they fortified as best they could, and there they themselves were compelled to endure the horrors of a siege.

Within their intrenchments the princes maintained for a time .with great heroism the unequal conflict. The coast was guarded, so that they could not reach their ships. Hunger and thirst tormented them, and when the enemy contrived to fire their camp, surrender seemed the only open course. But a torrent of rain extinguished the conflagration, and they still held their position with desperate stubbornness. Surrounded, however, by many thousands of Mohammedans (six hundred thousand, the Portuguese historians aver), surrender was inevitable, and the princes asked a parley. The enemy sent in conditions which demanded the cession of Ceuta. That agreed to, the Portuguese should be allowed to embark on leaving their arms, goods, and some hostages. The princes with down-cast hearts assented, and Henry sailed for Lisbon with the remnant of their army.

His brother remained as one of the hostages. He was not treated by the Mohammedans like an honourable foe and an Infant of Portugal. They loaded him with chains and cast him into a noisome dungeon. And when the governor of Tangier by-and-by transferred him to the charge of the King of Fez, a bloodthirsty ruffian, he was more evilly entreated still. He would have been tortured to death were it not for the hope of obtaining Ceuta as his ransom. His patient and forgiving spirit, his forgetfulness of self over the sufferings of his companions in misfortune, are pathetically described by his private secretary, a fellow-hostage, who afterwards obtained his freedom. Ferdinand and the others wore fetters perpetually. They were crowded by night in the suffocating atmosphere of a cell small and pitch dark. By day they were sent to the hardest and most menial work, to which they were literally goaded by pike-thrusts and driven by blows of heavy clubs.

Ceuta was not given up by the Portuguese. The feeling at home was decidedly against such a surrender of the national interests, and the ecclesiastical authorities insisted that the princes had no right to promise the cession of that town, so important not only to Portugal but to Christendom. It was agreed rather to offer a ransom price for the Infant. But before Portugal and the Moslems could come to terms, death stepped in and set the noble prisoner at liberty. Naturally more delicate than any of his brothers, his constitution at length gave way under the cruelties to which he was subjected, and, after seven years of the most dreadful hardships, succumbed. The King of Fez declared that if among the Christian dogs one righteous could be found, that solitary exception to the general depravity was the departed prince. "If he had been a Moslem," said the tyrant, "he ought to have been worshipped as a saint."

In 1438, five years before his hapless brother, King Edward (on opening a letter, it is said, sent from an infected district) was fatally stricken by the plague which scourged Portugal so persistently in the years of his rule. A better or more enlightened sovereign never occupied a throne than Edward ; yet he was sedulously visited by calamity, and died in his prime, heart-broken by the distress of his country and by the imprisonment among unbelievers of a beloved brother whom he was powerless to release. His undertakings were but attempts, and his beneficent policy was only in its experimental stage, hardly framed in detail, when he was summoned away.

His widowed queen, Leonora of Aragon, undertook then the government, which she intended to administer till the child-king, Alfonso V., who was only six years old at his father's decease, should be capable of assuming sovereign power. But this arrangement, though in accordance with Edward's testament, had not by any means the approval of the Portuguese. Leonora was a woman and a foreigner; and it seemed out of the question that the Infants, the late king's brothers, who had shown so much patriotism and capacity, should be deprived of authority in the state. The Infant Pedro, being the second son of King John I., should have succeeded to the throne had

Edward died without issue, and his distinguished qualities appeared to point him out as the best fitted to hold the regency. The public dissatisfaction with the sole authority of the queen became so pronounced that she herself could not fail to observe it, and certain notables of the court plainly told her, when she mentioned the matter of the government, that it would be well if she were to put the reins into Pedro's hand. Leonora, unlike her namesake, the spouse of Ferdinand, was naturally indisposed to strife and hatred. She was willing to follow the counsel which made for peace and the common weal, and as a token of her goodwill proposed to Pedro that her son Alfonso should be betrothed to Isabel, the Infant's daughter.

Things might have gone well had not the Count of Barcellos (later the Duke of Braganza), that son of King John I. already spoken of, with some others, manœuvred to imbitter the queen against the Infant. They were jealous of his power, and saw no hope of furthering their own ambition under his watchful eye. The weakness of the queen yielded to their representations of the indignity to which she would submit, and of what they called Pedro's self-seeking. She was persuaded that the Infant wished to rob her child of his right, and showed therefore a disposition to resume the undivided regency. But the people shouted for Pedro, and the Cortes at Lisbon declared for him as " Defender of the Kingdom." The queen was induced to publicly withstand the national will, and her attitude resulted in the removal from her of the child Alfonso. With the help of Pedro's enemies she permitted herself to carry on futile intrigues for the defender's displacement, and called upon Castile to support her scheme, till the Infant, now acknowledged chief magistrate of the nation, by a military demonstration before the fortress whither she had in rebellion withdrawn, compelled her retirement to Castile. Her hopes from that kingdom were vain, and in Toledo, after some years of fruitless endeavour to procure the downfall of Pedro, she died. Those who hated the Infant hinted at foul play on his part when the news of the queen's death was published; but the calumny, in the public view, redounded to the discredit of its authors.

Pedro faithfully carried on his work amid many discouragements. He grieved much when he heard of his brother Ferdinand's death in Africa, reproaching himself needlessly for not having taken better measures to avert such a tragic fate. Now only Prince Henry and he were left of the five brothers, for, one year before the decease of Ferdinand, Pedro had to mourn the loss of Prince John, the most faithful of companions and supporters. He had the more need of such a brother, since his foes, the Count of Barcellos at their head, were industriously occupied in blackening his reputation. All the faults committed by his government—and what human government is faultless?—were magnified. Every public step he took was represented as part of a self-aggrandizing policy. At length, when King Alfonso had reached the age of fourteen, the regent was tired of these machinations, and tendered his resignation. Alfonso, however, begged him earnestly to retain office, and, as a guarantee of his affectionate regard for his uncle, soon afterwards wedded Isabel, Pedro's daughter. The Infant Pedro having consented under such pressure to the king's request, carried on the administration for a while with confidence in Alfonso, who appeared to slight the accusations of the malignant opposition. But the one idea of Barcellos (now elevated to his dukedom) was the ruin of Pedro's name, and by dint of persistence he succeeded in infecting the mind of the young monarch with various suspicions of his uncle's good faith. So, just when the regent was congratulating himself on the auspicious aspect of affairs, the political sky was suddenly overcast. The Braganza party were triumphant, and Pedro, on learning the state of matters, went to the court and laid down the regency. "My lord!" said he to the king, "for ten years I have done the work as best I could. I desire now to live a private life upon my property. If occasion for my presence arises, you have only to summon me, and I am your majesty's obedient vassal and servant." The resignation was this time accepted, and with dignity and a clear conscience the Infant withdrew from the scene of his activity to his castle at Coimbra, from which place he derived a ducal title.

Great as was the malicious joy of his foes at this fall of the faithful regent, their scheme was not yet complete. Nothing less than the Duke of Coimbra's attainder for high treason could satisfy them. They suggested that his retirement to his fortress was only the preface to an insurrection, and that the king should order his uncle to give up all the weapons in the castle, upon pain of the royal displeasure. "If he be innocent," said the plotters, "he cannot be unwilling to afford such a proof of his peaceable intentions. His refusal will be equivalent to a conviction of guilt." Alfonso swallowed the argument with the inexperience of a boy, and accordingly sent a message to his uncle. Pedro protested his loyalty, but demurred to being deprived of the privilege held by all grand seigniors of keeping an armed garrison. It was manifestly treating him as a defaulter. When Alfonso heard his uncle's reply he sent the Duke of Braganza, at that noble's request, on a punitive expedition against the rebel. But this force was so decisively repulsed that stronger measures were seen to be necessary if the mutiny were to be put down. Queen Isabel recalled to her husband the loyal and efficient services of her father, and with all the ardour of a child's affection pleaded for one so dear to her and so little deserving of such a sorry reward. Yet though Alfonso would fain have drawn back, he was in the toils of his false-hearted advisers, and his honour was involved in the defeat of Braganza. So he took the field with thirty thousand men, and encountered the few troops of his uncle at the river Alfarrobeira. The king was victorious. The Duke of Coimbra fell pierced through the heart by an arrow, and of his little army few remained alive at the close of the engagement. Alfonso was so enraged at the resistance he had met with that he would not allow the body of the duke to be taken away for burial, but gave orders that as an additional mark of disgrace it should lie on the field of battle to be devoured by the wolves. Some compassionate souls, nevertheless, stole the beloved remains by night and interred them at a neighbouring church, and by-and-by the senseless fury of the young king abated so far as to allow his uncle's corpse to be carried with due honour to the noble edifice at Batalha, where King John I. had been laid.

The Duke of Coimbra fell in 1449. The country, though in mortal dread of the ruthless party now in power, loudly lamented the heroic man who had been recompensed with insult and violent death by him whose interests he had so carefully watched over all the time of his regency. Pedro deserves the highest consideration as a scholar, a politician, a soldier, and an honest, fearless, disinterested man. He had travelled over Europe and to the East, and was everywhere received with the respect which became him and those who offered it. At the English court, where he was invested with the Garter, he was a special favourite, both for his mother's sake and because, with his fair hair and blue eyes, he looked much more like an Englishman than a Portuguese. Able and industrious in affairs, kind to the weak and poor, pure in his private life, he was at once a buttress and an ornament of the state ; and Alfonso learned too late the wrong he had done the illustrious Infant. Pedro's daughter, the Queen of Portugal, died suddenly six years after her father, and the absence of any adequate cause for her decease led many to suspect the Braganza clique of having compassed it by poison, since Isabel was their steadfast foe, and ever ready to oppose their measures. But one must give the worst the benefit of a doubt.

Two years after the queen's death we find Alfonso on the old campaigning ground of Northern Africa. The Pope had called for a crusade against the Turks, who in 1453 had taken Constantinople. But the Christian sovereigns did not respond so readily as their predecessors had done to the trumpet-blast from Rome. Only Alfonso of Portugal seemed obedient, raising an army and a fleet, and striking commemoration coins.* Yet he could not go to Constantinople alone, and when the other princes excused themselves, he found himself prepared for an impossible expedition. Perhaps he had had Africa in his view all along, for he could easily have ceased his preparations so soon as he became aware of the general disinclination outside Portugal for the work prescribed by the Pope. At all events he had now a large and fresh army on his hands, and a fleet of some three hundred sail, great and small. He directed it to the north of Africa, where he had a remarkable success, taking Alcazar-Seguer, Arzilla, and, after a repulse, Tangier—that town whose former siege had been so unfortunate for his uncle Ferdinand. Alfonso, surnamed "the African," in memory of his triumphs in the Southern Gharb, subscribed· himself (and his successors on the Portuguese throne have imitated his example) "King of Portugal and Algarve on both sides of the sea."

After the capture of Tangier the king was drawn into a war with Ferdinand and Isabella of Castile, in which the Portuguese were no gainers. Isabella's right to the Castilian throne was challenged by the adherents of Joanna, reputed daughter of the late King of Castile. Few believed that the deceased Henry of Castile had left any issue, but Joanna made a good cry for selfish men who hoped to win something from an internecine struggle. Alfonso V. was inveigled into a matrimonial engagement with the pretender ; and marching to Zamora, a Leonese town on the Douro, took the place after a short siege. But on proceeding further up the river he was stopped at Toro

---

* The cruzado, so called because of the cross on its reverse ; a silver coin worth about two shillings and sixpence sterling.

by a Castilian-Aragonese force (1476). The result was un-
favourable to the Portuguese, though they retreated in good
order ; and they could no longer hold Zamora, which therefore
soon after the battle gave itself up to the Spaniards.

This reverse was so disappointing to the victorious "African"
that he determined to make an alliance with some enemy of
Spain, and so retrieve his fortunes. Louis XI. of France, the
most subtle and unconscionable of monarchs, was selected as
the likeliest to befriend him in his need. Louis made fair
promises, but as they were followed by no performance, Alfonso
set off for France, to settle in person terms of mutual support.
The French king met him at Tours, and led him thereafter to
Paris, still dangling hope before his guest, and laughing in his
sleeve. A visit paid by the King of Portugal, while he was at
Paris, to his friend and cousin, Charles, Duke of Burgundy,
who lay encamped at Nancy, opposite the troops of Lorraine,
ought to have opened Alfonso's eyes. King Louis was occupied
with an endeavour to break the Duke of Burgundy's power by
employing against him the Duke of Lorraine. Were Burgundy
the victor, he might bring pressure to bear on Louis in favour
of his Cousin Alfonso's scheme. But in the event of Burgundy's defeat, the dissembling Frenchman should certainly
drive his guest out of his fool's paradise. All this Charles told
his cousin plainly. But so much in love was Alfonso, not
certainly with Joanna, but with the crown of Castile, that
he retreated to Paris and was ensnared once more by the
blandishments of his royal host. The news came to the French
capital of the Duke of Burgundy's discomfiture and death, and
just as he had prophesied, the King of Portugal received a
polite dismissal, the reason assigned being the Pope's objection
to the maintenance of Joanna's claim. Louis would have
delivered him up to the King of Castile, and indeed had him
arrested on his way to the coast, with that view. But for
reasons of his own, the inscrutable and unscrupulous diplomatist

let go his prey again. Alfonso, however, was in no hurry to travel homeward. He had set his heart on the aid of France, and it seemed as if life were not worth living now. He would be a pilgrim, and seek *incognito* the holy fields of Palestine. He sent a message accordingly to his son and successor, John, announcing that intention, and desiring the prince at once to assume the crown. This atrabilious mood, however, passed off, and the king, who had just voluntarily abdicated, betook himself to Portugal, where he found his son already entered on the regal dignity and duties. Nevertheless, John immediately offered his father his old position, which Alfonso accepted, though at first he declined more than the sovereignty of the Algarves.

A few sparks of enthusiasm for his Spanish project still remained in the breast of Alfonso. So the contest was resumed and continued for two years. But the Portuguese were in 1479 compelled to come to terms with Ferdinand and Isabella, and Alfonso agreed to think no more of Joanna or her supposititious right. The pretender herself was offered the alternatives of life-long imprisonment or the veil. She chose the nunnery at Coimbra, and when its great iron gates shut upon her men heard the last of her claim. What was called an everlasting peace was sworn between Castile and Portugal. The document is interesting, particularly for the account it gives of Portuguese colonial possessions, "spheres of influence and projects," at that time. Portuguese rights were acknowledged by Castile all round the west coast of Africa, from Capes Nun and Bojador even as far as India, with the adjacent seas, coasts, and islands ; likewise in the islands of Cape Verd, Madeira, the Azores, and in all the north African conquests. Castile might not trade or fish in these districts and waters without permission of the King of Portugal. On the other hand, the Canaries were to be considered Spanish. Castile also reserved Granada for itself.

Henry "the Navigator," the mainspring of maritime enterprise in Portugal, died in 1460 at his villa overlooking the Bay of Sagres, near Cape St. Vincent. He had built for himself this place, in full view of that element he loved, at the nearest point to the continent with which in his hopes and plans the future of Portugal was so intimately connected. Other men, endowed with a like patriotic and adventurous spirit, were to carry out his plans in a scale beyond his fondest dreams; still the Infant Henry's genius conducted the Portuguese on the way he had indicated, long after his eyes were closed in death.

Alfonso did not live long to exercise his resumed sovereignty. The destruction of his darling scheme regarding Castile preyed upon his mind, and only a few years elapsed between his return from France and his death, which occurred in 1481. With all his physical intrepidity, there was something in him of his mother's inability to form a clear and independent judgment, which often induced him to vacillate in crises requiring instant and decisive action. An event of importance in his reign was the compilation of a statute book which gathered and condensed a multitude of edicts. But the people did not consider his legislation sufficiently progressive. There ran a common saying of him that he was a better king for the classes than for the masses. And without doubt he leaned in his frequent irresolution rather heavily upon the first two estates, and accepted too readily their biassed views. Alfonso V. was passionately fond of literature, and was the first among the Portuguese kings to accumulate a royal library. Yet, though unquestionably learned, his practical knowledge was limited. In the field he was a warrior rather than a general, and in politics an opportunist rather than a statesman.

John II., who in 1481 received a second time the homage of the Cortes, had seen with grave concern the numerous gifts, territorial and pecuniary, bestowed by royal hands upon the

Portuguese nobility, and no king had been more lavish in this direction than Alfonso V., who had indeed by his imprudent generosity considerably reduced the treasury of the state. Their extraordinary privileges also were a source of anxiety and dis-pleasure to the king, and he was convinced that strong measures ought to be adopted to adjust their claims on the national income, and their relations both to feudal inferiors and to the monarch as their head. The Duke of Braganza, because of his royal descent (from John I.), and of his immense wealth, assumed a position which the king felt to be incompatible with his own. How much so was immediately seen when, after a royal inquiry had been completed regarding the status and revenues of the nobles, regulations were drawn up which should have the effect of reducing them in both respects. The then Duke of Braganza, son of the Regent Pedro's relentless foe, took up an exceedingly presumptuous attitude on the publica-tion of the edicts, declaring against the ancient prerogatives of the peers being curtailed, and inflaming the pride of the grandees in a way most aggravating and dangerous to the throne.

John was indignant, and firmly resolved to compel the aris-tocracy to submission. He meant to begin with Braganza as the premier peer, and hoped that a successful beginning with him would be the end of the opposition. He had the duke watched, therefore, the more carefully, as he suspected that nobleman's hostility would as soon as possible assume a practi-cal form. Ere long the king got to know of a very pretty plot which was being hatched under the auspices of Braganza. The duke himself kept aloof at first, but his brother, the Marquis of Montemor, and other intimate friends were, under his auspices, conducting secret negotiations with Spain, whose object was to plunge their country into war with that power. They were urging Spain to demand the privilege of trading on the Guinea coast, which, as acknowledged by treaty, belonged to Portugal by right of settlement, if not of discovery. The conspirators were aware that such a demand would be repudiated by Portugal, and that declinature was to be a *casus belli.* The duke and all his party were to thwart their sovereign in such an event, and if necessary (safe, they said to themselves) should embrace the Spanish cause.

King John had information of the whole design; but not disposed to take extreme measures, could these be dispensed with, he commanded Braganza's attendance at the palace, and without revealing his special knowledge of the affair, exhorted the arch-plotter to patriotism and warned him regarding the peril of treason. Nevertheless the mischievous correspondence still went on, and the king at length gave orders for the duke's arrest. That step was necessarily delayed, even after it had been finally resolved on, till the return of Alfonso, the heir-apparent of Portugal, who happened to be in Castile and in the hands of Ferdinand and Isabella. Whenever the prince's safety was assured, John struck at the conspiracy with all his might. At his trial the duke employed the most eminent lawyers in Portugal, but they had no case, since the prosecution held some of his letters to the sovereign of Spain containing unmistakable treason. He was beheaded (1483), and the other ringleaders fled for their lives. The duke's brother, the Marquis of Montemor, was executed in effigy, as an advertisement of his fate should he dare to show his face in the country.

The common people were delighted with the humiliation of the nobles and the defeat of their treachery. The nobles of the Braganza party were in a state of mind which may be easily imagined. King John had still need to walk warily, for, baffled as to their Spanish project, they contrived another, this time directly against his life. The plan was to murder the king and the crown prince, and thereafter to set on the throne the young Duke of Viseu. That noble was connected with the king in a twofold way. The duke's father, in the first place, was the Infant Ferdinand, brother of Alfonso V.; and further, John's queen, Leonora, was Viseu's sister. As the king's cousin and brother-in-law, therefore, he might have been expected to decline being a party to the vile deed contemplated by the conspirators. But ambition smothered his conscience, and on the revelation of the cabal, nothing grieved John more than to see his cousin of Viseu, whom he had treated with affectionate regard, had, so to speak, warmed in his bosom, turning thus to inflict upon his benefactor a deadly sting.

The king had never gone from the precincts of the palace since the execution of Braganza without a faithful body-guard, and now especially that protection was extremely requisite. Several times he was informed opportunely of particular attempts to be made upon his life, and only escaped by the exercise of his own ingenuity or by reason of the force he kept about his person. He talked with the Duke of Viseu seriously about the danger of associating with the disaffected, and the good he might do if he turned his attention to the work of the state; the influential place he might hold as a relative of the royal family. But the bauble shining on the king's brow dazzled the lad's eyes and lured him to his destruction. He was infatuated by the vision of power with which his evil counsellors had filled his mind, and in his endeavour to snatch the crown his own life was sacrificed.

The Duke of Braganza had been formally tried and condemned; but in this new case the king, after the cruel mode of the time, considered himself justified in expediting procedure by becoming his own executioner. He sent for his cousin one evening to the castle of Setubal, where the court happened to be, and in the half darkness of the wardrobe slew the young duke with his poniard (1483). The body was exhibited to the public next day, and an announcement circulated by the king acknowledging and giving reasons for the deed. All the world should learn that John II. of Portugal was not a man to

be trifled with, since a member of his own family had paid
such a price for his treason.   John called his crime a sentence.
We cannot be content with the euphemism, and must catalogue
it among plain murders.   But let us remember as extenuating
circumstances the state of exasperation and terror into which
he had been thrown, and the fact that Viseu, according to
evidence indisputable, was busily urging and bribing miscreants
to accomplish the bloody plan of the conspirators.   But what
a short-sighted bungler the duke was after all!   Had he only
possessed his soul in patience, there should have been one day
given into his hands that very thing he was striving guiltily to
gain.   The rest of the traitorous band were most of them apprehended, and either executed or imprisoned.   So one more
danger was past.

But a very dark day was in store for the king.   Alfonso,
the heir-apparent, who was to have been the second victim of
the Viseu conspiracy, did not live to enjoy the crown which
his father thought had been firmly secured for him by the
violent despatch of a strong and perfidious competitor.   The
prince met his death in the flower of his youth, suddenly and
violently, as had the Duke of Viseu, but not by the hand of
man.   It was at Santarem on the Tagus, where the royal
family were residing about eight years after the explosion of
the last intrigue.   The king loved to frequent the banks of the
river in the twilight, and sent for his son one day to join him.
Alfonso rode thither on horseback, but in the growing dusk
the animal stumbled and fell, and the unfortunate young man
was found under his horse's body mortally injured.   Even as
those who had rushed to the spot were raising him in their
arms, he breathed his last.   They bore the corpse to the cottage
of a fisherman, and beside the rude pallet on which it was laid
the disconsolate father watched the whole night through, in
speechless agony, for some signs of returning life.   But the
spirit of the prince was as far away as that of the Duke of Viseu.

It was a terrible affliction. Alfonso had been a youth of great promise; his relations with his father had been most intimate and affectionate; and by his removal, as John had no other legitimate son, the next occupant of the throne should be a member of that very family to crush whose hopes the king had stained his hands with blood. Yet the effect of this deep distress upon the king's character seems to have been of a salutary description. It purged him of that princely *hauteur*, till then indomitable, which constrained him to trample upon the pride of the nobility, and to compel even the great Braganza to crouch at his feet. He could be kind to the commons—as in truth he was, and so earned their blessings—because they did not encroach upon his dignity; but woe to the man who should put on airs in the royal presence! The death of his son, however, evidently diminished his self-esteem; courtiers who had, perhaps, thought his dealings with the grandees too uncompromising to be wise, were often surprised in his later years by his humility. He lived only four years after his son. He is said to have received some time before, in his drink, a poison which produced little immediate effect, but crept slowly through his system. But whatever might be the proximate cause of his end, the king approached it in a desirable spirit, begging on his death-bed those about him to lay aside expressions of homage in addressing him. So, stripped of that loftiness brooking no check—a spirit which had affected the Portuguese nobles with chronic wrath, and made him once at least a criminal—he passed away (1495).

In the time of John II., the Portuguese continued in north Africa their attacks upon Mohammedan towns. But it was a difficult and costly affair, this persistent endeavour on the part of a small country like Portugal, which had few or no foreign mercenaries to swell her armies, to cope with the almost incalculable hordes of courageous and well-trained warriors who rallied round the banner of the Crescent in Africa. Varying success attended the Portuguese arms, more victories, on the whole, falling to them than defeats. But the project of subduing this region, thickly populated and well defended as it was, began to show itself to their ripened experience in its true colours, as something quite beyond the utmost valour and generalship which Portugal could devote to it.

Much better progress was made with discoveries in lands further off and less civilized. Already Portugal was beginning to recover, with interest, the money sunk in those expeditions which Henry the Navigator had advocated and directed. The trade with Guinea was by this time remarkably flourishing; and John II., rejoicing in the acquisition of such a productive country, styled himself " Lord of Guinea." But the Portuguese ventured much further south than Guinea in the reign of John. The discovery of the Congo and the doubling of the Cape of Good Hope by Portuguese mariners were two events in his day of first-rate importance, especially the latter achievement, which more than made up for the insignificance of the operations in the north of the African continent. And had Portugal only been more trustful and generous towards the great Genoese Columbus—and the king himself was most eager to patronize him—the glory of his famous western voyage should not have covered Spain.

Wealthy though the kingdom of Portugal was becoming, enormous disbursements were required for African work— campaigning in the north and discovery in the south. So John thought of a means of increasing his available funds. It happened in 1492 that all Jews in Spain were, by an edict of the " Catholic " king, commanded to leave the country unless they submitted to Christian baptism. It was a short-sighted policy on the part of Spain, for no more intelligent and peaceable subjects could be desired than were the Spanish Jews. But Granada had been taken from the Moors, and Ferdinand had leisure to exhibit his zeal for the Cross by persecuting those other unbelievers. John of Portugal was appealed to in this strait, by some leading Jews, to grant them a refuge in his country on payment of a large sum of money. The king closed with the offer, glad to obtain the sinews of war, and over twenty thousand Jewish families crowded into Portugal. But within a year, notwithstanding the heavy tax levied upon them, those who cleaved to the old form of faith were driven forth again, and many were not even allowed to leave the country but were sold into slavery there. It was the prevailing superstition to look on kindness to the Jew as dishonour to the Saviour; and an infectious disease, which had spread among the ill-fed Israelites, furnished the anti-Semitic party with a sufficient cry. Yet the treatment of the Jews in Portugal was altogether shameful, and John's permission of it, though we take into account the intolerance of the age, is one of the least pleasing episodes in his career.

With John II. the line of Avis terminated. That house had lived for a hundred years, and its century was noted for the astonishing rapidity with which the kingdom had marched to an excellent position among existing states, on account of its important and growing possessions abroad. It had not reached the zenith of its influence on the death of John II. Other lands, then unthought of, were to receive from Portugal an indelible stamp, to fill her coffers with treasure, and to make her still more prominent and powerful. Yet the house of Avis in its time saw more than enough to justify the fondest anticipations of the country's greatness.

CHAPTER V.

HOUSE OF VISEU.[*]

1495-1580.

AFTER the young Prince Alfonso's fatal ride, the next heir to the Portuguese crown was Emmanuel, cousin of John II., and younger brother of that Duke of Viseu who had gone to his long account by the same short way he had intended for the king. Emmanuel, a boy of fourteen at the time of his brother's death in 1483, became by that event second Duke of Viseu; but the king, desirous of obliterating, if possible, every memorial of the tragedy, abolished in the same year the dukedom, and created for his cousin the new title Duke of Beja, by which style he was known till his accession to the throne. As if to atone, in so far as that could be done, for the murder, though he did not choose to call it a crime, the king treated the boy with the greatest tenderness, gave him the best tutors whom he could find, and endowed him with the confiscated estates of Viseu, while he blotted the hateful peerage out of existence.

The new sovereign was crowned in 1495 without opposition. He ascended the throne at the age of twenty-six, and reigned for just so many years as he had lived before his coronation. They called him the "fortunate king," and no doubt the auspices were excellent when he assumed the government. John II. had made for his successor an easier seat by securing the favour

---

[*] So called; properly of Beja.

of the commons and checking the presumption of the nobles.
The rich and increasing foreign traffic rendered vexatious imposts at home unnecessary, and no irritating controversy with
neighbouring powers threatened hostilities. Nor did these
encouraging signs of the times change for the worse in Emmanuel's quarter of a century. Nevertheless the fact that the
best fortune may be marred by an incapable and unconscionable
man receives ample illustration from the career of King Ferdinand of Portugal; and if Emmanuel did not make his advantages, he at least possessed sufficient worth and ability to retain
and employ them.

The first representative of the house of Viseu was a man of
engaging appearance and affable, unaffected address. His intelligence and application had made the most of a very liberal
education. In classical and historical knowledge he was especially proficient. The refinement of his taste revealed itself in
many of his inclinations. He was exceedingly fond of music,
and is said to have supported the finest orchestra in the Europe
of his day. To state affairs he was extraordinarily attentive,
rising regularly with the sun, and giving himself to them immediately after his orisons. Even while hunting or pleasure-
sailing in the royal galley he kept one or two of his ministers
about him, with whom he conversed on public business. He
lived up to a high standard of morality, and swept the palace
clean of everything which savoured of the opposite. Yet he
was by no means austere. His cheerfulness banished melancholy, and life at the court was delightful. To his children he
was the kindest of parents, and after the death of his queen
Maria he caused his two motherless boys to sleep in his own
chamber, and showed them the most affectionate solicitude. So
much for a rough sketch of the man.

Before his first two years of kingship ended Emmanuel was
wedded to a Spanish princess, the Infanta Isabel of Castile,
widow of the late Prince Alfonso of Portugal. She had, after

her husband's sudden end, gone home to Castile, and now medi-
tated taking the veil. But the King of Portugal's suit induced
her to renounce her intention of retiring from the world, and to
become his queen. The marriage, one of warm personal attach-
ment, at least on Emmanuel's part, was important to both
peoples as a seal of international cordiality; but ere long it
became unexpectedly, by the death of the Spanish Infant, the
only son of Ferdinand and Isabella, of far greater consequence.
Isabel was now heiress to the throne of Spain. By the birth
of a son to Emmanuel and Isabel, the scruples of the Spanish
Cortes regarding the acknowledgment of a woman and her
foreign husband as their future rulers disappeared, and the oath
of allegiance to the new-born prince was tendered. But Isabel
shortly after died in her husband's arms, and the child whose
appearance had warranted the joyous expectation of a united
Peninsular monarchy followed his mother to the grave within
a twelvemonth. So did this bright project of Spanish and
Portuguese statesmen burst like a bubble. Yet Emmanuel felt
the blow rather as a husband and father, for he was not one to
be unmanned by the dissipation of a political dream.

In 1500 he married again. His second wife was Maria, the
youngest sister of his deceased wife, to wed whom he obtained
a Papal dispensation. This union, however, held out no such
hope as the other; for on the death of Ferdinand and Isabella
their monarchy, embracing Castile, Leon, Aragon, and Sicily,
should now pass to the house of Hapsburg, since the elder
sister of Maria, the imbecile Joanna, was the wife of Philip of
Austria.

Emmanuel's alliance with the Spanish royal house had one
unfortunate result. It stirred him up to a pitch of fanaticism
of which we should hardly have supposed him capable. In
Spain all who did not make a profession of the Christian faith
were treated in the most barbarous fashion, and the King of
Portugal was driven by entreaties and reproaches to suppress

Judaism and Mohammedanism within his dominions at any cost. He had meant to be tolerant. One of his first governmental acts was to arrange for humane dealing with the Jews (for the measures taken against these people by John II. had reference rather to the Spanish immigration, and there appears to have been a multitude of the race still in Portugal), and to all of that race who were at his accession still in slavery he presented their freedom. But his Spanish relatives and their ecclesiastics represented such humanity as weakness and wrong done to the Cross. Therefore, in 1496, the naturally benevolent Emmanuel treated his own feelings so violently for religion's sake as to repeat in his kingdom the policy of his neighbour towards Israelites and "Moors." All Jews must thenceforth be baptized. Those who declined must quit the land at once, leaving behind their children below fourteen years to be Christianized. Great was the lamentation among the wretched Jews. Many slew their offspring and some committed suicide in despair. Thousands nominally accepted Christianity, but of these a large number are said to have still practised their rites in secret. The rest left Portugal. The Mussulmans were in the same way compelled to conversion or exile.

Apart from the inhumanity of this blinded zeal, it was most impolitic to cause the withdrawal of such a host of quiet and diligent people. The Portuguese owed more of their national prosperity to the banished Jews than even the enlightened among them could estimate. The "Moors" too, whatever their ancestors may have been, were by this time law-abiding and industrious; and both Spaniards and Portuguese had the opportunity of learning later the folly of persecution, when the descendants of those Mohammedan exiles, become pirates, came again from Africa and harried the inhospitable shores from which their fathers had been cast out.

The idea of making north Africa Portuguese was still dominant in the time of Emmanuel, and under such brave leaders as Menezes and D'Ataide, both of whom met their death in this campaigning before his reign closed, various towns were taken; but the tide of Portuguese conquest in those parts was turned at the walls of Morocco. That city defied the utmost efforts of Emmanuel's troops, and the disappointment which they experienced through its stout resistance went far to shake the confidence Portugal had hitherto entertained in the ultimate triumph of her arms over Moslem Africa. Morocco was perhaps the key of the whole region, and without the possession of this place it was found almost as difficult to preserve other gains as to procure them. Once it seemed as if the Christian army could have had an easy victory over the King of Morocco, just after his army was put to flight by a faithful Mussulman ally of the Portuguese, Aben Tafuf. But the then Duke of Braganza, whose family had been recalled from their exile and employed by the King of Portugal, being in command of Emmanuel's troops, declined to take advantage of the situation. So Portugal lost Morocco, say her historians, and by consequence lost later all Africa. The real reason, however, of Portugal's inability to conquer northern Africa was, as has been already indicated, the ease with which the Mohammedan powers, out of their immense populations, could fill up gaps in their ranks, bring overwhelming forces into the field, and throw adequate garrisons into their fortresses.

While some of Portugal's bravest hearts were dashing themselves against the Moslem might in Africa, others as dauntless were risking their lives in perilous ventures on the ocean. Early in Emmanuel's reign, 1497, Vasco da Gama was intrusted with a small fleet wherewith to round the Cape of Good Hope and steer for India. This he did in less than ten months, having coasted the eastern side of the African continent as far as Mozambique, the future *entrepôt* of the Portuguese and halfway house to India. There he received pilots from the friendly sheikh, and in twenty-one days' sailing on the open sea reached

VASCO DA GAMA.

Calicut, on the Malabar coast of India. After two years' absence Gama arrived in the harbour of Lisbon with a wonderful tale of the Orient, which filled his sovereign with joy and greatly excited the Portuguese. The brilliant result of this venture induced Emmanuel to fit out a larger fleet and despatch it in the track of Gama's expedition. It was commanded by Pedro Cabral, and sailed the year following Gama's return. But contrary winds caused the ships' course to be directed far westwards into the Atlantic, where Columbus had steered eight years before and found a new world. Cabral also, to his amazement, discovered land, and making for it, sent a boat ashore. But the copper-coloured natives whom they saw could not comprehend the boat's crew. So Cabral's curiosity was unsatisfied. He named the region hit upon thus adventitiously Santa Cruz. It was destined to be, under the name Brazil, another Portugal across the sea.

Cabral at length reached Calicut as Gama had done, and with his greater armada commanded more respect for the Portuguese name. Continuing her discoveries and settlements in the East, Ceylon, the Maldives, the Malay Peninsula, and other parts adjacent, were visited, and marts founded wherever Portuguese enterprise could plant its foot with advantage. A governor of the Indies was appointed with much royal pomp and circumstance. So Portugal established herself in Asia.

Emmanuel's good fortune was noised throughout Europe. The Pope was delighted with the intelligence of Portuguese achievements abroad, for he saw in them a vast extension of the Church's influence. The King of Portugal sent a splendid embassy to Rome to acquaint the Pontiff with the particulars of the successful voyages. The ambassadors carried with them products of the far countries which they and their compatriots had visited. They especially astonished the Roman populace by the strange beasts which accompanied them—an elephant of extraordinary size, leopards, panthers, and other uncommon animals.   In return for these testimonies of consideration and respect on the part of the King of Portugal, Pope Leo addressed to that monarch a public letter of acknowledgment, and soon afterwards transmitted to him a consecrated rose. In addition, the Pope bestowed upon Emmanuel "all kingdoms, provinces, and islands which he might recover from the infidels, not only from Capes Bojador and Nun to the Indies, but in parts yet undiscovered and unknown even to the Pontiff himself."*

The course of home affairs in Portugal during Emmanuel's reign ran smoothly.   The kind of men who are wont out of wantonness or ambition to stir up mischief in a country found plenty of employment abroad; and though the historians of the period are so full of African and Asiatic conquest and settlement that they can scarcely afford time to look at the internal progress of Portugal, it is evident from what can be learned of it that the absence of so many wayward spirits was a real boon to the land.   Signs of a forward movement among the people are seen in the granting of enlarged civic rights and in the revision of the entire legislative code, which last, arranged in the reign of Alfonso V., had already, though only half a century old, become in great measure obsolete, through the rapid development of new needs and conditions.   The statute book of Emmanuel, a ponderous work, was undertaken by a distinguished lawyer in 1505, and is a distinct step on the way to political freedom.

In 1521 King Emmanuel died.   His eldest son, at once crowned as John III., was a man whose natural disposition was melancholy, and unfortunately the severe domestic affliction allotted to him thickened the gloom with which his spirit was shrouded.   His country was during his reign in the very zenith of its prosperity, and neighbouring monarchs might well envy the King of Portugal; but his home was desolated by the

* Roscoe's "Life of Leo X."

early removal of nearly all his large family. Three years before his own death he saw carried to the grave his only remaining son, who was cut off at the age of sixteen and a half.

The innate dejection of the king and the troubles which he met with threw him very much into the hands of his religious advisers. The church seemed to offer him the only refuge from despair, and in return for her consolation, he was ready to further her interests to the very utmost. His confessor, Diogo da Silva, was a bigot of the most intense order; and as John's low spirits necessitated the presence of this man in his character of ghostly physician more frequently than might otherwise have been the case, he had ample opportunity of insisting on his spiritual prescriptions. The cloud, he urged, might pass away from the soul of the king did he only fully implement his obligation as sovereign of a Christian realm. God was more honoured in Spain than in Portugal. The Spanish church had an engine at her disposal wherewith to cleanse the land and destroy the works of the devil which was wanting to the Portuguese. The power Da Silva desiderated was the Inquisition. In his pleading for the erection of this dreadful tribunal, he was vigorously supported by the Portuguese Dominicans, spurred by their Spanish *confrères* and by the Infant Henry, the king's brother, who was a priest, and filled the high office of cardinal.

The special object of Portuguese fanatics in proposing the introduction of the Inquisition was to have the means of sharply testing those who were known as "new Christians"—that is, Jewish and "Moorish" converts to the faith, many of whom were suspected, and no doubt justly, of having put on Christianity as a mere mask for prudential reasons. The suspicion often received confirmation when the converts made their way across the Mediterranean. Safe in Africa, they, in many instances, threw off their disguise, and the *quondam* "Christians" became Jews or Mussulmans again. Numerous "bad Christians" were believed to exist in Portugal, whose marks were irregularity of attendance at mass, carelessness in regard to saints' days, unwillingness to pay ecclesiastical dues, and a tendency to speak slightingly of the church. This heretical chaff must be sifted. No native Portuguese were imagined to be tainted with the plague of unbelief, or even susceptible of it. But stringent measures must be adopted to cure the disease, else its increase might appal the church one day.

The king yielded to these solicitations, and took steps for the establishment of the required ecclesiastical force in Portugal. He had indeed, soon after his accession, confirmed a law of his predecessor to the effect that the "new Christians" should be viewed and treated like other Portuguese; but clerical counsels operating on his gloomy spirit transformed him into a merciless partisan of the church, and altogether overweighted reasonable considerations.

John, accordingly, besieged the Papal chair with petitions for a bull to institute in his kingdom that inhuman ordinance which blinded zealots termed the glory of Spain. It was not often that kings found pontiffs reluctant to adopt rigorous measures in the church's behalf, but it was really so in this case. Two successive popes—Clement VII. and Paul III.—manifested extreme unwillingness to comply with the request of the Portuguese monarch. They thought it undesirable both for the church and state to inaugurate the bloody judicatory in Portugal, and were moved by the representations of the "new Christians" themselves, whose cause was advocated at Rome by a sagacious lawyer, Edward de Paz. But the fanatical party in Portugal were determined to attain their object, and stopped short of nothing for its sake. De Paz was set upon by their agents in the streets of Rome, wounded, and left for dead. A suit of chain armour, which he wore in anticipation of such an assault, was, however, the means of preserving his life from the rapier-thrusts of the would-be murderers; and on his recovery

from the effects of the attack, he charged the Portuguese fanatics with his attempted assassination. This *faux pas* delayed
the triumph of the Inquisitionists, for Paul III. was horrified
at the deed; but at length the persistent pleading of John
prevailed, strengthened as it was by the cordial support of his
brother-in-law, Charles V., Emperor of Germany and King of
Spain, who happened at that time to be in close alliance with
the Pope, and was a bigot as grim as the King of Portugal
himself.

In 1536, then, the Pontiff granted the wished-for bull, and
ere long the Inquisition was in full swing in three Portuguese
cities—Lisbon, Evora, and Coimbra. Also at Goa a similar
court was fixed, under which were placed all Portuguese possessions in Asia and Africa as far as the Cape of Good Hope.
Each establishment was provided with a large executive corps
after the Spanish model. There were Inquisitors, of whom the
bishop of the diocese was one, as presiding judges, deputies to
vote on the cases like jurymen, procurators fiscal to conduct
the cause for the prosecution, notaries to record the evidence,
commissaries to precognosce witnesses at a distance, familiars
to apprehend the accused, and many other officials. Those who
really got up the indictment were the visitors—human ferrets,
so to speak, who subjected the homes and business of the
people to the strictest espionage, and boarded all vessels which
entered Portuguese harbours for books such as would probably
be found in the *Index expurgatorius,* when that famous catalogue of literature objectionable from the Romish point of view
came from the press.

The Inquisitors did not lose time in beginning their work,
and the people had many an opportunity of witnessing the dismal pageantry of the *auto da fé,* that *spectaculum horrendum
ac tremendum,* as it is justly named by the Spanish Inquisitor
Pegna. The visitors were vigilant, having a commission upon
captures; to the process, verdict, and execution were lent the

united majesty of the state and the church. Many "new Christians" suffered confiscation of goods, imprisonment, torture, strangulation, burning. The very bones of some evil reported of were exhumed and consigned to the flames. A number of suspects who had scented danger and escaped were burned in effigy. Yet it is in evidence that after all this lynx-eyed scrutiny and relentless barbarity, thousands of "bad Christians" remained—"Moors" and Jews, who made glib lip-professions, while they burned inwardly with hatred of the Christian name.

The eager desire of the king to support the Romish propaganda led to an affair of great importance in the history of Portugal—the introduction there of the Jesuits, called at that time "the associates of Mestre Ignacio." The Portuguese ambassador at Rome became acquainted, in the year 1540, with a Portuguese disciple of Loyola at the Papal court. The envoy recommended to his master this devoted brotherhood as very suitable for the business of spreading Christianity in the Indies, and that same year the associate Rodriguez came to Lisbon on King John's hearty invitation, accompanied by the celebrated Xavier, to arrange the details of a foreign mission. Next year Xavier set sail for Goa, to carry on with marvellous energy that missionary work in the East which has made his memory so illustrious. His companion stayed in Portugal to recruit the ranks of the society, and so successful were his efforts that in two years he was able to send disciples all over the country to expound the tenets and objects of Jesuitism. Such was the enthusiasm evoked among the Portuguese for the new order by the preaching of these zealous agents of Rodriguez that the renown of the ancient religious fraternities grew pale in comparison. In the popular estimation Rodriguez and his associates were, as to their dignity and calling, above even the apostles themselves.

Nevertheless many in the realm looked with jealousy upon

the rapid rise of Jesuit power. They were angry with the king, who was bestowing abundant *largesse* upon the brotherhood, and granting them whatever privileges they craved. They disliked the arts by which Rodriguez was winning over numbers of the Portuguese youth to the membership of the society; and they of the council especially were affronted by the constant intrusion of the Jesuit leader in the royal cabinet. The Infant Henry, priest of Rome though he was, protested against Rodriguez's arrogance, and might have wrought his downfall, or at least been the instrument of more capable men in achieving that result. But his two brothers, the Infant Louis and the king himself, were entirely devoted to the brotherhood. So much was King John in subjection that Rodriguez could, with impunity, meet a request of his with a downright refusal, accompanied by vehement recriminations and threats of leaving Portugal, which always terrified the superstitious monarch into submission.

In John's day the Portuguese university was transferred to Coimbra, where it is at present situated; and at this seat of learning the Jesuits obtained the institution of a college of their own, independent of the university authorities. Thus they showed very early in the history of their order that desire to hold in their own hands the training of youth which has been the most distinguishing feature of their programme all along. Not only in the educational, however, but in many spheres, this remarkable society, by dint of shrewdness, diligence, and determination, obtained such influence that when, after centuries of occupation, a great statesman was strong enough to banish them from Portugal, his masterful dealing seemed like sacrilege.

John III. was suddenly seized in 1557 by an apoplectic stroke, upon which his death followed with startling rapidity. All his life he appears to have been a moody, discontented man. Nothing availed to cleanse his bosom of the " stuff which weighed upon his heart." It is remarkable that the king in whose reign Portugal reached the very height of her glory should have been possessed by such a soul-sickness—that he whom all congratulated and envied should have been the *miserrimus* of the Portuguese sovereigns.

Sebastian, now lord of Portugal and of its great possessions abroad, was a child of three years, the only child of that only son of John III. whose early death had been his father's crowning sorrow. King John, shortly before, and in case of his decease, designated his queen, Catherine of Austria, guardian of his grandson and regent of the kingdom till Sebastian should have attained his twentieth year. But desirous of nipping in the bud any mischief which might arise from those to whom the "regiment" of a woman, and especially of a foreign woman, was "monstrous," she called to her aid in ruling the realm the Cardinal-Infant. Many saw her take this step with disapprobation. For the cardinal was now nothing but a tool of the Jesuits. At first strongly opposed to the society, he had been completely won over by the subtlety of its members, and had sunk into a condition of abject submission to their orders. How exactly they achieved that triumph is not known. But the truth is, Cardinal Henry was a flaccid, gelatinous person, and had always been more or less subservient to some person or party.

The Society of Jesus knew how to push their advantage when Henry was installed as joint-regent. Everything was done to dishearten and annoy the queen, whose favour they could by no means obtain. The child-king was given in charge to Jesuit fathers, who should superintend his education and take care that he grew up a devoted slave of the society; and Catherine, in her well-meant efforts to carry on the government, was so baffled and brow-beaten that she was fain to lay down the burden of office. This she accordingly did after five years, during which she found herself, by the machinations of the Jesuits, becoming more and more of a nonentity. The Cortes were grieved at her decision; for she was a person of talent and uprightness, while the cardinal was little better than an automaton whose strings were pulled by the crafty associates of Mestre Ignacio. But she was determined to take refuge in a convent from her manifold vexations.

To the cardinal therefore fell, in 1562, the duty of administering the affairs of the country. He, of course, although nominal head of the kingdom, was practically relegated to the altar, while the Jesuit fathers transacted the business of the council chamber. Yet even the submissive cardinal was roused to a feeble indignation when documents which he had not read were put before him for signature, when his advice was pooh-poohed and his ecclesiastical and civil dignity trampled under foot. The wire-pullers tugged too roughly, and their puppet was to their chagrin transformed into a kind of man. No doubt he was instigated to rebellion by some stronger minds behind the scenes. But however that may be, the cardinal became recalcitrant, and the Jesuits, finding him intractable, bethought them of a means for putting him out of the way.

During his regency there was done almost nothing for the commonweal, but everything which directly or indirectly might conduce to the glory of the Society of Jesus. That the decrees of the Council of Trent, published at this period, should be accepted without question in Portugal, may be understood when one remembers who were her virtual rulers. Other governments were hesitating to receive this body of ecclesiastical decisions, not because of their doctrinal import, but because they confirmed clerical invasion of the secular sphere to a greater extent than was agreeable to statesmen. Against this sort of churchly pretension the enlightened John I. of Portugal had, through his ambassador, vigorously protested at the Council of Constance. But under the auspices of the Jesuit fathers the bull sanctioning the Tridentine articles ran unhindered through all the provinces of Portugal.   In fact the Jesuits, in ways too numerous for detail, wrought with a single eye to the spread of their order.   Their influence was fraught with woe to Portugal, as to every other land where it was legitimized.

One of the worst services the Jesuits rendered the Portuguese nation in the sixteenth century was their training of the young King Sebastian.   They had made a complete conquest of the boy's mind.   It seemed to the anti-Jesuits as if the society had cast a spell over Sebastian, so much did he view things through Jesuit spectacles.   It was evident that to him the society's plan of campaign was the only legitimate programme for the good of Portugal and the world.   Some influential men tried to disabuse him of his notions, but a questioning of his tutors' tenets was, in his thought, equivalent to the most shameless impiety. Sebastian was one who might, under enlightened discipline, have been touched to finer issues.   He reminded many, in appearance and some mental characteristics, of the great Infant Pedro, son of John I.   He had the same fair curling hair and blue eyes, introduced by Philippa of Lancaster, and reappearing for generations in scions of the Portuguese royal line in its various branches; the same sweet smile into which brief gusts of anger like April storms easily melted; the same integrity, moral purity, and dauntless bravery.   But if there were in Sebastian any germs of Pedro's *savoir faire,* it had been deliberately crushed by his pedagogues, who desired to form a creature of their own and not a statesman.

When the society then found the Cardinal-Infant a little intractable, they resolved to produce the young king as acting ruler, and so compel the regent's resignation.   Sebastian was now only fourteen, but the Jesuits managed to overbear all opposition to the premature assumption of sovereignty on the part of Sebastian, and had him proclaimed in 1568, six years before the time appointed in his father's will, as sole administrator of the affairs of Portugal.   It was with a very bad grace that the cardinal submitted to be laid in his political coffin, but nothing could withstand the will of the society. The game was in their own hands thenceforward, they thought, and they proceeded to play it with the utmost regard for the propaganda.

A proposal was made, now that Sebastian had actually come to the throne, for a closer political alliance with France by means of a marriage between him and the Princess Margaret, daughter of Charles IX. The Jesuits, on the other hand, supported the idea of a union with the Archduchess Isabella of Austria. Their object, however, was not an Austrian marriage, but to shilly-shally between the advocates of the rival schemes, and so to prevent any marriage. It did not suit them that a foreign power should have in Portugal an influence, though it might be indirect, such as a marriage with another reigning house would surely bring about. They had indeed looked before them and indoctrinated their royal pupil with a conception of celibacy as the most honourable state, that they might have him entirely to themselves. But to publish Sebastian's ascetic view would have been absurd. Therefore they carried on a policy of procrastination with an adroitness worthy of a nobler end, until a project possessed the king which shelved the marriage question effectually.

This new matter was a crusade which the king was to undertake single-handed. To be a soldier of the Cross was Sebastian's highest ambition. To discover a new world was nothing unless it were won for Christ. A Christian king who did nothing to hasten the ultimate triumph of the faith was undeserving of the name. Sebastian's apprehension of the process of conversion was the very crudest. He would simply with armed hand open doors in heathendom whereat Jesuit missionaries might enter and baptize unbelievers wholesale. In the East, vast, populous, and heathen—in the East, which God had evidently given to Portugal—he would make everywhere the truth victorious.

Yet he was destined to behold only in dreams that far-off land. Nearer Africa called him, and he sought that field in which to begin the work after his heart.

Things had not been going well with the Portuguese for some time across the Mediterranean. They had not been able to hold their own against the Moslems. In the beginning of the sixteenth century a family calling themselves the Xerifs, and claiming descent from Mohammed, rose into power. They possessed themselves, by the sword, by diplomacy, and by assassination, of a preponderating influence among their fellow-Mussulmans in northern Africa, and at length obtained the sovereignty of Fez and Morocco, which kingdoms they united under their sceptre. The Portuguese success hitherto against such an enormous population as north Africa contained had been owing in great measure to the want of close combination and efficient co-operation on the part of the various sultanates. But now the Xerifs could set in motion nearly the whole force of African Mohammedanism. The generals of John III. therefore, seeing the madness of scattering handfuls of troops over a wide region, asked and received permission to demolish several castles, and strengthening the others, watched from thence with anxiety the waxing of the new Moslem dynasty.

By-and-by there was a family quarrel among the Xerifs. A nephew seized the crown of Fez and Morocco, and exiled an uncle, the legitimate heir. The uncle, Muley Moluk, took service with the Sultan of Turkey, and distinguished himself so greatly in many engagements that his master gave him three thousand experienced soldiers wherewith to prosecute his own claim in Africa. With these, as the nucleus of an army, he reached the shores of his own country, and was joined by numbers of African Mohammedans. He met and overcame the troops of his nephew. The defeated usurper, Muley Mohammed, fled and threw himself upon the King of Spain for aid. That monarch declined to be drawn into an African campaign. But when Sebastian heard of Mohammed's purpose, he thought himself providentially summoned, and expressed his willingness to do battle with Moluk; not, however, with the view of setting up another unbelieving ruler, but as captain of a sacramental host to claim Africa for holy church. He had got together nine thousand Portuguese infantry and a thousand cavalry, to whom were added some six thousand Castilian, German, and Italian hired troops, and a few hundred volunteers of various nationalities. Mohammed with three hundred African horsemen came to support him when the Portuguese fleet, numbering about a thousand sail, arrived at Tangier.

Muley Moluk's forces encountered Sebastian's in the neighbourhood of Alcaçer in August 1578. The Mohammedan leader had to be borne to the field on a litter, being in mortal sickness at the time, and indeed died during the battle; but the fact was carefully concealed till the end, lest the Moslems should be discouraged. Sebastian was in the best of health and spirits, full of confidence in the piety of his enterprise and the valour of his soldiers. He was the victim of a fatal delusion. The army of the sick general was numerous and well disciplined. Many veterans were with him who had fought by his side at Goletta and elsewhere. The Portuguese were surrounded and slaughtered. Sebastian fell, fighting like a lion to the last. A number of Portuguese nobles were likewise slain, and others, made prisoners, were only ransomed at a great price. Mohammed, too, was taken in flight and lost his life. The victory was most important for the Mussulmans, and effectually dispelled the notion of a Christian north Africa. All that remained to Portugal after that disaster were Ceuta, Tangier, and Mazagan; and though these towns were so strongly fortified, they also might have been lost had the successor of Moluk understood, which he did not, how to employ his triumph.

The lamentation in Portugal over this tremendous misfortune was indescribable. There was a solemn procession

through the principal streets of Lisbon, headed by a rider on a
horse with black trappings, bearing in his hand a great black
banner, whose end hung over his shoulder to the ground.
Three venerable members of the municipal council, carrying
black shields, and a great multitude of the people, clad in weeds
of woe, followed after. At appointed places the procession
halted, and one of the shield-bearers cried with a loud voice,
" Citizens of Lisbon, bewail our King Sebastian, who is dead !"
then broke his shield in pieces. This ceremony was repeated
till the three shields were destroyed. Well might the Portuguese weep for the day of Alcaçer, so many of their noblest and
best had fallen with the king or been taken captive on the field.

Thus they mourned the loss of one who, in his twenty-fourth
year, perished by his own rashness and superstition, and precipitated his country, in its old and glorious campaigning ground,
into a depth of discomfiture from which it was impossible to
emerge. There were not wanting those who maintained that
Sebastian was not dead. They called him *O incoherto*, " the
concealed one," and trusted that he should one day reappear to
retrieve his fortune. To this the fact that the king's body was
so maltreated by the infuriated Moslems as to be scarcely
recognizable lent some shadow of reason. But it was too true
that the king had sold his life, though dearly, in the carnage at
Alcaçer. And as to the belief of his coming again, there is
scarcely any story of a nation where such a devout imagination
is wanting, from the days of Arthur, *rex quondam rexque
futurus*, till medieval mists had rolled away.

The removal of young Sebastian brought again to the front
Cardinal Henry, by this time sixty-seven years old. The unexpected happened to him. He had been discharged from the
regency without hope of being permitted to interfere any more
in state business, and now, by a sudden turn of fortune's wheel,
he was drawn from his obscurity and crowned King of Portugal ;
for upon him the dignity legitimately devolved, there being no

issue of Sebastian. There have been cardinal-ministers in France, Spain, and elsewhere—epoch-making men, such as Richelieu, Mazarin, and Granvelle—but a cardinal-king is a unique phenomenon. It was, however, a phenomenon whose early disappearance men reckoned with, for at the time of his coronation Henry required the constant care of his physician, and continued in a wretched state of health till the two years of his brief reign came to an end. Because of his age and rapidly increasing infirmity there was talk, even from his accession, of the succession. No less than eight claimants, some of whose pretensions were, to be sure, slender enough, were in the field, first and last.

By far the most influential of these was Philip II., King of Spain. He asserted his right, after Henry, to the Portuguese throne because he was a descendant of King Emmanuel, whose daughter, wife of Charles V., was mother of Philip II., and specially because his own queen was a daughter of John III. But by a law passed at Lamego, in the time of Alfonso Henriquez, and never repealed, a princess of the royal house marrying a foreigner lost her right to succeed.

The Duke of Braganza maintained that his wife, daughter of Edward, son of Emmanuel, was the true heir. That was so; but the succession had more to do with policy and the power of the claimant than with justice. Antonio, who held the ecclesiastical benefice of Crato, and the office, though no priest, of prior, claimed the crown, since his father, the Infant Louis, was a son of Emmanuel. But his claim was held to be vitiated by the bar sinister on his shield, he, however, stoutly maintaining his legitimacy. The Duke of Parma, son of that famous Alexander Farnese who played such an important part in the struggle between Spain and the Netherlands, insisted that, as son of Maria of Portugal, daughter of Edward, son of Emmanuel, his right was better than any; but to his case also that statute of Lamego applied.

The Duke of Savoy, another claimant, as son of Emmanuel's daughter, stood on the same ground as the Duke of Parma; but, for political reasons, he declared himself unwilling to press his claim, except in the case of the Spanish king's death before settlement of the question. The Queen of France preferred a claim on account of a descent which she could not prove, and which was not much believed in, from Matilda, wife of Alfonso IV. Queen Elizabeth of England averred that all the interests of the house of Lancaster in Portugal were hers. And, lastly, the Pope alleged that Portugal was a lien of the Papal chair, and that the Vicar of Christ should name the next sovereign; also that all property of a cardinal dying, as Henry did, intestate, belonged to him. The latter argument, as a matter of course, was not advanced till the king's death.

Here, then, was a considerable coil. The Cortes dreaded a war of succession, and various schemes were broached for averting it. One was that the king should marry under a dispensation from the Pope. The poor old cardinal told them he had never had such a desire, and at any rate could not entertain it now that he was well stricken in years and in such a precarious physical condition; but he was so pestered with importunities by his advisers that he consented to take the step. The widow of Charles IX. of France was named as a suitable consort. The haters of French influence, however, supported by secret agents of the King of Spain, did their best to thwart the party which made that motion. Others proposed a daughter of the Duke of Braganza, as a method of sinking the claim of the ducal house to succeed. But no marriage pleased Philip II. best, and he found means of rendering ineffectual at Rome the efforts of those who were pleading for the dispensation. Ever since the death of Sebastian the Spanish sovereign had been pushing his fortune in Portugal, using bribery or intimidation, as seemed most advantageous, in respect of different persons and parties of weight there. The Jesuits were helping him with might and main, though *sub rosa*, for Spanish rule was as abhorrent to the Portuguese mind as of old.

The marriage device being off the carpet, the cardinal was pressed to come to some decision regarding the succession. He invited accordingly all claimants to produce arguments for their views. Most of the would-be sovereigns of Portugal appeared either in person or by proxy to urge their pleas. Philip II. contented himself with a bare acknowledgment of the invitation, but by assembling troops on the borders argued his cause in a very effective way. Henry could not choose but confess that the Braganza claim was good ; but the Prior of Crato was a favourite with the people, and Philip, though weakened by his war in the Netherlands, was strong enough and determined to have his way, right or no right. The cardinal-king was bewildered, and wished himself well out of the clamour, perhaps also out of the world, as his shattered frame was little able to endure the torture of the continued controversy. Many of the Portuguese nobility had had their itching palms soothed by Spanish gold, and Philip, resolved not to have spent money in vain, commanded rather than entreated Henry to nominate him without delay or consultation with the estates ; for Philip knew that the estates would make preliminary trouble about their privileges, and he meant to be autocrat of Portugal.

Time sped, and the King of Portugal still wavered in his helpless way, till, in 1580, death put a welcome end to his bodily pain and mental distress—put an end too, in his person, to the old Burgundian dynasty. Of that line we see in Henry the attenuated and powerless extremity. He had a small and delicate frame and commonplace features, which entirely corresponded with his mind. He was blameless in his life, as became a priest, but for the rest of him, not admirable or significant—a respectable cipher. He had some theological and ecclesiastical learning, which was of as much use to him in attempting to guide the affairs of the nation as it would have been to Vasco da Gama in rounding the Cape.

It was a dismal year in which Cardinal-King Henry died. Drought robbed the people of their food, and the plague preyed upon their lives. In Lisbon, the whole summer through, biers were carried about incessantly through the streets. Politically, the affairs of Portugal were in a most critical condition, the country rent by parties and threatened with foreign invasion. In this melancholy way closes the story of medieval Portugal.

CHAPTER VI.

THE CROWN AND THE THREE ESTATES IN THE MIDDLE AGES.

WE propose in the few pages of this chapter to put together such notices of the Portuguese sovereign's position in the middle ages, and that of the three estates in his realm—namely, the Church, the Nobility, and the Commonalty *—as may help us to a better idea of the kingdom four hundred years ago than can be obtained by running over the lives of its crowned heads or conning accounts of its battles.

Although Alfonso Henriquez was the first to be called King of Portugal, the monarchy, as we have seen, had been in virtual existence for many years under Count Henry of Burgundy. Even before the death of his father-in-law, the count had exercised a vice-royalty which was scarcely subject to supervision, and had drawn to itself, without design on the viceroy's part, much of the homage belonging to the Castilian throne, under whose auspices it had been erected. The people had been accustomed to look upon Henry as their prince. To this view his circumstances assisted them—his close connection with, and at the same time his distance from, the seat of authority. When therefore his son's coronation took place, it seemed to them no violent and wonderful transformation of a seignior into a sovereign, but rather Alfonso's public investment with his legitimate dignity. Already Castilian claims upon their allegi-

* For remarks on this definition, see Freeman, " Growth of the English Constitution."

ance, and denials of their ruler's majesty, were branded as foreign insolence.

Thus the Portuguese could naturally tender their first formally chosen over-lord, and he could, without embarrassment, accept, the honours usually done occupants of the Spanish thrones. At first, as a matter of course, and so long as the "Moors" were in the land, the most important function of the Portuguese king was to lead his army in battle. Their sovereign was to his subjects, above everything, the general. He was the foremost defender of Portugal, sword in hand. His palace was a stronghold. But afterwards, when the country was purged of the aliens, it was acknowledged that as father of his people the monarch's commission included higher duties than conducting a cavalry charge or holding a fortress—that he was not disgraced, but acting kingly, when he sent others to the field, himself remaining at court to direct the council-board and foster the peaceful activities of the nation.

As might be expected, the _entourage_ of the Portuguese kings was, in the main, modelled upon that of Castile. For the maintenance of their independence, it seemed necessary that their throne should be surrounded by all the stately circumstance of the court from whose suzerainty it had torn itself away. The sovereigns of the Burgundian line in Portugal had their great military officers—high constables, inspectors-general of fortified places, and commissaries-general; for civil affairs, a chancellor. At court there were the major-domo or count of the palace, the great almoner, the receiver-general of the royal income, the high chaplain, and the king's physician, besides a number of "king's men" or lords-in-waiting. As ministers of his pleasures, the monarch retained such functionaries as a master of the hunt and a chief falconer. A body-guard of noble cavaliers attended him, riding in the van of the army when the king went to battle, and in times of peace keeping the palace, or forming their royal master's cavalcade when he fared forth for exercise or travelled through the provinces.

The king's revenue, small when the throne was founded, to be sure, for the people were few and poor, and even the nobles had little to spend from their bare acres, waxed rapidly after the conquest of all Portugal. The crown rights were many. To it belonged all highways, navigable rivers, and anchorages; the numerous salt-pans also and mines throughout the country. Custom and harbour dues, therefore, were payable to the sovereign, imposts on fishing and for transmission of goods by the highways. In like manner, the salt and minerals produced were the king's. Property of intestates, besides, of fugitives from justice, and of convicted heretics, fell to the crown. The king could levy a poll-tax on the occasion of a royal marriage or in war time. He could requisition vehicles, beasts of burden, or vessels of any size, whensoever he deemed it necessary.

Some of these rights were immemorial. The origin of others could be easily traced. One finds them all in the statute-book of Emmanuel, published at the close of the medieval period. But although never till his time put down together in black and white, most of them had long been recognized by the people as pertaining to use and wont.

Extraordinary privileges like these notwithstanding, the kings were forced for a considerable time to share the rule in Portugal with two classes—the clergy and the *noblesse*—through whose opposition the crown had to fight its way to supremacy. We have already spoken of that kind of friction which hindered the sovereign in the exercise of his functions; of the claims to local government which were insisted on by territorial magnates, religious or secular. Now it will be in place, and may be interesting, to draw more particular attention to those two estates which played in Portuguese history as important a part as they have done in the history of any Continental people.

And first, of the Church in Portugal. Under the Christian-ized Roman empire, and for a hundred years after the establishment of the Visigothic dominion, there were not many places of worship in the land, and the clergy were proportionately few; but with the termination of the Arian controversy, an impetus was given to the progress of the Portuguese Church. The Visigothic feudal superiors began to be diligent in erecting churches and convents on their estates. These churches were rude and diminutive—really chapels built close by the mansion of the landlord for his family and domestic servants, and for the labourers on his farm, who dwelt in neighbouring hamlets, named after the saint to whom the chapel was dedicated. That was the origin in Portugal, as in our own country, of the parochial churches. The parish clergyman of the Visigothic period generally wore the monkish habit, and lived as a solitary, the chapel being at first, in all probability, his hermitage. But sometimes men of like mind desired to share the religious life of a priest noted for sanctity, and thus a fraternity was formed, for whom a dwelling was reared not far from the church, and as primitive in construction. So convents arose. In the cathedral towns—Oporto, Lamego, Coimbra, and elsewhere—and in other centres of population, there were great churches even before the Arab conquest.

When the Mohammedans settled in the country, they might have been expected to sweep away every vestige of Christianity. But while they no doubt despised that religion, and made their own sacred edifices conspicuous in all towns of the subjugated territory, there is no evidence that, even under the fiercer successors of the Ommiades, the Christians were subjected to proscription or persecution. Yet the presence in resistless might of the unbelieving host so depressed and humiliated the Church that it was only the reminiscence of itself when at length the Crescent was vanquished in Portugal.

Then, however, was the beginning of its halcyon days. The

churches which, during the Arab occupation, had become ruins through violence, or, more frequently, neglect, were repaired, and many new ones erected, while every monument of Islam was, without compunction, razed to the ground. Those new or renovated ecclesiastical buildings were of the plainest description for a considerable time after the Visigothic reconquest. But as wealth began to pour into the Church's lap, she employed part of it in rearing cathedrals more worthy of the name and diocesan places of worship much superior to the barn-like structures with which circumstances forced her for a while to be content. Gifts to the Church became a fashion. Men of means could not die easily without putting its name in their testament as a legatee.

It was land which the Church principally received from these donors, for that kind of property was more plentiful than money. Warriors upon whom grants of land had been bestowed deemed it fitting that part of the spoil should be dedicated to the cause of God. The desire of divine pardon for crimes committed was a frequent incentive to liberality towards churches and convents. These latter edifices increased in number and size, and drew to themselves knights wearied of warfare or disabled in battle, who were entertained in them till their death, in which event the convent received all or most of their property. The bishops, becoming in time territorial lords, sallied forth on campaigns like secular barons at the head of their retainers, and won for their sees treasure and land. Such conduct of ecclesiastics was not deemed unseemly if the foe were the Moslem. The conflict with the Saracens gives to the narrative of the Portuguese (and of the Spanish) Church's enrichment a peculiar feature ; for otherwise it resembles what we are acquainted with from a perusal of other histories. The Portuguese clerical dignitary could, without scandal, put his own hand to the work of driving out the Arabs, since the war was a crusade, and claim, as a combatant, a share of the booty.

Apart, however, from this fact, which accounts for a certain, and by no means insignificant, proportion of the large revenue which it enjoyed from a comparatively early period, probably there never was a Church which received larger or more frequent donations than the Portuguese. But its enormous wealth, much augmented at the beginning of the twelfth century by the introduction of the system of tithes, did not, it need hardly be said, increase its influence for good. Rather it was more and more, the richer it grew, infected by an insatiable greed of temporal power. The bishops became the most troublesome of subjects. As lords of the soil, they exercised judicial functions to the damage, and often in defiance, of the royal supremacy. Moreover, they were so hedged about with the sacredness of their office that it was difficult for the secular arm to inflict chastisement upon them. Alfonso Henriquez, by his lavish kindness at Aljubarotta to dignitaries of the Church. had seemed to establish a principle against which it was hard to fight. Especially to the occupant of the see of Braga did the king cede great immunities and magisterial rights, which not only the successors of that prelate but other bishops also persisted too long in claiming, to the infinite annoyance of the reigning monarch, and not seldom to the distraction of the nation. Nothing less could satisfy some bishops and abbots than the transformation of their ecclesiastical spheres into little kingdoms, where the sovereign's writ could scarcely run. Bitter and prolonged was the struggle between Church and State in Portugal, and many were the bans which were hurled from Rome in its course at the Portuguese king and people.

But it was not only with ecclesiastical pretensions that the State had to deal. The arrogance of the second estate, the nobility, in like manner, taxed all the strength and prudence of the throne. The nobility of Portugal consisted of the grandees, or *ricoshomens*,* and the *fidalgos*, or lesser nobles. A

* Literally "rich men."

ricoshomen led hundreds of armed vassals to the field, and had borne before him a standard on which a caldron was embroidered, indicative of his ability to provide his following with the means of subsistence; so that humble utensil became the proudest emblem of a Portuguese grand seignior. The *ricoshomen* possessed the privilege of maintaining in his castle a force of retainers—squires and men-at-arms—and the right which the prelates claimed of judging causes, himself or by his appointed officers, within his barony.

The *fidalgo* was the minor baron; but the term was too elastic to convey a very definite conception of its holder's influence or wealth. At any rate, the *fidalgo* professed to be of pure Visigothic descent, for the title meant "son of a Goth"—no "peasant slave" of Celtiberian blood, no offspring of unbelieving "Moor," no mongrel. But he might be a man of considerable estate, with numerous dependants, of little less consequence in his own eyes than a *ricoshomen*, and covetous of a grandee's license, or one who had nothing save his charger and his sword. He was, however, always one of the aristocracy, fain to insist on time-honoured prerogatives, brimful of class likes and dislikes.

When as yet there were many kingdoms in the Peninsula, Christian and Moslem, with one or other of which sudden war might arise, it was necessary for the Kings of Portugal to conciliate by grants of land and various powers those whose local authority could place hosts of retainers in the field. Moreover, at a time when only the king's own feudatories were thoroughly subservient to him, and the baron's vassal rather to his particular lord-superior, the friendship of the noble whose will was law in his province was indispensable for carrying out any national measure of order. But time brought with it the contrary necessity. For the sake of the nobility themselves, who, as affairs with the folk beyond the border became more settled, for lack of an external foe, began to quarrel amongst themselves; for his peaceable subjects' sakes, who were disturbed by the collision of the great landlords; and for his own sake, lest he should be made the puppet of contending factions,—on all these accounts the king felt it incumbent on him to plant his foot firmly, to limit the authority of these turbulent patricians, and to proclaim his intention of reigning in fact as well as in name over his whole land.

Like the conflict with the encroaching Church, this with the nobility was a stubborn tussle; and one may say that it was not till the crushing defeat of the Braganzas, grown to be the head and front of aristocratic despotism, in the time of John II., that the sovereign obtained the upper hand of the peerage. Nor would the Portuguese crown have been at all successful in resisting such a powerful and high-spirited union as that of the secular magnates, if it had not been well supported by the third estate. Had not the commons often held up his hands when he was well-nigh exhausted, the forces of the king would have been discomfited, and Portugal, small enough for a separate nation, would have been cut up into a number of diminutive, semi-independent principalities. The complaints of the third estate regarding the exactions and imperious conduct of the second furnished the king with his best arguments with which to silence the cry of privilege from the titled order. The occasional breaches in that party were instrumental also, so far, in bringing about a material reduction of their influence; but these were apt to be closed up with alacrity when common danger threatened. To the communes, rural and borough, it was principally owing that a check was placed upon the extravagant pretensions of the barons; and as they were the means of lessening the weight of the secular arm, so did they conspire to prohibit the preposterous intrusion of the Church in the secular sphere.

To relate the history of the communes would require a volume. Here we can only give it in the barest outline.

The contest with Mohammedanism had left the country in a miserable condition. Much of the arable land had become waste. In every province one saw burned villages, and walled towns destroyed. The nobles who had distinguished themselves in driving out the Moslem received allotments of the recovered territory; and the Church, which had furthered the enterprise by its benediction, and not seldom by the presence of its priests at the seat of war in casque and breastplate, obtained rather more than its share of acres. But it was necessary to till the land and to restore demolished habitations. The case was urgent, and to attract settlers the offer of privileges was the only resource. The plan succeeded. The villages and towns rose from their ruins, and the soil, so long a stranger to the ploughshare, was gradually brought under cultivation.

But the laws which regulated these communities were various. The patrons from whom these edicts proceeded were ecclesiastical and lay; so there was one broad distinction between tributaries, as to rights and restrictions, according to the kind of superior, whether bishop or baron. But numerous differences, besides, are noticeable in those old communal laws, one code bearing traces of Roman, another of Visigothic, a third even of Arab origin. There was no general method of trying offenders, no uniform standard of penalties. In one district trial by combat or by walking on hot iron obtained; in another no such custom was in use. In some parts there existed what in this country was called the " branks," an iron instrument for fastening the tongues of slanderers and scolds. Elsewhere in Portugal those who possessed such unruly members had not to fear that physical restraint.

The diversity of legal maxims and practices could not but be fruitful of confusion and of many other evils. The communities were isolated, indifferent to each other, and often, from the clashing of their laws as much as from anything else, even hostile. Such an undesirable situation of affairs was, however, effectually dealt with by the introduction of Roman law in the reign of Dennis. The study of that code had been greatly stimulated in Europe by the discovery of Justinian's "Pandects;" and the attention of Portugal also was directed to it very specially by reason of the great law-pleas regarding royal *versus* ecclesiastical right with which the country was unfortunately familiar. Eminent lawyers, versed not only in canon but in civil law, were retained as counsel by the Portuguese crown; and it was felt to be a humiliation that foreigners had to be employed for the purpose, as no native had a reputation for that kind of learning.

But the disgrace was wiped out by the founding of a national university at Lisbon in the year 1290. Clerical personages were the foremost to urge upon the sovereign the pressing need of such a seminary. They saw in other countries seats of learning whose renown shed a lustre on the Church of those lands; for the university could not be conceived of except as a child in ecclesiastical leading-strings. The kind of knowledge which the Portuguese clergy wished to promote was, of course, theology and scholastic philosophy. They were far from desirous of seeing the study of the Roman formulary prosecuted in the proposed institution. That code was repugnant to their own canon law. Yet so soon as the chair of civil law was instituted, the university became more busy in that department than in any other. At Lisbon and at Coimbra, whither the university was transferred,* the prelectors

---

* The transference took place because of "town and gown" riots in Lisbon, which began to occur so frequently and to grow so much more serious that a change of air was prescribed for the university in 1307. The proneness of the medieval Portuguese student to turbulence and frivolity is illustrated by some early regulations of the university—one, for instance, to the effect that no courtier, player, or soldier should abide in the same lodging with a student. The first removal to Coimbra was not the only alteration of the university seat. Twice after its first disturbance the seminary was transported to Lisbon, then brought again to Coimbra. At Coimbra it finally settled in 1537. It is interesting to note that the illustrious Scotchman George Buchanan, incomparable Latinist, historian, and afterwards tutor to James I. of England, was for a short time on the professorial staff of Coimbra University, but was by-and-by deprived of his office and cast into prison for heresy.

had continually in training a large class who designed to give their lives to the legal profession as exponents of the resuscitated Roman legislation.

The code which made for a uniform legal practice in Portugal invested the king with the dignity of the Cæsars. Armed with such regard, he pressed more heavily on the two estates whose action tended to seriously impair his authority; and as the industrial pulse began to beat quicker in the third estate, it willingly saw the aggrandizement of the king to the disparagement of peers and prelates, who viewed the communes simply as their creatures. The people rejoiced, therefore, to see royal officials supplanting the episcopal and baronial judges in the various districts. Those magistrates, moreover, whom the communes, pursuant to old rights, themselves elected, had their spheres defined, and circuits were ordered for the hearing of appeals. The operation of a harmonious law was calculated to consolidate the scattered communes, and their voice had more influence in national affairs. The growing population and wealth of some of them made it the more desirable, but also the more difficult, for their superiors to keep them under. In the Cortes they began to occupy an important place.

From Visigothic times the Cortes—the name an echo of the Roman *curia*—had a being. But it seems at that early time to have been a clerical council more than aught else. The Cortes consisted of the clergymen, who advised the king. They only could read and write. The statutes were all of their composition, and not much would creep into them to the disadvantage of the Church. During the period of Mohammedan warfare, the ecclesiastical organization was so shivered that the secular barons learned to take a larger part in the management of state affairs; and though the Church was by-and-by mended and able again to make an impressive political appearance, the nobles bulked none the less in the Cortes. For a century subsequent to the Christian reconquest, these two estates were all who were represented in the council of the nation. It was still a mere assembly of notables. But from the beginning of the Portuguese monarchy we find deputies chosen by the communes sitting in the Cortes and giving voice to the views of their constituents. As middle walls between commune and commune gave way, the vote of the third estate became more solid; and as the exigencies of state service required the money of the commercial centres, the tone of the other orders grew more gracious. The advance of industry, the prosperous markets and numerous shipping, gave to the parliamentary commissioners of the commons a self-respecting spirit which was not confounded either by the mitre and crosier or by the pennon and caldron.

CHAPTER VII.

THE UNION OF SPAIN AND PORTUGAL.

1580-1640.

CARDINAL HENRY had before his death ratified the appointment of five notables who, in that event, should, under the name of governors and defenders of the kingdom, act as political tide-waiters, and utter a pronouncement as to the succession when matters should have ripened. The five were divided on the great question. Three were in favour of Philip—whether their goodwill was spontaneous or purchased, they knew best—and two were indisposed to accept a Spanish king. The people's deputies in the Cortes were all for the Prior of Crato. They thought of another semi-ecclesiastic, also with a blotted scutcheon—the Grand Commander—who had rescued them from the clutches of Spain, won for his country security and prosperity and for himself deathless fame. They believed such another era of glory might be inaugurated by Antonio. But the prior was not cast in the mould of John I. Selfish, base, and pusillanimous, he pushed himself to the front only to afford a demonstration of his unlikeness to the illustrious founder of the house of Avis, and of his incapacity to deal with national affairs, since his own were conducted with such palpable imbecility.

His rival, Philip of Spain, was one who fastened to his purposes like a leech, and could command immense resources in carrying them out. The "most catholic" king was a little,

meagre man, with an air marked by timidity and embarrassment. When he spoke he "looked continually on the ground;"
but he conversed as seldom as possible, preferring to employ
his pen rather than his tongue. He was a prolific writer of
letters and state papers, and had much facility in the use of
that artful language which conceals thought. He was one of
the worst men who figure in history. His sensuality and
gluttony are astounding. He was cunning and untruthful to
the last degree, and greedy of absolute power ; while of his cold-
blooded cruelty there needs no further proof than the incon-
testible fact that he ordained the death of his own son, the mis-
shapen, mad Don Carlos, round whom such a halo has been
thrown by Schiller in his immortal tragedy.*

The "governors" had no real intention of opposing the
powerful tyrant of Spain. Even the two who were not Philip's
partisans saw every day more clearly the futility of resisting
him. They could not, indeed, for shame's sake, invite him to
take possession. On the contrary, they felt themselves obliged
to make a show of patriotism by giving orders for the strengthening of the frontier fortifications and garrisons. But Philip
knew as well as they that this activity was very much a sham.
They said to the King of Spain that he should enter at once
on the declaration of their verdict, if that verdict were in favour
of his claim, and he was not slow to read between the lines of
their communication that the acceptance of his lordship was
with them a foregone conclusion. They wished him to understand that the way was not yet clear for him on account of
Antonio's popularity, but that they looked for the enthusiasm
of the prior's adherents melting away. They dreaded a rally
to the banner of Antonio, should Philip force his way in by the
sword, on the part of many who esteemed the prior little, but
would protest thus against the violent intrusion of a foreigner.

The Prior of Crato had imagined that he was going to have

* For a full-length portrait of Philip II. see Motley's " Rise of the Dutch Republic."

PHILIP I. OF PORTUGAL.
(Philip II. of Spain.)

a triumphal progress to power. He took up his abode in the neighbourhood of Lisbon in anticipation of a call to the throne, but as "the mountain did not come to Mohammed, he resolved to go to the mountain." He sent some of his adherents to the city, who should urge the authorities to accept and proclaim him as sovereign of Portugal. They returned, however, to say that their efforts had been in vain, and Antonio thought it well to retire in the meantime to Santarem, where his cause was strongest. It would have been much better if he could have got himself formally accepted in the capital; yet, since that seemed in the present circumstances impossible, he must try his fortune in the provinces. In Santarem, a public function— the laying of a foundation-stone—was, when he reached the town, appointed to take place immediately. The prior per- formed the ceremony, and was thereafter proclaimed King of Portugal by the assembled multitude. From Santarem, with a motley force which increased by the way, he marched back to Lisbon and took possession of the city. The governors were in Setubal at the time. So Antonio sent thither a confidant with a letter to these notables, informing them of what had occurred, and requesting them to acknowledge him as king. When they refused, Antonio's messenger managed to rouse the populace and even their own body-guard against them, and they fled for their lives, along with the procurators of the other claimants of the throne; for the farce of an investiga- tion regarding the succession was still being carried on by the governors. So far, then, the prior's course had run with tolerable smoothness.

The Duke of Braganza had been watching the proceedings of Antonio with intense disapprobation, and was especially indignant at an impudent demand that the Braganza claim should be waived in favour of the Prior of Crato's, who would bestow upon him, in return for homage, an important appoint- ment at court. The duke had been quietly asking aid for himself from various foreign powers, but had found them in-disposed to meddle.   He knew that without such help he could not hold out against Spain.   If he dared to challenge Philip, the result should be the plunging of his family into the miseries of exile and beggary, at the least computation of his penalty, and Braganza was the richest man and the greatest landlord in Portugal.   It was plain to him that the Spaniard was going to win in the meantime.   Antonio's rashness and insolence were but preparing his overthrow, and lending an appearance of justification to an armed interference from Spain.   The duke decided, therefore, not to risk his substance in pursuit of a shadowy prospect, and with mental reservation of his descend-ants' rights, tendered his allegiance to Philip.

The King of Spain was now at liberty, and believed it high time, to devote his attention to the Prior of Crato.   If the governors had not the courage of their opinions, his own sword should play his game.   He gave out that he meant to continue the various classes of Portuguese in the enjoyment of their national privileges.   The yoke of this *débonnaire* prince was to be easy !   The Portuguese should scarcely feel it !   There was not one grain of honesty in his promises.   Falsehood was Philip's element.   He revelled in it, like a dolphin in the sea. . It is said that he would sometimes concoct an elaborate fiction, even when the plain truth could have served him a shade better, he was so proudly conscious of being *facile princeps* in his specialty.   The bulk of the Portuguese swallowed the bait, and Philip, having bribed many of the nobles and gulled many of the people, had only to deal with the prior's party.   With a splendid retinue the King of Spain entered Elvas in Alemtejo (1581), and received the allegiance of the citizens.   Other places in the vicinity followed suit.   Meantime, the Spanish army had passed the king, and was marching Lisbonward to dis-lodge Antonio, receiving *en route* the submission of important towns.   At the head of the troops rode a tall, thin man with small head and dark sparkling eyes. He was the notorious Duke of Alva, the best general of his time, the partner of Philip's crimes and the willing instrument of his cruelties. Disdaining Philip's swinish pleasures, he was quite his master's equal in barbarity. During his administration of the Netherlands, he boasted that he had caused eighteen thousand persons to be executed.* That he considered more than sufficient evidence of his energy and assiduity, not to speak of the multitudes beyond reckoning who had perished through his action, "by battle, siege, starvation, and massacre." This man had been summoned from the quietude of his country-seat, whither he had retired for good, having drunk blood for sixty years, that he might do a last stroke of work for Spain.

The approach, with twenty thousand under his command, of a man like Alva, fearless as he was ferocious, and such an adept in warfare that he is said never to have been defeated or surprised, might well have induced Antonio to abandon hope and surrender with all possible celerity. But the prior was inflamed by self-conceit, and having added to his original ragged regiment a number of French mercenaries, whom he had purchased out of excessive exactions from the people, imagined that he could well withstand the Spanish commander. The withdrawal of Braganza had left him alone to represent the native as against the foreign cause, and he had given away decorations and created peerages with much generosity, so securing the interest of a number in his success; but many who at first had shouted for him were grumbling at the demands he was making upon their purses, and at the ruthless way in which he was forcing all sorts of men into his ranks. Half his followers were unwilling or faint-hearted, he was not gaining in popular esteem, and he had no means of carrying on a campaign. Estremos, Evora, and Montemor had already yielded, without a blow, to Alva, and Spanish war-ships had

* See Motley.

sailed round Cape St. Vincent to blockade the Portuguese fleet, which had declared for Antonio, in the Tagus.

The Lisbon magistrates entreated the prior to leave the town in view of Alva's approach, as his Spaniards would, it was believed, were they to get the upper hand, subject it to every kind of outrage. The burghers of Lisbon remembered the fate of those Dutch cities which had resisted the " Scourge of the Netherlands," and had afterwards unfortunately fallen into his cruel hands. Antonio agreed to vacate the capital, not for the reason adduced by the magistrates, but because he could not hold such a great place with the rout at his heels. He retired to Belem, and then to Alcantara, where, posted on a height, and having the Alcantara, whose steep banks here protected him like a moat, between him and the foe, he awaited the duke. Alva was never in a hurry, and when he came in sight of Antonio delayed operations for several days. He was all the more leisurely, inasmuch as his opponent's force was melting gradually away. It was the fear of being shot by their own officers which prevented many of the prior's soldiers from flying out of the danger of death from the Spaniards.

At last, after a little more resistance from the better part of the other side than he expected, Alva took the bridge over the Alcantara, and at the confluence of that stream and the Tagus inflicted a total defeat on the army of Antonio. The prior himself disappeared with celerity, and after the fight was nowhere to be found. Just before the battle of Alcantara the fleet of Philip had gained a victory over the Portuguese war-ships, and commanded the Tagus. Lisbon surrendered to the king, and suffered less than it expected. There was some plundering of the city, and more of suburban Lisbon, but since the Spanish monarch regarded the capital as his, he spared it for his own sake. Antonio endeavoured still to carry his point, and did indeed manage to collect something like a force at Coimbra. He had heard that Philip was at that time unwell, and anticipating an event which did not soon occur, put on mourning for the Spanish king. Thus the prior secured new friends on account of an imaginary change in the situation. For had Philip's decease really occurred, Antonio might have been able to lay hold of the sovereign power in spite of Braganza. But unfortunately for the prior, and certainly most unfortunately for the country, Philip lived for eighteen years longer as the worst enemy Portugal ever had.

In the meantime, however, the *ruse* about the King of Spain succeeded so far as to give Antonio the means of offering more resistance. From Coimbra he went with his following, mostly artisans and peasants, armed, many of them, only with cudgels, axes, and such-like weapons, to Aveiro, and thence to Oporto. A Spanish force was chasing him all the time, and by-and-by reached Oporto. But Antonio had decamped the previous night, hearing of the Spaniard's approach, and found his way to Viana. The citizens of Oporto did not strive to detain him, for he had borrowed of the magistracy a hundred thousand ducats, which they were convinced they should never see again, and they feared a demand for an additional loan. His people also, "flown with insolence and wine," had been making themselves under his patronage anything but agreeable guests. At Viana he proposed to embark, if the weather permitted. A fierce gale detained him, however, so long that some Spanish cavalry sent in pursuit had almost caught him. Between the Spaniard and the deep sea the prior was in a sorry plight. But choosing the lesser of two evils, he trusted himself in a small vessel to the warring elements, and thus eluded the clutches of his adversary.

Philip had been pushing his way in Portugal. At a meeting of the Cortes at Thomar, in Lower Beira, on the 19th of April, 1582, he publicly agreed to respect Portuguese statutes and usages, and comported himself generally in a manner, for him, extraordinarily affable. Of the foreign dominions of Portugal, the

African possessions, Madeira, Brazil, and the territory in India had acknowledged him. St. Miguel, the most important of the Azores, had also declared for him. But with the population of the remaining islands in the Azores group he was still to have trouble. Yet he believed he should ere long bring these stubborn islanders to their senses, and, happy in having accomplished so much, made a state entry into the capital on horseback, under a gold-embroidered canopy, in the presence of a great crowd, with the nobility of Portugal walking submissively behind the royal steed.

The terror of Alva's name had wrought wonders in the way of extinguishing the fire of rebellion in the land. But in the more distant Azores it was burning still. The Prior of Crato, after tossing about off the Portuguese coast in the rude smack which had afforded him refuge from the duke's troopers, landed once more in his native country, and was kept faithfully concealed by the peasantry, waiting for something to turn up in his favour. There were, however, no auspices of good fortune, and he slipped away to France to plead his cause with its government. He contrived to obtain a French fleet through the influence of the queen-mother, Catherine de Medici (who imagined she herself had a claim to the Portuguese throne, and called Philip a usurper), for the purpose of making an attempt, not upon Portugal itself, but upon St. Miguel, that, holding all the Azores, he might from thence strike at the King of Spain as he saw opportunity. The French ships accordingly, in 1582, sailed for St. Miguel, landing Antonio at Terceira, where his reception with royal honours was more congenial to him than the rough greeting with bullet and pike which his French friends might expect at the other island. The fleet debarked successfully the troops it carried, and took St. Miguel.

But while the French thus defeated the garrison, their fleet was attacked by Spanish war-ships which had been sailing in their wake and now unexpectedly came up. The result of the naval engagement was a victory for Spain. Her enemy's loss was heavy. The French admiral and two thousand men were killed. Antonio was bereft of his best adherent, the young Count of Vimioso, who received a mortal wound in the action. What was left of the French fleet sailed homeward, and the Spanish admiral retook St. Miguel with little difficulty. All Frenchmen who were found in the island he beheaded or hanged, and having thus executed his commission, left for Lisbon, leaving soldiery for the defence of the recovered place.

The tidings of his friends' misfortune had reached Antonio on Terceira, and he felt exceedingly uncomfortable. But he breathed freely again when he knew that the Spaniards had quitted the Azores for Portugal. Indeed, his relief was so great that he began to behave as if he had attained the summit of his desires. He lorded it more haughtily than Philip would have done in Madrid. His exactions exhausted the resources of the people; his dissipation disgusted and his imperiousness exasperated the simple islanders who had opened their arms to receive him. After some months of conduct loose and high-handed in the greatest measure, Antonio, unable to find pay for his strong garrison, sailed for France, though he was doubtful now of a friendly reception there, and so delivered himself from the obloquy of the starving soldiers. In the course of the next year (1583) a Spanish expedition was sent to Terceira, and, despite the steep rocks which made it exceedingly easy to hold, was able to effect a landing, and to deliver such a determined attack upon its defenders that they gave up resistance and yielded the island to Spain. All the Azores were thereupon Philip's, for none of the others were capable of withstanding Spanish forces.

Terceira having submitted to his yoke, Philip had not much fear of his authority being challenged anywhere on Portuguese ground. But that dream of Sebastian's return, which was still cherished by thousands of the illiterate Portuguese, gave rise now and again to some annoyance for the king, by reason of pretenders claiming to be "the concealed one" returned to resume his sovereignty. The son of a tiler, the son of a stone-mason, and the son of a sugar-baker successively gave themselves out as the long-lost Sebastian, and managed for a time to keep up the deception and to lead the credulous astray. But the imposture of each was in time unmasked, and a few companies of Spanish soldiers were sufficient to scatter the motley crews who followed the banners of these tricksters.

Another claimant, however, the last of them, who made his appearance in Venice, sustained his *rôle* so cleverly that he staggered even sceptics, and made himself the talk of Europe. He told how he, the veritable Sebastian, had been taken to Algarve to be healed of his wounds, and having thereafter journeyed far in Asia, was now sick of "land travel and sea-faring," and could no longer refrain from discovering himself to his people. Whoever the man may have been, he is said to have strikingly resembled King Sebastian in face and figure, and even in certain peculiar marks upon his person. (The story amusingly reminds one of claimants in our own day.) He disclosed secrets which none but Sebastian could have known. He recognized in particular a sword which had belonged to the deceased king, picking it up from a heap of similar weapons, and informed its owner that he should find the name Sebastian in minute graving beneath a gem on the hilt, which happened to be correct. But let him be Sebastian or any one else, Philip was not going to let the sceptre of Portugal slip out of his fingers. So Sebastian *redivivus*, at the request of the Spanish ambassador, was suddenly flung into the dreadful hold beside the doge's palace. The senate, however, released him upon the entreaties of influential Portuguese. He disappeared from Venice, only to be apprehended once more in Italy by the Spanish viceroy of Naples, and by him to be transported to Spain, where in the heart of Castile he died a close prisoner, without ever, so far as is known, bursting by a confession the bubble he had blown. A romance of history!

In 1588 the King of Spain suffered that humiliating defeat of his fleet which occasioned such unbounded joy throughout the length and breadth of England. We only allude here to the destruction of the Spanish Armada in order to connect with it a final effort which the Prior of Crato made to possess himself, by England's assistance, of the Portuguese throne. The year after the Armada's defeat he prevailed upon Queen Elizabeth, by grossly exaggerating his strength in Portugal, and by a promise of yearly tribute to the crown of England, to lend him a fleet under the command of the renowned Francis Drake. The English ships dropped anchor off Peniche in Estremadura, and the forces landing there marched to the capital. But the garrison repelled the invaders, and Drake, after waiting a considerable time for an uprising in favour of Antonio, saw that his mistress had been befooled, and embarked for home. This was the last public appearance of the prior, a disreputable and incapable creature, who succeeded as well as he deserved, and requited in the worst way the loyalty which better men than he were inconsiderate enough to squander upon him. He lived for some time in Paris, and spent his abundant leisure in raving about his rights and his wrongs, till he died there in 1595, little regretted by any who knew him.

It may excite some wonder that a person like the prior could maintain so long an opposition to such a powerful prince as Philip, and that charlatans such as the pseudo-Sebastians could from time to time set people by the ears through their fabulous representations. But the fact is, the king was almost everything which the Portuguese did not like. He was a foreigner and a Spaniard. He had threatened the nation into non-resistance while he climbed into the throne. He had in him not a drop of human kindness or even of geniality. And lastly, in spite of and not long after his ample protestations at Thomar, he began to ignore the ancient legislation and customs of Portugal, and to plainly show that he considered the Portuguese no better than bondsmen of Spain. The nobility who had tacitly admitted his claim saw by-and-by that his private promises to their advantage were made for the purpose of being broken. The Duke of Braganza, for instance, was bitterly disappointed by Philip's treatment of him. He had certainly not been bribed, but on his expressing a willingness to forego his own right, the king had spontaneously, though in vague terms, held out to him the prospect of substantial recompense. The recompense proved to be some office with a high-sounding title and no power. The governorship of the kingdom, which Braganza in all probability expected, was given to the Cardinal-Archduke of Austria, and the duke retired, deeply mortified, to his seat at Villa Viciosa in Alemtejo. His spirits were so affected that his physical constitution broke down, and he did not linger more than a few years longer in a world where he had been thus grossly deceived.

This is a specimen of the faith Philip kept with all classes of Portuguese; and his falsehood, together with the other faults which have been adduced, conspired increasingly to make the Spanish king the *bête noir* of the entire population, and to predispose them to accept rather such a Captain Bobadil as Antonio or that youngest scion of the house of Beja left on the field of Alcaçer, to whom they owed nothing but a tremendous military disaster.

As soon as the king left Portugal, where he remained only a short time, for Madrid, he opened a policy regarding the Portuguese nation which seemed to indicate the spirit, not of a king supposed to have peacefully and legitimately succeeded, but of a conqueror who desired to be revenged upon a prostrate foe. He garrisoned Portuguese fortresses with Castilian infantry, as if he could not trust the native troops. All decisions regarding important state affairs had to come from Madrid, and were

often inconveniently delayed. For the strengthening of the
Spanish fleet, ships, men, guns, and munitions of war were taken
without stint from Lisbon, and in consequence the naval force
at the command of the Portuguese government for the protection of her possessions abroad was notoriously insufficient.
Candidates for public offices must proceed to Madrid and purchase their places there. Philip, not content with the heavy
taxes he imposed, borrowed large sums from the Portuguese
treasury which he never remembered to repay. Under the
king's favourite system of espionage the persons of natives were
in jeopardy. Citizens of repute were imprisoned on incredible
indictments of disloyalty, and cruelly fleeced before they regained their liberty. Others who criticised too frankly the
condition of things, or were somehow objects of dislike to the
creatures of the king, found themselves unexpectedly apprehended and hurried to the tower of St. Jago, whence they were
flung into the water.*

Philip revised the statute book also, to its detriment, granting to the Church that very jurisdiction and many of those
various privileges which had been in the early history of Portugal so inconsiderately allowed, and had been withdrawn only
after an intense conflict protracted through many generations.
Yet did the "most catholic king" deliver, without compunction, to Islam the most important African fortress of Arzilla,
the glorious trophy of Alfonso V., as the price of Mohammedan
neutrality in the matter of the Prior of Crato.

The Portuguese had eighteen years of Philip I. (II. of Spain)
—eighteen years of his waxing tyranny and of their country's
waxing poverty. The state of the land did not annoy the
king; indeed it pleased him, for one of his wise saws was,
"Better a Portugal poor and peaceful than rich and restless."
Yet he was wrong in calling the desolation he had made peace.

* The fishermen of the Tagus complained of the number of corpses which they drew
up in their nets at that time.

There was peace in his own time; nevertheless a spirit dwelt still in Portugal which was by-and-by to manifest itself to the disestablishment of his house. That Portugal was declining before the days of Spanish lordship is undeniable. There was no reason in the world, however, for its fortunes breaking so rapidly, or why it should not have pulled itself together under a wise and energetic head. But before its rough embrace of Portugal, the great empire of Charles V. showed unmistakably its inability to hold its ground as it once had done; and the year 1588 saw it pushed over a steep declivity, down which it rushed helplessly, and with ever-quickening pace, to the valley of humiliation. Luckless Portugal, tied to its neighbour, was dragged along with it, and could by no means free itself from the fatal connection. The knot could not be undone. Only by the rude force of revolution could it be severed. But the time for that was not yet; and when it came, Portugal had fallen too far to indulge a reasonable expectation of regaining the height from which it had been precipitated.

Philip reigned exactly ten years after the terrible catastrophe which overtook his fleet, and in 1598 his son, another Philip, assumed the crown of Portugal; and he, in 1621, was followed by yet another of the same name. The similarity in the names of Portugal's Spanish rulers corresponded with the monotony of their Portuguese policy—a policy whose note was complete indifference to the interests of the country. At home, business stagnated, and the administration of the law was in the hands of corrupt officials who had bought their situations and looked to recompense themselves by underhand methods. Abroad, the magnificent acquisitions of the Portuguese were being laid hold of by the enemies of Spain. The Dutch, who were growing yearly in power, determinedly sought to extend their commercial influence on every hand. A Spanish decree was issued prohibiting them from trading with Peninsular ports; but the measure was a boomerang which struck Spain on the head.

PHILIP III. OF PORTUGAL.

For the bold merchants of Holland began thereupon to deal more directly and extensively with the countries whence those products came, which they had been content before to fetch from Lisbon. And from dealing with the 'Spanish-Portuguese possessions, they proceeded to lay violent hands upon them, and to drive out the Peninsular garrisons and officials. Thus were lost to the Portuguese one after another of the valuable territories and commercial establishments which their adventurous ancestors had discovered, and where the national flag had for centuries been flying. The Dutch had no scruples in spoiling the Spaniards. It was some small satisfaction for the barbarities they had so long endured at the hands of Charles V. and his son. But, unfortunately for the Portuguese, it was from *them*, who had done the Dutch no harm, and not from the tyrants of the Netherlands, that the compensation was obtained. Portugal was like a man who should be gagged and bound in his own house, and forced to witness thieves breaking open his receptacles and making off with his goods.

There is no need to expatiate further upon the period of forty-six years during which the second and third Philips of Portugal (III. and IV. of Spain) misruled the wretched Portuguese. The kings themselves are not worthy of any consideration whatever. Philip I. was in his evil way a personage. His successors and namesakes had, indeed, inherited his hideous vices, but in point of intellect were next door to imbecility. Regarding Portugal, they clung to the first Philip's programme, though it was growing more and more impossible. They had to leave the task of carrying it out, however, to ministers of the worst kind, who had received *carte blanche* from their masters' laziness and stupidity. Portugal seldom saw its Spanish kings. The visits which the last two Philips condescended to pay it were quite angelic in their rarity. But the analogy halts painfully. When they came, it was only to receive the fulsome homage of flatterers, and to stare about in a bewildered style, without once taking in the situation or knowing what to do.

The time was very " weary, flat, stale, and unprofitable." But there were still those who dared to hope against hope ; who believed that the old yearning for independence had not yet been utterly crushed out of the Portuguese by the iron heel of Spain. And they were right. The oppression of Spanish officials, their monstrous exactions, their insolence, and their severity were at length somewhat too much for flesh and blood to endure. The people slowly braced themselves to insurrection. It was in Evora, the capital of Alemtejo, that the first outbreak occurred. The citizens were in a state of high indignation at the ruthless conduct of the *corregedor* (the principal functionary of the government) at Evora. There was a rebellious demonstration in the streets, and the *corregedor* fled for his life. The revolt spread through the whole province, and months elapsed before it could be put down, though a considerable military force was employed for the purpose. The ringleaders were executed, and many were sent to the galleys.

Margaret, Duchess of Mantua, a relative of the royal family, had been appointed vice-queen of Portugal in 1634, and was in office when the Alemtejan insurrection took place. She trusted that her stringent measures in the province had tranquillized the country, and wrote in that confident mood to Madrid. It was not so. The rising in Evora was but the beginning, not the end, of the matter. It had only whetted the appetite for rebellion.

The Spanish prime minister, the Duke of Olivarez, a man of insight and resolution, and a relentless hater of the Portuguese, believed, from information which his spies were continually bringing him, that the vice-queen was deceiving herself. He saw that something must be done to quell the agitation effectually, else the fire, only apparently extinguished, should burst out again with redoubled fury. He thought out a policy of coercion stricter than had ever yet been applied to Portugal ; and, with that view, took steps to secure what was a necessary preliminary to his plan, the reduction of Portugal to the position of a Spanish province. He determined to use the trouble in Alemtejo for the furtherance of his designs. The king might now, in consequence of the disloyalty of the Portuguese, consider himself released of the oath he had taken to respect the constitution.

In accordance with the crafty project of Olivarez, a great number of the most influential persons in Portugal were invited to Madrid in 1638 to a conference regarding important Portuguese state affairs. At its opening, vows of secrecy were extracted from those who attended it ; but it is indubitable that the notables were asked to pledge themselves to support a plan for stripping their country of its rights, and leaving it at the absolute mercy of Spain. Now, considering the damage which Spain had already inflicted on Portugal, even when protected by its constitution, what result might be expected were it denuded of its armour and exposed to every method of assault which the diabolic ingenuity of the Spanish government chose to employ? The scheme was so atrocious that the Portuguese who were present at the conference knew they dared not divulge it at home. They could only say to Olivarez that the matter was one for the Cortes, and take their departure as speedily as possible.

All Portugal heard of the conference, and saw more or less clearly that a gigantic evil was intended by the odious Spanish minister, which only united action and desperate resistance could suffice to avert. Sixty years before, the blood of the Portuguese would have run cold at the thought of rebellion. But now they were familiarizing themselves with the idea. The Alemtejans had taken the first step, and had not been easily repressed. What if the whole nation should take the next together? And, supposing the insurgents successful, what then? Who should wear those insignia of Portuguese royalty in which, for half a century, foreign princes had been masquerading? They wanted a name to conjure with—a person round whom their conspiracy should circle—an illustrious Portuguese whom even the aristocracy would consent to acknowledge as a sovereign, and who should, nevertheless, be native enough to keep in touch with the heart of the people. Through such an one they might hope to repair, as far as that could be done, the infinite loss and disgrace which, as a nation, they had suffered. The man they wanted was not far to seek. There was only one who could fairly satisfy all classes of Portuguese—the Duke of Braganza.

The Braganzas were connected with the throne of Portugal in more ways than one. The first duke of the long line was a son of the Grand Commander, founder of the house of Avis; and another, it may not have been forgotten, was husband of the Princess Catherine, grand-daughter of Emmanuel, first monarch of the Beja family, and in her name claimed the crown. The wealth of the Dukes of Braganza was, for those days, enormous. As territorial magnates there were none who came within a long distance of them, the sum of their acres being about equal to one-third of the land in Portugal. At the time when the nation stood on the threshold of revolt against the Spanish dynasty, the holder of the Braganza title was the grandson of the above-mentioned Princess Catherine. His father and grandfather fretted without ceasing under the necessity of foregoing the distinction to which they considered themselves entitled, and probably shortened their lives by indulging their feelings of mortification. But their successor, though he hated the Spaniards like a true Portuguese, little "vexed his bosom" about the crown. The excitement of the hunting field, the pleasures of society filled his cup. If he had ambition he kept it very much to himself. The Spanish government apprehended no danger from his own motion. But the whole nation was for him, and it seemed extremely desirable to those who supported the existing government that the downfall or exile of the duke should be somehow procured.

Spain happened just then to be involved in war with France, and the Duke of Braganza was appointed inspector-general of Portuguese harbours and fortifications. He was also to board Spanish-Portuguese ships of war which should enter the harbours of Portugal, and ascertain their seaworthiness and fighting strength. The first part of the duty Braganza performed, but while waiting for the approach of the fleet, which was delayed by stormy weather, he wearied, and withdrew to his country seat. Perhaps he had a suspicion of a plot against him. At all events it was well that he took himself away, for Olivarez had given orders to the Spanish admiral for the detention of the duke whenever he should step on board one of the war-ships, and for his conveyance with all speed to Spain. That stroke having missed, the ingenious minister prepared another. The Catalonians were at the time in a state of revolt against the government, in consequence of the same high-handed dealing of which the Portuguese complained. Braganza received a direction to repair with a Portuguese contingent to Madrid, that from thence he might march into Catalonia and assist the king in chastising his refractory subjects. The business was not congenial to the duke or to the Portuguese. Moreover, he guessed that if he went to Madrid he should never see Portugal again. So he sent an evasive reply to the summons.

Olivarez quite overreached himself in ordering Braganza to the capital. Not only did the duke disobey it, but the minister's evident desire to lay hold of his person precipitated the crisis in Portugal. The Catalonian insurrection favoured the Portuguese party of revolution, since the attention of Spain was necessarily directed to that serious disturbance, and a peremptory repetition of the injunction to the duke to appear in the capital of Spain showed them that the time had come for raising the standard of independence.   Many influential persons waited upon Braganza and besought him to accept the crown.   He was himself reluctant, but the duchess, a spirited and intelligent lady of the Medina Sidonia family, urged him to cast in his lot with the insurgents, as his fate was sealed at Madrid.   He should lose all by refusing the offer his countrymen were making him, and on the other hand the chances of revolt were great.   He was convinced that he must choose between the royal palace at Lisbon and a Spanish prison, and agreed to the proposal of the revolutionists.

That night, 26th November 1640, the conspirators met in the Braganza palace at Lisbon and made their final arrangements.   On Sunday, December 1st, a crowd of armed men were seen in the vicinity of the royal palace, and at the first stroke of nine o'clock there was a rush into the building. Some overpowered the guard, and others sought the vice-queen and certain obnoxious Spanish officials.   The worst hated of these individuals was Vasconcellos, the Duchess of Mantua's private secretary, who had been very assiduous in communicating to Olivarez everything he knew, and much that he did not know, to the disadvantage of the Portuguese.   Vasconcellos was drawn out of a cabinet where he had hidden himself, pistolled, and thrown out of the window.   The duchess was found at another window calling for help.   The conspirators bade her be silent, else they should be compelled to treat her with less respect than her eminent position deserved.   "How?" said the vice-queen.   "By throwing you out of the window, gracious madam," replied one of the ringleaders, with a profound obeisance.   The duchess held her peace and retired.

The conspirators appeared on a balcony waving their swords and shouting, "Long live Dom John IV.!   Freedom for the Portuguese!"   The cries were answered by the voice of a great multitude gathered in the courtyard of the palace.   Orders for the delivery of all the strong places about Lisbon were forced

from the poor vice-queen.   Ere long every fortress in the kingdom was surrendered to King John, and the revolution was
complete.   A message was sent to the Duke of Braganza, and
on the 5th of December he entered the capital of Portugal and
received an extraordinary ovation.   On the 15th of December,
the grandees tendered their homage to the duke, now John IV.
of Portugal, while he sat upon a stage erected before the
palace, holding the sceptre which the Grand Commander had
taken from the King of Castile at the battle of Aljubarotta.

Thus, by means of a revolution, almost bloodless, because of
the unanimity of the people, the family of Braganza were set
upon a throne which they have occupied to the present day.

CHAPTER VIII.

HOUSE OF BRAGANZA.

1640.

THE first sovereign of the Braganza family could bring to his work neither genius nor experience in state affairs, but he possessed a tolerable amount of common sense, which sometimes gets over a difficulty by looking into details beneath the attention of genius. And having that "far-off touch of greatness to know well he was not great," he determined to be off completely with the *dolce far niente* mode of his existence as Duke of Braganza, and as King of Portugal to "live laborious days." His excellent queen, moreover, conducted him by her sagacious counsel safely through many a difficulty; and it is one of the best traits of John IV. that he endured advice when a lesser man would have attempted to save his dignity by obstinate self-assertion. There was another upon whom the king justly depended for wise suggestions, Antonio Veigas, an old and faithful retainer of his house, who, though such a martyr to gout that he had to be carried in a chair about the palace, more than made up for his physical impotence by the vigour of his intellect. Veigas and the queen understood each other well, and both had the interests of the sovereign at heart. Historians speak also of the king's happy fortune. The conjunction of things seemed often to promise a crash, when suddenly, without any apparent cause, it turned to his advantage. Portugal was in a lamentable state when he ascended the throne, and relations with various foreign powers were much strained; but somehow the reign of John IV. was as satisfactory as reasonable men could expect.

One of the first acts of his reign was the summoning of the Cortes in the beginning of 1641. It met at Lisbon, and consulted about the defence of the kingdom against a Spanish invasion. A number of taxes imposed by the late government had to be abated or abrogated, so that the revenue, and consequently the means of resisting the enemy, were considerably diminished. But the king showed himself ready to make great personal sacrifices for his country's sake—offered to reduce the royal expenditure to the lowest possible limit, and to contribute to the cost of the war all the money he could spare, and all the royal valuables, as well as those belonging to the house of Braganza. His generosity touched and stimulated the Cortes. Through them the whole nation learned how nobly the king was supporting the cause of Portugal, and money flowed into the state coffers in quite surprising abundance.

The foreign dominions of Portugal acknowledged the Braganza dynasty one by one. Madeira first, then St. Miguel; soon afterwards most of the possessions in Africa, America, and Asia. But Portugal itself was threatened by the Spaniards, and the Dutch were resolved to ruin the commerce of the Portuguese abroad. In Portugal, before the new taxes imposed by the Cortes of 1641 were paid, the treasury was empty. Trade, too, was at the opening of the reign almost stagnant. Then there was no army, no arsenal—only a few ships and guns. Some influential nobles also went over to Spain, and others who did not openly desert occupied themselves in intriguing against the king's government and life. Yet a fortunate congeries of affairs delivered the king and Portugal out of the majority of their straits.

Those envious members of noble Portuguese families who

could not bear the extraordinary elevation of the Braganzas, and left their country rather than accept the situation, were outlawed and had their property confiscated. But the conduct of a number of disaffected persons who remained in Portugal was much more difficult to deal with. Under the mask of acquiescence in the new order of things, they contrived a plot which had for its object the murder of the sovereign, the overthrow of the new dynasty, and the restoration of the kingdom to the Spaniards. The Archbishop of Braga was the moving spirit of the conspiracy. He had been the chief adviser of the ex-vice-queen, and suffered unspeakable annoyance when, at the revolution, he saw his occupation gone. The archbishop gained over some noblemen who had been or fancied themselves badly used with regard to the distribution of government places. But in the endeavour to win more adherents, the agents of the conspirators made the mistake of dropping a hint to one or two for whom they were angling, without having tested the feelings of their men beforehand. The result was that the plot was blown upon. The king quietly arranged for the apprehension of the traitors. He ordered a muster of military in the vicinity of the palace on a certain day, on the pretext that he wished to review them. He judged this precaution necessary because he did not know the strength of the malcontents. For the same day he arranged a meeting of the council of state. The incriminated nobles came to the meeting, and were arrested as they made their appearance. On the 28th of August 1641 followed the execution of the three most distinguished lay conspirators, the Marquis of Villa-Real, the Duke of Caminha (his son), and the Count of Armamar. Others, found guilty, were sentenced to various terms of imprisonment. The Archbishop of Braga and another influential clerical conspirator, the inquisitor-general, had their lives spared on account of their sacred calling, but were placed in strict confinement. The archbishop died a prisoner. His companion, however, was, out of misplaced pity, released two years afterwards and reinstated in his office.

The storm having burst, the kingdom was calmer than it had been since the accession. Many who were for various reasons disposed to favour Spain were now terrified into the repression of their inclination. The affair was of real benefit to the king and the realm. The sympathy of the people was aroused for their sovereign, and their hatred of Spain being refreshed by the discovery of these desperate machinations, they were the more eager to proceed with operations for the national defence. The king, after his deliverance, carried on the more zealously negotiations with other powers for their support and assistance against his natural foe. Richelieu, whose policy was continually directed towards the weakening of Spain, cordially joined hands with John IV., and promised twenty ships of war to assist the Portuguese fleet in blockading Spanish ports and capturing Spanish vessels. The cardinal, moreover, caused information to be conveyed to the United States of Holland that they should be welcomed in the anti-Spanish league. But, unfortunately for Portugal, the great minister died in the end of 1642, and his successor, Mazarin, was too much under the influence of the French regent, Anne of Austria, to adopt decided measures of hostility to Spain.

About this time (1642) that congress of European powers took place in Münster regarding a general peace which concluded the Treaty of Westphalia. Portugal, like the other states, was represented by a plenipotentiary. But the Spanish commissioner objected to the words " King of Portugal " in the credentials of the delegate of John IV., and threatened to withdraw if the independence of that country were recognized. The delegate of France attempted to settle the dispute, but, Mazarin being minister, not with all his heart ; and the diplomatic haggling over this matter was so protracted and vexatious that the Congress of Münster, terminating so happily for the rest of Europe, was ever after a very sore point with John.

Holland was certainly a declared and determined enemy of Spain, yet it pursued its attacks upon Portuguese possessions in the East and West notwithstanding the severance of the two Iberian kingdoms. But the Portuguese would not go to war with the Dutch for their dominions abroad with Spain waiting for an opportunity of invading their home. So a ten years' truce was arranged between King John and the States of Holland, for the purpose of engaging in a united attack on their common enemy. The wording of the treaty was much in favour of the Dutch, and those articles which seemed disadvantageous to them they knew how to cleverly steer clear of. And further, they used the time which was to elapse before the publication of the bond for seizing all they could lay hands on abroad belonging to Portugal. Thus, even when their fleet was on the way to assist King John against Spain, the States were robbing him with might and main in foreign parts. England, aflame with civil war, and Denmark in alliance with Austria and dependent on Spain, could render no aid. So Portugal was left pretty much to its own resources. Holland was a peculiar kind of ally, for, as we have seen, it was smiting the king with one hand while it helped him with the other.

At Rome also the Spanish ambassador strove to prevent a recognition of the Braganza line, and with such success that only on the conclusion of a peace with Spain, twenty years after King John's accession, was the desired acknowledgment obtained from the Pope. The worst of this complication was that it put back the hands of the clock in Portugal with regard to ecclesiastical affairs, since it afforded the Pope a pretext for interfering with the Portuguese Church *pendente lite.* The king could not exercise the prerogative of presentation to benefices till his right to the throne had been allowed by the

Romish see, and the head of the Church himself proceeded to exercise that function. John III., Sebastian, Henry, and especially the Philips, had suffered Rome to regain much power which had been wrested from it in the national interests by former kings. Now John IV. saw the Portuguese Church made more dependent upon it than ever. Even after the king had been received as sovereign prince, the hand of Rome, which cannot be easily shaken off, pressed more heavily on the Church of Portugal than on any other communion. It was the inquisitor-general who pointed out to the pontifical chair its opportunity of magnifying itself in Portugal—that plotter against the king's life and the liberties of his country who had been justly incarcerated, and as unwisely set free to use his craft for enslaving Portugal in one way or another.

The inevitable fight with Spain began in earnest in 1644, not to speak of previous skirmishes with various results. The Portuguese army was willing though small, and the fact that the flower of the Spanish soldiery were busy in Catalonia told greatly in favour of Portugal. The troops which could be employed against it were indeed superior in numbers to its own, but were mostly raw recruits who had never smelt powder. The first important encounter took place near Badajoz. The Portuguese, under the intrepid and experienced Albuquerque, had their ranks at the beginning of the fray broken by the enemy's cavalry, and the Spaniards, thinking the day theirs, had already begun to plunder the Portuguese baggage and dead, when Albuquerque rallied his infantry and drove the Spanish army across the Guadiana after six hours' fighting. The Spanish lost three thousand men, and left on the field a great quantity of weapons. The Portuguese loss was about nine hundred.

The following year, however, a severe defeat was suffered by the troops of Portugal near Villa Viciosa ; and again in 1646, after he had taken the fortress of Telena, Albuquerque met with a disaster at the hands of a Spanish force, which retook the place and forced him to retreat. Eight hundred Portuguese fell or were made prisoners at the affair of Telena. From that time, during the remaining years of John's reign, the war was continued on a smaller scale. Skirmishes, such as marked its beginning, took the place of pitched battles. Had Spain been in a better condition, Telena might have been followed by the conquest of Portugal. But the Catalonian revolt had not yet been suppressed. On the contrary, it had grown more serious. There was now also trouble in Naples and the Netherlands, and even in the court at Madrid a dangerous turmoil of parties. All these things used up the strength of Spain and spared its neighbour the disgrace of the Spanish yoke.

Though Philip could not subdue Portugal by force of arms, his malignity found a means of striking a blow at the heart of his rival. King John had a brother Edward, who, as a volunteer in the army of the Emperor Ferdinand, had served the Austrian cause with distinguished courage and faithfulness. Him the King of Spain caused Ferdinand to imprison, in contravention of all the laws of hospitality and gratitude. There was nothing against Edward but the mind of Philip. Yet that was enough. The King of Portugal by persuasion, the offer of money, and the good offices of foreign powers, sought to compass the freedom of his brother, but in vain. Edward was conveyed from prison to prison, and after eight years of confinement, which grew always more rigorous, died in a Milanese fortress just before the sentence of capital punishment which Philip had obtained against him could be executed. His death was a grief to the King of Spain, because the noble prisoner had so escaped the axe. Edward was, by all accounts, a person of worth—a scholar, an amiable, brave, and pure-minded man. That such as he must endure treatment of this sort from the ignorant, licentious, and "most Catholic" king, for no offence except that he was brother to the King of Portugal, is one of the grossest scandals in the scandalous story of Philip IV.

While the attitude of Spain necessitated constant watchfulness on the frontier—though from various causes Philip was providentially kept from accomplishing his nefarious designs upon Portugal—fighting was going on between the Dutch and the inhabitants of Portuguese colonies in different quarters with very different results. In Brazil the colonists had succeeded, before the publication of the truce already mentioned, in recovering a fortress or two; and when Prince Maurice of Nassau had withdrawn, pursuant to the treaty, with the best part of the Dutch garrison, the Brazilian Portuguese, not considering themselves bound by an agreement entered into without their knowledge or consent, rose *en masse* and drove their masters completely out of the territory. Thus Brazil, which had been in the possession of Holland for thirty years, was in 1649 restored to the Portuguese. Angola in Africa, the island of St. Thomas, and other places were, in a similar way and about the same time, recovered from the Dutch. When the news reached Europe, Portugal was delighted and the States-General correspondingly enraged. Fearful of an attempt on the part of the Dutch to retake what they had lost, John IV. appealed to England for help. He was promised aid, but instead Cromwell sent Admiral Blake with a fleet to threaten him.

The reason of the hostile demonstration was this. The King of Portugal had afforded Prince Rupert, so celebrated in connection with the civil war in England, and his brother Maurice a refuge in his realm. Admiral Blake came to demand the persons of the princes. King John would not deliver them up after they had fled to him for protection, and Blake thereupon captured fifteen ships of the Brazilian fleet, which, unconscious of any danger, was nearing Lisbon. John's troublesome guests left Portugal of their own accord, and so ended the dispute; but the Protector would do nothing for a country which had been an asylum for his enemies. Nevertheless, as war broke out in 1652 between England and Holland, the object of Por tugal was gained and Brazil preserved. In the East, however, it did not go well with the Portuguese. One place after another fell into the hands of the Dutch, and when peace was concluded with England in 1654 reinforcements from Holland were despatched to India. Colombo, the capital of Ceylon, was taken by the troops of the States-General in 1656, and two years afterwards the whole island was theirs. The loss of Ceylon gave the Portuguese influence in India a deadly blow. The king had heard enough about his "fortunate star," but now, he thought, it seemed to have paled. "Would God," he said, "I could give up the East Indies with honour!" As a devotee of the Romish faith, he shuddered at the idea of heretics lording it in those regions where the Kings of Portugal had been charged with the duty of protecting the true religion. But he could not help fearing, to quote his own expression, "that the number of Portuguese states, separated from each other by such great distances, would lead to the loss of them all."

John IV. died in 1656, the year in which the Dutch successfully besieged Colombo. He was predeceased by his eldest son Theodosius, Prince of Brazil (which title of Portuguese kings' sons and heirs this prince was the first to bear). Taken away at the age of nineteen, his case reminds us of Alfonso's, the son of John II. Like Alfonso, Theodosius was one whose opening career prophesied the very best things for Portugal. He was remarkable for his scholarly attainments, particularly in languages and mathematics; showed great aptitude for the science of war; to all was constant and genuine, and his morals were blameless. John IV., however, was not, like his predecessor and namesake, without an heir on the death of Theodosius. He had other two sons, and a daughter, who is known to readers of English history as Catherine of Braganza, wife of Charles II. But, unhappily, the son who should succeed the admirable Theodosius was in character diametrically opposite. The nation lost the hope of a Hyperion and obtained a satyr.

Alfonso VI., so was the young king named, was from his childhood intractable. His chief playmates were the street arabs of Lisbon. In stealing away to join them he exercised an ingenuity which got over every impediment placed in his way. The favourite haunt of his boyhood was the royal stables, where he delighted in witnessing dog-fights and encounters between representatives of the dregs of the population with fists and knives. He was only a little over thirteen years when he became king. But for some time his sovereignty was merely nominal. The queen-mother, according to use and wont in such circumstances, was the actual ruler, and, considering the objectionable proclivities of her son, was naturally anxious to retain her power as long as possible. But when Alfonso had reached the age of eighteen his mother was forced to resign the government into his hands. The queen's discharge came about in this way. A sly Italian of the shopkeeper class had by flattery and pandering to his vices wormed himself into the king's favour so far as to seem indispensable to the vicious lad's enjoyment. The pecuniary gifts by which Alfonso testified his affection for his odious favourite were enormous, and these lavish rewards, or the intimacy between the king and such a man which they betokened, roused the extreme displeasure of the queen and her counsellors. Accordingly the object of their antipathy was arrested and transported to Brazil. The king was beside himself with rage. One of his lords-in-waiting, a man of talent and ambition, thought he might improve the opportunity for making his own fortune. He expressed sympathy with the king therefore on account of the affront, and advised him to assert his independence forthwith and snatch the sceptre from his mother's grasp. The king consented, and permitted his crafty mentor, the Count of Castello-Melhor, to arrange the details of the scheme. Castello-Melhor soon gained a party among the nobles out of office, and when at a specified time Alfonso announced his intention of reigning now in fact as well as in name, the queen-mother was compelled to sign her abdication in 1662.

Many regretted the queen's withdrawal from affairs, for all along she had shown herself capable of dealing with state matters firmly and prudently. She quickly saw through difficulties, and adjusted them with credit to herself and advantage to the nation. A Castilian by birth, she was true to her adopted country, and stood like a rock against the pretensions of Spain. But Castello-Melhor thought nothing of the injury which this noble lady sustained by her abrupt dismissal. He was consumed by thirst for influential position. Kicking his heels in the royal ante-chamber did not suit him at all. He saw an open door, and entered, reckless of aught but his own chance. The place he gained was a splendid one. Of course he became first minister of the crown. Any other appointment was impossible. And the disposition of the king made him as great as a minister could be, for Alfonso had no ideas about governing. He was simply led by those who knew how to humour him. His tastes were as depraved as ever. He associated with the most notorious profligates of the capital, and was himself not behind the worst of them. He was in the habit of sallying forth after nightfall with a gang of villains, who perpetrated all sorts of outrages upon harmless citizens. In short, he was hopeless, and after the resignation of his mother, as vile as ever. Shakespeare's roistering prince could throw off his loose behaviour with increase of responsibility, that—

> "Like bright metal on a sullen ground,
> His reformation, glittering o'er his fault,
> Should show more goodly."

But not so Alfonso. He was radically bad. What might not a man like Castello-Melhor do with a king of this stamp—one whose heart was in midnight brawls and revelry, whose speech was the dialect of loafers and thieves, who had so obstinately refused to receive even the beggarly elements of knowledge that he could neither read nor write!

The count, however, was an efficient minister, and by the wisdom he evinced in the conduct both of home and foreign affairs undoubtedly won respect from many who detested the unscrupulous manner in which he had clambered into office. Plots were hatched to overturn him; but he got timely intimation of them, and they were adroitly circumvented. Much of the satisfaction which existed with his *régime* arose from successes achieved against Spain in the field. These put the Portuguese into high good-humour; but Castello-Melhor had little even indirect merit in the matter. If fortitude and sagacity could have done much for Portugal against its old enemy, the ex-queen, in whom these qualities were conspicuous, would have kept the Spaniard at bay. But, considering the condition in which the country stood, she needed greatly the backing of foreign powers. This she could not obtain, for France, in which she trusted most, was a broken reed. The wily Mazarin had fair speeches for her and nothing else. So, though she would not bate a jot of Portugal's right of independent existence, she saw to her sorrow, and without adequate means of resistance, Spanish sieges and ravages on Portuguese soil.

The situation was much improved in Castello-Melhor's day. Mazarin's death had broken the close relations of France with Austria, and, through Austria, with Spain. Louis XIV. had no objections to crush Spain and everybody else, and willingly lent Portugal not only troops, but also his marshal, Count Schomberg, one of the greatest military leaders of the period. The marriage of King Alfonso's sister Catherine to Charles II. of England had also secured for Portugal the interest of the English Government, and three thousand auxiliaries were lent by them to support Schomberg's operations.

Don John of Austria, who was not much behind his name-sake, the hero of Lepanto, in talents and renown, commanded the Spanish forces, and, Schomberg notwithstanding, pressed into Alemtejo, and took Evora, its principal town. On receipt of the intelligence the populace of Lisbon lost their heads. The Spaniards, in their panic-stricken imagination, were already at their gates. The city was in an uproar, and the baser sort were about to institute a pandemonium; but the government managed to calm the people by getting the king to put his head out at a window of the palace and assure them that all was well. It was a quack medicine for their trouble, but it served. Soon afterwards news came of a tremendous defeat which Schomberg inflicted upon Don John at Amerial in June 1662. Four thousand Spaniards fell on that field; six thousand were made prisoners.*

The Portuguese followed up their victory by retaking Evora, and an explosion of the powder magazine in the castle of Avronches, also held by the Spaniards, ruined that fortress, and caused the death of many of the garrison. Thereupon Don John, having had enough of the Portuguese campaign, left the country in 1663. On his disappearance numbers of the mercenaries whom he had left to guard the frontier deserted to Schomberg. Next year another great fight occurred at Montes Claros, near Estremos in Alemtejo. It ended in the discomfiture of the Spaniards, and may be said to have extinguished the war. Spain had neither money nor able-bodied men enough to continue the contest, and no general who could take the field against the indomitable Schomberg.

But though the Count of Castello-Melhor made capital out of these brilliant military exploits, his ruin was impending. The ex-queen could not bear him, and she saw that he was virtual sovereign, the king being but his tool. She wished that her second son, Pedro, had been her elder. The Infant Pedro far

---

* In the battle of Amerial, by the way, the English rendered splendid service. But as they were only heretics, the Portuguese considered three pounds of snuff to each company sufficient wages. The heretics were ungrateful enough to receive this reward with scorn and maledictions. They were paid eventually out of the English treasury.

surpassed his brother, as indeed he might well do without being anything extraordinary, in ability, culture, and conduct. The wish was impossible, but the question remained, Why should not the Infant supplant one who was so plainly inefficient—a mere senseless instrument in the hands of an upstart? The suggestion was made, and Castello-Melhor heard of it. He knew that Pedro's rise would be his own fall, and he resolved to checkmate the queen's or the Infant's party. In the ex-queen's time a project had been mooted of marrying Alfonso to the French princess Marie, daughter of the Duke of Nemours. The count took steps to carry out this project, judging shrewdly that France would, in the event of that union, take care of the king's interests. The marriage took place, but the result had not the least correspondence with the minister's expectations. The princess did not know the kind of creature to whom she was going to be wedded, and when she discovered his character was naturally disgusted. Yet for a time she made no protest, because she was not only the wife of Alfonso, but a political agent of Louis XIV. She had the secret commission to gain access to the Portuguese cabinet, and report what occurred there to her relative the French king. The count resented her intrusion when she asked to be present at cabinet meetings, and complained to his nominal master. Alfonso obeyed his minister like a child in things political, and bade his queen, on the count's suggestion, mind her own affairs. Alfonso's rudeness knew no bounds, and the young queen felt she had been tied to an ogre, and was now denied the only compensation she could obtain for his repulsive companionship, that of being known at the court of France as an important personage.

The party of the Infant, becoming aware of the estrangement, rejoiced. They used every art to widen the breach. The Infant himself condoled with the poor young queen, in a strange land, with a hateful husband, whose minister was allowed to trample on her feelings and make a cipher of her where she had intended to shine. It was dangerous for her to accept the Infant's condolences. She was young, and he was very kind. They grew more and more intimate. The king paid no attention to his wife. He preferred the company of drunken debauchees. The end of it all was that the queen and Pedro were enamoured of each other. She threatened to return to France, and in the meantime retired to a convent. The French court saw that matters could not possibly be smoothed over, and took the side of the Infant. Here, then, was a resistless coalition, on the strength of which Pedro could demand the dismissal of the obnoxious minister. The king, stupified as he usually was in a crisis, and associating the count with that bad business of his marriage, was half persuaded, half forced to consent, and Castello-Melhor fell. And then he was exposed to his foes— surrounded by them as by angry waves—like a shipwrecked sailor on a bare islet in mid-ocean, helpless and wretched. He had not a friend.

Now the game was in the hands of Pedro. He got his brother declared incapable of ruling, as indeed he was, and taught Alfonso to scrawl his signature at the bottom of a deed of abdication. History is silent as to how the king was led or dragged to surrender his crown. At all events, in November 1667, he did so, and, in the following January, Pedro was nominated at a meeting of the Cortes "curator of the king's person, prince and governor of Portugal." Alfonso, in the first place, endured a period of imprisonment in the palace, was then banished to Terceira, and from Terceira brought to the castle of Cintra, where, in 1683, the curtain fell upon his disgraceful life. Nobody missed him—his wife least of all; for not long after the abdication, she obtained a divorce, and emerged from her asylum to become, by the usual Papal dispensation, obtained through her uncle's mediation, the Cardinal de Vendôme, the bride of the Regent Pedro.

It was France which smoothed Pedro's path to the regency.

The influence of France is also easily seen in the marriage of a Portuguese princess to the English monarch. Such a union was plainly in the interest of Louis, for England at that time was pretty much in his hands, and by bringing that country and Portugal together, he discouraged Spain, the discomfiture of which was his fixed purpose. Louis XIV. was not yet the terror of Europe, but already he had become a great factor in the politics of the Continent. It was he also, though not consciously, who brought about peace between Spain and Portugal. Sir Robert Southwell, the English ambassador, was the direct agent, and used in his negotiations the fact that Spanish prisoners of note, who should be given up in the event of peace, were held by the Portuguese, as a chief reason for the establishment of an understanding between the belligerents. He might not have made much capital of the point, but Spain, having struggled in vain to avert the English marriage, was aware that Louis had won the game, and assented not only to a cessation of hostilities, but to a permanent peace, and to the acknowledgment of Portugal as an independent sovereignty. Louis, for his own part, would rather have had the strain sustained a while, to give Spain enough work on its western border, but he could not openly object to the turn which affairs took under Southwell's guidance. So, in February 1668, there was an end of the twenty-six years' war which had inflicted so many wounds upon both countries.

England and Portugal were at this time on the best terms. Charles II. had got Princess Catherine, and England, through her, Tangier and Bombay, with their spheres of influence. These slices of its foreign possessions were granted by Portugal on condition that England should help it to defend the rest. The friendly footing on which Portugal stood with Britain was not without influence on the attitude of the States-General. Holland, too, entered into a treaty in 1661, resigning Brazil in consideration of a money payment, and stipulating for the retention of all former Portuguese possessions in the East and West Indies which the Dutch held at the date of the bond. But the Dutch East India Company were not content with the terms, and proceeded to take Portuguese towns on the Malabar coast. In 1669, however, the difficulty was arranged, and an agreement signed at the Hague.

The party which had lifted Pedro to his high place, and the people who had rent the air with their acclamations when they saw the wretched Alfonso overwhelmed, were inclined to drop, in remembrance of their service to him, that respect for the regent's person which Portuguese rulers had been wont to expect and obtain. Sir Robert Southwell feared that half a century would be required before the due order would prevail in the relation of vassals and populace to the seat of supreme authority. John I. had come to the throne in a way somewhat similar; but he was a commanding figure, and Pedro only a very ordinary individual; and, moreover, John I. swam into power on the crest of a wave of victory. Yet Pedro II. was a long-headed, patient, and reasonable man. He could wait for the growth of subordination, and meantime held his own quietly, without demanding too much. So, although there was a possibility in Alfonso's lifetime of revolt, whenever this clique or that did not get all its own way, the grumbling of malcontents never set the heather on fire, and on his brother's decease no opposition to Pedro's coronation made itself well heard.

His friends were apt to magnify Pedro's qualifications, which was natural when they compared him with Alfonso. But taken out of the rosy sheen of eulogy, and seen in daylight, there was nothing remarkable about him. He spoke good Spanish and Portuguese, whereas his brother knew only the slang of the streets. He could conduct himself with propriety in public, understand affairs, and speak to the point. He minded his business, and put on no airs. He cared for the administration of justice, put down highway robbery with a firm hand, and would not permit those Mohock raids in which his predecessor delighted to engage. One could go anywhere at all hours of the night in Pedro's time without insult or injury. As to his private life, his dress and his table were plain. He ate very moderately and of the simplest dishes, and in these days of temperance reform it is interesting to note that Pedro II. was a total abstainer from fermented liquor—would, in fact, on no account allow it to be placed on his board. He was strictly attentive to the offices of the Romish Church; could be often heard whispering to himself Hail Maries and Paternosters; and showed considerable zeal in sending missionaries to the heathen. Tall, and of astonishing corporal strength, he liked to take part in manly exercises—hunting of wild oxen and so forth. So much was he addicted to dangerous sports that his queen, whose affection for him was as sincere as her disgust for her former husband, constrained him to give them up on account of her dread that his bleeding corpse should be brought home after one of these escapades.

There is another part of the king's life over which we would willingly draw a veil. It would not be a correct portrait of the man, however, were we to omit the statement that he was frightfully profligate, probably as much so as his brother, although Pedro had tact enough to be a serious politician in his council and a gentleman in refined society. It is somewhat amazing that there is no record of a domestic breach in consequence of his flagitious behaviour.

The influence of France was very great in the regency of Pedro and the earlier part of his reign. The queen's French extraction brought many ladies of that nationality to Portugal. Not a few of these Frenchwomen were married to Portuguese persons of quality, and Queen Marie and her fellow-countrywomen pushed vigorously the cause of France. Those marriages were encouraged, at the instigation of Louis XIV., by the queen and the French ambassador, in order to further the

French king's design of succeeding to the throne of Spain. It was desirable, in the event of his seeing his opportunity, to have Spain's next neighbour well bound to him. The Jesuits, too, rendered Louis every assistance. They had been zealous partisans of Spain in the day of its strength. Now they had fled from a falling house. This coalition of women and Jesuits to win Portugal over to the side of Louis did not, however, meet with success. Pedro and the Portuguese wished to remain neutral; for if Portugal were a party in the strife when the great powers collided, it would be likely to meet the fate of the earthenware pot between the vessels of iron. The matter by-and-by developed into the famous contention which had to be settled by the War of the Spanish Succession, wherein Marlborough covered himself with glory.

It was briefly this, for, except in so far as it touches Portugal, we have nothing to do with it here. Louis should have had a double right to the Spanish crown—the then King of Spain, Charles II., being without issue—as husband of Charles's sister and as the son of Philip IV.'s sister (Charles's aunt). But he had renounced that right for himself and his heirs. The Austrian was a rival claim. The emperor, Leopold I., had married a younger sister of Charles II., and had made no renunciation. His right was good therefore. During the life of his grandchild, the Electoral Prince of Bavaria, however, it was understood that he did not design to prosecute his own claim, having regard to the jealousy with which the great powers would view a union of Spain and Austria, but preferred that the prince should succeed. Yet the prince's claim was also vitiated by his father's renunciation in his name, and had the Bavarian claimant lived, Louis would have been as much in order as he. But the electoral prince died in 1700, and Leopold then put himself forward as true heir, through his mother, Philip IV.'s youngest sister. Nevertheless, the emperor designated for the conciliation of Europe his second son, the Archduke Charles, as successor to the Spanish sovereignty. Louis, not to be outdone in policy, named the Duke of Anjou, second son of the dauphin, as representative of the French claim, and manœuvred so that Charles II. was induced to approve the duke's candidature in his will. When the King of Spain died, Philip of Anjou entered Madrid, and was well received. But England, Holland, and Austria, as the Grand Alliance, declared war against France in 1702, as it was completely patent that Louis XIV. had the control of Spain, and that Philip was a mere nonentity.

The King of Portugal's design to steer clear of the troublesome succession question was by-and-by broken through by force of circumstances. Events drew him more and more to the side of Austria. The queen died in 1683, and with her much of the French influence in Portugal. Louis, now less hopeful of Pedro, began to use stronger arguments to draw him over. The harbours of the Portuguese and various other resources would be useful to him in the event of an outbreak of hostilities. But Pedro was well aware of the endeavour, on the part of Louis, after despotic power in Europe, and believed that after swallowing Spain, the voracious Frenchman would not be satiated without little Portugal. So in 1703 he joined the Alliance. The campaigns of Marlborough convinced him that he had been wise in doing so, for when less than three months had elapsed Blenheim was won, and two years thereafter the allies had another first-rate triumph at Ramilies. In 1706, some six months after Ramilies, Pedro II. died. The Spanish succession affair was still far from a settlement. (There were, in fact, yet nearly eight years till the Peace of Utrecht.) In 1704 the archduke landed at Lisbon, and was received as Charles III. of Spain. Next year the brilliant Earl of Peterborough arrived with an English fleet and five thousand Dutch and English soldiers, took on board the Austrian claimant, and sailed for Barcelona, with whose capture he began his series of magnificent exploits. But Peterborough's enemies at the En-

glish court procured his recall.   Charles himself was found to
lack energy, and all Castile was for the Bourbon king.   Pedro,
however, continued to believe in the cause of the archduke, and
with his dying breath exhorted his heir to cleave to that side.

Another international agreement, of date December 1703,
the celebrated "Methuen Treaty," so called after the English
ambassador, entered into with Great Britain, had an important
and disadvantageous bearing on Portugal.   According to that
bond, one-third of the import duty on wines was to be remitted
to Portuguese consignments at the English custom-house (while
French wines were still to be charged at the higher figure), in
consideration of woollen goods from England being permitted to
enter Portugal on too easy terms for the latter power.   This
arrangement crippled for half a century the sheep-breeding and
woollen industries of Portugal.   But the prospect of stimulating
the vine culture in the land was an alluring one, and blinded
the Portuguese signatories to the danger of depressing other
great interests upon which many were dependent.   Undoubtedly
a remarkable fillip was given to the cultivation of the grape,
chiefly in the Douro district, by the "Methuen Treaty;" yet
the gain was not, by a great way, equal to the loss which the
agreement entailed.   It must be remembered, however, in ex-
culpation of those who, in Portugal, assented to the bargain,
that 1703 was the year in which that country joined the Grand
Alliance, and being now in a position of hostility to France,
Portugal was extremely anxious to purchase a friendship which
could fend off French reprisals.

The Prince of Brazil, on whom his father enjoined fidelity to
the Alliance, was as good as his word to the dying man, till
the Alliance itself went to pieces.   Scarcely out of his boyhood
when, as John V., he received the homage of the Cortes, he
was aware of his inexperience, and leaned on men who had a
good report for astuteness and familiarity with public matters.
One adviser whom he chose was Castello-Melhor.   But John V.

was not likely to follow the course of his uncle, and let himself be made a tool of even by Castello-Melhor. The king gave himself, under the guidance of these men, to the study of practical politics. Then he broke his leading-strings, and showed a decision of character which much astonished the statesmen in whose circle he had till that time expressed himself with a certain amount of hesitancy. That irresolution ceased with his political apprenticeship. Thenceforward he showed a determination which often amounted to stubbornness, and exercised a masterful sway, which was only now again possible, for Sir Robert Southwell's half-century was just about run, and the turbulent and self-assertive spirits who clamoured for recognition were pretty well subdued. Of the determination in upholding his authority which John V. displayed, sometimes at considerable hazard, there are many illustrations. On one occasion, when an English man-of-war, lying in the Tagus, had impressed a few Portuguese seamen, he ordered the vessel to be detained till the captives were given up, and the forts on the river to fire on the ship till they sank her should she dare to put to sea without acceding to his wish. Considering the relative strength of Portugal and England, such a nailing up of his colours indicated a doggedness akin to temerity. At another time, when the once all-powerful Society of Jesus in Portugal declined to meet his views, he threatened to ship every man of them away to one of those bare rocks which are found outside the Portuguese coast, unless they submitted, which they accordingly did with the best grace possible.

The Abbé de Mornay, French ambassador, has drawn the king's portrait for us in a despatch to his government. John V. was a well-built, handsome man, if somewhat swarthy, with lively, piercing eyes, and a majestic bearing. His mental vision also was penetrating. He knew how to select the best men for special work. His ambassadors, for instance, were chosen with a fine perception of qualifications necessary for the

particular court to which each was accredited. It must not be
forgotten that it was John V. who found and employed as a
diplomatist Sebastian Joseph de Carvalho, afterwards the Marquis of Pombal, one of the most capable of ministers, a man as
eminent as any to whom Portugal has given birth. The last
king had been a man of fair education, but John V. would have
passed as a well-educated person at a time when the schoolmaster
had gone much further abroad. He had a special predilection for
mathematics, and took up that study as a recreation whenever
he was wearied with official burdens. As might be expected
from a man of this stamp, John V. was a great patron of
learning. He founded the " Portuguese Royal Society of
History," built and stored a magnificent library at the University of Coimbra, and in many other ways promoted the
intellectual growth of his kingdom.

His great fault was extravagance, especially in the matter of
building. The colossal edifice at Mafra, some eighteen miles
north of Lisbon, proves that his passion for such work fairly
ran away with his judgment. Mafra took about sixteen years
to build, from ten to twelve thousand labourers were employed
in its erection, and the expense was enormous. It was intended for a monument of the new Portugal, and is a palace,
church, and convent in one, adorned with every shade of
marble and the most exquisite mosaics, and dazzles the eyes
with the manifold and brilliant play of colour of lapis lazuli,
porphyry, amethyst, chrysolite, alabaster, silver, and gold.
Upon another building, the miniature chapel of St. John
Baptist at Lisbon, whose dimensions were only seventeen feet
by .twelve, he laid out £225,000. The splendour of John's
court, too, was in striking contrast to that of his father. In
fact, the regal pomp maintained in the first half of the eighteenth
century probably eclipsed anything of the kind ever seen in
Portugal.

But while all this cost was being incurred, the land was

suffering from poverty. The gold mines of Brazil were yielding immense sums, and diamonds from thence were coming
into the country in fabulous quantities,* nevertheless all
the king's income and more was squandered for the most
part on buildings like Mafra, on his majesty's household, or
in lavish gifts to his friends. Moreover, all the treasures from
Portuguese colonies destined for the royal coffers did not reach
them. There were many itching palms. Still there was .
abundance for the king to spend; and if he was in some
respects a good ruler, and cannot be charged with immorality
like his father's, there is occasion in regard to his misuse of the
royal revenue for a charge against him of the most senseless
prodigality. Though the financial condition of Portugal grew
so distressing that the people had to be withheld by stringent
legislation from fleeing in thousands out of the country, the
king calmly scattered his gold as if the treasury at Lisbon had
been the purse of Fortunatus. Even works of a useful kind,
such as the aqueduct at Alcantara, were carried out in a style
that corresponded little with his limited resources. His taste
for display was evinced also in the elevation of the See of
Lisbon to the rank of a patriarchate—a privilege which he
procured for his capital from Pope Clement XI. The succeeding Pope gave to the Patriarch of Lisbon the dignity of a
cardinal, and his chapter were ranked with bishops. That step
in the ecclesiastical peerage which the Bishop of Lisbon obtained
only strengthened the Romish Church, always too strong in
Portugal; by so much weakened the civil authority; and cost a
good deal of Brazilian gold, which had to be minted for the establishment and endowment of the patriarchate. For his generosity to the Church, John V. was granted the right of calling
himself the " most faithful king," a reward which cost the Pope
nothing, and gave much pleasure to the devout Portuguese.

* Many valuable diamonds came into and still remain in the possession of Portuguese
noble families. The celebrated Braganza diamond, however, weighing 1,680 carats, is
said by some connoisseurs to be only a topaz.

Resolutely clinging to the Grand Alliance, the king married, as an emphatic declaration of his policy, the Archduchess Maria Anna, sister of the emperor, in spite of Louis XIV., who opposed the union with all his might. But the Austrian claimant succeeded to the imperial crown, and England, which could not contemplate with equanimity an Emperor of Austria as King of Spain, withdrew from the Alliance in 1712. This move which England made necessitated an agreement on the part of Portugal, in 1713, to a truce with France and Spain. Still the two Peninsular kingdoms were not fast friends, and every now and again the danger of a rupture became imminent. Louis XIV. was indefatigable in his efforts to keep the peace between these irritable neighbours, because he feared that, though Portugal would probably make a poor fight alone, England, tired, in 1712, of war and Marlborough, was inclined now to support that country in a Spanish quarrel. In 1715, however, Louis died, and the antipathy became immediately more pronounced. The correspondence between the governments was far from conciliatory, and the dogs of war were evidently straining at the leash.

An occurrence at Madrid in 1735 brought the estrangement to a point. In the rescue of a prisoner from the officers of justice, some footmen of the Portuguese ambassador took part. The Spanish government, in consequence, sent a company of soldiers to the envoy's house, arrested all the servants whom they could find, and put them in the jail. The cabinet of Portugal, retaliating, arrested in Lisbon a corresponding number of the Spanish ambassador's lackeys, and bade the Portuguese minister at Madrid withdraw from the court. Great Britain, hearing of the jangle, promised Portugal, if it should take the field, two thousand men and twenty war vessels, and did actually send a fleet to the Tagus. But the mediation of France, while the two nations at variance were just on the brink of a campaign, succeeded in laying the storm, and in

1737 a peace was subscribed, to the real satisfaction of John V., who, anticipating warfare, had been compelled for the time to cease his building operations while he looked into the state of his army and navy ; and he had found, to his amazement, that his forces were in the most wretched condition. There is no doubt that the Spaniards knew better than the King of Portugal the state of his defences, and, if England had not kept them off, would have broken them in pieces. Spain and France, however, were much too weak at that time to brave the wrath of England. Had Spain understood, as France did then, that England saw in the independence of Portugal the balance of power in Europe guaranteed, it would not have been so ready to take umbrage.

The peace was kept during the rest of the "most faithful king's" reign, and when at his death in 1750 Joseph, Prince of Brazil, succeeded him, there was no special apprehension of hostilities from Spain or any other quarter. But the financial affairs of the country had been left, by the extravagance of the last sovereign, in a pitiable and indeed almost desperate state. It was a crisis in which a statesman of more than ordinary power was required to stop the immense leakage in the treasury and banish the fear of national insolvency. King Joseph himself, an amiable and upright man, was one who could not stand alone. In a crisis he was subject to intellectual paralysis, a result, perhaps, of his father's treatment. John V. had utter confidence in himself, and disliked interference from any. He was jealous of his sons, and peremptorily forbade their taking even a small part in public business. When Joseph, therefore, received into his hands the charge of affairs, he felt himself utterly ignorant of politics. He had hitherto principally given himself up to the pleasures of the chase and to the study of music. To the exercise of his new vocation he could only bring honesty and good-will.

In these circumstances, he had the fortune to light upon one of those men whom his father had engaged in the service of the country, Sebastian Carvalho, than whom he could not have found a stronger prop though he had travelled through the length and breadth of Europe. Carvalho, the son of a country gentleman of moderate means, had even in youth devoted himself to public life. He had read sedulously in political science and history, always with a view to practical work; and, as a young man, had such a reputation for proficiency in these subjects that he was elected a member of the Portuguese Academy, and invited to prepare a historical pamphlet, with which King John was delighted. The king kept his eye on Carvalho, and in 1739 sent him as ambassador to London. For six years he represented Portugal at the English court, and was then despatched on a special mission to Vienna. He discharged his functions with so much credit to himself and benefit to his country that Joseph, a few days after his accession, appointed him Secretary of Foreign Affairs.

Carvalho had learned much in England. That country was his best book. He had seen how the prosperity of a nation depended rather on the cultivation of its own resources than on great possessions abroad. He understood, with England as an illustration of contrast, how foolish Portugal had been in staying itself on the spices of the East and the gold of the West, while its own acres were untilled and its industry declined. The condition of Portugal had got to be so unhealthy that the resources of even a genius would be overtaxed to discover a panacea; still whatever lay in mortal power Carvalho could achieve. He threw himself with the zeal of one conscious of a providential calling into the duties of his office. But a man like Carvalho could not confine himself in the cabinet to one department of the government. He looked into every portfolio and mastered its contents. To each minister he made himself indispensable, and became premier in fact, though not in name.

In the year 1755, something occurred in Lisbon of which

everybody has heard—a catastrophe with whose awful results no one knew how to deal except Carvalho—that great earthquake which laid the beautiful city in ruins. It was on the first of November, about nine o'clock in the morning—a lovely morning, bright, cloudless, and still. The magnificent palaces and churches of the capital were reflected in the mirror of the Tagus, which glided without a ripple to the sea—a picture of peace which was, without a moment's warning, suddenly transformed into a scene of indescribable horror! A tremendous shock, lasting six or seven minutes, followed, after an interval of five minutes, by another of about three minutes' duration, and all was over. For one short quarter of an hour "the earth was shaken out of her place, the pillars thereof trembled," and the capital of Portugal was destroyed. The terrified populace, half of whom were out of doors—for it was All Saints' Day and a holiday—rushed hither and thither at the first convulsion to escape the impending doom, only to be crushed by falling buildings or swallowed up by the chasms which yawned beneath their feet. Many fled to the Tagus, but the river had risen about thirty feet, and its waves, lashed into fury by the violent disturbance of its bed, were contributing to the disasters of the day. Great ships were seen spinning wildly round like a child's top, then to disappear in the vortex. Some vessels were dashed against each other and went to pieces, others were tossed in the air and hurled into the town. As if to make the calamity complete, fire burst from the rents in the ground and burned fiercely for five or six days. Many perished in the flames who had remained alive after the earthquake. The massive walls of the prisons had also given way, and set free a number of criminals, who, joining their kind in the streets, and profiting by the prevailing confusion, indulged in plunder and every possible mischief and violence.

There are various estimates of the mortality resulting from the earthquake and its concomitant evils, but the best authorities maintain that the number of victims was at least thirty thou-sand. Not only the capital, but other Portuguese towns—Setu-bal, Oporto, and places in Algarve especially—suffered severely from the earthquake. Indeed, the shock was felt in parts beyond PortugaL But nowhere was there seen anything approaching the pitiable desolation which befell the city of Lisbon. Buildings of the most costly and elegant description, the royal and patriarchal palaces, numerous churches and convents, were demolished. Whole streets were transformed into heaps of broken masonry. The damage to property in Lisbon could not, it was estimated, be made good for less than seven millions sterling.

No wonder that men were at their wit's end in the face of such a gigantic and unprecedented disaster. The king, who was with his family at Belem,* two miles down the Tagus, had abandoned himself to despair, and as Carvalho entered his apartment, cried to his minister in a voice stifled by emotion, "What is to be done?" "*Enterrar os mortos, e ciudar nos vivos*" (Bury the dead, and care for the living), replied Car-valho, with such calm resolution that Joseph gazed at him in astonishment and admiration. The minister received full powers for the work, and carried it out, so that his will became thenceforward his master's law.

The ruins were explored; the corpses found were for the most part taken out to sea and lowered into its depths to pre-vent an epidemic from so many burials on land; the injured were placed in temporary hospitals, and the thousands rendered homeless gathered together and put up in huts rapidly con-structed for their accommodation. The necessaries of life were procured and distributed among the poor; and finally, in view of the depredations daily committed by unconscionable mis-creants profiting by the general confusion and calamity, the city was placed under martial law, and all apprehended *in flagrante delicto* hanged without delay at the nearest convenient

* Now a suburb of the capital.

LISBON.

spot. The panic for a time was so great that Carvalho " was employed night and day," so runs a despatch of the British consul, in the business of allaying it and inducing the people to return to their duties—no easy task, since shocks of earthquake, though less and less violent, recurred at intervals till January of the following year. The minister was looked upon almost as a being of an order superior to mortals, so acute was his perception, so indomitable his energy, so impregnable his serenity.

The day of national misfortune was Carvalho's opportunity. He revealed himself as a spirit of order and life in the state. He won for himself, by his conduct in the crisis of 1755, such respect with sovereign and people that during the twenty-two succeeding years of Joseph's reign nothing could shake his authority. Following up his measures to alleviate the distress among the population of Lisbon, he proceeded to restore by degrees the city itself, or rather to construct a new capital much finer than the old. The former narrow and uneven streets were replaced by broad, level thoroughfares and handsome squares. The new public buildings surpassed the old in size and splendour. Had the minister's plans been completely carried out, Lisbon would, considering its advantages of situation, have been one of the grandest capitals in the world. But so far as it was accomplished, Carvalho's scheme of reconstruction corresponds in its excellence with every public undertaking to which he devoted his attention.

But this capable and indefatigable minister, so well deserving of his countrymen's support, had a number of inexorable enemies, who endeavoured to thwart and misrepresent every step he took. Chief among his opponents were the Jesuits. The brotherhood believed they saw in his policy a desire to minimize ecclesiastical influence in Portugal, to disregard the voice and the interests of the Church. According to this view of theirs, they made Carvalho responsible for the earthquake, declaring it to be a judicial visitation of the people on account of the secularizing lines along which he was conducting the administration. They even went to Belem and required the king to do penance for the wickedness which, by his sanction, his minister was perpetrating, and to deprecate the divine vengeance. But Joseph's firm conviction of his minister's capacity was proof against attacks from this or any other quarter. Carvalho was not only permitted to go his way and work his will, but as a significant token of his master's unimpaired confidence, particularly in recognition of services to the nation beyond all praise or reward, was created Count of Oeyras.

The Jesuits were foiled for that time, but the Count of Oeyras knew them too well to think they would accept their defeat and refrain from further hostilities. He was sure they were forging new weapons wherewith to wound his reputation, and that he must succumb, unless he fought them until they were permanently disabled as well as disarmed. He was one man ; they were many—masters, too, in strategy. Nevertheless they were by-and-by doubly delivered into his hands.

The first definite charge which Oeyras was able to make against the Jesuits regarded their conduct in South America. Since the end of the sixteenth century the Society of Jesus had carried on mission work in the then Spanish province of Paraguay, and had gradually acquired in that country civil as well as ecclesiastical authority. They used their power to enrich themselves by a trade monopoly, and considered themselves absolute masters of the territory which was covered by their missions. In 1753, under a treaty with Spain, Portugal obtained possession of Paraguay in return for relinquishing Portuguese claims upon Nova Colonia (Sacramento). Oeyras proceeded in due course to assert the right of his master to rule Paraguay, like the other colonies of Portugal, by a governor receiving orders from Lisbon. The Jesuits opposed what they termed an encroachment on their privileges, forbade commercial dealings with Portugal, and even the use of the Portuguese language. Representing Portuguese government, moreover, to the Indians as tyranny, the society roused them to an armed resistance of its establishment. The behaviour of the Jesuits abroad afforded the Portuguese minister an opportunity of adopting sharp measures with them at home. He persuaded the king that the Jesuit influence at court must be put down, and accordingly the confessors of the royal family, who were then all of that society, were suddenly dismissed, and replaced by members of the Franciscan and other orders. Carvalho, however, felt that he must go much further than that, having committed himself so far against the Society of Jesus. He formally complained, therefore, of their doings to the Papal chair, with the design of obtaining an edict suppressing the order. Yet the Vatican was friendly to the Jesuits, and it seemed as if little heed would be paid to the representations of Oeyras.

But in 1758 the count was furnished with a fresh indictment against the Jesuits, which, together with the fact of their contumacy in Paraguay, justified him in expelling them from Portugal. This new crime was nothing less than an attempted assassination of the king. Joseph was driving home one evening in September of that year from a visit, when two shots were fired from behind his carriage. The king was fortunately only slightly wounded; nevertheless the audacious attack indicated a plot of the most dangerous kind. Carvalho was convinced that the prime object of the conspirators was his own overthrow, and that they had unscrupulously contemplated making a victim of King Joseph only for the purpose of procuring the downfall of the obnoxious statesman who held the sovereign so completely in his hands. As at the time of the earthquake, so now the great minister showed few signs of discomposure, but, with the perseverance and ingenuity of an experienced detective, unearthed the cabal. In consequence of his investigations, certain members of two families, among the most important in the country, were apprehended and charged with complicity in the outrage.

The Duke of Aveiro was the highest in rank of those to whom the treason was brought home. He was not a man of much ability, but most ambitious and malignant. He attributed his want of success in obtaining the royal favour to the opposition of Carvalho, whom, in the pride of an illustrious ancestry, he scorned as a vulgar upstart; for the Count of Oeyras belonged by birth to a family of squires who had no connection, as we should say, with "the strawberry leaf." Among the duke's papers was found a document which maintained the advisability of getting rid of King Joseph, in order to the ruin of King Sebastian (Sebastian de Carvalho was intended), and other writings containing damning proofs of his share in the intrigue. The house of Tavora, related to the Aveiro family, participated in the guilt of the duke. The Marquis of Tavora, who had been viceroy of Portuguese India, was indignant on his return, after his term of office had expired, to find Carvalho installed in a place at court from which the Tavora influence, once so great there, was rigidly excluded; and his wife, who had undoubted political talent and coveted a large sphere for its exercise, was no less vexed to think that she and her husband were to be relegated to the obscurity of their country seat.

These two, therefore, countenanced and helped to arrange the crime, and dragged into the plot their two sons and their son-in-law. All the conspirators above-mentioned were found guilty, and condemned to be executed in various ways at Belem in January 1759. The Duke of Aveiro and the elder Marquis of Tavora were broken alive on the wheel. The elder son of the latter nobleman, called likewise Marquis of Tavora, and the younger, the Count of Atouquia, and their brother-in-law, were strangled. The old Marchioness of Tavora was beheaded.

The king wished her to sue for grace, and sent a message to her hinting that in such an event her punishment might be mitigated. But the high-spirited lady would beg no boon. "Tell him who sent you," she replied to the messenger, "that as I followed my husband to India, so I shall follow him to the scaffold." Of the two men, both servants of the duke, who actually fired at the royal carriage, one was burned alive and the other in effigy, since he had eluded arrest.

The people generally approved these severe sentences, and when, two days after the executions, the king appeared in public, he was received with indescribable enthusiasm. As he floated on the Tagus in his barge the river was crowded with every kind of craft, whose occupants rent the air with shouts of rejoicing. The warm reception of the king was meant and understood as a commendation of his measures and a testimonial to his minister; for the conspiracy was felt to be an effort of reactionary politicians filled with bitter hatred of the advanced principles which Carvalho was persistently applying in his administration. The Count of Oeyras was well known to be the *bête noir* of the old nobility, and therefore the more entitled to the support of the commons. Many shook their heads when they saw or heard of the traitors' fate and became aware of the arrests and punishments which followed the executions of January. They called the minister inexorable; yet he declared that if he erred it was on the side of indulgence, for that unless he had tempered justice with mercy he should have made the streets of the capital run with blood, so many were implicated in the horrid plot.

But, as has been already indicated, it was not the aristocracy who were at the bottom of the affair. Carvalho claimed to have proved that the Society of Jesus were its real instigators. Those subtle priests, he maintained, had worked upon the selfishness and vanity of Aveiro and the Tavoras. So those who had met their fate had been urged to the front. But had it not been for the machinations of the Jesuits, there should have been no attempt on the sovereign's life. The process against the society was conducted in secret, but this much is indisputable, that before the king was fired at certain Jesuits in various countries of Europe had spoken in such a way as to suggest afterwards their intimate knowledge of the dark business, predicting particularly that in September 1758 — the very time of the attempt—the king's life should come to an end; and, moreover, that the Duke of Aveiro, as indeed an Italian Jesuit chronicler of the society's history acknowledges, stated that the assassination had been advised by the Jesuits. It is also matter of fact that Gabriel Malagrida, a Milanese by birth and a member of the society, occupying the position of confessor to some influential families of the ancient *noblesse*, had expressed himself treasonably, both verbally and in his writings, and was actually named by the duke as one who had urged him to the action which he took.*

A number of Jesuits were apprehended as the result of an inquiry into the connection of the order with the outrage; and at the same time a circumstantial account of the plot was transmitted to Rome, as an additional reason why the supreme ecclesiastical authority should, in the interests of peace and good government in Europe, declare itself against the intriguing Society of Jesus. But Pope Clement XIII. would not listen to the accusation, and forbade the trial by the civil court of the Portuguese Jesuit prisoners. Oeyras, thereupon, finding Rome deaf to his appeal, not only did not hesitate to try the incriminated priests without leave of the Vatican, and to inflict

---

* Malagrida was a fanatical enthusiast who looked upon the Count of Oeyras as nothing better than Antichrist. He was subject to hallucinations, one of which was that he possessed the gift of prophecy. He perished at the stake two years after the expulsion of his brethren, but the Inquisition, and not Carvalho, was responsible for the sentence. Intoxicated by his prophetical bent, he had made statements at variance with the articles of the Romish faith, and on that account was given up to the tribunal which condemned him. So, though clearly a traitor in so far as he was responsible, he suffered as a heretic. In these days he should have been more suitably dealt with in a lunatic asylum.

capital punishment upon them, but he furthermore procured a royal decree banishing the Jesuits entirely from Portuguese territory at home and abroad; and when the members of the society absolutely declined to move, he called out the military, who ejected them by force, and drove them on shipboard at the point of the bayonet. They were carried from the shores of Portugal to Papal territory, and there debarked. Thus did Carvalho purge the land of his enemies.

The Pope was incensed beyond expression, and caused his nuncio to threaten Portugal with extreme ecclesiastical penalties. Yet the minister stood firm, and did not once wince at the roar of Rome's artillery. He bade the nuncio follow the Jesuits out of the country, as he would suffer no interference with his conduct of the national affairs, and calmly proceeded with his work. Carvalho's serenity reassured the Portuguese in their natural dread of the Church's ban. Foreign ambassadors in their despatches expressed themselves as somewhat amazed to observe how little the dovecots were fluttered by the Papal commination. But the people trusted the minister. They remembered how his heroism chased away their fears during the calamity of 1755, and they submitted without a murmur to his policy now. Yet it was remarkable that Portugal, which of all Catholic lands had been so much under the influence of Jesuitry, should make the first undisguised fight against it. Other countries in a few years followed its bold example. France, Spain, and the Italian states, one after another, proscribed the society, as it had almost everywhere made itself intolerable. And in August 1773, the new Pope, Clement XIV., who was not unwilling to take the step, since his hostility to the Jesuits was pronounced, issued the bull of suppression which the Portuguese minister had so long desired. So the breach between Rome and Portugal was healed. Carvalho, now by a grateful master made Marquis of Pombal, saw one of his greatest designs eventually accomplished, and rejoiced in the belief that the nation should be thenceforward freed from the mischievous interference of the Jesuits, and from those dangerous intrigues in which, if it did not always originate them, the society was so frequently involved.

The work which Pombal did for Portugal was wonderful both in amount and kind, when we take into account his great disadvantages. The nation was depressed, and very much dependent upon England; and the statesman had many relentless foes, particularly in the Church and among the aristocracy. He encouraged agriculture, fishing, and other industries; enlarged Portuguese commerce; organized the army, and created a navy; improved every educational institution, from the primary school to the university; granted more liberty to the press, and curbed the Inquisition; reduced the number of convents and the enormous income of the Church; arranged the administration of justice and the national finances; abolished serfdom in Portugal. This is a tale of labour which will compare favourably with that of many statesmen furnished with far greater resources. But one must remember that Pombal was in office for more than a quarter of a century, and like King Dennis, "did what he pleased." He was, nevertheless, though possessed of such unrestricted power, a practical man, and knew how many steps to take at a time. Accused by his opponents of precipitate radicalism,* he called himself a Conservative, and professed his anxiety to go about an obstruction if he could, rather than cause an explosion by its violent removal. And at all events it was agreed by impartial and capable critics that no one during the Pombal administration had shown himself fit to take the helm of affairs out of the illustrious statesman's hand.

As a patriot he was grieved to see the commercial ascendency of England over Portugal, and endeavoured to give his own

---

* Pombal was no Radical, but an autocratic reformer. He never dreamed of summoning a national assembly for its sanction of his projects.

land more weight in this regard. His hope of adjusting the balance by the granting of subsidies and the imposition of duties was, however, doomed to disappointment. Nevertheless, under his rule, a spirit of activity took possession of the nation, and he lived to see its trade in a better condition than it had been for many a day. After all his dislike of being so completely overshadowed by England, he was too wise to pick a quarrel with her. Once, indeed, he stood to his guns and insisted on satisfaction from the British government until he got it, when, after the victory over the Toulon fleet, Admiral Boscawen captured, Portugal's neutrality notwithstanding, those French ships which had taken refuge in the bay of Lagos. But in proportion to his distrust of France and Spain did Pombal desire to maintain cordial relations with Great Britain, unless she distinctly invaded the honour of his country.

The French statesman, Choiseul-Amboise, filled with the bitterest envy of England's greatness, conceived and concluded with Spain in 1761 the celebrated Family Compact, according to which the Bourbon kingdoms were to make common cause (against Great Britain in especial). Lisbon was besieged by importunities from Versailles to break with England. But the minister of Louis XV., *"cocher de l'Europe"* though he was called, could not drive Pombal into the arms of France. The marquis knew that in the event of his joining the Franco-Spanish Alliance he should have to brave England's wrath, and should secure little help from his would-be friends; and that, in the improbable event of Great Britain suffering from the compact, the Bourbons would assuredly use their power to deprive his country of its freedom. Pombal's reply to the allies' overtures was a preparation for war, which he expected would be declared when the Duc de Choiseul had grown tired of his solicitations. The Portuguese army was diligently recruited and brought up to a strength of something like sixty thousand.   The frontier defences were repaired.   The Spanish government complained of these preparations, but Pombal said that if one's neighbour did not intend to commit robbery, he need not take umbrage when one locked one's door.

In June 1762 the French threw down the gauntlet.   But the marquis had already apprised Great Britain of his danger, and within fourteen days after the declaration of war, an excellent general, Count William of Schaumburg-Lippe, having been sent from England for the purpose, landed at Lisbon to conduct the campaign for Portugal.   The English contributed also five or six thousand cavalry and infantry to the force destined to engage the enemy.   Of the Portuguese only four-teen or fifteen thousand were available to meet the combined French and Spanish armies, together forty-two thousand strong, which assembled in the neighbourhood of Ciudad Rodrigo. The rest were guarding the north and employed as garrisons on the frontiers.   At first the Franco-Spanish troops were fortu-nate.   They took Almeida, twenty miles from Ciudad Rodrigo, a place garrisoned by the rawest of recruits, who surrendered almost on demand ere the count was able to march to their relief.*   This, the principal success of the invaders, no doubt postponed the result of the contest.   But the manœuvres of Schaumburg baffled them, and before they could come to a pitched battle the rainy season began, and their provisions gave out.   Drenched and starving, there was no more spirit in the invading troops.   So, in less than a year after its opening, the campaign ended, and peace was concluded at Paris (Feb. 1763).   The aggressors were no gainers by their pains, and according to the treaty were bound to restore the places which they had taken and damaged to their former condition.   In this way England proved once more what her friendship was

---

* On the whole, however, the Portuguese soldiers did their duty in the war.   Carlyle's remark ("Frederick the Great," bk. xx., chap. x.) that Schaumburg "got from his Portuguese army next to no service whatever," is hardly fair, and is flatly contradicted by the general's own testimony.

worth, and Pombal was abundantly justified in fighting shy of the Family Compact.

The semi-jubilee of King Joseph's reign (1775) was celebrated by the unveiling of his statue in the principal square of Lisbon. The work was a colossal bronze casting, and on its marble pedestal there was placed, by express command of the king, a bronze bust of Pombal. The medallion was most appropriately placed, for the reign of Joseph would have been nothing without his minister. Just before the inauguration of the memorial the marquis had a narrow escape of his life. An infernal machine was discovered, intended to be stowed beneath the seat of his carriage, and timed to explode during the procession on the festal day. Pombal had the miscreant who meant to destroy him arrested, and kept silence on the matter till the rejoicings at the unveiling were over. Then the conspirator, an Italian resident in Lisbon, was tried and executed. There were some behind him whose names were not made public—some of the minister's old antagonists among the aristocracy, to whom the public triumph of the "upstart" was gall and wormwood. But Pombal's adversaries missed their mark a second time.

His fall was, notwithstanding, at hand. His master's health was already declining, and in February 1777 he died. Joseph left no son. His daughter Maria therefore became queen. She was the wife of her own uncle, the Infant Pedro, a declared enemy of Pombal. So the brilliant politician, by trusting whom so well the commonplace Joseph had done himself honour, was forced to realize that he was at length *de trop.* It would be strange if he were allowed to retire without an impeachment. He tendered his resignation, which was as a matter of course accepted, and to his surprise he was permitted to leave for the country. His enemies, however, were busily seeking for materials on which to found an indictment against him. It had been supposed by those who might have done so in his place, that he was enriching himself during his term of office. But an investigation revealed him as one who had contented himself with less than his due. Foiled in their purpose of making out against the late minister a charge of malversation, those malignants obtained from the queen a decree acquitting all who had been executed or imprisoned in connection with the attempted assassination of 1758 ; and in the next place they tore down the bronze medallion from the pedestal of the king's statue. They could do no more. Pombal's end was approaching. He was fifty years old when he became minister, and now he had passed his eightieth year. In 1782 he expired, one of the most noteworthy men of his day. He procured, it must be admitted, the passage of questionable fiscal measures ; and he was sometimes ruthless in his dealings, as, for instance, with the Society of Jesus : but he was a true man and a great one. He impressed himself deeply on the minds of his countrymen. To this present the Portuguese are heard dating events from " Pombal's time."

Queen Maria I. was a woman of a mild disposition, a good judgment, and a cultured intellect, but too nervous and timid to wear a crown. She and her husband were thoroughly devoted to the Church, and surrendered themselves to a set of fanatical ecclesiastics, in whose eyes the reform policy of Pombal was essentially wicked, particularly where it touched the revenues of the Church. In obedience to these spiritual advisers, Maria restored as speedily and completely as possible the ecclesiastical privileges which the late minister, in the interests of the state, had taken away, and generally strove to make up, as a strenuous and liberal devotee, for her father's neglect of the duty which devolved upon a "most faithful" king. With the ecclesiastics the aristocracy came into power, and out of that party, so distrusted and repressed by the great marquis, the new ministry was formed. While using without acknowledgment many of the patent advantages secured by

Pombal, they maligned his memory, and endeavoured to over-turn anything he had done which seemed to militate against the prerogatives of their order. Nevertheless the new administration was often unconsciously under the influence of the dead statesman's spirit. He had awakened feelings and cravings in the people which his mediocre successors could not stifle, and in spite of their conservatism and their hatred of the marquis, the current carried them along in the channel dug by his hands.

The queen was favoured with a peaceful time. France and Spain, after their last lesson, showed no longer that aggressive mood which forced Portugal to put itself on the defensive. England's hands were full of its rebel colonies in America, and it did not exercise over the country a too paternal supremacy. Portugal's relations with other powers were, therefore, freer, and the export trade flourished. Almost every industry made considerable progress. Travelling within the kingdom, too, was rendered somewhat easier by the making of new roads, the most important of these additions to Portuguese highways being one between Lisbon and Oporto by Leiria and Coimbra. Nor was learning neglected in Maria's time. Ministers, indeed, cared little for it, but the queen herself was an accomplished lady, and her uncle, the Duke of Tafões, zealously patronized the advancement of science. To him, probably, is mainly due the credit of such institutions as the Portuguese Royal Academy of Sciences and the School of Design and Architecture, which began their existence in Lisbon during the queen's reign.

The time was not, however, remarkable for political events. Until the tumult of the French Revolution, while other nations were pouring out blood and treasure in conflict by land and sea, the kingdom was left alone in the maintenance of its neutrality and in the furtherance of its material interests. And when the first mutterings were heard in Portugal of the tremendous political tempest which made itself felt throughout every European state, the sceptre had already been taken out of the queen's hands. Maria's superstition had, under the treatment of her ghostly monitors, developed into a religious mania. She is said to have brooded on the thought that her father had wronged the Church, and that she could not repair the damage. A deep-seated melancholy was the result of her reflections, which rendered her utterly unfit to give any attention to affairs. The probability is that her tendency to mental alienation was the cause rather than the effect of her self-accusations. At all events her son John, Prince of Brazil, had, from 1792, to act first as his mother's temporary substitute, and then, in 1799, since the queen's case grew more and more hopeless, as regent of the kingdom. The prince had not devoted himself to politics, for, until the death of his promising elder brother, it was not expected that he should occupy the throne. Moreover, he was quite as feeble as his grandfather, and there was now no Pombal to lean on. But even with so strong a minister, it is hard to say what could have been made of Portugal in the storm and pressure period which John was to see.

Just before France declared war against England in 1793, a French emissary appeared in Lisbon to require from the Portuguese government a recognition of the republic. Portugal declined, and immediately joined Spain in the first coalition with England against France. Portuguese troops were with the Spanish army which made the campaign of 1794. But the Spaniards, being defeated, concluded with France the Peace of Basle in the following year. Soon there spread rumours of a secret arrangement between France and Spain for the delivery to the latter kingdom of some Portuguese territory, on condition of a slice of Spain in the region of the Pyrenees being ceded to France. The news was very disquieting; but it was quite supposable that France should advance such a proposal, since she was continuing after the Peace of Basle to commit depredations on Portuguese merchandise, capturing richly-laden vessels from Brazil and elsewhere, and making many bankrupts in Lisbon and Oporto.   Portugal was losing money every day, and it is estimated that from the beginning of hostilities in 1794 till the Peace of Madrid in 1801, the country suffered to the extent of ten millions sterling.   Exactly that sum had been saved for the treasury by Pombal in his long administration, and in seven years of trouble it was all consumed.

With the rapidly-growing power of Buonaparte the situation of Portugal became more and more serious.   Its government saw the country to be in peril whether it clung to England or broke away.   Still it remained faithful to the English side, and so annoyed the French with a squadron at Malta and before Alexandria, that the future dictator vowed he should make Portugal weep bloody tears for its conduct to the republic.   In November 1799 Buonaparte became first consul.   Six months thereafter he won the battle of Marengo, and in 1801 compelled Austria to accept the Peace of Luneville.   Then he turned his attention to Portugal, that, through it, he might strike a blow at England.   He concluded a convention with the court of Madrid to force Portugal to give up its ally.   The ports of the kingdom were to be occupied by French and Spanish troops, for the purpose, as he said, of "giving back to Portugal its independence."   Thereupon Spain declared war against Portugal, and sixty-five thousand French and Spaniards prepared to invade the land.   Portugal called for English aid, but England, having sufficient work for her soldiery in Egypt, sent no men—only a subsidy of £300,000.   Portugal, however, needed men as well as money, and after some resistance saw nothing for it but to sign a peace in 1801 which ceded Olivenza to Spain, and closed Portuguese harbours against British shipping.   In retaliation for this action of her old ally and debtor, England occupied the island of Madeira.   Portugal was indeed in a hard case between the two stools of France and England.   France was strong and masterful, and there is little wonder that Portugal bowed to its demands, since, next year, England itself concluded with its enemy the Peace of Amiens (March 1802).

The Amiens treaty was repudiated in fourteen months by the British government, after Napoleon had shown in various ways his contempt of its provisions, and by his audacious annexation of Piedmont and Parma and his occupation of Switzerland had made still more clear his designs against the freedom of Europe. In May 1803 hostilities recommenced between England and France; and Buonaparte obtained from Portugal, besides a formal declaration of neutrality, an agreement, as a condition of his friendship, to pay him one million francs per month so long as the English naval operations should last, which was something more than neutrality. The Portuguese hoped that with the payment of a tribute at the rate of £600,000 a year, the requirements of the first consul would stop. But they had to deal with an insatiable man. On Napoleon's assumption of the crown, the Prince Regent of Portugal was one of the first potentates to congratulate him on his new dignity, and to acknowledge the empire. This haste to please was ill rewarded by a peremptory order that Portugal should not only shut English vessels out of her harbours and unite her fleet with the ships at Napoleon's command, but also arrest all Englishmen in the country and confiscate their property. Such an outrageous demand roused even the weak nature of the regent to indignation. He replied that he should comply with the request in so far as the closing of ports was concerned, and even to the extent of joining the empire in naval warfare, but that to fall upon subjects of a power with which he was at peace, and spoil them of their possessions, was a thing to which he could not bring himself.

Because of the regent's refusal to deal so barbarously as was desired with the English residents, Napoleon concluded with Spain, at Fontainebleau (27th October 1807), a treaty, accord-

ing to which Portugal was divided between the neighbouring
kingdom and the French empire. This intended partition of
the country was as yet a secret, but it was now a matter of
certainty to the not very intelligent regent and his government
that the emperor would employ every means to force his will
upon them. Therefore, though sorely against the grain, the
prince agreed at last to sequestrate the property of the English.
But notwithstanding this degrading submission to the tyrant's
order, the regent learned that the French marshal Junot had
arrived with an army at Abrantes, eighty miles north of Lisbon
(24th November). Junot's commission was to take possession
of Portugal in the name of Napoleon, pursuant to an edict,
published in the *Moniteur* of November 13th, dethroning the
house of Braganza.*

The prince was driven to his wit's end (no great distance) by
the appearance of Junot. An English fleet under Sir Sidney
Smith was blockading the Tagus, and now he was caught between the forces of the two great powers. He had revolved
more than once the idea of fairly running away from the
country, rather than remain as the football in the game which
the French and English were about to play. The suggestion
had been expressed, and his English correspondents, when they
were acquainted with it, warmly approved ; for they understood
quite well that in his recent action he had not been a free
agent, and thought that, in the event of a collision with France
on Portuguese soil, the prince were better out of the way. As
soon then as the British ambassador, Lord Strangford, who was
now with the fleet, heard of Junot's march to Abrantes, he
went on shore and visited the king, taking with him a copy of
the *Moniteur* containing the edict of dethronement, which had

---

* The proclamation is an example of consummate insolence. " Le Prince Régent de
Portugal," it runs, "perd son trône ; il le perd influence par les intrigues des Anglais ;
il le perd pour n'avoir pas voulu saisir les marchandises anglaises que sont à Lisbonne.
....La chute de la maison de Bragance restera une nouvelle preuve que la perte de
quiconque s'attache aux Anglais est inévitable."

been put into his hands that very day.   The sight of the news-
paper was enough to confirm the prince in his resolution, and
to persuade the council of state to let him go.   So three days
thereafter (27th November 1807) the royal family, and fifteen
thousand Portuguese with them, took ship for Brazil, the regent
leaving a decree for publication to the effect that, for the good
of the kingdom, and until a general peace, he had resolved to
establish himself at Rio de Janeiro.

CHAPTER IX.

THE PENINSULAR WAR.

A S soon as the French government had been warned of the prince's intention to flee, Marshal Junot received orders to intercept the exodus, principally for the sake of preventing the removal of the wealth which was to be carried in the regent's fleet. Junot, by a forced march, which had thoroughly exhausted his men, entered Lisbon on November 29th, just a day or two late. The bird had flown. So he resolved to make the best of it by carrying out with what speed he might the rest of the emperor's arrangements. What these were, the people soon got to know, through the indiscretion of certain Spanish commandants in Portugal, who were proud to think and to tell that the country was to become a province of Spain. Junot, on the contrary, preserved complete silence on that point, and issued a proclamation to the effect that he had come simply to save the land from the mastery of England. "Le grand Napoleon, mon maître," the proclamation said, " m'envoye pour vous protéger ; je vous protégerai."

He began his beneficent work by hauling down from the towers of Lisbon that old Portuguese banner under which so many victories had been won, and running up the French flag in its place, amid salvos of artillery. Next, he proceeded to weaken the native forces by discharging nominally a third, but really a much larger part of them, and by sending a corps of about ten thousand men to join the French army. (They acquitted themselves well by-and-by at Saragossa, Wagram, and elsewhere.)   After in this manner draining away the nation's physical strength, he further "protected," to use the Napoleonic vocabulary, the pockets of the Portuguese, by first imposing a small war-tax of five million francs, then a larger property tax of fifty million.   The people might well wonder what was the difference between Buonaparte's friendship and his enmity.

While Portugal was thus in the talons of the imperial eagle, the Spaniards were ceasing to congratulate themselves on the French alliance.   Napoleon's fresh moves sufficed to convince the blindest that he meant evil by Spain ; that he did not intend to make it a present of the western kingdom, but to seize the whole Peninsula.   What Junot was doing in Portugal seemed about to be repeated across the border.   The emperor held the northern Spanish frontier, and now a French army had traversed the Pyrenees and was threatening Madrid.   The King of Spain, in his reasonable alarm, was inclined to imitate the prince, whose pusillanimity had made him the butt of the Spaniards, and to seek refuge in some Spanish dependency beyond the seas.   But the populace rose on hearing of his project, and to still the tumult he gave it up, and removed the crown altogether from his uneasy head by abdicating in favour of his son.   The new sovereign's policy was to comply unreservedly with Napoleon's will ; and, as a proof of his confidence, he sent a large Spanish contingent to co-operate with Junot's troops in Portugal.   The will of the emperor ere long became painfully manifest when, sending for the Spanish royal family to Bayonne on the pretext of an interview, he informed them that the Bourbon rule in Spain was over.

The king and his father were helpless, and surrendered at discretion ; but in Madrid the news of the deposition was immediately followed by an insurrection.   The French general Murat, however, took the capital after a short but furious resistance on the part of the inhabitants, and inflicted bloody chastisement upon the " rebels." On the taking of Madrid, Napoleon, considering Spain his own, gave it a puppet-king in the person of his brother Joseph, whom he commanded to exchange the crown of Naples which he wore for that of Spain and the Indies. Yet Spain was not subdued. Several provincial representative assemblies or juntos proclaimed their Bourbon king. Soon all Spain caught fire from their example. English aid, which the patriots now implored, was readily promised ; and fortified by the expectation of this support, the country resolved on war to the death.

The disturbance in Spain roused the Portuguese from their lethargy. They felt that now there was a reasonable hope of shaking off the oppressor's chains. With two nations against him, and England at their back, they should certainly be able to face Napoleon, who had so many other interests, and to drive his soldiers out of the Peninsula. Encouraged by the spectacle of the Spanish troops in Portugal turning against the French, insurrections took place in quick succession at Oporto and other northern towns. Evora, too, in the south, was in arms against the emperor. Junot, however, received reinforcements. The uprising in Evora was put down by General Loison with terrible slaughter. But in the north the patriots were still masters of the situation, and ere effective measures could be taken for their suppression, the promised help from England arrived. Sir Arthur Wellesley landed at the mouth of the Mondego with a division of the British army, numbering ten thousand men (July 1808). Wellesley, however, was not in this expedition commander-in-chief. That place was assigned to Sir Hew Dalrymple, Governor of Gibraltar, with Sir Harry Burrard next in command. But those generals had not yet arrived.

There was great enthusiasm along the coast of Portugal on the landing of the British troops, an enthusiasm increased by intelligence which had just been received of King Joseph's flight from Madrid and the retreat of the French army to the Ebro. Wellesley's men were pleased with their welcome, and stimulated by the latest news regarding the situation of the French in Spain. The British opened, therefore, their Peninsular campaign in the best possible spirits. On August 14, they saw from their position at Caldas, sixty miles north of Lisbon, the French general Laborde take up a position on the heights of Rolissa, two miles off. Laborde was waiting for Loison to join him in giving battle to the English. But Wellesley advanced without delay, and, notwithstanding the advantage of the enemy's position, dislodged him, and compelled him to retreat upon Lisbon. This affair was succeeded by a much greater fight at Vimiera in Estremadura. Junot himself commanded, and his force, including the divisions of Loison, Laborde, and Thiebault, amounted, Napier says,* to fourteen thousand men. The British troops, now augmented from England, numbered sixteen thousand, but not more than the half of them were actually engaged at Vimiera. The French, though showing the greatest courage on this field, were, notwithstanding, defeated with a loss of two thousand men and much war material. Wellesley would have pursued, but was forbidden by his superior, General Burrard, who had just joined him. So Junot was permitted to make his way back to Lisbon.

After the battle, the French leader held a council of war, and it was determined, as the imperial army was incapable of prolonging the contest, to come to terms with the British. He offered to evacuate the country, provided that his troops were conveyed to France by English ships, and allowed to take with them their arms, horses, and baggage. General Dalrymple was by this time at the front, and thought well of the proposal. So in the end of August the treaty, celebrated as the Convention of Cintra, was concluded at that place by the chiefs of the two armies, and immediately ratified at Lisbon. Byron waxes very

* " History of the Peninsular War."

indignant over the convention.* Many in England thought the French had been let off too easily. The Portuguese were especially angry that more humiliating terms had not been imposed. But it was desirable that the land should be at once freed from the burden of the French soldiery. And Wellesley was certainly in nowise ashamed of the convention, though it had been subjected to so much criticism and branded as disgraceful, for he testified in its favour at the inquiry ordered by the British government regarding the matter of the Cintra arrangement. Portugal was once more under the authority of the regency designated by the prince before his departure. The national flag again floated where an alien standard had been insulting the self-respect of the Portuguese.

But the convention did no more than secure a breathing time for Portugal. When Wellesley left for England after Vimiera, Sir John Moore remained in the Peninsula. He had landed the week following the victory of his compatriots. On the supposition that the Spaniards still held Madrid, he had marched the troops which had come with him into Spain, with the view of encountering the division of Marshal Soult. But Moore on the way learned that Buonaparte himself had retaken the capital, and was now with an immense army advancing westward. It would have been suicidal for General Moore, with only twenty-five thousand men, to have met the force which was represented to be approaching. He turned, therefore, to seek a place of embarkation. He was, however, overtaken at Coruña by the French under Soult, after his long and difficult march to the coast of Galicia; and seeing he could not embark without fighting, he accepted the enemy's challenge. The action (January 1809) resulted in the defeat of the French with great loss, and, unfortunately, in the death of the British commander.

The troops which inflicted this temporary check upon the

---

* " Here Folly dashed to earth the victor's plume,
  And Policy regained what arms had lost. "—*Childe Harold, I. xxv.*

French had only struck in desperation, and immediately sailed for England. So Soult, after recovering himself, joined Marshal Victor, and took possession of northern Portugal, the fine soldiers they had brought with them being more than a match for the most strenuous opposition of the patriots. Only three or four months had elapsed since the Convention of Cintra, yet the case of the Portuguese was nearly as lamentable as before. Sir Arthur Wellesley was therefore again ordered to Portugal. He found himself in command of forty thousand British, thirty thousand Portuguese regulars, twenty-six thousand native militia, and some thousands of *ordenanzas* or guerillas. The number of these last cannot be ascertained. The regular troops of the Portuguese army were exceedingly raw to begin with, but under the training of General Beresford, and educated by contact with the English soldiery, they turned out so well as to win great respect from Wellesley, who declared that, setting aside the British, there were no finer troops in the world than the Portuguese. Marshal Junot paid them the compliment of saying "that they fought like Englishmen in Portuguese uniforms."

Invested now with the chief command by the British government, and appointed from Rio Janeiro general field-marshal of the Portuguese army, Wellesley could make his dispositions at his entire discretion. He employed the less efficient native regiments, with the militia, as garrisons, and distributed the more excellent among the British to bring up the strength of the brigades. Then he proceeded to make an attempt at dislodging Soult from Oporto. Marching to the Douro, which at Oporto flows between steep banks with great rapidity, he saw that the French had demolished the bridge of boats, and left opposite the town not the smallest craft which could convey an enemy across. The capture of the place seemed a hopeless undertaking. Yet Wellesley meant to have Oporto. He had some guns planted on an eminence of the south bank which hid his army from the view of the French. And as a citizen of

OPORTO.

Oporto had managed during the night to come over in a skiff, volunteers were not wanting for the service of bringing in by this means other boats for the transport of the English. As soon as the boats which were found by the search-party touched the river-side they were filled with gallant men, who crossed the Douro, and scrambling up its north bank, took a great building which had attracted Wellesley's attention, and held it in spite of the vigorous endeavours which the French, now roused and marching to this point, were making to carry it. The enemy were much hindered by the deadly fire of the British guns from the other side ; and meantime the people of Oporto, taking advantage of the confusion, were sending boats across for the use of their deliverers. The English, thus continually reinforced, entered the town, and at length forced Soult to retreat into Galicia, sacrificing his baggage and artillery. The taking of Oporto (May 1809) was one of the most remarkable exploits of the whole campaign.

When the news of this disaster reached Marshal Victor, who commanded another French division in the Peninsula, he hastened to the assistance of his brother-in-arms. Wellesley, who had intelligence of Victor's movement, conceived a plan by which he could circumvent him with the help of the Spanish general Cuesta, and hastened westward to meet that leader. But unfortunately the Spaniards had not intrusted the British commander with the same military power which he possessed in Portugal, and Cuesta, doubting the feasibility of Wellesley's notion, refused to fall in with it. The British had accordingly, as the next best expedient, to remain with the Spaniards till the French should make their appearance. They met Marshal Victor at Talavera. A most sanguinary battle ensued, lasting for two days (July 1809). Much of the fighting was bayonet work, and both sides showed stubborn bravery. The French, however, were defeated ; but Wellesley, on attempting a pursuit, was checked by the division of Marshal Soult, which had marched from Galicia to join Victor. Considering the tremendous force in front of him, and the impossibility of depending for carrying out his schemes on the co-operation of the Spaniards, who with the pride of their race were jealous of his mastery, he was compelled to fall back upon Badajos, and from thence, annoyed at the want of confidence in him which was shown by the provisional government, left Spain in the meantime altogether, and resolved to devote his whole attention to the defence of Portugal.

This important strategical problem Wellesley—since Talavera raised to the British peerage as Viscount Wellington—had worked at diligently and solved. He had succeeded in covering Lisbon from a descent of the enemy upon it, whatever the strength of that enemy might be, by constructing the celebrated lines of Torres Vedras. In October of the previous year the work was going on, and in November 1809 this extraordinary piece of military engineering was ready to afford him an impregnable asylum. There were three lines of fortifications, the first, about thirty miles long, stretching from Alhandra, on the Tagus, to the mouth of the river Sizandro, on which the town of Torres Vedras stands. The second and stronger line extended within the other for twenty-four miles, also from the Tagus to the coast. The third, placed at the mouth of the Tagus, was only intended to protect the British troops in case they should be compelled to embark. For that purpose thirteen ships of the line and a number of smaller vessels lay ready in the river. The physical conformation of the district favoured Lord Wellington's plan of turning it into a fastness. But the undertaking was immense. Ten thousand men were employed at the making of the lines. Hill-slopes were cut into precipices; rivers were dammed and inundations produced; roads which might be useful to the enemy were destroyed; wherever an attack might be expected, cannon were planted (there were in all four hundred and forty guns mounted on the works);

and when the labour was complete Wellington was satisfied that he had provided himself with a means of defying the tyrant of Europe.

To a general of renown and a prime favourite of Napoleon, Marshal Massena, was committed the task of, for the third time, invading Portugal. Under him were three French divisions, commanded respectively by Ney, Junot, and Reynier, in addition to the cavalry of Montbrun—an army beside which Wellington's troops were ridiculously few. The French were fortunate at the outset. They invested Almeida in Beira, and, happening to throw a grenade into the powder-magazine, which exploded and made a great breach in the walls, were able to take the fortress, much to the vexation of Wellington, who lay not far off. The unexpected surrender of Almeida forced Lord Wellington to retreat across the Mondego. Massena, elated with his success, marched westward to the town of Viseu, and sat down before it for a siege. But no one was visible on the ramparts. After waiting in vain for some signs of life in Viseu, its gates were broken open. The French soldiers, however, discovered neither man nor beast within the walls. They entered the houses, and found everything of value removed. Worst of all, there was not a particle of food to be had in the town. The place had evidently been abandoned.

This was Massena's first disagreeable surprise. The reason of the condition in which he found Viseu was an order of Lord Wellington for the complete evacuation of a large district within a certain radius of Torres Vedras so soon as the enemy's approach should be perceived. The region to which the order referred contained two thousand square miles. Massena discovered as he pushed on towards Lisbon how well the British commander-in-chief had been obeyed. He found on his line of march no people, no cattle, no provisions. The very fruits of the ground had been destroyd. He saw bridges broken, mills demolished, and in fact every precaution taken which could render

his progress next to impossible.   Over rugged mountain passes
and through desolate valleys the troops of Massena pursued
their toilsome way by roads so wretched that it required almost
superhuman exertions to drag their guns and waggons along.
Every now and then a piece of artillery or a waggon would fall
over a precipice and be damaged beyond repair.   The French
soldiers were exhausted.   Provisions were growing scant.   In
the towns and villages on their route, where they sought for
something to stay their hunger, no one was to be seen from
whom they could beg or steal.   There was not even a dog left
to bark at them.

Lord Wellington had taken up his position across the Mondego, on the high ground of Busaco, which covered the city of
Coimbra.   It was a splendid position.   To turn his flank was a
long way, and no guns or cavalry could be brought up the steep
slopes in front of him.   He had only fifty thousand men, half
of them Portuguese, but he had such advantage from the heights
he occupied that he watched with equanimity the approach of
Marshal Massena's host.   The French encamped at the foot of
the sierra and held a council of war.   Ney advised a retreat to
Viseu or Almeida and a message to Paris for reinforcements.
Others recommended an attempt to gain the other side of the
British position.   But Massena resolved upon an immediate
attack.   Wellington was prepared.   The Portuguese as well as
the English behaved like heroes, and Massena had to confess
himself discomfited after the second day's fighting (September
1810).   The French loss was over five hundred ; the British about
half that number.   Now Massena made up his mind to seek a
way round the crest of Busaco.   Two peasants whom his scouts
captured were terrified into furnishing him with such information
as he desired, and in the darkness the French army set out for
Coimbra.   Wellington noted the movement, and was in the city
before Massena.   The population fled at the bidding of the British leader, whereupon he directed his course to Torres Vedras.

Marshal Massena had been all along under the delusion that Wellington was flying to a place of embarkation, and that he should soon chase the British out of Portugal. He knew nothing at all about that gigantic bulwark by which the wave of aggression was destined to be stayed. Only when he advanced beyond Coimbra, which he had entered on the day after the British quitted it, did he become aware that the task he had thought well over was scarcely begun. Junot, who was pushing forward in the van of the imperial army, had ventured, ignorant of his danger, near the formidable batteries of Torres Vedras, and the roar of Wellington's twelve-pounders was the first intimation the French received that any serious obstruction existed to their seizure of the capital. When Massena came in sight of the British works he could hardly believe his eyes. But he was too able a soldier not to understand, as he surveyed the long lines, with what sagacity his opponent had laid his plans, and how vain all his own calculations had been.

The British were comfortably established behind their defences. Provisions were sent daily up the river to them in abundance. A very large supply was indeed required, for Lord Wellington's forces had greatly increased. With fresh detachments from England, two Spanish divisions, militia and irregulars, he had within the lines one hundred and thirty thousand men. The camp was in good order. Signalmen posted on elevations telegraphed every motion of the enemy. The French, on the other hand, were in a condition which became more and more deplorable. The ground where they lay, sodden with the autumn rains, was little better than a slough with the constant trampling of so many feet. They were ere long pinched with hunger, and in the neighbourhood not a morsel of food could be obtained. Parties were sent out to scour the country for the means of subsistence. These hunted down the peasantry, and threatened them with death if they did not reveal their stores. Many unfortunate Portuguese were murdered by the desperate foragers. Massena's men, unable to endure the state of matters in his army, began to steal inside the fortifications, and were transported to England. In the month of November about four thousand deserters had been received and thus disposed of.

By the middle of November, the situation had become intolerable to Massena himself, and he withdrew his troops to the neighbourhood of Thomar. Immediately Wellington issued forth in pursuit.

The feelings of Massena must have been anything but enviable as he broke up his encampment and marched eastwards. He had firmly believed that he had but to chase Wellington to the British ships; and now he himself was a fugitive, wishing his army well over the borders of a land where the rain, during his dreary retreat in the midst of winter, was falling with relentless constancy, and where the foresight of his great antagonist had swept away from him all means of physical support.

Gradually he fell back further and further, his soldiery marking, in retaliation for their disappointment, by the most shocking cruelty and devastation, the stages of their progress to Spain. These excesses, however, the Portuguese irregulars often revenged upon individuals and small bodies of the French army in a manner as sanguinary as it was unexpected. The guerillas knew every inch of the ground which Massena was traversing, and had many hiding-places of which the enemy knew nothing. They were able, accordingly, to waylay unfortunate French soldiers, to intercept communications, to fall upon outposts, and generally to pester the retreating army, without much fear of punishment. Lord Wellington dogged the footsteps of the retiring foe, advancing and resting according to the movements and halts of Massena, but without engaging in a pitched battle, till in April the imperial troops crossed the frontiers. There was now not a single French soldier left in Portugal, with the exception of the garrison which occupied

Almeida. The British, having invested that fortress, pursued Massena's army into Salamanca, and at the village of Fuentes d'Onoro, in that province, the two forces met in fierce conflict (May 1811), which left Wellington master of the field, and the French in such a condition that it was impossible for them to succour Almeida, Massena's sole trophy in this, to him, inglorious campaign. Yielding, therefore, to the inevitable, the French marshal bade the commandant destroy the town's defences and rejoin the army. The orders were obeyed, and the third French invasion of Portugal came to an end.

Thereafter the Peninsular War was confined to the neighbouring kingdom. But further than Fuentes d'Onoro it is not necessary here to follow the distinguished British commander-in-chief through that series of victories terminating in the blow which crushed Soult at Toulouse in 1814, just after the "adventurer had paid his vows to fortune," and the allies were triumphant in his capital. It was to the British soldiers, those men who would go anywhere and do anything, and to the British officers, who could so well comprehend and execute their leader's wishes, that, after the genius of Wellington himself, the brilliant success of his arms was owing. Nevertheless, while dwelling with pride on the achievements of his fellow-country-men, Lord Wellington, with characteristic fairness, acknowledged everywhere the services of the Portuguese contingent, which he reckoned much better than the Spanish, if not in bravery, at least in discipline, endurance, in all those qualities which, besides brute courage, go to make up the efficient soldier.

The population of Portugal suffered extremely and in many ways from the invasion. As the British troops marched after Massena, numbers of poor creatures, who had scarcely maintained their lives through the hard winter, emerged from their places of concealment among the hills and woods; and the emaciated aspect of these unfortunates so stirred the pity of Wellington's men that the generous fellows were often constrained to give away their own rations for the relief of such crying need. Many perished, many had their constitutions utterly broken down, some even became insane under their hardships. At the end of the war, the inhabitants of the country were found to have become fewer, during its course, by about a quarter of a million. That number, no doubt, includes those who emigrated with the regent, and the men slain in battle. Still, there must have been multitudes of non-combatants who owed their death to sheer hunger, or to their houseless state in the inclement weather.

The condition of Portuguese agriculture, manufactures, and commerce, after so many years of fighting, was, as a matter of course, lamentable. The national debt was monstrous, the borrowing power of the nation at the lowest ebb. Such a price Portugal had to pay for its deliverance. But England was at charges more extraordinary still for the Peninsular War. Yet her outlay was most essential and profitable. For the blow struck at the Iberian kingdoms was only preliminary to an attack upon herself. "To seize the whole Spanish peninsula, to develop its resources by an active administration, to have at his command not only Spain and Portugal, but their mighty dominions in South and Central America, to renew with these fresh forces the struggle with Britain for her empire of the seas —these were the designs by which Napoleon was driven to the most ruthless of his enterprises."*

* Green's " History of the English People."

CHAPTER X.

LATER HISTORY.

1816-1890.

THE prince regent, established since 1807 at Rio Janeiro, became, after the final breakdown of the French empire, John VI. of Portugal, for his mother, Queen Maria, died in 1816 ; and it was naturally suggested in Portugal that he should immediately return to Lisbon, seeing that the peace of Europe was secured. But he was not disposed to fall in with the proposal. He liked the climate of the colony. He had lived there for now eight years, and felt quite at home among his Brazilians. Besides, he had, yielding to the wishes of the Rio merchants, consented to repudiate the monopoly of trade which Portugal had hitherto enjoyed with its transatlantic dependency, and on that account would be less a *persona grata* to the home traders than before. So he let the old country wait for him. But the Portuguese could not endure the king's absence, which meant the substitution of Rio Janeiro for Lisbon, and the supreme authority in the kingdom of those confidants of the king who were with him there. They were being governed by a colony. Portugal was now, in fact, the dependency, and unfilial Brazil had snatched away the rod of correction.

Marshal Beresford, too, who held the chief command of the forces in Portugal after Wellington's withdrawal, gave umbrage especially to the army—in the first place, because he was a foreigner; and further, because his bearing was unfortunately the reverse of affable. Beresford's distinguished services were forgotten in view of what was deemed his despotic severity. Moreover, the commission of the regency, as it was still called, though the regency had of course terminated at the queen's death, did not possess the confidence of the people. It was not the old body appointed by the prince regent on his departure from Lisbon, but a new one created by Sir Hew Dalrymple. Its origin accordingly was a matter of annoyance to the Portuguese, and the vacillating conduct of its members did not tend to procure for it any feeling of respect. What with an absent king, therefore, who seemed now more Brazilian than Portuguese, and an unreliable regency, the discontent grew daily; and so, when in 1817 an order was communicated to the regency from Rio Janeiro that a detachment of troops should proceed to Brazil, its issue was followed by a downright refusal on the part of several regiments to embark. They retired in bands to the hill country, and maintained such an attitude of resolute defiance that the regency had actually to suffer the humiliation of countermanding their order.

To the mutiny in the army succeeded the same year a plot to promote a revolution in Lisbon. Its leader was Lieutenant-General Feire d'Andrade, a man of good family, and well spoken of as a soldier. He had been slighted, he imagined, by Beresford, and for his sake attributed all the evils of Portugal to the English influence. That influence he meant to dismiss, and to destroy the regency as a thing which in nowise represented the feelings of young Portugal. But the commander-in-chief was advised of the conspiracy, and the ringleader, with four others, was executed at Lisbon. Yet this stern measure did not stay the current which was flowing through the country. The soldiers were elated with their victory, and Feire d'Andrade represented thousands of dissentients who had not seen their way to a hopeful plot. Marshal Beresford was scant of the sinews of war for fighting against a revolution which he never-theless saw impending. He hastened, therefore, to Brazil to express from the king a sum of money wherewith to pay the troops (to whom the regency were in debt, as to every one else), in order to keep them on the side of the government in case of a rebellion. But before he could return to Portugal, that which he dreaded had occurred.

The submission of the Spanish king to a reformed constitu-tion in 1819 gave an impetus to revolutionary ideas in Portu-gal, and taking advantage of the commander-in-chief's absence, in August 1820 an insurrection took place at Oporto. The municipal government perhaps connived and certainly winked at the demonstration ; but the ostensible leader of the revolution-ists was the Portuguese general Sepulveda, who, supported by the military, declared against the existing *régime*, and marched for Lisbon. The large reinforcements which he received on the way showed the amount of sympathy with which the movement was hailed in the country. The regency did not know how to treat the matter. One day they issued a bold denunciation of the revolt, and cancelling their edict the next, summoned the Cortes for deliberation. The army as a whole ere long let its mind be known ; for on the annual September holiday, to cele-brate the evacuation of Portugal by the French, the soldiers, Sepulveda's contingent having by this time joined them, paraded the streets of Lisbon, though the government, in con-sideration of the troubled time, had expressly forbidden any military display. On the motion of their commander the troops voted the discharge of the regency and the appointment of an interim national administrative council.

The Oporto insurgents had nominated a junto, who accom-panied them to the capital. These delegates, whose Liberalism was of an extreme type, wished the new constitution of Spain to be adopted *simpliciter*. But the council which had just taken office objected to such a long and sudden step, and proposed to take the voice of the Cortes.* The army being with the council, the ancient assembly of the nation convened in 1821, and began the work of modelling a constitution in accordance with the spirit of the times, accepting hints from the Spanish articles, but having regard to the special needs of Portugal.

Meanwhile, Count de Palmella, the president of the regency, crossed the Atlantic to lay before the king a narrative of what had occurred, and to plead for his instant return to Lisbon. John, whose constant fate was a deadlock, wished to lose neither Portugal nor Brazil. It was plain that he could not keep the first if he remained in South America; and on the other hand, if he left, he feared an insurrection in Rio would ensue. Brazil was already by royal edict no more a colony, but on a level with Portugal, by which arrangement John VI. was styled sovereign of Portugal and Brazil. Not content, however, with having their country made an integral portion of the Portuguese monarchy, a large number of Brazilians craved an independent government on the basis of those new-fangled constitutions which were the note of the time. What should the king do? He compromised, as he had done more than once before, and without saying whether he intended to quit America for good, appointed his eldest son Pedro Viceroy of Brazil, and set sail for Lisbon in March 1821. When his ship reached the Tagus, it was boarded by a deputation from the Cortes, who demanded from the king an assent to the principles of that reformed government upon which the nation had determined. John was informed that unless he agreed he should not be permitted to set foot in the capital. Seeing

---

* The Cortes had not met since 1697. The king had during that period been absolute. The people had no voice in the legislation. The work of the government was directed by four ministers of state—the president of the treasury, the minister of the interior, the minister of marine and of the colonies, and the minister of war and of foreign affairs. There were also five supreme courts or councils, from which no appeal could be taken—two at home in Lisbon and Oporto, two in Brazil, and an Indian council at Goa.

that his deposition would succeed his declinature, he subscribed
the required declaration, and entered Lisbon as the sovereign
of a people who now enjoyed an amount of freedom which
their forefathers would scarcely have thought compatible with
the idea of law and order.   At the outbreak of the revolution,
which was happily bloodless, Portugal got rid of that direct
English influence whose introduction, indeed, saved it from
absolute ruin, but whose continuance seemed more and more,
an intolerable incubus.   The administration of affairs and the
control of the national defences were now entirely in Portuguese hands.   It looked as if the morning of a promising day
had arrived.

But this desirable state of affairs was only transitory.   The
fruits of the revolution of 1820 were destroyed by a counter-
revolution in 1823.   The changes effected by the new constitution were detested by the Conservatives in Portugal.   Dom
Miguel, the second son of the king, was a leading spirit in
that party—an out-and-out opponent of reform.   He and his
friends therefore set themselves to bring about a return to the
despotism of the past.   They found the military and the
people generally suffering from a political relapse, and fearing
the tendency of those enlightened principles to which the royal
seal had been adhibited.   The Portuguese had been too long
accustomed to Absolutism to understand at once how, under a
Liberal constitution, national and personal security could be
maintained, how trade could live and grow in freedom.   The
enthusiasm of their uprising had cooled, and now they were
disposed to think that in their zeal they had overstepped discretion.   They had panted for liberty, and then having brought
it into existence, felt towards it somewhat as Frankenstein did
in the presence of his monstrous creature.   Freedom had not
" broadened down " slowly enough in Portugal " from precedent
to precedent " that so they might love it steadfastly and believe
in it fully.   They required just then for the completion of

their political education a fresh object-lesson on tyranny, and they found, in the sequel, the Infant Miguel a very competent instructor.

The reactionaries had already on their side the priests and the nobles, who, with the army, were one-fifth of the population; and by representing to the military the dangers of a Radical programme, the Infant's party gained them also. The restoration of Absolutism in Spain by the intervention of a French army under the Duke of Angoulême enabled the Por tuguese Conservatives to turn the wheel more easily; so, not long after the Liberal reverse in Madrid, the Infant executed his movement. As in the case of the change in 1820, this revolution also was accomplished without any fighting; and so far as the abrogation of the three-year-old constitution was concerned, the people and the king seem to have looked on in silence. But when the triumphant party demanded from him a public declaration of his absolute sovereignty, John demurred. He was cautious enough not to plant himself on a height from which he should in all probability be incontinently hurled headlong. It was too late by a century at least for that sort of thing. Nevertheless, the proclamation in question was insisted on till John, in his trouble, bethought him of his former flight into the arms of the English, and wished to repeat it, which he could indeed do without much trouble, since from his windows in Lisbon he was able to see a British war-vessel floating in the river. But his purpose being suspected, he was detained a virtual captive in his palace; while Miguel, presuming on his father's weakness, began to execute some important royal functions. At length John gave his jailers the slip, and on board of a foreign man-of-war resumed that authority which was denied him in his own capital. When the audacious Infant knew that his father had found such a retreat, he took alarm. If the English should not only harbour the king but defend the royal decision, Miguel's position would be certainly untenable and ruinous. So the rebel, betaking himself to the outraged parent and sovereign, sur-rendered at discretion, received forgiveness, and was banished the realm, his exile being euphemistically expressed as a " per-mission to travel." John, therefore, during the three remaining years of his life, administered the affairs of the kingdom accord-ing to that style of compromise which was so dear to his heart—the constitution of 1820 being set aside, while the name of absolute king was avoided like the pest.

When the king realized his approaching end, he arranged that the regency should at his death be placed in the hands of his daughter Isabella. On her father's decease therefore, in 1826, she took up the government, to carry it on in the name of her elder brother Pedro. The reason for the employment of the Infanta as regent concerned the relation in which Dom Pedro stood to Brazil. That country had, in the year of the counter-revolution, quite broken loose from the fatherland; and though John VI. had made every effort to recover the South American dominion, it persistently adhered to the de-claration of its independence. A constitution was framed, many elements of which were derived from England and the United States; but the monarchical form of government was retained, and the crown given to Dom Pedro. The courtesy title of emperor was, from motives of respect for the old home, allowed to the King of Portugal; but his son was thenceforth the independent King of Brazil.

Now the ancient laws of Lamego, which have been more than once referred to, bore that no foreign potentate should sit on the Portuguese throne; and in case these statutes should be raked up when he died as an occasion of disturbance, John, no doubt to save the country from the unreasonable Miguel, put forward his daughter, who might be elected to succeed him. Or, as there was a possibility of the Brazilians consenting to share their king with Portugal, Pedro could quietly succeed in

the event of nothing being said about that inconvenient legislation of the far past, and leave his sister as the visible head of
affairs at home.   As it turned out, no objections were raised
to the King of Brazil's succession on the score of the ancient
statutes.   The Infant Miguel, who was then at Vienna, sent
congratulations to his brother and loyal professions.   It appeared as if the power of Pedro IV. were to be peaceably
established.   Yet in four months after his accession Portugal
was in an uproar.

The Brazilians would by no means consent to a reunion of
the crowns, and Pedro, emperor now of Brazil, had to choose
between his South American dominion and the ancient throne
of his fathers.   He drew out a scheme, therefore, which he
imagined would allay all discontent both in the empire and in
Portugal.   He proposed to resign the Portuguese crown on
condition that his Peninsular subjects accepted as queen his
daughter, Maria da Gloria, with whom his brother Miguel, the
plan further bore, should contract a matrimonial alliance.
Pedro believed that the Infant had learned wisdom by the
failure of the counter-revolution, and, at any rate, would have
his future action fettered by a constitutional charter on the
French model, which, it was finally stipulated, should be recognized as the basis of Portuguese legislation.

As soon as the news of these conditions reached Portugal
there was consternation among the privileged classes.   Nothing
could reconcile them to the adoption of such a charter.   Immediately a conspiracy was organized to formally repudiate the
sovereignty of Dom Pedro and to enthrone the Infant Miguel,
the fast friend of the old order.   The laws of Lamego were
flourished in the faces of Constitutionalists.   The Emperor of
Brazil, it was said, was a usurper.   The crown was not his
either to wear or to give away.   Dom Miguel was the rightful
king.   The excitement in the country was extraordinary.
Spain, too, helped to swell the tumult.   The Absolutist

Ferdinand, deprecating the advance of Liberalism across his borders, sent an army to the assistance of the Miguelites. The priests everywhere, with as much enthusiasm as if they were preaching a crusade, bade the people rally to the side of Dom Miguel. The Constitutionalists, on their part, were not idle. Especially indignant at Ferdinand's impertinent demonstration against their liberties, they sought to throw a weight into the other scale, and made urgent overtures to the British government for succour in their distress. England responded by sending a force to the capital, and Miguel, who was by this time at the scene of action, and had a wholesome fear of the British power, agreed, sinking his larger claim, to take the position of his brother's lord-lieutenant in Portugal.

But no sooner were the English gone than he raised his standard once more. Spain, remembering the late British intervention, did not again venture to send troops to the frontier, but still energetically supporting the Infant's cause, employed her agents in attempts to provoke a mutiny of the Portuguese army. Nevertheless, with the exception of a regiment or two, the troops remained this time faithful to King Pedro. The priests, however, were admirable recruiting-officers for Miguel, and large numbers of the fanatical apostolic bands flew to his side. These societies, existing both in Spain and Portugal—the Spanish section afterwards swelled the ranks of the Carlists—were composed of ultra-Catholics and Absolutists, who deemed no ways too dark or bloody for the attainment of their objects. Besides these unscrupulous partisans with the incongruous name, the landlords were with the Infant; and the illiterate peasantry thought with the landlords and the priests. Had it not been for the civic population, the cause of Pedro would have been doomed.

For four years after the departure of the English—that is from 1828 till 1832—the Miguelites had wonderful success. Absolutism was supreme in Portugal. As lord-lieutenant the

Infant convened the Cortes' according to its constitution at Lamego; and that old-fashioned assembly, realizing the work emphatically suggested by its convocation, trampled the charter under foot as the worthless document of a pretender, and declared Miguel absolute monarch.   The Constitutional troops took the field in opposition to the settlement, but were defeated in an engagement by the force which the Infant had got together.   Now opened a period of merciless severity which savoured rather of the Middle Ages than of the nineteenth century.   It was the Portuguese " reign of terror," only its ministers were in this case Conservatives.   The extreme bigots gave no quarter to any who were known or suspected to hold Liberal views.   Men were arrested by the dozen and the score. Fifty thousand persons are said to have been thrown into prison by order of Dom Miguel's cabinet, a clique of the narrowest - minded and most frenzied upholders of the *ancien régime* who could be found in Portugal or out of it.   The Constitutionalists made one or two desperate efforts to rouse the people against the insolent faction in power, but in vain.   The voice of Lisbon seemed to be smothered, the country to lie bound before the Miguelites.   Thousands of Portuguese, almost as many, it is said, as John VI. took with him to Brazil, shook the dust of the land off their feet and wrathfully quitted it, seeing the people's inertness in degradation.

But Pedro had received not a few packets of intelligence from Portugal, and, well acquainted with what had transpired and was daily transpiring there, only waited for an opportunity of dealing in some effectual way, on his daughter's behalf, with the Miguelites.   He was, however, impaled on the horns of a dilemma, as his father had frequently been before him.   He did not wish, for his own sake and for the sake of his infant son, the future and only recently-deposed Emperor of Brazil, to estrange himself from his subjects.   And the Brazilians would certainly view with jealousy his interposition in the affairs of Portugal, and see in it a patent sign of an affection divided between the two sides of the Atlantic. Yet he could not resist the call to defend his Liberal principles and his daughter's cause where his brother was showing himself such a determined enemy of both. Moreover, there was no other, failing him, who should be able to strike in there with the highest authority, since he was still, in fact, King of Portugal, his abdication having depended on the acceptance of the charter. He made up his mind, therefore, to achieve at any cost the redemption of the old country, for which he cherished an inextinguishable regard, and to that end renounced for ever his Brazilian dignity in favour of the five-years-old Pedro, his son and heir.

There was indeed another reason for this step. A powerful and, as he thought, too progressive party in Brazil had been for some time calling his caution Conservatism and making him uncomfortable by their clamour for sweeping reforms. That party, he felt, was bent upon overthrowing him, and the announcement of his intention to take part in the Portuguese struggle would be the signal for an insurrection. The charge preferred against him seems somewhat strange when we reckon up the trouble, expense, and risk so readily borne by Pedro in support of Portuguese Liberalism. But it showed that there were other differences than that of latitude grown up between the Portuguese and their kindred over the sea during the long years of separation. The half loaf which more than satisfied in Europe was no bread in the freer West.

Having, then, been allowed to doff the purple on the terms he suggested, Pedro made his appearance in England, and met there Doña Maria, who had been on her way to join her uncle and prospective husband in Portugal, but, learning what had occurred, had wisely avoided its shores and sought an asylum at the English court, where she was entertained with the honour due to her high rank. Her father, who travelled as Duke of Braganza, a resumption of his youthful designation, threw himself with all his heart into the task he had set himself. From sympathizing Englishmen of wealth he borrowed a large sum of money. Thus provided, he had little difficulty in procuring ships and some thousands of fighting-men in England and on the Continent. Then finding that Terceira, the island which so long harboured the Prior of Crato's followers, still held out for him, and that the regency he had nominated was established there, he proceeded thither, and soon afterwards captured St. Michael, the principal place in the Azores group. From the Azores, Pedro, having issued a proclamation against the Absolutists, sailed for Portugal.

In 1832 he landed, and found that his forces mustered, with the addition of his friends in the country who came to share his fortune, about ten thousand strong. He marched to Oporto, the stronghold of Constitutionalism in Portugal, and was received with enthusiasm by the populace. Dom Miguel thereupon advanced and attempted to take possession of the city. The efforts of the besiegers were fruitless. The suburb of Villa Nova was all upon which they could lay their hands. Holding this, and blockading Oporto, they hoped to starve the garrison into surrender. For eleven months the blockade lasted, when it was at length raised by Dom Pedro's fleet, under the command of Sir Charles Napier. Miguel lost in the engagement five vessels of his small navy, two of them ships of seventy-four guns, and from that day the downfall of his power was assured.

About the same time a reinforcement for Dom Pedro landed in the south, and the Lisbon people, learning of their approach, rose as one man against the Miguelites. When Pedro, therefore, heard of the Lisbon movement, he left the Douro by ship for the Tagus, and was conducted into the capital in triumph. Doña Maria was immediately sent for, and received a most gratifying welcome. Her father's original proposal was carried out. She was proclaimed queen (1833) amid the plaudits of an immense concourse, Pedro taking, for the time being, the name and duties of regent. Miguel endeavoured a while to maintain his claim; but his naval force having been dispersed by Napier, and having met with another defeat on land, he had to confess, after trying to hold a position fifty miles up the Tagus, that his cause was lost. So, in 1834, he subscribed a treaty at Evora, by which he agreed to interfere no more in Portuguese affairs, and to leave the country, in consideration of an annual income of £15,000. Thus Miguel, one of the most intolerant of men, was, though crushed and exiled, dealt with much more mercifully than he deserved, after having indulged for years with impunity in the most barbarous conduct towards the Portuguese.

The regent was not slow to turn the tables on his late assailants. Since ecclesiastical persons had made themselves very conspicuous in the ranks of the Miguelites, he thought fit to punish the Church severely for the sins of its emissaries; and for this purpose he did that which was enough to make his devout ancestors turn in their graves. He dissolved the monasteries. These houses were, for the size of the kingdom, exceedingly numerous, and in many cases wealthy; for during centuries it had been the delight of Portuguese kings to rear and endow them with lavish hands. Nevertheless he broke them up everywhere, without hesitation, and appropriated their lands and incomes. Herein the regent is convicted of ruthlessness; for although some of his worst enemies had undoubtedly found harbourage in them when the fall of Miguel became manifest, it was probably not the inmates of the religious houses but the secular clergy who had been so active and bitter against him. Granting, however, the necessity of dissolving the monasteries for reasons of state, the thing might have been accomplished more gradually and humanely. The government indeed, to a certain extent, acted on the principle of compensation for disturbance, but the sum distributed was notoriously insufficient. One palpable benefit the country obtained from this great eviction. Much cultivable ground came

by means of it into the market, and being purchased for the
most part by energetic farmers, the value of crops in Portugal
was signally enhanced. This and other repressive measures of
Dom Pedro fairly cowed the Absolutists, and showed them that
no time-honoured custom or institution whatever should be
allowed to stand in the way of that liberal administration
which the spirit of the age required.

The regency of the ex-emperor was of short duration. He
died in 1834. It seems unfortunate that he should have been
removed before his ideas of government had time to work
themselves out in the practical administration of Portuguese
affairs. He had a good deal of destructive work to do before
proceeding with his task of construction. But just as he was
laying the foundations of a political edifice, according to his own
conception of symmetry and stability, he was called away. He
was probably the right man for Portugal. That Whiggishness
which was so obnoxious to the forward party in Brazil, and
showed itself in the charter he gave to the Portuguese, was
perhaps, for the time then present, the most fitting means for
moderating between rabid Democrat and dogged Absolutist.
But he had to leave the difficult concerns of his country in the
hands of a woman who had not sufficient experience, perception, or strength of mind for anything that was worthy the
name of political work.

Queen Maria II., in 1835, wedded Charles, Duke of Leuch-
tenberg, son of Eugène de Beauharnais, Buonaparte's step-son.
But the duke survived his marriage only one year. In 1836
she married again. Her second husband was Prince Ferdinand
of Saxe-Coburg, cousin of the Prince-Consort of England.
Ferdinand, however, belonged to that branch of the family
which adhered to the Romish faith. The king-consort was
not allowed to afford her much support in the exercise of her
office. The ship of state drifted in a perilous strait. The
queen was distracted by the outcries of rival factions,. adjuring

her to shape a course for this point or that. Her ministry was composed of self-seeking men, who gave no satisfaction to the people. There was, besides, a great cleavage in the Liberal party. On the one hand there stood that section of it which called itself the Septembrist, in memory of the soldiers' revolt in September 1820, when a demand was made for an advanced form of government. This was the Democratic party; and against them the Chartists or moderate Liberals strenuously held the instrument of Dom Pedro to be the safer basis for a national settlement. Amid the bickering of these parties the extreme Conservatives, somewhat reduced but united, determined, and vigilant, sometimes stole an advantage, and were always ready to do what they could to make a coalition of Septembrists and Chartists impossible. Maria was unable to lay down the lines of a judicious arrangement, and was fain to concede its whole demand to whichever party seemed for the time to have the upper hand. This too generous dealing with temporary victors only made the return to power of their opponents more certain and speedy. Such continual shuffling irritated the people, and as the extremity of Liberalism is Absolutism's opportunity, the reactionaries had well-nigh obtained once more a general acceptance of their fetters. They were indeed baffled, but all the time of Maria the nation was thoroughly discontented with the see-saw motion produced by the alternate success of the two Liberal parties. Conspiracy followed conspiracy; money was consequently frightened away from Portugal, and the country approached the abyss of insolvency. Trade was paralyzed. The police was so feeble that roughs and broken men were permitted to form robber bands and to make the highways extremely dangerous for travellers.*

With no foreign nation was the government of Maria da Gloria on very cordial terms. In one matter, the slave trade,

---

* "In the provinces, even thirty miles distant from Lisbon, the country is in a state of almost lawless barbarity and outrage."—*Lord Londonderry's Steam Voyage in 1839.*

Portugal's backward attitude provoked the great powers, especially England, which had taken the subject of slavery so much
to heart.   Just after the general peace, Portugal had frankly
adopted an abolition compact ; but its inclination to resile from
its treaty position became so evident in the reign of Maria,
that Great Britain, where abolition was now triumphant,
moved for and took part in a warlike demonstration against
Portugal (1847).   The imminent danger of a rupture with the
powers, and particularly with Great Britain, which had so
often lifted the nation out of the pit, brought home to the
people the prospect of friendless isolation, which politicians
were helping to make certain by their intemperate behaviour,
and ministers by their bad conduct of affairs ; and it exercised
for a time a soothing influence upon party dissensions.

But the calm was brief.   By-and-by the tempest raged
fiercely as before.   Public indignation was stirred by the
manner in which the head of the ministry, Count Thomar, was
flouting the mind of the people.   (Pombal's day was gone by,
nor was Thomar a Pombal.)   So the Marquis (afterwards
Duke) of Saldanha, procuring the mandate of the army, insisted
on the deposition of the obnoxious minister.   The soldiers rose,
and the demand was conceded.   By the elevation of the chief
conspirator to office, the abdication of the pithless sovereign,
which had been part of the cry, was avoided.   The Saldanha
insurrection was followed by a revision of the constitution, by
which two houses of parliament, resembling the double chamber
at Westminster, came into existence in Portugal.   But the new
machinery did not readily get into working order, and in 1852
the cabinet published its intention of legislating, *pro tempore*,
on urgent matters without extraneous advice or sanction, trusting to obtain the national approval at a future day of reckoning.   Portugal was thus practically under an oligarchy when
the queen died in 1853.

Pedro V., Maria's eldest son, was a lad of eighteen on his

mother's decease. The regency, therefore, was undertaken by the king-consort. The good work of Ferdinand, as regent of the kingdom, showed what a public loss had been sustained through his absence hitherto, in deference to Portuguese etiquette, from official life. He took hold of difficulties with such a strong hand, dealt so prudently with violent party politicians, and revealed so much skill as a financier, that when his son Dom Pedro came of age and entered upon the active duties of his position, the state was in a happier case than it had been since the French aggression.

Pedro V. wore the crown after his majority only a few years, and his story is a sad one. Politically unimportant, his short reign was marked by the invasion of a more dreadful enemy than Napoleon. Pestilence in a double form scoured the country and slew thousands of the inhabitants. Asiatic cholera, not long after the king-consort had resigned the regency, paid its periodical visit to the continent of Europe, and nowhere did it secure a greater number of victims, in proportion to the total population, than in Portugal. And when the power of that fell plague was spent, yellow fever made its appearance, and committed more havoc among the people, who had already suffered so severely. In that trying time the young sovereign showed himself a man of the most heroic mould. Insufficient sanitary arrangements were, of course, to blame for the rapid spread of disease through the land; and recognizing the need of improvement in that regard, Dom Pedro made it his business to personally inspect the districts most infected, that he might note their state and what they stood in need of, and to stimulate by his presence the battle with the foe. He would not be restrained from what he considered his duty. He protested that, as a king, he must stand by his people in calamity and share their sorrow. Thus he endeared himself to the Portuguese, and by his constantly evident sense of responsibility, by his goodness and grace.

His marriage, in 1856, to the Princess Stéphanie of Hohen-zollern-Sigmaringen was a very happy one; but in a twelve-month after he had led her to the altar she was snatched away by death. It was a heavy blow, and though he bore up manfully and never allowed his private grief to divert him from the task which lay before him, there is reason to believe that it did not cease to gnaw his heart, " like a worm i' the bud," and so lowered his physical tone that he fell an easy prey to the sick ness which carried him off in 1861. He had that year just returned to his capital from one of those benevolent journeys of observation which good kings of Portugal had been for centuries in the habit of making through their land, but in which duty none of them had ever showed themselves more conscientious than Pedro V., when he found two of his brothers, the Infants Ferdinand and Augustus, struck down with fever. Pedro tended them personally and affectionately. His loving service resulted in himself taking the malady. Dom Augustus recovered. The other prince died. And in a few days after the king had been seized by the fever, he also was taken away. Pedro lay on his death-bed, it is said, conscious that his hours were numbered, in a frame of the deepest religi-ous composure. The whole country mourned the loss of such a good man and true king, removed so young from a sphere where, without adulation, he may be said to have walked as a spirit of compassion and helpfulness.

The tragedy was complete when yet another of the royal princes, the Infant John, succumbed to the fever. Louis, the brother next in age to the late king, it did not touch, and he ascended the throne of Portugal as Louis I. At the beginning of his reign he found some difficulty in obtaining a ministry who could pull together and inspire some measure of public confidence. His official troubles seemed to culminate, however, in 1870, when the Duke of Saldanha, now an aged man, but still desirous of playing a large part in politics, was sent out of the country as ambassador to the Court of St. James's. Saldanha had questioned the wisdom of the reform policy advocated by the statesman Loulé, to whom the king was very well disposed ; and remembering the success of his former determined stand against a minister, requested Loulé's removal, and announced his intention of repeating the movement by which he crushed Thomar, unless Loulé were dismissed. It is probable that the duke would this time have failed, but the king was a man of peace, and parted with his adviser. He took care, however, to rid himself at the same time of the restless Saldanha. Thereafter things went on in Portugal with remarkable smoothness, and the political quietude was extremely congenial to Louis, who, though he was by no means destitute of aptitude in dealing with state problems, was a scholar rather than a politician. He fully appreciated the saying of Prospero, " My library was dukedom large enough." Dom Louis cannot be classed with profound or original thinkers, but he was a devout lover of literature and art ; and as, in his later years, physical weakness caused him to withdraw himself to a considerable extent from the " strife of tongues "—to decline the burden of affairs—he gave himself up more and more to the companionship of books. He had a special relish for the great English writers. Of Shakespeare he was a diligent student and successful translator.

In his reign Portugal advanced on the path of reform, one of the most notable changes effected being the substitution of life-membership for hereditary right to occupy a seat in the upper chamber of the legislature. The country's financial position, never very flourishing, became at times embarrassed ; but there were evident signs of improvement in the national commerce during the time of Louis which have not disappeared, and even now, amidst much which is depressing, are encouraging Portuguese statesmen and patriots. The relations of Portugal with foreign powers were, on the whole, friendly, although at the time of the civil war in the United States a rupture was threatened in consequence of a misunderstanding with the American government; but danger was happily averted. The Spanish conspirator, General Prim, on the outbreak, in 1866, of the insurrection which resulted in the flight of Queen Isabella, pressed hard the idea of joining the crowns of the Peninsular kingdoms under Louis of Portugal. However, the head of the Braganzas had no ambition of that sort, and knew, besides, that his acceptance of the Spanish throne would open the door to violent disturbances both in Spain and Portugal, and would meet with decided objections from the other European governments. So the thought of an Iberian union was dismissed.

Dom Louis found an excellent helpmeet in his queen, Maria Pia, daughter of the late King Victor Emmanuel of Italy; a lady who, coming to Lisbon as a stranger to the Portuguese and their ways, nevertheless ere long commanded the respect of her own circle by her faultless manner, and won the love of the poor by her patronage of all kinds of organizations for their benefit, and by the kindly visits she paid to the most squalid quarters of the capital. In her husband's last illness she waited on him with untiring devotion. There is no more deservedly popular person in the kingdom than the dowager-queen.

The decease of Louis I. in 1889 gave the crown to his eldest son, Carlos I., the present ruler of Portugal, who married in 1886 Princess Amelie, daughter of Philippe, Comte de Paris. At the time of his wedding there was an attempt in France to invest it with some political significance, especially since a month or two previously there had been a union between an Infanta of Spain and Prince Anthony, son of the Duc de Montpensier. But it is not at all likely that this connection of the Orleanist Bourbons with the Peninsula will have the slightest effect upon the affairs of either kingdom.

Carlos was comparatively unknown when he succeeded, having lived mostly in the country, occupying himself with field-sports, like the first sovereign of his line, and at the same magnificent old seat in Alemtejo, whence his ancestor emerged at the revolution of 1640 to found the house of Braganza. Nevertheless, the young king was not, like John IV., called to a position of whose duties he knew absolutely nothing, since he had for a time acted as his father's substitute during the absence of Dom Louis abroad. He afforded then a sufficient guarantee that, though deficient in those brilliant qualities which are necessary for sustaining a great *rôle*, goodwill and frank expression of his mind will be conspicuous in his direction of affairs. It is too soon to form a judgment on the conduct of Dom Carlos on the throne; but it may be hoped that, so far as he can keep it, the Portuguese will have peace in his time, since he is believed to be free from that "vaulting ambition which o'erleaps itself and falls on the other," and to understand that crowned heads are safer and more dignified when they do not come within the reach of the blows which partisans are zealously raining upon one another.

CHAPTER XI.

THE PORTUGUESE IN AFRICA.

THE invasion of the African continent from Portugal began in the first quarter of the fifteenth century. Various causes stimulated the Portuguese to this enterprise. Besides the passion for renown, they held that the possession of north-western Africa was required to round off their conquest of Algarve. Southern Algarve was in fact the received name of the north-west corner of Africa, having been so called for centuries by its Mohammedan inhabitants. Further, an African expedition presented itself in the light of an easier crusade. It was not such a far cry to Africa as to Palestine, and the people of Algarve *trans mare* were unbelievers as rank as the lords of the Holy Sepulchre. Finally, the thought of pecuniary gain fired the aggressors' zeal: the towns in north-west Africa, opulent through the tribute paid them for serving as depositories of wares from far, would fill the coffers of Portugal, and be the means of rapidly developing Portuguese commerce.

So in 1415 we find the Portuguese in Africa for the first time, bent on striking down the Crescent and spoiling the Mussulman. That year saw the great fortress and town of Ceuta fall into the hands of Portugal. Ceuta provided a rich revenue for the Peninsular kingdom. There it sat and taxed all foreign ships and goods coming within its reach. There it established a bazaar, where it could buy and sell with merchants of many countries. The Mohammedans made desperate efforts to retake the place, but in vain. The Portuguese drove back the unbelievers from the walls of Ceuta again and again, erected it into a bishopric, transformed its mosque into a cathedral, and kept it as a Christian town. It is Spanish now, since the usurpation of 1580. Tangier was the next place against which Portugal sent a besieging army; but the attempt upon it in 1436 was a disastrous failure, which cooled the desire to prey upon the Moslems for some twenty years. In 1457, however, an expeditionary force successfully stormed Alcazar-Seguer. A second attack on Tangier in 1464 was as unfortunate as the other; but the neighbouring fortress of Arzilla being taken in 1471, the population of Tangier evacuated the city, and the Portuguese at length entered in triumph. It also was created an episcopal city. (Arzilla was returned to the Mohammedans by Philip as the price of their neutrality. England received Tangier with the bride of Charles II.) These were the chief Portuguese gains in north Africa.

The country behind these places was subdued in the time of Emmanuel as far as Mount Atlas, and tribute levied throughout that circuit, but the annexation of all southern Algarve was never accomplished. On the contrary, outside the walls of the Portuguese strongholds the Mussulmans showed themselves invincible; and in the time of John III., as the dominion of the Xerifs extended, it became necessary, lest Portugal should lose its footing in Africa altogether, that it should strictly confine its power to its great fortresses. Its resources, besides, were now required in another region of the globe. Alcazar-Seguer, therefore, and some lesser towns were demolished, and by the middle of the sixteenth century, Ceuta, Arzilla, and Tangier were the only fruits which remained to the Portuguese after so much blood and treasure had been sown on the soil of north Africa.

Yet it must not be forgotten that very much through this intercourse with north Africa, costly and hostile though it was,

Portugal came to a more intimate knowledge of the riches with which the interior of the continent was teeming. Precious wares were brought from the south and laid down in the Portuguese markets on the coast. The question then naturally presented itself why Portugal should not do something more with such goods than simply buy them, or take toll as they passed through her hands. But to get at the source of that wealth by land meant forcing a passage through swarms of fierce Mohammedans. The sea passage, however, by the west coast might solve the problem. This was the idea which eclipsed the project of mastering Algarve across the sea. By-and-by it was to become a passion with the Portuguese.

But Prince Henry "the Navigator" was the first to grasp the conception and to set about realizing it long before it had penetrated the duller minds of his contemporaries. He had been present at the taking of Ceuta, and was astounded at the sight of the valuable articles which its warehouses contained. He questioned Mohammedan prisoners and merchantmen, and learned from them much of western and inner Africa, which made him eager to push at once the fortunes of his country in those parts. He had by this fresh intelligence confirmation of a thought which he had entertained for years—that far beyond the southern Algarve lay an El Dorado which beggared any miser's dream.

Filled with the purpose of establishing the commercial greatness of his country, and impelled in the same direction by the pious hope of Christianizing the parts of the infidels, the Infant on his return to Portugal fitted out and sent forth a vessel to explore the west coast of Africa. Before his day Cape Non had been, as its name implies, considered an impassable barrier. "*Quem passar o Cabo de Não,*" the Portuguese said, "*ou tornará ou não*" (He who rounds Cape Non knows not whether he will return). But the prince had already falsified the old word, since ships which he fitted out had in 1410 not only rounded that headland which had for centuries been an object of exceeding dread, but he advanced as far as Cape Bojador. There, however, the progress of the explorers for the time was stayed. The strong currents and foaming breakers of the latter promontory were too much for them, and they were glad to make for smoother waters. It must be remembered that though (thanks to the inventive genius of Flavio Gioja) navigators had possessed the mariner's compass since 1302, until the researches of Columbus into the nature of its variations the instrument was often practically useless. Nor were the early Portuguese discoverers able to make use of astronomical observations for the purpose of ascertaining their position when out of sight of land, and they were unprovided with charts of their course. When, therefore, one thinks of these things, and considers also the superstition of the age, one is surprised, not at their timidity, but at their boldness.

In 1418 two noble Portuguese, Vaz Tereira and Gonzalves Zarco, companions-in-arms at Ceuta, offered to adventure the rounding of Cape Bojador. This they failed to do, being caught in a violent tempest and carried westwards; but their voyage was of the greatest importance, in that they lighted upon the little island of Porto Santo (as they named it), four hundred miles off the coast of Morocco. They found the place fruitful and salubrious, and returned with the good news to their patron. The prince, overjoyed, sent settlers thither from Portugal, and provided them with seeds and plants and whatever else was required for the infant colony. Unfortunately Perestrello, one of the most influential immigrants, whose daughter afterwards became the wife of Columbus, in his intense desire to reproduce in Porto Santo some of the features of the old country, had brought with him some Portuguese rabbits, which ere long carried out the scheme of reproduction so completely that they were numerous enough to eat up all the fruits of the colonists' labour. Extraordinary exertions were necessary to deal with the effects of Perestrello's unwise importation.

The immigrants were soon after their arrival struck by an appearance like that of a dense motionless cloud on the western horizon. To satisfy their curiosity they sailed towards it the year following their landing on Porto Santo, and found it to be an island much larger than the other, with steep shores and thickly covered with trees. This new discovery, twenty-five miles from Porto Santo, was called Madeira (timber), since the island was from end to end one vast wood. A clearing was made by fire near the site of the present capital, Funchal, but the conflagration spread so much that the greater part of the trees was burned down. Its remarkable fertility drew many settlers from Portugal to Madeira. Corn sown there yielded, it is said, sixty-fold; Cyprus vines and Sicilian sugar-canes throve at once beyond expectation. The Madeira group still belongs to Portugal, and forms a province of the kingdom. The greater island is chiefly known as a place whither invalids flee for their lives, and where the wonderfully equable temperature frequently prolongs existence to the diseased, if it does not entirely restore their health. The trade of Madeira is inconsiderable. The value of its exports appears to have been almost stationary for some twenty years past. The occasional fluctuations to the extent of a few thousand pounds sterling have been due to the success or failure of the vintage, wine being the principal article shipped from its shores.*

Delighted as Prince Henry was with the discovery of the Madeira group, he did not allow himself to be diverted for a moment from his original design. His eye was still fixed on the west coast of Africa. The prince was far before his age,

---

* According to the report for 1890 of Mr. Keene, H.M. Consul, Madeira, the value of the wine exported in 1889 (£151,250) was nine times that of all the other exports put together. The imports, owing to excessive duties, have decreased in twenty years by over £100,000. Madeira's best market is the English, the tonnage of British ships entering and clearing at Funchal considerably exceeding the combined tonnage of vessels belonging to all other nations trading there.

and his ideas met with scant encouragement. On the contrary, he had to contend with no little opposition. To approach the tropics was believed to be a tempting of Providence. Human beings could not exist, it was said, in the sweltering heat of the torrid zone. It was the height of cruelty, Henry's critics insisted, to send men in frail barks so far upon the ocean. But the enthusiastic "Navigator" was not to be discouraged. He summoned to Portugal Jacome of Majorca, a great authority on navigation, caused him to instruct Portuguese seamen in that art, and with his assistance prepared hydrographical charts, in which work the prince was perhaps helped by his brother, the Infant Pedro, who had travelled far in Europe and Asia, and had during his stay in Italy enjoyed much intercourse with Venetian shipmasters.

Henry found that in the light which he was disseminating the mariners of Portugal were growing less reluctant to launch into the unknown deep, and in 1433 Gilianes of Lagos, in Algarve (a town which has produced since that time many a brave sailor), after touching at the Canaries, successfully accomplished the rounding of that terrible promontory, the tail of the black mountains, nameless till then, but called by him Cape Bojador (the springing-out cape), from the immense length of its projection into the north Atlantic. Gilianes landed on the southern side of the headland, and saw not the sandy waste of the popular imagination, but a fertile country, showing, however, no sign of inhabitants. He sailed again for Portugal, and took home with him some specimens of vegetation from the region he had visited. The prince was thus furnished with the means of dissipating another prevailing delusion, and stimulated to further adventure.

Next year Gilianes and another advanced a considerable distance beyond Cape Bojador, and in 1435, sailing still further southward, landed, and despatched two of their companions on horseback a little way into the interior. Here for the first time were encountered some of the natives, who fell upon the strangers with their spears. But the white men being mounted were able to escape and relate their experience to their chief.

Political troubles interrupted thereafter for six years the explorations directed by Prince Henry, but in 1441 Tristan and Gonzalves, gentlemen of Portugal, commanded an expedition to the west coast of Africa. Tristan sailed as far as Cape Blanco (the white cape), whence he returned because of the stormy weather and for lack of provisions. Gonzalves, stopping short of the cape, landed, and made prisoners of ten natives, whom he took with him to Portugal; for Gilianes' story of their attack on his party of observation had created there a desire to see the savage Africans. This was the earliest importation to the kingdom of the children of Ham, and naturally their swarthy figures created a great sensation. These were the first-fruits of that multitude of the negro race who were destined to be "hewers of wood and drawers of water" for the Portuguese in their future vast dominions.

Now at length the Infant began to win golden opinions from his countrymen. The merchants of Portugal were awakening to the advantage and the possibility of laying the first hand on those valuable commodities with which caravans of Moslems and Jews entered their African emporiums; and now the testimony which the captured Africans gave in signs and broken sentences regarding their goodly land made the popular mind catch fire, and Lisbon clamoured for the continuance of those adventures which once it decried. The tables were turned. Hitherto the great Infant had been mocked as a dreamer, hindered, and, when he brushed aside obstructions, pursued with caustic criticism and obloquy. Now he was lauded to the skies as the benefactor of his country. He had spent his own money freely in his enterprises. It had become evident that his outlay had been no prodigality, but the wisest investment. Henry was one who could afford to stand alone. He fought not for himself but for the fatherland.   Yet he was human enough to rejoice in a majority.

The prince was, with all his eagerness to accomplish his daring object, so free from jealousy that he assented with the greatest pleasure when, in 1443, a wealthy Lisbon merchant desired to fit out an expedition in his own name for the work of exploring the African west coast.   The result of that overture was the discovery of Cape Verd (the green cape).   But the pilot did not run the risk of rounding the headland.   Two years thereafter Cadamosto, a Venetian in Henry's service, and Vicente Dias of Lagos, advanced to the mouth of the Gambia; and in the same year Gonzalo de Cintra sailed some distance along the Gold Coast.   The prince hearing on Gonzalo's return that the land contained a considerable population, sent thither, in 1446, three caravels, with orders to the masters that they should attempt the conversion of the heathen whom they should find.   They had, however, no success in that direction, and sailed homewards.   But Fernandes, one of the voyagers, being, at his own request, left behind, stayed among the natives for nearly a twelvemonth; and when his fellow-countrymen returned for him they found him living on the best of terms with the people, and in possession of much information about the interior, where he had travelled further than any European before him.   They took back Fernandes, some negroes, and a quantity of gold dust.   The prince was deeply interested in Fernandes' intelligence, and in the human and mineral specimens which his explorers had brought.

The remaining years of Prince Henry's life, which ended in 1460, show incessant activity in African voyaging.   In 1446 the above-mentioned Cadamosto, turned aside from his course by a storm, discovered the Cape Verd islands, passed Cape Roxo (the red cape), arrived at the mouth of the Rio Grande, and landed at the Bissago islands.   The increasing boldness of Portuguese mariners is illustrated by the fact that in the same year no fewer than fourteen ships sailed together from Lagos, and coasted Africa as far as Cape Verd. That year also saw an endeavour on the part of a Portuguese expedition to ascend the Rio Grande; but the intruders were met by a shower of poisoned arrows from the natives. All but five of the voyagers died of their wounds. The ship's clerk and four youths alone remained alive to take the vessel home. How they managed it they could not tell, for they were all ignorant of navigation. Nevertheless they at length, though in a very exhausted condition, entered the harbour of Lagos. At more and more frequent intervals vessels set out from Portuguese havens on the African voyage, yet the explorers did not get much beyond the Rio Grande all the prince's day.

It was about this date (1446) that the Portuguese established themselves at the Azores, though the exact time when they were discovered is uncertain. It is not to the Portuguese that the credit of finding them belongs, but to Vanderberg, a merchant of Flanders, who was driven thither by a storm. Seamen of Portugal, however, on hearing of the islands, hastened to visit them and to take possession in their country's name. The Azores, a volcanic cluster of nine islands in the north Atlantic, being eight hundred miles from any coast, cannot be properly assigned to any continent, but this seems to be the most convenient place for taking such slight notice of them as our space affords. Those who first landed there from Portugal found them desert indeed, but not by any means barren. The vegetation was luxuriant, the picturesque heights green to their summits. The glowing accounts which the sailors gave when they returned regarding the fine climate and scenery of the group, and the splendid prospects of any who should till its soil, induced numbers to quit the fatherland and seek a home in those isles of the west. At this day the Azores are a province of Portugal, and their population, usually reckoned with that of the peninsular country, is one-sixteenth of the whole, the proportion of inhabitants to the square mile being more than double that of continental Portugal. The capital is Angra, in Terceira, the central, though not the largest of the group, that island whose inhabitants so obstinately resisted Philip of Spain. The islands are isolated, and none of their harbours are good, Fayal having perhaps the best. Yet the record of their exports and imports is excellent, considering the various disadvantages under which they labour.

After Prince Henry's death the public interest in maritime adventure rose to the height of a passion. The spirit which animated the "Navigator" seemed to be diffused in the nation. Men of the highest rank considered it a privilege to be employed in the dangerous task of discovery. During three successive reigns the sovereign of the day made it a point of honour that something should be added, by his patronage and at his expense, to the list of achievements in this kind. The mariners of Portugal had now banished much of their old timidity, and rivalled the famous sailors of Genoa and Venice.

The Portuguese trade on the west coast of Africa had even in the prince's lifetime begun to assume respectable dimensions. A merchant company had planted a factory on the island of Arguin, twenty-five miles south of Cape Blanco, and carried on a lively commerce there, exchanging the goods of Europe for such commodities as negroes, gold, and ivory. Treaties were concluded with native chiefs, and by an embassy to Mecca in 1448 a *modus vivendi* was sought with the Arabs, who were at work in the interior, and came coastwards to barter. Ten years after the prince died, the Portuguese Cortes resolved that the privilege of dealing under the Guinea Coast commercial agreement with persons influential there should be knocked down to the highest bidder, a fact which reveals how valuable the privilege was, since competition for it was expected.

Alfonso V. was so anxious to secure his possession of these trading rights that he obtained a bull of confirmation from the

Pope in 1452, and, armed with that instrument, was able to beat off the claim which John II. of Castile preferred for a share in the booty. This dispute between Spain and Portugal about the coast of Guinea was the occasion when the Canaries, about whose lordship there was a Spanish-Portuguese quarrel of some standing, were ceded to Spain in 1481, on condition of that country renouncing any claim, supposed or real, to traffic by the side of Portugal in Africa.   .

When John II. of Portugal ascended the throne in the year of the treaty with Spain, Portuguese discoverers had become acquainted with Sierra Leone, Cape Mesurado, and the coast to Cape St. Catherine (the most southern point of progress in Alfonso's time); also with the islands known as St. Thomas, Prince's, and Annobon, along with the (now Spanish) island found by Fernando Po, and since called after him, having lost the name Fermosa which he originally bestowed upon it.

To make his footing sure in Guinea, John II. caused to be erected on the coast in 1481 a fort, which was named St. George da Mina ; and by-and-by, as many Portuguese who came to settle and trade chose the neighbourhood of the stronghold for security, the houses clustering round it grew into a town. It was this royal establishment which occasioned the king and his successors to assume the style of "Senhor do Guine." The year 1484 was memorable by reason of Diogo Cam's voyage to the Congo, where he left behind several Portuguese who should gather information regarding the country, and whence he carried home some natives to converse with the king. In 1485 Cam returned to the Congo, passed the mighty river, and fared some hundreds of miles further, and there, in the twenty-second degree of southern latitude, he set up a pillar on a headland, which, accordingly, he named the Cape of the Pillar.

The Congo region was found to be very populous. The people lived under a native king, and had a town of a sort (or a collection of huts) named Banza, which, however, the Portuguese, after their manner, called San Salvador. They were quite approachable, indeed demonstratively cordial, and were ready not only to trade with the white men but even to receive from them the Christian religion. The early Portuguese were zealous propagandists. They sailed out of their havens for those *partes infidelium* with the double object of commercial advantage and the increase of the Church. They considered that to search for worldly gain and to neglect the opportunity of spreading their religion was to invoke a malediction on their heads. They sought therefore to consecrate every hundred miles or so of the African shore by raising at conspicuous points the symbol of the faith. Beside their fortress of St. George da Mina a church was immediately reared, and wherever they established a market abroad they did not rest satisfied before the introduction of Christian priests and sacraments. In Congo-land and elsewhere in Africa many thousands embraced Christianity ; but as the fruits of this ecclesiastical activity long ago disappeared from the region, it is not difficult to arrive at an approximate estimate regarding the quality of those numerous conversions which are the boast of sixteenth century chroniclers.

The mind of John II. was now possessed by the conception of another enterprise which he believed would yield even better results than the African. He was resolved upon finding an ocean passage to India. He was assured, by communications he had received from north-eastern Africa and from Asia, and by the stories of travellers visiting his court, that the great continent, whose western side was already becoming familiar to the Portuguese, terminated southwards in a promontory ; and that if this were passed by a vessel, there would be nothing but water between its prow and the wonderland of the Orient. The thought wrought like leaven in his mind, and gave him no rest until he had prepared an expedition for the purpose of seeking the south cape, rounding it, and pursuing the route to India.

The chief command was given to Bartholomew Diaz, who in 1486 set out with three ships upon that voyage which was to make him famous.

Diaz, a Portuguese of gentle blood, was considered one of the most skilful and daring navigators of his time—a man who, the king was well aware, would do honour to the confidence reposed in him. But to reach the most southerly point of Africa was a tremendous ordeal even for the ablest mariner afloat. Easy though it be to take advantage of the westerly trades, and so make the Cape of Good Hope, the pilots of four hundred years ago did not in the least understand the theory of those constant currents moving across the Atlantic; so, in ignorance of a matter with which every schoolboy is in these days familiar, the great Bartholomew Diaz struggled with the elements in his attempt to execute the orders of his master. It required the greatest steadfastness to resist the impatient demand of his sailors that he should give up an apparently impossible task. But Diaz was able to contend both with the passions of men and with the dangers of seafaring, and courageously held on his way, alternately becalmed and tempest-tossed, till he passed the cape now called "of Good Hope." But at the time he was absolutely unaware that he had reached the termination of the continent. The cape was to him but a headland of the coast, where he was made the sport of the gale as he had never been before, for which reason he named that promontory the "Capo of all the Storms." He visited the islet of Santa Cruz, on which he piously erected the holy rood, and cast anchor at length where the Great Fish River debouches near Algoa Bay. Here the endurance of the crews, whose exertions had been prolonged and excessive, gave out entirely. They threatened mutiny if their leader persisted in his voyage. Diaz was not unreasonable. He saw the inefficient state of the men, and agreed to turn back. But anxious not to return without having accomplished some part at least of his commission, he persuaded his associates to proceed for yet two or three days' sail in search of that cape which he had in fact left behind him. He was of course disappointed, and fulfilled his promise to return. He looked mournfully, as he sailed by it, at the cross on the island, the sole memorial of his expedition. Yet his heart was lightened in no small degree when, on reaching the Cape, he observed that he had actually rounded the continent, and had been skirting its south-eastern side. After an absence of sixteen months Diaz arrived in the Tagus. The king received him with cordial thanks for the great service he had rendered ; and looking on the rounding of the point as the practical solution of the problem which had long been occupying his thoughts, declared that the south cape should not bear the ill-omened title which the explorer had given it, and renamed it *Cabo de Boa Esperanza* (Cape of Good Hope).

It was not the will of Providence that the last sovereign of the house of Avis should satisfy his heart's desire by achieving the eastern passage to India. That honour was reserved for the founder of a new line. But John II., when he saw his end near, was sure that the better part of the work was done, and that his country stood on the way to incalculable wealth and influence. Therefore he quitted the world in a spirit of resignation, saying, " One plants and another gathers the fruit."

King Emmanuel did not lose sight of his predecessor's cherished design, and got ready, soon after his accession, four ships for the Indian voyage. They were built under the eye of Bartholomew Diaz, whose experience, especially of his former expedition, was of great value to the shipwrights. The conduct of the venture was given to Vasco da Gama, a native of Sines, in Alemtejo, whose family belonged to the ranks of the lesser nobility. Da Gama had already an honourable reputation for fearlessness and good seamanship. But now he was to leave his record far behind him, to traverse an ocean which no European keel had ever ploughed, except when the ships of

Diaz had crept into it a little way and then withdrawn.
Brave Diaz! He had shown the path. His had been the
pioneer work, the most difficult and dangerous of all. He had
provided the evidence that the work to which Da Gama was
called lay within the power of a careful and intrepid navigator.
But it was Da Gama who should wave the palm, whose
exploits should be enshrined in the pages of the immortal
"Lusiad." * Another advantage the later discoverer had.
Though the accurate nautical instruments of the present day
were not yet invented, the astrolabe had in the later years of
John II. been applied to the purpose of taking the sun's altitude at sea; and provided with an astrolabe, as no doubt he
was, Da Gama must have felt much more at ease than Diaz in
guiding his fleet round the stormy Cape.

In July 1497 he set sail, and after much wild weather
steered with his own hands the foremost ship of his command
round the Cape of Good Hope in November of the same year.
The sea was calmer than when Diaz had made it ten years
before, and Da Gama's men saluted the promontory with
huzzahing and trumpet blasts. He passed Algoa Bay, and
coasted a charming country, which, because it had been sighted
on Christmas day, he named Natal. Sofala,† where an important trade in gold was carried on by Mohammedans, he did not
observe, being at the time of his sailing by too far from the
coast; but in March 1498 he sighted Mozambique, and moored
at that island, which was destined to be the great *entrepôt* for
the Portuguese in connection with their Indian trade. Da
Gama found there a commodious haven filled with vessels, some
of them large, and, to his surprise, as well provided as his own

* Camoens, however, does not altogether neglect Diaz, though Da Gama's voyage is
the theme of that fine epic which has often been placed beside the *Gerusalemme Liberata*.
Diaz found a watery grave just outside of the Cape of Good Hope, after many dangers
passed; and the poet, speaking of him warmly, imagines the spirit of the Cape to
have conjured up the storm in which the navigator perished in revenge for the invasion
of its rest by the expedition of 1486.

† Perhaps the ancient Ophir.

MOMBASA.

with charts and nautical instruments. The population were Mussulmans, and imagining the Portuguese to be their co-religionists from north-west Africa, the sheikh gave them a hearty reception, sent them a pilot for their further voyage, and supplied them with stores. But discovering ere long the mistake they had committed, the people began to make a hostile demonstration, and Da Gama took his ships out of the harbour, upon which, however, he by-and-by opened fire. The thunder of his artillery and the damage it wrought soon brought the Sheikh of Mozambique to his senses, and constrained him to sue for quarter. Da Gama obtained another pilot, for the first had fled while the vessels lay in port, and the expedition left Mozambique. But the pilot proved a traitor, and had nearly wrecked the fleet by conducting it among shallows.

Dreading, therefore, more roguery, the Portuguese, after happily extricating themselves from their dangerous situation, would not put the helm into the man's hands again, but ran further northwards along the coast, and arrived at the island and town of Mombasa. The island had a beautiful appearance from the sea, with its numerous gardens of tropical fruit-trees. The climate was found so excellent, and the drinking-water so wholesome, that those of Da Gama's sailors who had been on the sick-list became speedily convalescent. Into the town, however, the Portuguese did not venture, mindful of their experience at Mozambique. Mombasa was a well-built place, standing on a rocky height by the sea, with handsome houses and regular streets. There was much shipping, also, in its harbour, as in that of Mozambique. It invited a visit, but having cause to suspect the good faith of the inhabitants, Da Gama quitted the neighbourhood and cast anchor at Melinda.

Melinda was at that time a large and fine town lying in a fruitful plain, its air, and the quality and quantity of its vegetable productions, reminding the voyagers of Mombasa. All these Mohammedan settlements had a thriving business connection with India, and many Indians had established themselves in them as merchants. The King of Melinda, less of the fanatical Moslem than the Sheikh of Mozambique, showed the Portuguese much kind attention, and learning their purpose, willingly provided them with a skilful pilot. So the expedition which was to bear such abundant fruit left the shores of Africa, and Da Gama committed himself to the Indian main.

Believing that, if it were peopled at all, they should come across in east Africa the same kind of people as those with whom they were acquainted on the other side—unclothed men of the negro type, outside of civilization—the Portuguese could scarcely credit the evidence of their senses when they saw, north of Natal, places not inferior to the average European city, with large populations of that race with which they and their fathers had so long contended. They found a multitude of Arabians there, speaking the language and using the customs, religious and other, of the obnoxious "Moors." Da Gama wanted nothing when he came to the eastern shores of Africa but provisions and a pilot. He had no commission from Emmanuel to explore the region, and did not contemplate at first an establishment there. But the good of such a half-way house between Portugal and India was soon evident. So for the sake of the Indian trade the Portuguese determined to plant themselves on the African east coast. To this end they began to eject its Mohammedan ruling class as soon as the foundations of their Asiatic dominion had been laid. In the west it suited them to live at peace with the followers of the prophet. They were glad to use the Arabs there as middlemen, who saved them the trouble and danger of penetrating the interior. Here the commercial interests of Portugal were staked upon the downfall of that race, which to oppose and crush was moreover a religious duty.

In 1505 Kilwa was taken and plundered by Francisco d'Almeida, and thereafter Mombasa fell into his hands. Town after town was captured. Some with which the Portuguese had a special quarrel were treated with great barbarity. Others, like Melinda, which had shown themselves friendly, were exempted from attack, and simply placed, meantime, under the suzerainty of Portugal. But gradually the grasp of the European conquerors tightened even upon these, till the Arab lordship was a shadow and the Portuguese over-lordship all in all. That supremacy, as the sixteenth century ran its course, came to be exercised over almost the entire stretch of the east African littoral. Before the middle of that century the Portuguese colonies in these parts were in a most flourishing condition. The abundant harvest they yielded, of that very kind which had been reaped for a hundred years in the west, made them now remarkably interesting on their own account, apart altogether from the consideration of their usefulness as halting-places between two oceans.

But the incubus of the Castilian usurpation pressed the life out of these settlements everywhere. The colonial income was insufficient to meet the demands of Spain, whose expenditure for her military operations was enormous. European enemies of Spain preyed not only upon her own dependencies, but upon those of her sister or rather vassal kingdom. And though the east African possessions were not directly attacked from Europe, the withdrawal of Portuguese war-ships and troops to other waters left them comparatively defenceless. The Mohammedans, therefore, seeing their advantage, disputed vigorously with Portugal the possession of the upper half of the coast line, from Cape Delgado northwards, being the portion nearest the headquarters of the Arab race. The fight was protracted for years with varying fortunes; but its effect was to steadily contract Portugal's sphere of influence, till the Imaum of Muscat, on repudiating the Portuguese yoke in 1648, put himself at the head of the Moslem forces, and so shook the rival power in the north that its decay there was greatly accelerated. Between Juba and Kilwa, the towns which acknowledged the sway of the Portuguese were rapidly recovered by the Mohammedans; and from the middle of last century the Portuguese maritime territory in east Africa has been confined to the line between Cape Delgado and Delagoa Bay.

The province which is known as Mozambique extends for about thirteen hundred· miles along the sea-board, nearing the equatorial line on the north, and reaching southwards to the temperate zone. It covers an area of three hundred and eighty thousand miles. The chief river is the Zambesi, a mighty stream whose length is estimated at fourteen hundred miles. Unfortunately the heavy surf makes the delta perilous, a circumstance which has no doubt told against the progress of the colony. Its whole neighbourhood abounds in shallows and hidden coral cliffs. Up the river for five hundred miles there are here and there Portuguese forts and stations. The climate of the province is accounted unhealthy, but those who have had experience of both east and west coasts of Africa maintain that although intensely hot, Mozambique is preferable to the other side of the continent. South of the Zambesi the country consists of steppes covered with mimosa bushes. Further inland, nut-woods are found, and the borassus palm. On the other side of the river the land is for the most part higher. Here and there throughout the province are sugar and cotton plantations and groves of tropical fruit trees.

The capital of the whole district is Mozambique, on the island of that name, a town of seven thousand inhabitants. It is a place which pleases the eye. Some of the churches, government edifices, and private residences may even be called imposing. There is a large and sheltered harbour where are always to be seen a number of war and merchant vessels. The importance of the place is maintained by reason of its being the seat of the colonial administration, at the head of which is a

QUILIMANE.

governor-general, usually a naval or military officer of high rank, who is assisted by a council. The commercial standing of Mozambique is, however, diminished by the want of a navigable river on the opposite shore, and the consequent necessity of conveying goods to the interior by the slow process of portage.

Quilimané, about three hundred miles further south, on the river Quaqua, is the business capital of the colony, though it has not half the population of Mozambique. Quilimané, though fifteen miles from the river's mouth, is nevertheless accessible to great ships, which there lay down their cargoes from Europe. Thence the imports are taken by boat up the Quaqua, which rapidly narrows above the town, as far as it is navigable. From that point to the Zambesi, since the Quaqua bends towards the great river, a portage of two miles only is necessary. At the Zambesi a steamer waits to take the boat-loads up and down its waters, or up its tributary the Shiré, to the Murchison Falls, over which the goods must be carried by bearers. Again shipped on the Shiré, they can be conveyed to Lake Nyassa. Thus from Quilimané the commodities of civilization are continually being introduced to the interior, and in the same way are brought down to the port the hides, the rubber, the ivory, and other products of Africa. Perhaps one day the waters of the Zambesi will break down the thin wall which divides them from the Quaqua and sweep away this Portuguese emporium lying on a low, wide morass, in which case another and greater town will rise at what will be then the northern mouth of the Zambesi; but meanwhile Quilimané as it is thrives, as African east coast towns go.

Lorenzo Marques, at the extreme south of the province, is a place with a future. It is the natural outlet for the flourishing Transvaal state, and probably the republic will eventually purchase the fifty miles of territory between its frontier and Delagoa Bay. A company received a concession to construct a railway from the bay to the interior; but a party in the national house of representatives at Lisbon viewed with jealousy an undertaking entirely in foreign hands, and persuaded the home government to refuse an extension of the time for finishing the works which the contractors saw necessary to ask. Lord Salisbury, for the sake of British interests, sent therefore three men-of-war to Delagoa Bay. But the dispute was happily adjusted, and the Portuguese government took over that part of the railway which runs through their own province. Already, although the track is far from complete, Lorenzo Marques is feeling the better for the railway. Nor is there much room for doubt that this, the first line ever laid on the east coast, will be found of inestimable advantage when the Transvaal shall have further developed, and attract a great business to Lorenzo Marques.

A much larger bone of contention between Great Britain and Portugal was the question about the standing of the latter country in the interior. The former position of the Portuguese there is one of the dark things of history. It would be as easy to stake off the paradise of Prester John as to delimit Portugal's old-time sphere of influence in the *hinterland* of Mozambique. Her patriotic children, intoxicated with the idea of their country's former glory, would claim that Portugal had a thoroughfare in Africa between the Atlantic and Indian Oceans, and was monarch of all she surveyed from this pathway; that Nyassaland was hers; and that south of the Zambesi she owned the immense tract known in these days as Matabeleland and Mashonaland. But when evidence was demanded in support of these extraordinary assertions, nothing was produced which could endure the light of reason.

As to the Portuguese claim upon a horizontal strip of the entire continent, it is certain, in the first place, that the countrymen of Vasco da Gama had no knowledge of the east coast when he arrived there in 1498. No one had, in the in-

terest of Portugal, pushed through from the west by that time.
Nor was it likely that an advance should have been made from
thence. Their employment of the Arabs as jackals in that
quarter exempted them from the necessity of journeys inland.
And if it was from the other side that Portuguese adventurers
set out to plant the wooden cross—their favourite method of
taking possession in those days—there was only a short time in
which this kind of activity could have prevailed, for only in
1505 did the work of reducing the eastern sea-board begin.
May we not believe that time was wanted to set their conquests
in order, during which they must have had little to give up
to making excursions westwards? What they held north of
Mombasa, moreover, required all their spare courage and care
to keep. Then in 1580 Philip II. laid his cold hand on
Portugal, paralyzing her enterprise at home and abroad. It is
not the least likely that any Portuguese ever accomplished the
arduous task of crossing Africa.

It is quite as improbable that Portugal once occupied Nyassaland. It may be doubted whether its explorers even saw the
magnificent Lake Nyassa. "Many indeed believe," says Captain Lugard, "that the ancient Portuguese discoveries of a
great lake with a mountain rising out of it referred to the
swamps of the Shiré, then flooded, and not to the real Nyassa."
The argument on behalf of Portuguese rights in the interior
south of the Zambesi rests upon an arrangement which, it is
insisted, was entered into with the representatives of Portugal
by a native sovereign named Monomotapa. There is no reason
to doubt the existence of this potentate (though the name was
perhaps a designation of honour, like Abimelech, Pharaoh, and
the like). Proofs of it are to be had from other than Portuguese
sources. His rule extended over the district called Matabeleland and Mashonaland, and the story goes that more than two
hundred and fifty years ago he made over his lands or that
portion of them to the Portuguese. But it is not easy to see

what could have induced him to do so—what advantage the Portuguese could have offered for the grant; or is it possible that they could have had the means of compelling Monomotapa to such action—that they led an army up the Zambesi and per-suaded him by a demonstration of force? The alleged date, too, strikes one as peculiar. It was in 1630, ten years before the revolution, just when Portugal was being robbed of her pos-sessions all over the world, and had no power to arrest the spoilers. The claim, in short, is eminently unsatisfactory.

But even if it could be more clearly proved that Nyassaland and an indefinite number of square miles south of the Zambesi were once owned and occupied by the Portuguese, they must be held to have forfeited their possession by long-continued neglect. They are like a parent who has deserted his child in its infancy, and who by-and-by claims kin, when the child has scrambled into a position of influence. The importance of Nyassaland and the immense tract on the other side of the Zambesi is palpable, and one can understand the feeling of a Portuguese when he thinks of his country's splendid history, when he remembers that Portugal was first on African ground, and sees enormous slices carved out of the continent by this nation and that, com-paratively late comers to the field. Yet outside of Portugal it is with justice maintained that if that country had long ago a forward colonial policy while other peoples were slumbering, her centuries of inaction do her the greater dishonour; and that, if others have entered into and laboriously cultivated the ancient so-called possessions of Portugal, they are entitled to reap the fruits of their pains—have, moreover, earned a moral right of pre-emption in respect of territory as yet fallow lying convenient to the spheres they have worthily occupied.

To a person of ordinary candour, without a jot of English bias, this is especially the case of Great Britain in Africa. If dis-covered long ago by Portuguese, certain portions of it were, at the very least, after having been lost for centuries, found by

SERPA PINTO.

Livingstone; and the conduct of Britain wherever it has planted its foot on the continent guarantees its capacity and will to do the best for its acquisitions. Probably no white man ever stood on the shores of Lake Nyassa till the time of the great Scottish explorer. His countrymen have since made the whole region, by the most energetic missionary and commercial enterprise, peculiarly their own.* But Portuguese *amour propre* has been apparently deeply wounded by seeing British influence established there. The same sentiment was excited when the native chief Lobengula, the present ruler of Matabeleland, which stretches from the Zambesi to the Transvaal, gave a charter to a British trading company. "The grasping spirit of the English must be checked," a party at Lisbon were resolved, and an officer of some distinction as an explorer, an ardent patriot, moreover, received a commission to do whatever lay in his power for the establishment of Portuguese and the suppression of British interests in Nyassaland.

This officer, Major Serpa Pinto, visited the chief M'ponda, a man who was known to be hand-and-glove with slave-dealing Arabs, at the foot of Lake Nyassa, and persuaded him to conclude a treaty with the Portuguese, to cede them also a certain location where they could block the mouth of the Shiré. Mr. H. H. Johnston, British consul at Mozambique, thereafter procured at Lisbon an arrangement which acknowledged as British a kind of semicircular line running from the Zambesi to Lake Nyassa, and from its northern shore to Lake Tanganyika; and as Portuguese, the tract on the east of Lake Nyassa, between the Ruo and the Rovuma. The Portuguese should, in accordance with the agreement, forego their demand for Mashonaland. By this treaty the Upper Zambesi and Shiré and the highlands of that river were given to Portugal—that is, the very district where British missionaries and merchants had been working so vigorously. The protests in England against the transaction

* See Professor Drummond's charming book, "Tropical Africa."

were so loud that it was not ratified, and Mr. Johnston received orders to proceed to the region in question and bring it under British influence. But the Portuguese were, on the other hand—the terms arranged being repudiated in London—bent upon doing everything they could to secure for themselves that district and Mashonaland besides. One agent of theirs was therefore detailed to advance their interests in Mashonaland, and Major Serpa Pinto was ordered to perform that service in Nyassaland.

The British consul, on his mission above mentioned, passed on the Shiré the Portuguese officer, who professed to be engaged in peaceful exploration, although the large armed force of Zulus he had with him looked more like war than science. Mr. Johnston, pursuing his way, reached the district between the Shiré and Mozambique, and received from the people assurances of their desire to live under British protection. The progress of the Portuguese emissary, who appeared on the scene after the consul had made his exit, was accordingly checked by the Makololos.* But Major Pinto, strengthened by some thousands of additional Zulus and a few pieces of field artillery, again advanced on the Makololos and inflicted terrible punishment upon them. The tribe was thereupon terrorized into submission.

Meanwhile the Portuguese had proclaimed their protectorate over Mashonaland, and Lord Salisbury had protested against the intrusion. The butchery on the Shiré, however, caused the British government, on their receipt of the news, to change their civil protest into a scarcely veiled threat of hostilities. Lord Salisbury demanded that the Portuguese troops should be immediately withdrawn from the Shiré, the Makololo country, and Mashonaland. British war-vessels were sent to Portuguese waters, and the British minister was required to quit the capital

* These Makololos, the headquarters of whose numerous tribe are in the heart of Africa, their capital being Linyanti, on the Mamele river, had marched towards the Indian Ocean with Livingstone in 1854, and established themselves on the Shiré. They have been all along friendly to the British.

of Portugal within a specified time, if the request of his government was not complied with. Great excitement prevailed, and violent indignation against the English was expressed at Lisbon. The persons and property of English residents were for a time imperilled. The ministry could not endure the storm, and tendered their resignation. But the wish of the British government was acceded to, pending negotiations. These negotiations have borne fruit in an Anglo-Portuguese agreement which, it may be hoped, will put an end to strife and misunderstanding between the two powers in east Africa.

By that treaty, concluded in August 1890, Portugal receives a portion of Lake Nyassa's eastern shore, but is excluded from the south-east and south end of the lake and from the Shiré highlands. Portuguese territory, after skirting Lake Nyassa from the German sphere to $13\frac{1}{2}$ degrees of south latitude, runs south-east by the eastern shore of Lake Shirwa ; thence southwards to the Zambesi, between Tete and the Kebrabassa Falls ; up the Zambesi, ten miles beyond Zumbo ; southwards again to 16 degrees of south latitude ; then eastward, taking in a slice of Mashonaland ; and southward, passing the eastern frontiers of the Transvaal State and Swaziland, till it emerges at the sea by the Maputa river, at the extreme south of the Mozambique province. (Britain has thus an unobstructed course from the Cape to Lake Tanganyika.) The Zambesi, the Shiré, and their affluents are free to the ships of every nation, and all rivers in the delimited territories to the vessels of the treaty powers, Portugal being allowed to construct roads and railways, and to lay telegraph lines, between the eastern and western possessions, up the Zambesi's north bank, "across the territories reserved to British influence." The settlement of Zumbo and the surrounding district within a radius of ten miles is declared Portuguese, but it shall not be transferred to another power without the consent of Great Britain. Transfer of Portuguese territory south of the Zambesi is fettered by the same condition. Great Britain will have free passage between the Ruo and the coast. Portugal will make a railway from Pungwé Bay to the British sphere of influence. Transit dues to the protectorate of Great Britain are not to exceed three per cent. *ad valorem.* Differences will be adjusted by arbitration.*

Portugal has room for a colonial enterprise of considerable magnitude under this arrangement, though she hold no more than its articles allow. But in addition to her eastern sphere, she still remains mistress of an extensive area in the west of Africa. To be sure she is no longer sovereign over all the coast. Other powers are entered into portions of that ancient heritage delivered to her by those hardy seamen whose names adorn her annals. Yet, not including her smaller possessions, such as the Cape Verd and other islands, there still belong to her Portuguese Senegambia and the great province of Angola, that long strip of coast territory stretching from the south bank of the river Congo to the north of Damaraland. Interior Angola is also by international agreement Portuguese, but as a matter of fact the power of Portugal is there only skin deep. The unhealthy coast of Benguela, the southern portion of the province, has repressed commercial activity, and so directed attention from its interior; but though the cool breeze which blows over the western verge of Angola proper renders it much less of a " white man's grave," and the country behind is consequently better known and in subjection, the whole province is a standing evidence and example of Portugal's colonial inertness. The soil is very fertile, and might be made to yield great harvests of cotton and sugar, but almost

---

* Since the above paragraph was written, the Anglo-Portuguese Convention has been cancelled. Its terms, on being made known in Portugal, were so objectionable to the patriotic party there that the ministry responsible for it were driven from office. The new cabinet repudiated the compact, but have agreed with the British Government, pending a final settlement, to a *modus vivendi*, valid for six months, which recognizes the territorial limits laid down in the broken treaty. From the reasonable lines of the first convention, however, it may be assumed that Great Britain will not be induced to move.

nothing has been done by the government to promote tillage. The palm-oil, gum, and rubber exported require no husbandry to produce ; and a small quantity of coffee, tobacco, and sugar sent out of the country is nearly all which speaks of farming. The chief commodity brought from the interior is ivory, which the Portuguese have been taking from west Africa for more than four hundred years ; but things are very dull in Angola. The truth is, the province has not recovered from the blow which fell upon it on the stoppage of the slave-trade. In the days of slavery, St. Paul de Loanda, the capital of Angola, was a flourishing town, for a long time the only place in Africa built in European style, with churches and streets which were intended to recall the old country. Now it is only the shadow of its former self. Its once splendid harbour gets more and more silted up, and the town generally has an air of having seen better days. On the cessation of the slave-trade the province was made a penal settlement, and no one liked to go home and say he had been in Angola. The convicts by-and-by received donations of land to cultivate ; but the heavy export and import duties damaged industry, and the colony still languished.

That, in fact, has been the mistake of the Portuguese in their management of the country's dependencies on both sides of Africa, and, indeed, elsewhere. In their desire to derive quick returns to the treasury, they have heaped imposts on the colonies which have not yielded the government what was expected, but have effectually smothered trade. Then the remarkably low salaries of officials have tempted them to corrupt practices ; and the permission given them to eke out their starvation allowances by appropriating certain dues and a proportion of others, as commission, has been often very liberally interpreted, which is the less astonishing since the pittances on which they are supposed to live have not been always forthcoming at the proper time. If it were not for the glory of ownership and for the hope of future success, the Portuguese might well drop their African colonies. They are far from self-supporting.* But the home treasury sadly disburses each year a subsidy large enough to meet colonial debts. So things move on in an artificial way. There is no question of turning or even wishing the Portuguese out of Africa. If, however, they are to make any way, they must needs reduce their customs tariff. And they will no doubt have convincing demonstration, when the low scale arranged by the Anglo-Portuguese Treaty shall have had a little time to show its effects, that the fall of duty means the rise of trade. In these circumstances, they will probably be constrained to liberalize their rates all over their African colonies; and the lesson may be even more widely applied. The present population, largely half-castes, negroes, and, on the east coast, Indians, as in Da Gama's day, demoralized by their association with the slave-trade, will be succeeded by a generation better, it is to be expected, because engaged in a cleaner business; and when they see, as no doubt they shall, their more energetic neighbours in the east and west using machinery, mining and farming, putting on the interior the dress of civilization, a superior class of immigrants will be summoned from Portugal to give the name of their country more moral weight in Africa.

* In Mozambique, for instance, the expenditure for 1880-90 was £193,910, and to cover it there was only available an income of £137,684, showing a deficiency of £56,226. The figures are from Consul Johnston's report. Comparing this statement with reports of Mr. O'Nell, the former British consul, one notes an increase of revenue, owing, of course, to the development of trade with Nyassaland and the Transvaal; but the expenditure leaps up surprisingly by the side of the income, and the gain is, after all, trifling.

CHAPTER XII.

THE PORTUGUESE IN ASIA.

FOURTEENTH and fifteenth century books of geography were not complete without an account of the empire of Prester John. The theme was celebrated throughout Europe. It was doubtless one of those "wonders of the world" wherewith William Wykeham bade his students of New College entertain themselves when they gathered round the evening fire. It was well known to John II. of Portugal, and it became to him a matter of the greatest importance in connection with his desire to obtain a footing in the Orient. A puissant sovereign like Prester John, whose dominions lay in northern India, and who was, moreover, a Christian, would, he thought, be an invaluable ally. Between them they might reduce the entire East.

But how to find the mysterious potentate was another question. Sir John Mandeville's travels (which the Portuguese king probably possessed, for they were published in Latin and French by the middle of the fourteenth century), and other narratives equally veracious, spoke of the immense extent of Prester John's realm, of his fabulous wealth, and of his Christian faith, in token whereof a cross was carried before him when he went abroad, whether in peace or in war. But in their description of his whereabouts medieval books are amusingly vague. Mandeville says only that "the land of Prester John is more far, by many dreadful days' journey, than Cathay" (Tartary). The

whole affair was a chimera. If it had any foundation, it referred
to the King of Abyssinia, for Ethiopia and India were strangely
mixed in people's minds long ago. Yet if that were so, the
Abyssinians, curiously enough, themselves retailed the story
and directed eastward those travellers who would search for
the "local habitation" of Prester John. The King of Portugal,
believing implicitly in the existence of a Christian monarchy
across the Indian Ocean, sent by land to the East Pedro de
Covilhan, who visited Calicut and Goa, travelling thence by
Aden and Cairo, and voyaged with Arabs to Sofala on the east
coast of Africa ; then staying for some time at Ormuz, at that
day the depôt for the spices and other rich products of the
East, gained much information regarding the Oriental trade.
From Ormuz he sent a companion with a caravan "to Aleppo
bound," that the messenger might thence pursue his way towards Lisbon, where the king was impatiently waiting for
advices.

It was a happy thought so to do, for Covilhan himself, in
assaying to journey homewards through Abyssinia, was made
a prisoner, though not ill-treated, by the king. Even in Emmanuel's time he was still detained in that country. The news
he conveyed to Lisbon was of consequence. He had found, of
course, no Prester John, but he had discovered that by a promontory named the Lion of the Sea, or the Head of Africa, a
voyage could be made from the western to the eastern sea.
This information arrived before the return of Diaz from the
Cape of Storms ; and when the brave mariner came home and
related his experience, the king shrewdly suspected that the
cape of Diaz and Covilhan's Lion of the Sea were one and the
same, and that was the reason why he would have it called
the Cape of Good Hope. We must not forget Covilhan when
we reckon up the noble hearts who risked their lives for their
country's good. His land travel had its awful perils no less
than the seafaring of Diaz ; and it was the news coming from

him which, combined with the story of the navigator, enabled Emmanuel to appoint the expedition of Vasco da Gama with much hope of success.

We have seen how Da Gama's fortunes sped on the east coast of Africa, and how from Melinda he was piloted to the other side of the Indian Ocean. Before Calicut he anchored on May 20th, 1498. The elements had been so favourable to the voyagers that they traversed those two thousand miles of open water in twenty-two days. The Portuguese had hitherto hugged the shore in their expeditions. They had been often driven out a considerable distance, but had never willingly ventured into unknown seas. Now, however, they had proved their courage notably by crossing the wide Indian deep, and were rewarded by the spectacle of that dreamland which so stirred the imagination and tempted the ambition of the fifteenth century. Arrived at their destination, the crews of the Portuguese ships gave way to the most extravagant demonstrations of joy. The vessels were gaily decorated with flags, and a deafening clamour of trumpets filled the air. It seemed to the voyagers as if they had reached the gates of Paradise.

The Portuguese found the coast of Malabar divided into various principalities, the most important of which was the domain of the Samudri-Rajah (sovereign of the coast), a title shortened into Zamorin. In the land of the Zamorin, whose capital was the important city of Calicut, as elsewhere in Malabar, the Brahmins were the ruling caste; but besides the low-caste natives, Arabs, Jews, Persians, and other Asiatics formed part of the population, and these immigrants from other parts of Asia were the commercial class in that region, some of them being persons of considerable wealth. Da Gama was at first entertained by the Zamorin in a friendly manner; but the merchants of Calicut, particularly the Arabs, whose influence there was the greatest, seeing their business in danger, stirred up the prince against the expedition. The Portuguese leader, perceiving that a conspiracy threatened his safety, and that he was too weak for successful resistance, shipped his men, and embarking with them, left Calicut and sailed as far as Goa, the future capital of the Portuguese possessions in India. From Goa he recrossed the Indian Ocean, and after encountering a tremendous storm at Cape Verd, reached the Tagus, having spent fifteen months altogether in his voyage.

Da Gama received an ovation at the capital. The king bestowed upon him a large sum of money and the privilege of engaging in the Indian trade, gave him the honourable title of Dom, named him Admiral of the Indies, and built in memory of the fortunate expedition the convent of Belem (Bethlehem) at that point of the river from which Da Gama had set out for the East.

It was not to Da Gama, however, but to another Portuguese navigator, Pedro Alvarez Cabral, that the duty of conducting the next fleet fitted out for India was intrusted. In March of the year 1500 it left Lisbon. It consisted of thirteen vessels of the best type which floated then, carrying fifteen hundred soldiers and mariners, a sufficient armament, and abundance of provisions. We have already spoken of Cabral's remarkable adventure in the earlier part of his voyage, when he was drifted far westward and discovered the land known afterwards as Brazil, and shall discuss at greater length in the next chapter the transatlantic settlement of the Portuguese. Here, however, let us follow the fleet as it rounds the Head of Africa and steers in the course of Da Gama. In attempting to pass the Cape of Good Hope it encountered a dreadful tempest, in which no less than four of the vessels went down, including one commanded by Bartholomew Diaz, the pioneer of the Eastern voyage, who perished thus in sight of the promontory the discovery of which had brought him well-earned fame.

On the east coast of Africa the Portuguese admiral was well received at Mozambique and Melinda, out of fear in the one

case and out of friendship in the other, and thence arrived at
Calicut in September. Cabral desired the Zamorin to allow
the Portuguese the privilege of trading with the natives, and
with that object to permit the erection of a depôt for the
storage of European wares. But again the Arabian merchants
prevented a treaty between the prince and the strangers, and
succeeded in creating such an uproar in the town that the
Portuguese were attacked and fifty of them slain. Cabral in
retaliation burned fifteen vessels in the harbour and bombarded
Calicut for two days. After this summary vengeance he sailed
southwards to Cochin. There he was agreeably surprised to
find a king and people ready to welcome him and to afford him
all those commercial facilities which had been denied him at
Calicut. The reason of this kind reception was the animosity
which existed in Cochin, as Cabral discovered, towards the
Zamorin on account of his trade monopoly. And not only at
Cochin, but in the other principalities of Malabar, the Portuguese found a disposition to put down the Prince of Calicut.
Thus the benefit to the Portuguese of the political divisions
along the Malabar coast was demonstrated. They, in consequence, gained a footing where one mighty prince would have
been able to keep them at arm's length.

From Cochin, Cabral took a full lading of spices, and could
have loaded his vessels three times over, being entreated by the
other coast rulers to run into their harbours and trade. Delighted with the progress he had made, and promising to return
for the purpose of dealing with the other towns, the admiral
departed from Malabar. The Zamorin had got together a
fleet of twenty-five vessels to check the homeward progress of
the Portuguese ; but they passed it within reach of its guns,
and such was the fear of them among the seamen of Calicut
that not a shot was fired. Cabral reached Portugal in June
1501. But Emmanuel was so determined to prosecute the
Indian trade that he had not waited till the return of Cabral's

fleet. He had despatched another three months before under John da Nova, a Galician settled in Portugal. Da Nova arrived at Cochin and came back safely, laden with Eastern wares, having discovered on the way the islands of Ascension and St. Helena.

The King of Portugal had sufficient information before him to show that if the Portuguese were to maintain a business connection with India, they should have to plant a garrison as well as factories on the Malabar coast, and give their power visibility by investing it with some state. To this the natives were accustomed, and without it they should fail to respect the Portuguese name. Thus the notion of an Eastern vice-royalty took shape. The expense of upholding such a dignity might be considerable, but Emmanuel considered it worth the cost, since his ambition did not concern itself with Malabar alone. That quarter was in his plan to be only the centre of an immense empire, over which the viceroy should, in his name, exercise authority. Already the king called himself by anticipation "Lord of the Navigation, Conquest, and Commerce of Ethiopia, Arabia, Persia, and India."

But ere the vice-royalty was instituted, Emmanuel resolved to send Da Gama with a powerful fleet once more to Malabar. His commission was to ingratiate himself with or to terrify the maritime princes, and to clear away all opposition to the introduction of Portuguese influence on a grand scale. He was also to leave at the coast some ships, which should be stationed there permanently as a floating defence of his country's interests. Da Gama, therefore, left the Tagus with a fleet of twenty sail in 1502. Finding the Zamorin still hostile, he again subjected Calicut to the fire of his artillery, proceeded to Cochin and other parts, concluded treaties with the authorities, giving to each locality a detachment of Portuguese soldiers for the protection of the factories, and placing the prescribed number of vessels under the command of his relative, Vincente Sodré, on the Malabar station. Then he left for home; and, although satisfied that he had done everything possible to impress the Indians with the idea of Portugal's power, had to inform the king that yet further efforts must be made to finally break down the stubborn opposition of the Zamorin and his Arab advisers.

He was right; for scarcely had he quitted the Indian coast when the ruler of Calicut advanced against Cochin with an army of fifty thousand men. The King of Cochin fled with his people. The defence of the place had to be conducted by the small Portuguese garrison. They had almost perished; for Sodré had taken it upon him to vacate his station and sail to the coast of Arabia in search of something to fight with. The elements gave him more than enough to do. Two of his ships went down, and the other three had not sufficient provisions to take them back to Malabar. But the valorous Francis d'Albuquerque, sailing to the East with six ships from Lisbon, came upon all that was left of the Malabar squadron, provisioned it, and conveyed it to Cochin, where he was able to relieve the handful of Portuguese. The Zamorin's forces fled. He sued for peace, which was granted, but D'Albuquerque fined him heavily for his attack on Cochin. More Portuguese factories were now established, a fortress of considerable strength was erected in Cochin, and an excellent soldier, Pacheco Pereira, was appointed commandant.

As soon as D'Albuquerque had sailed for Portugal, the irrepressible Zamorin invested the new stronghold. But its governor, with his force of one hundred and sixty Portuguese and eight thousand native auxiliaries, sustained the siege with remarkable bravery; and thereafter, assuming the offensive, he opened his gates and pursued the enemy, upon whom he had just succeeded in forcing a humiliating peace when the greatest fleet which Portugal had ever sent to that region made its appearance. It numbered fewer vessels than Da Gama had commanded on his second voyage to Malabar, but all were of the largest size. The king had laid the counsel of Da Gama to heart, and, resolving to do his utmost with the view of putting an end to the obstruction of his Eastern trade, had fitted out this armada and intrusted it to Lopo Soares, a man whose qualities as a navigator and soldier entirely justified his appointment. He astonished the Indians by his feats of seamanship and arms. He procured the submission of the whole sea-board of Malabar. The influence of the Zamorin was so reduced that his allies fell away one after another. Soares, moreover, proclaimed a Portuguese commercial monopoly in the ports of Malabar; menaced with destruction the vessels of any other nation which should come thither for trade; and, to show that his threats were not vain, cut out of a harbour belonging to the Zamorin, and burned to the water's edge, seventeen great ships of Mecca. This he accomplished with two caravels and fifteen boats, while his large vessels were receiving their cargoes at various ports on the coast.

The expedition of Soares advanced so much the interests of his country that on his return, in 1505, Emmanuel judged the time had come for sending out to the East a lieutenant invested with a certain amount of regal splendour. That very year, accordingly, Francis d'Almeida was designated as first viceroy of India. As a knight and royal councillor, D'Almeida had won the esteem of the Portuguese court, and as Indian viceroy he maintained his excellent reputation. He was incorruptible where the temptation to fill his private purse was great. His sway was mild where he might have played the tyrant with impunity. If danger had to be faced, he was there; and when it came to a division of booty, he would choose for himself a simple memento, and give the more valuable treasures away with a generous hand. Under his fostering care the Portuguese influence made sure progress. His operations, offensive and defensive, during his tenure of office resulted in securing the position of his nation so firmly that its enemies' idea of dislodging it by force was now well-nigh abandoned.

A few years were considered by the king long enough for any subject to exercise in India an authority so closely resembling his own. A longer term might afford an ambitious man an opportunity of constructing for himself an independent and impregnable position. Therefore, in 1509, Alfonso d'Albuquerque went out to supersede D'Almeida. Of a somewhat sterner cast than his predecessor, D'Albuquerque was as honest and patriotic, as brave and unselfish. But there was in the second viceroy, combined with the will and the capacity to perform present duty, also the power of understanding the far-reaching plan which his master cherished, of adopting practical measures for its realization, and of carefully arranging a thousand details in subordination to the main issue. D'Albuquerque was indeed the greatest of all the viceroys. The occupation of Malabar was to him, as to Emmanuel, only a step to the empire of the Orient. He was appointed just when it became possible for Portugal to lengthen its cords—thanks to the vigilance of D'Almeida, who had procured from native potentates a real, though in some cases a notoriously unwilling, acceptance of the situation.

From his base at Malabar, D'Albuquerque seized, in his master's name, the best commercial positions in that quarter of the world. First of all, he took the town of Goa, which, because of its good climate and great convenience for shipping, he considered much better adapted for the capital of Portuguese India than Cochin, the seat hitherto of the viceregal government. Then faring eastward, he obtained possession, in 1509, of the peninsula and town of Malacca. Malacca, founded two hundred and fifty years before the coming of the Portuguese, was in D'Albuquerque's time the richest and most populous place in the East Indies, where the merchantmen of China, Japan, and other countries on the east, and those of Ceylon,

Coromandel, and Bengal on the west, resorted to exchange their commodities.

In 1515 the island of Ormuz, which commanded the entrance of the Persian Gulf, fell into his hands. It had been a province of Persia, and the Shah, in accordance with his custom, demanded the annual impost from the Portuguese, who he expected would recognize his suzerainty. But D'Albuquerque, it is said, presented the Shah's tax-collectors with a handful of bullets as a grim warning of the kind of payment they might look for if they troubled him. On the bare isle of Ormuz rose by-and-by, under the auspices of the Portuguese, one of the most opulent cities in the Orient, a magnificent emporium where the valuables and delicacies of India were deposited for sale to the provinces of western Asia.

Thus the Portuguese empire in the East grew, until the name of the little slip of territory in the European peninsula became celebrated throughout the Asiatic continent. The sovereign of Portugal possessed Malacca and Ormuz, the two great gateways of commerce in the eastern peninsula. These points, well watched, were worth kingdoms. This was the work of D'Albuquerque. And it was the chief part of the scheme for getting the East into Portuguese hands. Whatever else was obtained in after days, it was insignificant compared with the mastery of the Persian Gulf and the Strait of Malacca.

D'Albuquerque was allowed to remain as viceroy some years longer than D'Almeida, for Emmanuel was aware of his magnificent powers; but "whispering tongues" at Lisbon were doing him damage. Many envied him when they saw the Oriental treasures which came home in ever-increasing quantities, testifying to the progress the Indian colony was making through his administration. They turned his very successes to his disadvantage, insinuating that all his exertions had a selfish object —that in due time he meant to set up a monarchy of his own. Nothing was further from the mind of D'Albuquerque, but

Emmanuel was persuaded of his servant's treason, and recalled him. The king's want of confidence in him—shown most unkindly, as he thought, in the appointment to succeed him of one who had never been on good terms with him—was the death of D'Albuquerque. His indomitable spirit, which no danger could frighten or tòil deter from its purpose, succumbed to the breath of suspicion. He died of a broken heart on board ship, in sight of that town of Goa which he had made the head-quarters of a flourishing dominion.

Lopo Soares, the next viceroy, the same who burned the vessels of Mecca, was a fighting man second to none, but a miserable colonial governor. He established the power of Portugal in Ceylon in 1517, a feat worthy of record; for that island, with its fruitful soil, its fine harbour of Trincomali, its rubies, and its elephants, contributed afterwards a considerable quota to the Portuguese revenue. That sort of work was in his way. To the rest of his office he was not so equal. D'Albuquerque had been stern, even merciless, some said, as warrior and judge, but courteous, and unwilling to use force if tact could serve his purpose. Soares, on the other hand, was rough to brutality, not only with his subordinates, but with native rulers. He rooted up thus much of that respect for Portugal which his predecessor's moderation had planted. Bitterly did Emmanuel regret that he had made a viceroy of one who was only fit to storm a fortress, and disgraced a patriotic statesman, for now he knew the true character of the charges against D'Albuquerque. Nor did any subsequent holder of the dignity show himself capable of filling the shoes of the captor of Malacca and Ormuz. How the redoubtable Da Gama, who was one of the number, would have borne himself in the viceregal chair, we know not, for he died soon after his landing in 1525.

One or two conquests were made by the successors of D'Albuquerque. The Moluccas or Spice Islands were taken in 1522, and the island of Diu (now in the Bombay presidency) in 1546; but their gains, and indeed the whole dominion, were lessened in value by the mediocrity of the viceroys. And the greater number of them, adding to incapacity an unscrupulous avarice, diverted to their own coffers a portion of that stream of wealth which should have flowed uninterruptedly to the Lisbon treasury. A charge, which seemed too true, of grossly immoral living is also preferred against some of these representatives of the Portuguese crown. Thus, while surrounded with a pomp which far outshone the simple state of D'Albuquerque, the later viceroys, by their weaknesses and vices, lowered the prestige of their country in the East, and when the reign of John III. closed in 1557, the empire began to show unmistakable signs of decay.*

Another cause for the decline of Portuguese influence in Asia was the establishment at Goa of the Inquisition by John III. in 1536. That institution pursued heretics in India with a ruthless ferocity which surpassed the proceedings of its European model. Quiet and diligent Jews and Arabians could not live within its reach. Even "new Christians," converts from Judaism and Mohammedanism, or children of such converts, were subjected to impertinent surveillance and examination, to bonds and spoliation. In this way ecclesiastical zeal clipped the wings of enterprise. So the political and clerical officials of Portugal unconsciously co-operated to wreck the authority on which they depended. But it took a good many bad viceroys to sensibly damage the splendid fabric of Portuguese sovereignty in the Indies. Nor could even the Inquisition bring it down at once, though it certainly did its worst in Goa.

The palmy days of Oriental empire were the later portion of

* Notwithstanding that, in this very year the Chinese, in testimony of their gratitude for the defeat of a pirate who had long been the scourge of the coast, conceded to Portugal the peninsula and town of Macao, a place where an extensive trade developed, which only left it on the rise of Hong-Kong.

Emmanuel's reign and the opening years of the next. The Portuguese monarch was then unrivalled and uncontrolled in the Indian Ocean. He issued commercial laws to the native rulers. He forbade other European nations to intrude on his immense preserve. Even Portuguese merchants had to pay him for a permit to trade at most of the ports where the royal factories existed.

Venice and Egypt conspired to annihilate his power, but in vain. The Venetians, who saw their once lucrative trade with the East destroyed by the discovery of the Cape of Good Hope route, and the Soldan of the Mamelukes, then dominant in north-east Africa, who found his Red Sea passage to India blocked by Portuguese ships of war, were equally desirous to sweep away the spoiler. The soldan undertook the task. Venice gave him wood from her Dalmatian forests for the building of war-vessels; and thus enabled to meet the enemy, the Mamelukes advanced with a powerful navy against the fleet of Portugal. But the resolute courage of their antagonists withstood the attack of those fierce Tartars, so renowned in warfare. The Portuguese battered and sank some of the soldan's ships, boarded others, and after a desperate and bloody fight came off victorious. The Mamelukes, beaten thus at sea, could no longer hold their own in Egypt, but were forced to surrender their dominion to the Turks. Venice courted the new Egyptian power as she had the old, and incited the sultan to fall upon Portugal. He did so, and was chased ignominiously away. Thus Venice was humiliated, and the famous League of Cambray against the republic succeeding this disgrace, dashed all her hopes to the ground.

Portugal, triumphant, received attention on every hand. The Shah of Persia sent an embassy to her. China made friendly advances. The kings of Pegu, Siam, and Sumatra sued for an alliance with her. She monopolized the trade with Japan. So flourished the Portuguese dominion in Asia; and, thinking of it at its best, " whether we consider its extent, its opulence, the slender power by which it was formed, or the splendour with which its government was conducted, there had hitherto been nothing comparable to it in the history of nations." *

Though we have here no room to do more than touch the subject, we must not omit from the sketch of the Portuguese in Asia the work of the Jesuit missionaries initiated by the celebrated Navarrese, Francis Xavier. Inclined in early life to more liberal views, Xavier's mind had been completely transformed by the influence of Ignatius Loyola. Thenceforward he was filled with hatred of the reformer's "godless tendencies," and devoted himself as an ultra-Catholic to the Romish propaganda. His overflowing enthusiasm despised every danger and was ready for any sacrifice. On coming to Lisbon, he was designated as missionary to the Indies. A considerable number of Franciscan friars had gone thither with the armadas, and had settled or itinerated as Christian teachers in various parts of the empire; but their progress had been unsatisfactory, and the Society of Jesus were believed to have a special calling to the work of converting the heathen. So with De Sousa, who had just been appointed viceroy, Xavier and some companions arrived at the capital of Portuguese India in 1542. Many of the Portuguese had lapsed into practical heathenism in the East; and them, as well as the natives, the Jesuit fathers earnestly endeavoured to win to a moral and devout life. The Jesuits occupied themselves with incessant zeal in street preaching, visiting, healing the sick, and baptizing. The seminary in Goa for orphans and converts was handed over to them; and when Xavier had set matters in order there, he sent for more "fathers" from Portugal, and began his journeyings by land and sea for the ingathering of the heathen to the Church. He laboured for some years in

* Robertson's " Historical Disquisition concerning Ancient India."

southern India, in Travancore, where he is said to have baptized ten thousand persons in one month, and on the Coromandel coast among its pearl fishers. Thence he betook himself to Malacca, Ceylon, and Japan, everywhere making converts. He died in 1552, near Macao, when he was on the eve of pursuing his missionary toil in China. His life presented a fine example of purity and self-denial; the attractiveness of his presence and his preaching was amazing. Some of his followers continued the religious labours of Xavier with remarkable success, and many of them met with heroic fortitude persecutions and hardships of the most trying description. Not a few of Xavier's converts, companions, and successors suffered martyrdom for the cause of Christ. Yet the more admirable the zeal of those devoted Jesuits, the more does one regret that the creed in whose propagation they so willingly spent themselves was no better.

Of the empire in whose interests Xavier wore himself to death, where Portugal maintained such a lordly state and such extensive commerce, only a poor remnant exists in our day. When Spanish jealousy forbade the Netherlands to buy at Lisbon the products of the East, the Dutch East India Company found its way to those foreign fields in which the Portuguese had so long exclusively reaped harvests of incalculable value. Portugal, with her hands tied by Spain, was no longer able to punish trespassers in the Indian Ocean. The founding at the beginning of the seventeenth century of the Dutch Foreign Shipping Company, and later, by advice of the sagacious Oldenbarneveldt, of the Dutch United East India Company, the rise, moreover, about the same time of the English East India Company, drove Portugal, weak as she was, into the background. The Dutch by force and diplomacy gradually stripped the Portuguese of nearly all their possessions. Malacca they took, and in Ceylon they also, some years later, established themselves, though not without a desperate struggle. From the

Moluccas, too, they drove the Portuguese; and the Shah of Persia recovered Ormuz. The British, making treaties and planting factories at several points on the Gujerat coast, insinuated themselves till they obtained the magnificent position which they hold at this day.

The territory which the Portuguese have been able to retain in Asia consists of Goa and a piece of adjacent country; the island of Diu, off the southern extremity of Kathiawar Peninsula; and the settlement of Daman—all on the west coast of Hindustan, containing an area of thirteen hundred square miles, and a population of half a million, two-thirds of whom are Roman Catholics, the remainder being Mohammedans and Hindus. In the Malay Archipelago one-half of the island of Timor is Portuguese, a district which includes six thousand square miles, inhabited by some three hundred thousand people. The Chinese gift of Macao Portugal still holds. It is now, however, a comparatively valueless possession. The island, of twelve square miles and a population of sixty thousand, most of whom are in the town, was once a famous resort of ocean shipping, but in these days the only craft which visit it are coasting vessels. These are the relics of Portugal's astonishing acquisitions in the sixteenth century—faded patches of a gorgeous imperial robe.

Goa is the headquarters of Portugal in the Indies. But the ancient capital is well-nigh desolate. It is in Panjim or New Goa, nearer the sea, that one finds the population (twenty-five thousand), a mere fraction of the multitudes who filled the princely Goa of the past. The old city was devastated by cholera in the end of the seventeenth century, and in consequence abandoned. It affords a most depressing spectacle, with its dilapidated palaces, warehouses, and edifices of every kind, its grass-grown streets, its death-like stillness. In former days its grandeur eclipsed that of any other city in the East. Now "Ichabod" is plainly written on its ruins. It is still the seat of archiepiscopal power, or the ghost of it. The primate of the Indies has his seat there, and his clerical *entourage* compose nearly the entire population of the venerable derelict.

Rice, cocoa-nuts, and some cotton are the principal articles of export, and these in no great quantities. The imports are likewise few, the population consisting for the most part of uncivilized and semi-civilized natives, and of half-castes not far above their level in the scale of humanity. The Portuguese colonies have not been successful in this quarter of the world, any more than in Africa, for many a day. Corrupt administration, ecclesiastical bigotry, want of enterprise, want of capital, high tariffs—all these things have had to do with bringing these possessions to their present pass. The Portuguese seem to imagine that their vanished greatness here will one day come back to them, knowing "how to wait." But they have played the waiting game too long, while others have been up and doing. They have, it is true, been an unfortunate people, but they might have extracted more "honey from the lion." It may be the nation shall awake to juster conceptions of government, both domestic and foreign, and strive to keep and cultivate that which they have retained, instead of mourning over their irretrievable losses.

CHAPTER XIII.

PORTUGAL lost and Spain obtained in the fifteenth century the services of two distinguished men, Magellan and Columbus. The first was a Portuguese born, a native of Oporto, who had sailed in Indian seas, and fought there for his country; but believing she had overlooked his claims to important command, he offered the benefit of his skill to her neighbour. Columbus was no Portuguese, but had from his early manhood much intercourse with that nation, sailing often with Portuguese, and coming to the Tagus again and again from longer or shorter voyages. At last he settled in Lisbon, and there found respectable and tolerably lucrative employment as a chart-maker. There also he married, his wife being daughter of the then recently deceased Perestrello, first governor of Porto Santo. From his mother-in-law Columbus received many charts and nautical instruments belonging to her late husband, and the Genoese navigator, pondering these, and talking with mariners and geographers, with both which classes Lisbon at that time swarmed, believed it certain that India could be reached by the Atlantic.

It is well known that he wished to make the attempt under Portuguese auspices, but found his notion received with incredulity. The king was more willing to listen to Columbus than were his councillors, and would, the Portuguese say, have given the adventurer the commission he desired, but that such an exorbitant price was demanded in the event of success as to bar the way of an arrangement. However this may have been, it is undoubted that, probably without King John's sanction, the crafty Bishop of Ceuta endeavoured to profit by the hints of Columbus by sending a caravel across the Atlantic on a pretended voyage to the Cape Verd Islands, really to discover, if possible, the western route to Asia. The voyagers returned, protesting they had been sent on a fool's errand, and Columbus, indignant at the treachery, shook the dust of Portugal off his feet.

It must have been exceedingly galling to that country, which had been all along the foremost in such enterprises, when its Spanish rival acquired the distinction reflected from the discoveries of Columbus and Magellan. Yet Portugal, too, was able to connect her name with America. Between the discovery of a new continent by Columbus and, twenty years after, of a new ocean by Magellan, the Portuguese, at the opening of the sixteenth century, found Brazil. Adventitiously, lamenting the hard fortune which had taken him so far west, Cabral came in sight of its shores. He sailed a whole day along the strange coast, where he had not dreamed of touching land. He dropped anchor at a likely place, went ashore with a number of his people, and celebrated mass, to the wonder of the natives. Then rearing a wooden rood as a sign that the region—he knew not its extent—belonged thenceforth to Portugal, he named the new possession Santa Cruz, and sent a ship with tidings of the discovery to Portugal, while he pursued his appointed way to India.*

The news of Cabral's discovery created in Lisbon a joy proportioned to the chagrin with which the Portuguese had seen the Spaniards pressing into the lands opened by Columbus. Moreover, this latest acquisition was within the sphere of

---

* The name Terra de Brazil, from the dye-wood with which the land abounded, exported afterwards in great quantities to Portugal, supplanted soon the original designation.

Portugal, as set forth in an agreement between that kingdom and Spain brought about by the Vatican at the close of the fifteenth century.* So Portugal might enjoy the honour and profit of her South American prize without fear of Spanish interference. Yet Spain would fain have broken the compact when the good fortune of Portugal across the Atlantic became public, since in point of fact her own mariners—some who accompanied Columbus to the Bahamas—had coasted from Cape San Roque almost to Trinidad before Cabral sighted South America. But Portugal was suffered, without any serious resistance on the part of Spain, to retain Brazil, because that region was not deemed to possess treasures such as were to be found farther west. Nor did the poor savages who inhabited it seem to promise lucrative trade.

The heads of the Portuguese were, however, at this time full of India. Brazil was a trifling matter compared with their Eastern empire. They thought with the Spaniards that there was nothing in the interior of their South American possession worth taking away but its timber, and had the same views regarding the utility of opening commerce there. Land in Brazil therefore was at the beginning of the sixteenth century at a discount. To settlers was sold for a song as much as they would. Among them were freely and inconsiderately dispensed magisterial powers—captaincies of such authority that, though only after many days, the home government awoke to see the folly of their too generous grants. These unrestricted officials, appointed irrespective of their character or capacity, exercised so much tyranny over the Indians (as the natives were called, because of their resemblance to the people of the East) that these savages learned to detest and shun the Portu-

---

* By the treaty referred to a vertical line was drawn on the map about eight hundred miles outside of the Cape Verd Islands. Of the hemispheres thus indicated, the western was granted to Spain, the eastern to Portugal. Portugal's division thus included Brazil. The humour of such an audacious halving of the globe between two peoples of the European Peninsula was not then apparent.

guese, for whom they prepared much trouble, and never could be brought in numbers—scarcely at all, except by force—to help the invaders. Nevertheless, the work of colonizing did go on slowly. Towns and villages were founded in every captaincy. Sugar-planting was the first kind of general industry occupying the colonists. The climate was suited for the cultivation of the cane, and there was abundance of water-power to turn the mills which were ere long numerous in Brazil.

But when its hold of India began to be more precarious, the attention of the mother country was more earnestly directed to South America, and it was evident that a better policy was decidedly wanted there. The co-ordinate authorities of the magistrates scattered over the colony impeded its growth. There was need of one superior power or chief captaincy to regulate the relations of the others and issue general orders. A rising of the aborigines, encouraged, it was believed, by French pirates to destroy Portuguese influence, had besides assumed dangerous proportions before it could be suppressed, and threatened to repeat itself if more complete defensive co-operation of the various governors were not secured. Another reason for active interference from Lisbon was the vast range of territory accessible in Brazil to Portuguese colonists. The voyagers of 1500 had of course no notion when they reared their cross at Porto Seguro that they were laying claim, in the name of Portugal, to a land whose boundaries might be extended unopposed till they included half the South American continent. But now, though its limits were as yet not defined, it was known at home that the Portuguese possessed in that quarter a great and goodly land, fruitful and well irrigated, the climate on the whole excellent. This was theirs without encroaching on the claims of Spain, without any opposition which could withstand the march of disciplined soldiers and the fire of modern weapons.

Finally, the Spaniards who had planted the settlement of Buenos Ayres, and now held both sides of the La Plata estuary, were pushing their commerce with some vigour and making headway. At first the Spanish colonists had been content with the southern shore, but time revealed to them the great importance of both sides to their advancing trade. So they settled on the south coast of what is now Uruguay, and the adjacent Portuguese *capitania* was not strong enough to forbid them. The thing would probably not have happened so easily had the provincial governments of Brazil been consolidated under one head. But now that it was an accomplished fact, the expulsion of the Buenos Ayreans would be rather unmanageable. And though the loss of the Plate was a heavy one, the Portuguese had compensation in the north of Brazil, that part of the Sierra Parinié which adjoined the valley and basin of the Amazon having been taken from the French Guiana colony as a trophy of hostilities between the forces of France and Portugal ten years after Cabral's landing.

Many things, in short, combined to rouse Portugal to a clearer perception of its responsibility regarding Brazil, and in 1549 John III. sent Thomas de Sousa thither as governor-general of all the *capitanias*, with supreme power in civil and criminal cases. On his arrival at his destination, De Sousa was to set about the erection of a capital of the Brazils in the province of Bahia. The town was to bear the name of San Salvador. It was to be so strongly fortified as to excite the fear and astonishment of the natives, and be a sufficient protection to its garrison against all attacks. A squadron of three vessels bore to Brazil the new governor-general, officials, soldiers, craftsmen of various kinds, and priests of the Jesuit order. The natives were sufficiently impressed with the spectacle of the Portuguese fleet as it anchored off the shore and disembarked its force, clerical, military, and civil. They seemed to feel their impotence in the face of such an array, and came unarmed to meet the procession from the boats—a procession which, headed by the priests, each with a great cross hung at his side, the rest following in dignified order, must have numbered about four hundred, including the governor's staff. The town was immediately founded, and its limits surrounded with a rampart on which were mounted pieces of artillery. This place, San Salvador or Bahia, as it was alternatively called, after the province, remained for a long time the capital of the Brazilian colony.

Matters went more smoothly after the subordination of the *capitanias.* Trade prospered ; the mineral wealth of the country was discovered, and the work of bringing it to the surface began. As the business of mining increased there was urgent need of hands. It was naturally expected that the Indians could be easily utilized as labourers. But the old proverb, " One man may take a horse to water, but twenty will not make him drink," was fully exemplified in the case of the Brazilian aborigines. Driven in gangs to the mines, they for the most part refused to touch the work. They were flogged, imprisoned, starved, tortured. Many were executed as a frightful warning to the rest. Every expedient which diabolic ingenuity could suggest was tried with the intractable savages. But nothing could induce the bulk of them to lift spade or pickaxe for the tyrants. They were dismissed with imprecations, and the more docile race of Ham summoned to dig for the treasures of Brazil. This was the beginning of negro slavery in America. Shipload after shipload of Africans were transported from Guinea to the Brazilian mines. The miseries of the voyage in the wretched vessels of that time may be imagined. Many a slave found a grave in the ocean, and many who reached the American continent and experienced the hardships of labour in the mines were sorry that they had not died like their fellows at sea. The scanty nourishment provided by their masters, the pig-sties in which they were housed, the incessant drudgery, the cruelties of the overseers, made up for these unfortunates a life of untold suffering. The African slaves were put to all kinds of menial labour, not only in the mines but in the fields. But it was principally in raising the precious metals that they were used.

This kind of industry, which partakes so much of the nature of gambling, the Portuguese pursued with such avidity as to leave them too little time by far for the less intoxicating occupation of agriculture. From the enormous metalliferous deposits of Brazil there were by-and-by extracted annually on the average silver to the value of one million sterling and gold worth a million and a half. The diamonds for which Brazil became so famous were not exploited for two hundred years after the settlement of the colony. But the silver and gold were a sufficient curse to the Brazilians. Fallow or badly-tilled fields, frantic activity at the diggings, the honest, hard work of which was done by bondsmen treated like brutes, did not contribute to the health of the colony, and if the increment of the ground had not been so extraordinary, the Portuguese in Brazil would have been badly off. Nevertheless, the soil and clime were so kindly that the colonists throve better than they deserved. The *morale* of the Portuguese grew, as in India, very bad; but the plain living and assiduous teaching of the Jesuit fathers had a wonderful effect in restoring a sense of decency. The wild natives, too, came in some degree under the influence of the Order of Jesus, whose work among them might have been more successful had the colonists been better specimens of Christians.

The Spanish usurpation of the Portuguese throne rendered Brazil, like the other old dependencies of Portugal, a prey to the enemies of Spain. The Dutch West India Company resolved to drive the Portuguese from South America. The "High and Mighty" States despatched their Admiral Willekens to the Brazilian coast to carry out the wishes of the company. He stole into the harbour of Bahia unsuspected, by hoisting the flag of Spain at his masthead, and soon had the place at his mercy. This was in 1624; and though two years later a combined attack of Spanish and Portuguese war-vessels resulted in the recovery of the town, the Dutch took Recifé (Pernambuco) some time afterwards, and the French appropriated the magnificent haven of Rio de Janeiro. That distinguished general, the Stadtholder Maurice of Nassau, then devoted his energies to the seizure of the entire colony. It is a wonder that he did not completely achieve his object, considering the crippled state of the Portuguese fleet. As a result, however, of his operations, a great part of Brazil came into the possession of Holland. Desperate but fruitless attempts were made to eject the Dutch. They held Portuguese America for fourteen years after the revolution of 1640. The Brazilians, left very much to themselves, had been able, even before the Dutch were compelled to a general surrender, to attack and expel their enemies from various fortresses. These advantages were possible to them because of the war between Holland and the English Commonwealth, which engaged the finest Dutch ships. But in 1654, just before Cromwell brought the struggle with Holland to an end, the Portuguese commander, Francis Barreto, bombarded and took Recifé. The other Dutch garrisons were forced to yield in consequence of this victory. Brazil—the French also having been obliged to evacuate the Bay of Rio—was once more placed under the Portuguese sceptre; and the Count of Atouquia, the new *viceroy*, so the governor-general was now called, showed himself quite able to deal with the immense difficulties which the condition of his charge presented.

The mother country, having lost her great empire in the Indian Ocean, began to esteem very highly her transatlantic dominion. The infant manufactures of Brazil were fostered, and experiments were made in planting all kinds of food-stuffs to which the climate was adapted. The coffee-bean, introduced from the East, was found to be specially successful. The population, too, increased by immigration from the time when the country was released from the power of Holland.   But the immemorial bad feeling between Spain and Portugal increased tenfold after 1580, and now allowed full play by the separation of the two kingdoms, occasioned some trouble in South America. The history of ancient disputes in the Peninsula regarding boundary lines repeated itself here.   These contentions were settled at no little loss of life, time, and treasure.   Provincial insurrections and inter-provincial brawls sometimes took place, and unless the viceroy were a strong man, tranquillity was not easily restored.   Such disturbances, though they doubtless lessened the country's pace, were not sufficient to effectually check its progress.   It had elasticity enough to recover from the shocks of war as well as to hold on its way under the burden of that extravagance, profligacy, and laziness in which many of the colonists lived.

In the beginning of the seventeenth century the mining industry of Brazil received a remarkable impulse from the discovery of diamonds.   While they were searching for gold, diggers had stumbled upon the valuable jewels, and pleased with their lustre, but ignorant of their worth, had sent some to the old country as curios.   They were duly appraised, and at once the diamond fever infected thousands of Portuguese on both sides of the Atlantic.   Many hastened across the ocean to join in the hunt for these exquisite gems.*   Those who first found Brazilian diamonds did not confer an unmixed boon on the land.   Agriculture was neglected on account of the glittering baubles, just as it had been before and was still for the sake of gold and silver.

Nothing reveals the Marquis of Pombal's large-mindedness better than the efforts he made to improve the condition of Brazil.   He saw and deplored the mania for raising precious stones and metals, while field-work and manufactures languished.

---

* The mines were royal property, but many officials and private individuals in Brazil soon became adepts in the art of legerdemain, and diamonds to the amount of millions sterling were successfully "conveyed."

DIAMOND WASHING, BRAZIL.

"What kind of wealth is that, great God," he writes in an official paper, "which brings with it the ruin of the state!" One sees how far he was above the follies and passions of his day. He interested himself in Brazilian agriculture—in the cultivation of Indian corn, rice, and cotton—that a better source of riches than the mines might be opened for the colony. He regretted exceedingly the persistent savagery of the natives and their numerical decrease, and insisted on kindlier dealings with them, that they might be encouraged to give themselves to regular industry and to acquire the habits of civilization. He caused Indian schools to be erected, and was particularly anxious that the girls should receive instruction in the use of the needle and the spinning-wheel, and in other womanly employments which should win them from the wild customs of their people.

The conduct of the Jesuits in Paraguay, and Pombal's connection with them, have been referred to in a previous chapter—the cession of the seven missions there by Spain to Portugal in 1750, and the expensive war for the establishment of his government which the marquis had to carry on. But by the boundary treaty of 1778 Paraguay was given up to Spain, with the exception of its eastern side, which Portugal retained.* This convention defined the South American possessions of Spain and Portugal. Under its articles Portugal received, besides a part of Paraguay, eastern Peru and a section of Guiana as far as the Rio Negro. To Spain was ceded Uruguay, with the navigation of the Plate and Uruguay rivers.

Of the events at the opening of the nineteenth century we have also spoken—events including the transference of the Portuguese court to Rio de Janeiro, which succeeded Bahia as the metropolis of Brazil ; the change of Brazil's position as a colony into that of an empire under the Portuguese crown ; its repudiation of the Portuguese government ; the accession to the

* After the independence of Paraguay the (now Brazilian) territory between the rivers Paraguay and Parana had again to be fought for and wrested from that state as an indemnity.

independent Brazilian throne of the male line of the Braganzas in the person of Pedro I. of Brazil (Portugal retaining as its ruling family the female line); and the first emperor's abdication in favour of his son, who became by that means Pedro II. when only six years of age.

The reign of Pedro II. was long, and the sovereign himself performed the functions of his office in an exemplary manner. Nor was any fault found with his private character. Nevertheless, the whole fabric of imperialism in Brazil came down with a crash in 1889 (November 15th), and Dom Pedro, after occupying the throne for fifty-eight years, was forced to take his departure from Rio with the sorrowful knowledge that the empire had been abolished and a republic proclaimed under the name of the United States of Brazil. The ex-emperor, it is said, used to boast of the security of his throne, and to compare the South American republics with a fly-wheel in motion, because of the frequency of their "revolutions." But now the empire which for its steadfast adherence to the monarchical principle was such a notable example to neighbouring states has wearied of standing alone on the continent, and adopted the prevailing system of government.

The revolution may be termed a peaceful one. There were indeed disturbances at Bahia and Rio, but they were speedily put down, and the mass of the people seem to have acquiesced in the change. A provisional government was formed, by whom a constitution was drafted for presentation before a constituent assembly, to be elected by all citizens above twenty-one years of age able to read and write. The provisional government produced a favourable impression abroad at the outset by taking over the liabilities of the country—no small burden, for the amount of the national debt is something like one hundred million pounds sterling. The constitution follows generally the lines of that by which the United States of America are governed. The presidential term of office will be six years.

There will be a triennially-elected chamber of deputies, consisting of two hundred members ; and a senate, elected every nine years, of sixty-three members. Church and State are to be completely separated ; titles of nobility are to be abolished ; local government will exist in each state ; the banks are only granted rights of issue to the extent of their paid-up capital.

Hard financial work will require to be done, since the average annual deficit is two millions sterling. Yet, if strict retrenchment is practised, if capital can be induced to tap the unused riches of Brazil, and a tide of immigration flows, there is no reason why it should not in time rival the great Anglo-Saxon republic.

The twenty states of Brazil, and the "neutral municipality" of Rio de Janeiro, with its surrounding district of five hundred square miles, form an immense country, more than twenty-six times as large as the British Isles, more than three times the size of British India, including Upper Burma. Within 'its area of three million two hundred and forty thousand square miles there is a population of only twelve millions, mostly on the sea-board. Inland the inhabitants are few and scattered. Besides the native Brazilians, many European nationalities help to make up the number of the white residents, one-third of the whole population.

There are six million negroes. Thirty-five years ago the transport of that race from the opposite coast of Africa came to an end. A gradual Emancipation Act was passed in 1871 declaring all children of slaves born thereafter free. The object of the act was to avoid those ruinous effects upon the slave-owners which had been produced in the United States by immediate and total emancipation. Two years ago, however, slavery was completely abolished in the Brazils. The negro, after his involuntary servitude, has been unfortunately so fond of his liberty that he has generally, since the abolition, declined hard work. But that was to be expected. The ex-emperor, being very much responsible for the measure of abolition, fell under the displeasure of the Conservatives, who on that account raised no objections to his deposition. But the Brazilians cannot return to the slavery platform, and must make the most of their negro by education, for which there is much room in a country where the vast majority are unable to read or write. However, if the new constitution stands, and the negro is qualified by a little schooling to exercise the franchise, he will be able to do what he likes in Brazil, unless white immigration take place on a hitherto unprecedented scale. So the African race will be indemnified for their centuries of bondage.

The aborigines have resisted all attempts to drag them within the pale of civilization. They have had too much reason to dread the lash and chain of the Portuguese. Now the attempt to induce their removal out of the wilds where they dwell far from the homes of the white man is probably too late a while.

Less than one-thirtieth part of the country is under cultivation. In the north, where the unparalleled river system of the Amazon furnishes abundance of water, there are dense forests and a floral *embarras de richesse* more wonderful than is seen anywhere else on the face of the globe; yet in that enormous valley only one hundred thousand people are to be found, though it might yield to millions the means of livelihood. Farther south are those rolling prairies which compose the greater part of the Brazils. But north or south the soil is generally unbroken by the hand of man, except where shafts have been sunk for the exploitation of minerals. Coffee is very extensively grown in Brazil, which, indeed, raises half the coffee produced in the world, and exports annually, chiefly to the United States, from six to eight million hundredweight of the bean. Sugar, tapioca, cotton, caoutchouc, and other articles are produced in large quantities for export; but the total value of the exports, some thirty millions sterling, shows

RIO DE JANEIRO.

both how little the resources of Brazil have been utilized, and how badly the Brazilian husbandman has managed even that fractional area which he has planted. There is no better mineral field than Brazil. Not only the valuable metals and stones, but iron, coal, and petroleum might be obtained in abundance there. Yet the mining industry is now so depressed that gold and silver for the coinage have actually to be imported.

The climate, although the country lies for the most part under the equator, is much more tolerable than might be imagined. The surface of Brazil is high, and the sea-breezes to which its extensive littoral is exposed alleviate the tropical warmth so enervating to the natives of more temperate countries. There are often epidemics in the coast towns, but these could no doubt be speedily put an end to by a more particular attention to health laws.

The chief towns are Rio de Janeiro, with a population of three hundred and fifty-seven thousand; Bahia, having one hundred and forty thousand inhabitants; and Pernambuco, a place containing one hundred and thirty thousand people. Rio de Janeiro is the capital, the largest city, except Buenos Ayres, on the South American continent. Rio stands on the shore of a magnificent bay, the entrance of which is narrow but safe for the largest vessels. The buildings are as fine, the streets are as well lighted and paved, as in most cities of Europe. The educational establishments of the Brazilian capital are well equipped, and there is a public library of one hundred thousand volumes. The Roman Catholic Church, with which nearly the whole population of Brazil are nominally connected, practises its rites with the greatest pomp in Rio. The religious festivals present most brilliant scenes in the churches and in the streets, where long processions of devotees, carrying lighted candles and attended by bands of music, the performance of *al fresco* Biblical dramas and pyrotechnic displays in the

evening,* supply the populace with an entertainment completely to their mind.

The balmy air and kindly soil have contributed much to
make the people of Brazil careless, light-hearted, and laughter-
loving, more ready to gape at a spectacle than to strive for a
living.   What the too charming climate would have made of
Anglo-Saxons after four hundred years we cannot tell, but it is
certain that a large influx of sturdy Saxons, or of some other
nationality with more grit than the native Brazilian, is urgently
required to make his country what it might be.

* As much as £15,000 is said to be expended annually in Rio on fireworks and wax-
candles for the *festas.*

CHAPTER XIV.

MODERN PORTUGAL.

THE Portuguese nation, as it is, reminds one of Francesca da Rimini's woful shade flitting about the Inferno, the memory of her days of sunshine thickening the gloom of the "purple-black night." Portugal looks back in exceeding bitterness of soul to the "happy time" when, basking in prosperity, it was the envy of the world; when "Lisbon was the great European emporium of Indian goods; its warehouses filled with silks, cotton, spices, and pearls, ivory, and gold dust; Dutch, German, and English merchants making it their rendezvous, and taking away costly freights."* The sight of Portugal in its nineteenth century degradation, deprived of its vast and wealthy dominions and reduced to the rank of a third-rate power, is not wanting in pathos. But it would be absurd to view the picture only from the sentimental side. The decline and fall of Portugal are as admonitory as its early history is inspiriting. The consideration of its reverses is fitted to impress on other peoples a very essential principle.

The Portuguese ransacked the wide world for the means of satisfying their overweening pride and insatiable greed, while all the time the resources of that little corner of Europe which Providence had specially allotted to their care were utterly neglected. They seemed to imagine they should, without doubt, be able to go on for ever fetching home cargoes of "barbaric

* Yeats, "The Growth and Vicissitudes of Commerce."

pearl and gold," wherewith to maintain themselves in luxury, forgetful of the thousand and one possibilities of failure in the foreign supply. They were like a community which should forbear to dig wells at its doors, and prefer to provide itself with water by emptying into a tank the contents of numerous pitchers in which the element was being carried from a distance.

No country can afford to depend on colonies as Portugal did on hers. Sooner or later a people committing such a folly will be brought to "a piece of bread." What did the Portuguese, after all, gain by bringing to the Tagus innumerable cargoes of spoils from the East and the West? The treasure-heap rapidly diminished, and it is a remarkable fact that "while gold and silver increased in Amsterdam, and there was scarcely a European state which did not increase in wealth, the possessors of the trade with India, like the conquerors of Peru and Mexico, were so troubled for want of money that they had to resort to a great issue of copper coinage."* There was sufficient to sustain in comfort more people than ever inhabited Portugal at any given time in its fertile soil, in its grassy uplands, so well suited for pasture, in the mineral wealth which lies beneath the surface, and in the ample harvest of its waters.

There was a time in the history of the kingdom when it seemed, after the expulsion of the "Moors" and the settlement of its boundaries, to be resolved upon making the most of the land for agricultural purposes ; but, in the first place, the campaigns in north-west Africa, and then its discoveries in that continent and elsewhere, called it away from the work which lay nearest. So much was the country diverted from the humble, unromantic business of the plough, that not all the strenuous efforts of the "great marquis" sufficed to arouse in it an abiding sense of simple duty. Even at this day, only one-

* Yeats.

fifth part of Portugal is under cultivation. And as the methods employed by Portuguese farmers are still of the most primitive description, the annual yield is much less than it ought to be. The rotation of crops is not understood; the plough used in Portugal is of rude construction and little weight; harrowing is rarely done; and the style of separating the grain from the husk is that of last century. In Minho, husbandry has always enjoyed a better reputation than in the other provinces, the tolerably level surface and plentiful water supply affording considerable natural advantages. But speaking generally, Portuguese agriculture is quite two hundred years behind what it is in our own country.*

There is great variety, however, in the produce of the ground, as may be easily imagined when it is remembered that five degrees of latitude intervene between the north of Minho and southern Algarve. Besides cereals, flax and hemp are grown in the north, while in provinces of a warmer temperature one finds rice, maize, and many semi-tropical fruits, such as olives, oranges, and lemons. But the chief department of Portuguese husbandry is the culture of the grape for the manufacture of wine. There are many vineyards in Portugal, but the wine district *par excellence* is Alto Douro, in Tras os Montes, where the celebrated liquor is produced which, from the fact of its being shipped at Oporto, is familiarly known as port. For two hundred years this wine has been esteemed and exported, principally to England. Pombal, who left his mark on most things in Portugal, directed his attention also to the condition of vine-culture there. His measures regarding the vineyards of the Douro are particularly important. He found that they urgently required improvement, and that the proprietors were unable to raise capital for the purpose, having fallen into a state of abject poverty. He procured, therefore, the organization by royal edict in 1756 of the Wine Company of Alto Douro, with a

---

* Latouche, "Travels in Portugal."

capital of £150,000, in shares of £90 each. A price was fixed which should afford a reasonable profit both to the husbandman and the wine merchant.

There was no little excitement over the matter of the new company. The publicans of Oporto, who had been taking advantage of the destitution among the owners of the vineyards and purchasing at a very low price, making, besides, a further profit by adulterating the liquor, were highly incensed. They were especially offended by an article of the edict, which said that only a certain number of wine-sellers of good character were thenceforth to be licensed to supply their customers with port. The publicans stirred up the mob, and there was a riot in Oporto. The soldiery were called out. The populace resisted them fiercely, and reinforcements had to be sent for. Much blood was spilled, but the revolt was put down at length. Seventeen persons were executed for taking part in the uproar, and a hundred and thirty-six others sent to the galleys, banished, or imprisoned. A tremendous storm about the price of liquor! It was long before the people of Oporto forgot the port wine riot. The Jesuits too, for the sake of destroying the marquis, endeavoured to turn the people against the new company's wine by declaring that it was not suitable for the mass. But Pombal heeded neither priest nor publican, and ere long the agitation subsided.

The company whose birth was thus made memorable founded the prosperity of the port wine trade, and raised Portugal, as regards the quality of the article, to the rank of one of the principal wine countries in the world. At this day the Alto Douro business gives employment to thirty thousand persons annually to dress the vines and gather their fruits. The annual value of the port wine exported is something like one million and a quarter sterling, nearly one-half of the whole value of the wine which is sent out of the Portuguese dominions, including Madeira.

But such devotion to the vintage has had an effect which Pombal would have deeply regretted. It has helped other causes to throw the culture of cereals into the background. A luxury has thus usurped the place of the necessaries of existence, and the Portuguese are compelled to procure from abroad an extraordinary quantity of that staff of life with which their own agriculture ought to have provided them, at least in a much greater degree. It appears, moreover, as if overwhelming disaster overhung that wine trade which the people have considered the stay of their country. Nemesis, in the shape of the phylloxera, has visited the vineyards. It is said the merchants have on hand so much wine that for some time exporting will go on as usual. But long before they feel the pinch, the husbandmen and labourers will be reduced to the penury out of which Pombal lifted them, and that in far larger numbers.

The mining industry in Portugal has fallen lower even than it has done in the neighbouring kingdom, which is saying a great deal. As a metalliferous country, Portugal is hardly behind any in Europe. From the earliest times mines have been worked by the various races which had possession of the land. In Tras os Montes there is one of immense size, opened probably by the Romans, or even earlier than their time. The mouth of this excavation is nearly a mile and a half in circumference, and the mine is sunk for nearly five hundred feet. After the establishment of the Portuguese kingdom, various metals were wrought with spirit, some of the ancient drifts being re-entered. But the sixteenth century put an end to the work, and the few mines which are in use at the present day are leased for the most part by foreign companies. There is an incalculable revenue under the feet of the Portuguese. The scarcity of coal in Portugal, it must, however, be observed, is a serious matter in respect of the national progress.

The passion for ocean voyaging which depressed many useful occupations in the country had, for a time, the opposite effect

on one calling, that of the fisherman.   Much was done for him,
since it was essential that plenty of hardy seamen should be at
hand to man the vessels of Portugal.   The fisher-tribe increased,
therefore, greatly, and ventured far, even to the Banks of Newfoundland, whither, in 1578, it is recorded, a Portuguese fishing-
fleet of fifty craft sailed, and returned with great catches of cod-
fish.   In the same year only thirty fishing smacks left England
for Newfoundland.   But as the age of discovery advanced, the
Banks and other distant fishing-grounds were forsaken of the
Portuguese, who bought then from the English the fish which
formerly they had for sale.   Yet the trade of the fisher lived
when other vocations were gone or going.   A long coast and a
teeming sea have made many fishermen, but sustained them also.
They could supply their own table, if purchasers failed for a
time, with their daily haul, or from their dried stock hanging
from the rafters.   Moreover, after wars and voyages, the fisher
could speedily return to his lines and nets as if his business had
never been interrupted.   In our day, the fisheries of Portugal,
and especially the tunny fishery of the Algarve coast, are
carried on vigorously; and this of all Portuguese industries is
the one which may be called most thriving.

Portugal has long borne the evil reputation of being one of
the most poorly furnished European countries, as far as the
means of internal communication are concerned.   It has many
rivers which, though dangerous by reason of bars at their
mouths, have navigable channels; and were they connected by
canals, easier intercourse would be afforded between the various
districts.   But such engineering has not been undertaken.
Bridges and roads are fewer and worse than one is accustomed
to in lands pretending to so much civilization.   Of late much
effort has been directed to the task of transforming the rugged
interior into a tolerable thoroughfare.   But the task of thus
opening the country is no sinecure, for so late as half a century
ago it was as expensive to convey goods from the Spanish

frontier to the capital as to bring them from Brazil. But now-a-days we are not so dependent on carriage roads; and the railway, twelve hundred miles of which are in operation in Portugal, has thrown some life, to which no doubt the improved highways have contributed, into various branches of Portuguese industry. The cattle breeders of Minho and the sheep farmers of Beira can now, with less delay, convey their stocks to Oporto or Lisbon for sale there or transport thence.*

As a manufacturing nation, Portugal is nowhere. Nor was it ever distinguished in this respect. It was, to be sure, hampered by the policy of Great Britain while that power exercised a commercial monopoly in Portugal. But the Portuguese have never responded to the ardent wish which government after government have expressed, to see the country on the path of progress in manufactures. Bounties and protective tariffs, every method of encouragement which could be devised, have hitherto effected only a small result. Last century, and at the beginning of this, John Bull was said to be the clothier of the Portuguese, and that is still very much the case. Textile fabrics, pottery, and some other goods, Portugal produces on a limited scale, the only considerable manufactories being in the capital and in Oporto, the great town of the north.

There are in the country no more than three towns with thirty thousand inhabitants—Lisbon, Oporto (the wine depôt), and Coimbra (the university seat).† The next place in respect of population is Braga (the capital of Minho), the ancient archiepiscopal residence. It has a little less than twenty thousand inhabitants.

Lisbon, as it rises like an amphitheatre from the north bank of the broad Tagus estuary, presents to one looking from the south-east its best aspect, and from that point of view is universally admitted to be one of the most picturesque cities in

* Portugal, after its manner, was a laggard as to a railway system. In 1800 only forty miles of rails were laid.

† Population of Lisbon, 246,000; of Oporto, 105,838; of Coimbra, 33,967.

Europe. It is now a long time since travellers, who had been in raptures with its distant beauty, were rudely disenchanted with "its filthy streets and still filthier inhabitants," and supremely disgusted when their midnight slumbers were banished by the howling of a canine multitude, its only scavengers. No doubt it has, like every Continental town, its disagreeable odours (though one might not be able to distinguish them with the accuracy of Coleridge). But they manage things better in Lisbon now than when Byron so fiercely anathematized it in "Childe Harold." Even the old town is kept tolerably clean, and the new town, with its broad streets and splendid squares, a native need not blush to compare with Paris or Vienna.

Through what vicissitudes has not the fair capital of Portugal passed? Found by the Romans a busy town with a history behind it of which there lives no record; held by the Moslems; taken by the Portuguese; defended against a mighty Spanish army; elevated to the highest rank among the cities of the earth; devastated by a most fearful convulsion of nature; protected from the occupation of an imperial dictator by extraordinary fortifications, hastily prepared, but discovered to be impregnable,—there is no spot on the globe which is more full of interesting and romantic associations.

Lisbon, though shorn of its beams, is still an important commercial centre. As a noble "haven of ships," it is continually thronged with the flags of every nation. In Lisbon also is carried on the central government of the kingdom, and from it issue general orders for the conduct of affairs in all that are left of the Portuguese dependencies abroad. The Cortes or parliament consists of two houses, the Chamber of Peers and the Chamber of Deputies. The upper house differs from the corresponding British chamber in that it is not composed exclusively of peers and is not hereditary. The king, with advice, nominates its members for life. The number is not strictly limited by any enactment, but practically it is a chamber of one hundred and fifty. A peer of the Portuguese realm may, according to this system, never happen to be chosen to serve in the parliament of his country.

The Chamber of Deputies has one hundred and seventy-five members, chosen for four years by all registered male citizens of twenty-five years of age who can read and write and are in receipt of an annual income of £22. The Azores and Madeira, as integral parts of the kingdom, send deputies to the lower house. The parliament meets at statutory periods. No mandate from the king is required. Every deputy receives out of the national revenue adequate pecuniary compensation for his services. A Privy Council of life members exists to advise with the sovereign, but the working ministry consists of six members of the Cortes, who are the cabinet of state.

A ministry which undertakes to guide the affairs of Portugal ought to be eminently distinguished by the quality of hopefulness. Otherwise their position is far from enviable. For every year they have to face a deficit.* But though depressed, Portugal is not dead or dying. The gross tonnage of the shipping entering and clearing at her various ports, which affords a considerable indication of a country's progress, is decidedly on the increase, as we see from the tables of the most recent British parliamentary abstract. Fifty years ago, the entire tonnage was under half a million; ten years ago, it had risen to nearly five millions; and now it is well-nigh eight millions. What Portugal appears to want is to have her interior engineered with vigour and thoroughness, that her people may move conveniently about, her tariffs lowered both in the Peninsula and abroad, and the masses furnished with at least the elements of education.

---

* The national debt, therefore, which fifty years ago amounted to only eighteen millions sterling, has now become nearly one hundred and twenty-three millions. The revenue is small—nine millions sterling—out of which the army and navy seem to annually require one million and a half, and the colonies, on the whole a dead loss to Portugal, a heavy subsidy.

At the ancient and sole university of Portugal there are scarcely seven hundred students. As to primary education, a compulsory act was passed in 1844, by which every child from the age of seven to fifteen was bound to attend a public school if there should be one within a mile. Failing such attendance, the parents should come under a penalty. But in too many cases there was no school within the prescribed distance; and when such a school did exist, there was no effective search for absentees. So in 1861 there were only eighty thousand pupils in the public schools. Now, with better school accommodation, defaulters also being more strictly dealt with, the number has swelled to two hundred and forty thousand. The contrast between the educational condition of Portugal and that of other countries in Europe—Holland, for instance, which contains nearly the same population—is glaring. A comparison of the flourishing Dutch universities, secondary, elementary, and infant schools, with her own corresponding institutions must be exceedingly odious to Portugal.

The physical characteristics of the Portuguese vary in a remarkable degree in different parts of the country. The Arab is seen in the face and figure of many a peasant of Algarve and Alemtejo. In these provinces, too, there is a considerable intermixture of negro blood, recalling the fact that numbers of Africans were transported to the southern home provinces for agricultural labour, as well as to the colonies. The easily-recognizable Jewish features are observed frequently occurring in some districts of Portugal, especially in the town of Braganza, a place whose excellent situation for frontier trade induced many Jews to settle there. Moreover, it is certain that even where the lineaments have been modified in the course of generations, Jewish blood runs in the veins of many Portuguese. The dreadful alternative offered the Jewish settlers by Emmanuel, of conversion or banishment, and his detention and baptism of their children on the event of the parents choosing exile, then the cruel hand of the Inquisition, forced many into the position of ostensible Christians, and to secure their safety by seeking matrimonial alliances with families above suspicion. Farther north, one arrives at an approximate idea of how the ancient Celtiberians looked as one comes across the shorter and fairer peasantry of Beira and Minho. Only the modern Portuguese has so much per cent. of the Visigoth, which reduces the accuracy of the estimate. Everywhere in the kingdom, finally, are met the Visigothic seigniors, squires, and squireens.

It is not easy to label a mixed people like this—to say it is an honest, a frank, a selfish, a vindictive people. This much may be set down, however, that the isolation of the country population has kept them simple and very superstitious. The Romish Church has not anywhere a class which more unhesitatingly reverences it than the Portuguese peasantry. Travellers receive ungrudging hospitality in the rural districts, but are always astounded at the ignorance of the natives, at whose notions of the world a British schoolboy would smile, who retail the wildest vagaries of folk-lore as if they were sober science.

The townspeople are excessively fond of ostentatious display. That has probably been created by the former Oriental wealth of Portugal, and by the knowledge of and interest in the pageantry of the East which thousands of Portuguese visiting or residing at Goa brought home. To this taste for stage-effect the Church of Rome diligently caters, as in Brazil, by providing splendid services and appointing more holidays than is good for the business of the country, on which the populace, tricked out in their best, may visit the pleasure-garden or the theatre. The charming climate enables the Portuguese to live a great deal in the open air. The houses, therefore, even of the better classes are not so comfortable or tastefully arranged as those to which we are accustomed. Works of art are scant in Portuguese homes. Indeed, there is a strange want of the artistic sense in the nation. The "Academy of Fine Arts" collection at Lisbon is a contemptible affair; and both the town residences and country seats of the grandees are generally unfurnished with those valuable specimens of master-hands which make a visit to such places in our own land a delightful privilege.

Portugal has a very tough Conservative party, including, of course, the *titulados* and *fidalgos*, who are still steeped to the lips in the feudal traditions; and there is also a section which would take advantage of any public excitement to substitute a republic for the monarchy. Occasionally a fear is spread of a revolutionary rising, a danger more real since the events in Brazil, and the Spanish government masses troops on the frontier against the contingency. The Moderates have difficulty, when the Radical fever is in the air, to keep the peace, particularly as the Conservative nostrum for unrest is the antiquated *coup d'état*, the very mention of which is enough to goad advanced politicians to fury. What has happened in South America of late has of course stimulated the craving for a constitutional change in Portugal. But for the Brazilians the dissolution of the empire was comparatively easy. It was not old, and it was a thing of their own creation, when they might have made anything they pleased of their state. But in the hearts of many Portuguese there reigns a feeling towards the venerable throne which is akin to superstition. One dare not prophesy unless one knows, but the likelihood is that the Portuguese Braganzas will not soon be ousted without bloodshed, like their cousins in Rio.

Who can tell, considering the prevailing irritation in Portugal, what in a week or a day may be seen transpiring on its political stage? But apart from this external form of government or that, and although Emmanuel's golden prime be a thing of the past, the resources of Portugal are not exhausted. With energy and economy she may yet occupy an honourable and useful place among the peoples of Europe.

I. GENEALOGICAL AND CHRONOLOGICAL TABLE OF THE PORTUGUESE SOVEREIGNS.

HOUSE OF HENRIQUEZ (9)—1129–1383.

ALFONSO I., son of Count Henry of Burgundy........1129–1185 = 56 years.
SANCHO I., son of Alfonso I. ....1185–1211 = 26
ALFONSO II., son of Sancho I...............................1211–1223 = 12
SANCHO II., son of Alfonso II................................1223–1245 = 22
ALFONSO III., brother of Sancho II.......................1245–1279 = 34
DENNIS, son of Alfonso III....................................1279–1325 = 46
ALFONSO IV., son of Dennis ....1325–1357 = 32
PEDRO I., son of Alfonso IV ....1357–1367 = 10
FERDINAND, son of Pedro I. ....1367–1383 = 16

INTERREGNUM—1383–1385.

HOUSE OF AVIS (4)—1385–1495.

JOHN I., son of Pedro I..1385–1433 = 48 years.
EDWARD, son of John I..1433–1438 = 5
ALFONSO V., son of Edward ....1438–1481 = 43
JOHN II., son of Alfonso V...................................1481–1495 = 14

HOUSE OF VISEU (4)—1495–1580.

EMMANUEL, cousin of John II...............................1495–1521 = 26 years.
JOHN III., son of Emmanuel.................................1521–1557 = 36
SEBASTIAN, grandson of John III.........................1557–1578 = 21
HENRY,* brother of John III.................................1578–1580 = 2

HOUSE OF HAPSBURG (3)—1580–1640.

PHILIP I., grandson of Emmanuel.........................1580–1598 = 18 years.
PHILIP II., son of Philip I.....................................1598–1621 = 23
PHILIP III., son of Philip II..................................1621–1640 = 19

* The cardinal.

HOUSE OF BRAGANZA (12)—1640.

John IV., husband of Emmanuel's grand-daughter...1640–1656 = 16 years.
Alfonso VI., son of John IV..................................1656–1667 = 11
Pedro II.,* brother of Alfonso VI.......................1683–1706 = 23
John V., son of Pedro II. ....1706–1750 = 44
Joseph, son of John V...1750–1777 = 27
Maria I.,† daughter of Joseph ....1777–1810 = 33
John VI., son of Maria I............................ ....1810–1826 = 16
Pedro IV.,‡ son of John VI...............................1826—a few months.
Maria II., daughter of Pedro IV. ....1826–1853 = 27 years.
Pedro V., son of Maria II. ....1853–1861 = 8
Louis, brother of Pedro V ....1861–1889 = 28
Carlos, son of Louis..1889.

  * Regent from 1667 to 1683.
  † Her husband was styled Pedro III., King-Consort.
  ‡ Emperor of Brazil.

II.—DESCENT OF FIRST VISEU KING.

EDWARD, King of Portugal.

- ALFONSO V.
  - JOHN II.
    - Alfonso.
- Ferdinand.
  - Leonora, Queen of John II.
  - Isabel = Duke of Braganza.
  - Diego, Duke of Viseu.
  - EMMANUEL, Duke of Beja.

III.—DESCENT OF THOSE WHO CLAIMED THE SUCCESSION IN 1580.*

EMMANUEL = Maria of Castile.

- JOHN III.
  - John.
    - SEBASTIAN
- Isabel = Charles V. of Spain.
  - Maria = Philip II. of Spain.
- Beatrix = Charles, Duke of Savoy.
  - Emmanuel, Duke of Savoy.
- Louis.
  - Antonio, Prior of Crato.
- Edward = Isabel of Braganza.
  - Maria = Prince Alexander Farnese of Parma.
    - Ranuccio, Duke of Parma.
- HENRY (Cardinal).
  - Catherine † = John, Duke of Braganza.

---

* The names of claimants are printed in italics.

† The Duke of Braganza was not only by marriage connected with the Portuguese royal family. He was the sixth in descent from Alfonso, son of John I., who married the daughter of Nuno Pereira, Constable of Portugal; and as will be seen from the foregoing table of Emmanuel's descent, the grand-daughter of King Edward wedded a Duke of Braganza.

INDEX.

Works of Travel and Research.

Journal of a Voyage round the World of H.M.S. "Beagle." By CHARLES DARWIN, M.A., F.R.S. With 16 Full-page and 6 Double-page Illustrations. 8vo, cloth extra. Price 4s.

Wanderings in South America, etc. By CHARLES WATERTON, Esq. With 16 Illustrations. Post 8vo, cloth extra. Price 4s.

The Land of Greece. Described and Illustrated. By CHARLES HENRY HANSON, Author of "The Siege of Troy, and the Wanderings of Ulysses," etc. With 44 Illustrations. Imperial 8vo, cloth extra. Price 8s.

In this handsome volume, the present condition of the "historical localities" and ruins of Greece is well described, along with interesting sketches of their past history.

In the Holy Land. By Rev. ANDREW THOMSON, D.D., F.R.S.E., Minister of Broughton Place Church, Edinburgh. With 18 Engravings. *New Edition.* Crown 8vo, cloth extra. Price 4s.

The aim of the author has been to record such customs among the people as shall be found to shed new or increased light upon the Word of God.

Kane's Arctic Explorations: The Second Grinnel Expedition in Search of Sir John Franklin. With a Chart and 60 Woodcuts. Crown 8vo, cloth extra. 4s.

A record of heroic endurance and courage, and of providential deliverances.

Maury's Physical Geography of the Sea. With 13 Charts and Diagrams. Crown 8vo, cloth extra. Price 4s.

A book of scientific information in regard to ocean depths, currents, temperature, winds, etc.

On the Desert. A Narrative of Travel from Egypt through the Wilderness of Sinai to Palestine. By HENRY M. FIELD, D.D., New York. Author's Edition. With 16 Illustrations. Crown 8vo, cloth extra. Price 4s.

CANON FARRAR says of this work:—"I found it so interesting that I could not lay it down till I had finished it."

MR. SPURGEON pronounces this "a book of the first order."

Mountains and Mountain Climbing. Records of Adventure and Enterprise among the Famous Mountains of the World. By the Author of "The Arctic World Illustrated," etc. With 33 Engravings. Post 8vo, cl. ex. 4s.

A delightful record of mountaineering adventures and experiences in all regions of the globe, with many beautiful illustrations.

Egypt Past and Present. Described and Illustrated. With a Narrative of its Occupation by the British, and of Recent Events in the Soudan. By W. H. DAVENPORT ADAMS. With 100 Illustrations, and Portrait of General Gordon. Post 8vo, cloth extra. Price 3s. 6d.

In this volume are brought together the principal facts in connection with the history and monuments of Egypt. The illustrations are from authentic sources.

The Mountain. By JULES MICHELET, Author of "The Bird," etc. With 17 Illustrations. Crown 8vo, cloth extra. Price 4s.

A volume of graphic word-pictures, along with beautiful engravings, of the most striking features of mountain scenery, including glaciers, lakes, forests, the Alpine flora, etc. The scenes described lie mostly among the Swiss and Italian Alps; but there are also glimpses of the Tropics, and the mountains of Arctic ice.

Library of Historical Tales.

Dorothy Arden. A Story of England and France Two Hundred Years Ago. By J. M. CALLWELL. Crown 8vo, cloth extra. Price 4s.

A story of the dragonnades in France in the time of Louis XIV. Also of the persecutions in England under James II., the Monmouth rebellion, the Bloody Assize, and the Revolution.

How they Kept the Faith. A Tale of the Huguenots of Languedoc. By GRACE RAYMOND. Crown 8vo, cloth extra. Price 4s.

"No finer, more touchingly realistic, and truthfully accurate picture of the Languedoc Huguenots have we met."—ABERDEEN FREE PRESS.

The Lost Ring. A Romance of Scottish History in the Days of King James and Andrew Melville. Crown 8vo, cloth extra. 4s.

"The plot of the romance is skilfully constructed, the dialogue is admirable, and the principal actors in the history are portrayed with great ability."—U.P. MISSIONARY RECORD.

The City and the Castle. A Story of the Reformation in Switzerland. By ANNIE LUCAS, Author of "Leonie," etc. Crown 8vo, cloth extra. Price 4s.

Faithfully portrays the state and character of society at the time of the Reformation (in Switzerland).

Leonie; or, Light out of Darkness: and **Within Iron Walls,** a Tale of the Siege of Paris. Twin-Stories of the Franco-German War. By ANNIE LUCAS. Crown 8vo, cloth extra. Price 4s.

Two tales, the first connected with the second. One, of country life in France during the war; the other, life within the besieged capital.

Under the Southern Cross. A Tale of the New World. By the Author of "The Spanish Brothers," etc. Crown 8vo, cl. ex. 4s.

A thrilling and fascinating story.

Alison Walsh. A Study of To-Day. By CONSTANCE EVELYN. Crown 8vo, cloth extra. Price 4s.

La Rochelle; or, The Refugees. A Story of the Huguenots. By Mrs. E. C. WILSON. Crown 8vo, cloth extra. Price 4s.

Wenzel's Inheritance; or, Faithful unto Death. A Tale of Bohemia in the Fifteenth Century. By ANNIE LUCAS. Crown 8vo, cloth extra. Price 4s.

Presents a vivid picture of the religious and social condition of Bohemia in the fifteenth century.

Helena's Household. A Tale of Rome in the First Century. With Frontispiece. Crown 8vo, cloth extra. Price 4s.

The Spanish Brothers. A Tale of the Sixteenth Century. By the Author of "The Dark Year of Dundee." Crown 8vo, cloth extra. Price 4s.

The Czar. A Tale of the Time of the First Napoleon. By the Author of "The Spanish Brothers," etc. Crown 8vo, cloth extra. Price 4s.

An interesting tale of the great Franco-Russian war in 1812–13; the characters partly French, partly Russian.

Arthur Erskine's Story. A Tale of the Days of Knox. By the Author of "The Spanish Brothers," etc. Crown 8vo, cloth extra. Price 4s.

The object of the writer of this tale is to portray the life of the people in the days of Knox.

Pendower. A Story of Cornwall in the Reign of Henry the Eighth. By M. FILLEUL. Crown 8vo, cloth extra. Price 4s.

A tale illustrating in fiction that stirring period of English history previous to the Reformation.